Shattered

Hannah Till

Other Works by Hannah Till

The Celestra Series

This is a work of fiction. References to real people, events, establishments, organizations, and/or locales are intended only to provide authenticity, and are used fictitiously. All other characters, and all incidents and dialogue, are drawn from the author's imagination and are not to be constructed as real.

Published in the United States by Hannah Till

Cover design and all associated artwork: Marcia Godfrey of PlusInfinityArt
Editor: Marcia Godfrey
Developmental Editor: Rachel Bunner
www.instagram.com/rachels.top.reads7

ISBN 979-8-9857674-1-4 PB
ISBN 979-8-9857674-4-5 HB
ISBN 979-8-9857674-5-2 EC

To receive special offers, bonus content, and all other information related to works completed by
Hannah Till, please visit the following websites and sign up for the newsletter.
www.hannahtillauthor.com
www.instagram.com/hannahtillauthor

Content Warnings:
Panic Attacks
Abandonment
Sexual Assault/Rape
Mentions of previous child sexual assault
Mentions of suicide

Shattered

Dear Reader,

First and foremost, I want to thank you for wanting to read this book. Before you dive in I want to specifically state that this book is intended for adults only. It is my job as the author to make sure you know what you are getting into when you pick up my books. If you do not wish to have scenes spoiled and are okay with various triggers with no need for warnings then stop reading here. If you would like to have trigger warnings please continue below.

Please know this book contains explicit consenual sexual content, adult language, mentions of suicide/past child sexual assualt/rape and current depictions of rape. These sensitive situations may be triggering or inappropriate for some audiences.

If you or anyone you know is suffering from domestic violence, please reach out to the National Domestic Violence Hotline at 800-799-7233 or text START to 88788

If you or anyone you know are contemplating suicide, please reach out via call or text to the National Suicide Prevention Hotline at 988

If you or anyone you know is experiencing sexual assault, please reach out to the National Sexual Assault hotline at 1-800-656-4673.

To my most favorite booksta-besties
in the whole wide world. May you
always find your sex master. ;)
IYKYK

Shattered

Shattered

Prologue - Sam

Can anyone ever really belong without truly accepting who they are in the first place?

That was the question Sam should have been asking herself. In reality, all she was contemplating at this moment was how fast she could get out of the room. Out of the building. Out of the state.

In fact, had an alien spaceship landed on the pristine grounds before her, trying to scoop her up and carry her off into oblivion, she was sure she would have gone running to meet it.

The air had become stifling and the summer heat wave hadn't even truly begun yet. Summers in South Carolina were meant to come with permanent air conditioning, and even though she eyed the vent sitting to her right and knew it was blowing practical flurries of ice in her direction, she couldn't stop the sweat that continued to form at her brow.

She didn't want to be here. She wanted to be anywhere but here.

A quick look down at her nails proved she shouldn't have let Kristin talk her into getting a manicure the previous day. Half of the polish was already chipped off from her nervous picking habit. She reached up to twist her fiery red curls around her finger—another nervous tic—and then remembered she had it perfectly pulled back into a proper bun.

She just needed to stay still. Still and quiet and perfect. Per usual.

She was so busy planning her escape, she didn't even hear him at first. When he spoke the second time, a little louder and from directly behind her ear, she jumped in surprise. The ice water in her hand splashed slightly on the marbled floor below.

"Huh?" Sam turned, finding Christian staring down at her, a worried look plastered on his perfectly shaven face. She knew that face all too well, considering they had spent more time than not circling through the same foster homes.

Sam had lived in six counties and eight foster homes from the time she entered the system at birth until she'd aged out at eighteen. She'd almost been adopted twice, but both attempts had fallen through.

She'd never known her parents. She didn't feel bad about it, most people in her situation didn't know their parents. Instead of nightly dinners and parents who cheered her on from the sidelines, Sam got indifferent foster mothers and creepy foster fathers who, at times, stepped over the line. Sometimes, thinking back on the inconsistency of her childhood made her head spin.

But there was always a silver lining in every story. That's what she told herself. And maybe learning how to cope with the inconsistencies thrown her way over the years as opposed to panicking through them was what had gotten her to where she was at this moment. Which was preparing to begin her junior year of undergrad with a declaration of pre-med, plans to submit applications to seventeen med school applications she'd end up spending most of her savings on submitting, a 4.0 GPA, a mediocre part-time job, $47.82 in her bank account that was somehow supposed to last her the next ten days, and absolutely no social life.

The last part didn't bother her as much as the rest. She'd never really cared to be part of some big group of people who focused more on what they were doing from Thursday through Saturday than on wondering where their next meal would come from.

"I said, 'Are you okay?'" Christian questioned further as he reached out to tuck one of her wayward red curls back into submission.

Ugh, she thought as she tried to subdue the curl back around the bun.

"Oh, yeah. Yeah, I'm fine. It's just hot as hell up there." Sam eyed the stairwell that led to the upper ballroom full of people she knew she could never truly impress.

"Sam, this room is practically an ice box." Christian swung his hands out as if the motion would magically reveal the invisible crystals that lingered in the air. "Are you sure you aren't sick or something?" He placed his beer on the counter beside them and reached out to sweep the back of his hand across her freckled forehead; a trick they had seen so many guardians do over the years.

She quickly batted him away.

"I'm fine. I promise," she all but groaned.

"Is this about your speech later?"

"What? No. No." She placed her drink beside his and began fussing with the hem of her dress, the one she had found the previous week at a secondhand shop. She was hoping no one would notice she'd had to mend it in seven different places to hide the fact it was most definitely not new. "I'm completely fine with that speech," she lied. "I've been working on it for weeks, and I'm sure—"

"Samantha Williams?" the gratingly high-pitched voice came barreling down the stairs along with the clicking of heels and a shockingly short designer dress.

Mrs. Saunders.

The dreaded Mrs. Saunders had a face that barely moved due to years of plastic surgery, but was still somehow able to form a perfect scowl.

Mrs. Saunders was the current head of The Giving Hearts Foundation board, which oversaw her scholarship, making sure recipients met all standards and expectations. Thankfully, this was the last luncheon that would be held while she still presided over the board. That single thought was what kept Sam from fleeing the room. In another week, the new board members would take over and Mrs. Saunders would no longer have control over her. *Thank fuck.*

"Right here!" Sam called out.

"We're ready for you."

"R-Ready for me? Now? Already?" Sam swallowed, not knowing if she was just throwing some PVCs or if her heart was really about to give out.

"That's what I said." Mrs. Saunders' perfectly polished fingernails glistened in the light from the chandelier as she clasped her hands together in front of her.

"We'll be right up. Just giving Sam here a little pep talk," Christian said as he waved at Evil Incarnate with a massive smile, looking about as much of the beautiful dork that he was.

Sam punched him in the arm.

The barely visible lines on Mrs. Saunders's face tightened just that much more.

"I'm coming," Sam amended with a disingenuous smile and watched as the woman stalked back up the steps toward the ballroom. Sam made sure to dig her heel into the polished toe of Christian's fancy shoes as she passed him.

"Ow! Sam!" he feigned annoyance. In reality, being that he was at least twice her size, she doubted he even felt her attack.

"Oh, sorry," she said with as much sarcasm as she could muster as she cut her eyes down to his foot. She could barely hold in the surprised squeal as he lunged for her, wrapping an arm around her neck from behind and placing her in a perfect chokehold.

"Don't tempt me. How many times did I take you down when we were kids?" he whispered in her ear before pushing her away from him.

"I let you beat me," Sam countered as she steadied herself, not completely comfortable walking in heels.

"Ha! You wish," Christian said as he grabbed their discarded drinks and made to step in line beside her.

They walked in flawlessly coordinated movements, a task they had perfected over the years. Had it not been for the fact that they were complete physical opposites in most every way, many would have assumed they were twins.

Sam, who, when her fiery red curls were at their fullest, could almost pass for five foot three (at least, that's what it said on her driver's license), had a face filled with freckles, and a slim build that could give most models a run for their money, was in stark contrast to the man who now walked beside her.

Christian, who at close to six foot three was made of pure bulky muscle (how he was able to pay for as much protein as he must've needed to eat she never knew or questioned), had a head full of perfectly coiffed blonde hair that could make anyone fall to their knees, and a heart of pure gold.

No, they were about as different as two people could be. But beyond their obviously contrasting physical features, both were constantly seen by those who knew them as one half of the other's whole.

Sam had never liked that comparison. It was strange for someone to assume you were related to the only boy you'd ever let fill your scandalously explicit dreams.

Sam coughed at the memory of one of those dreams. She could *not* afford to have those thoughts running through her mind right now. Not when she was about to speak in front of a hundred of the university's highest officials who oversaw the Giving Hearts Foundation. The exact officials who would be deciding if she was worthy enough to receive increased funding, which would allow her to live on more than stale bread and ramen noodles for the remainder of her undergrad career.

Actually, that was a bit of an exaggeration. Sam liked the ramen noodles, and the bread only went stale when she forgot about it. And it's not like Kristin let her want for anything. She was constantly bringing home goodies and delicacies, and she kept their freezer stuffed with ice cream.

"You'll do great." Christian leaned down and kissed her brow as they reached the top stair.

Sam lingered in the way his lips felt against her skin. This was all she would ever get from him, and she had to be okay with that.

She'd pushed it once, a few years back. Shortly after a stint of hopping from place to place, just looking for somewhere they could stay long enough to learn the other kids' names. He'd been sent to another foster home for a few months, and they'd had no contact during that time. Something about poor service out in the country. It was then that she'd realized how much he truly meant to her—how much she'd missed him. She'd, of course, dated a few other guys in highschool, but it wasn't until that moment when Christian was no longer there that she'd realized he was hers and she was his.

He hadn't returned until the week before they graduated from high school. She'd had one more week of living under a roof she had never considered her own and she'd fussed when he spent a portion of his earnings to rent a room at the motel down the street from her. But, honestly, she'd liked having him so physically close. She had initially planned on couch surfing with Sara until college started, but then those plans had been shattered and she'd moved into that motel room with Christian, taking a summer job at a local pizza place to help with expenses.

When he'd first come back, he had initially given him some space, but then she had bared her heart to him while sitting on a playground swing set. He'd, in turn, shut her down so fast she couldn't even complete the next breath before he hopped up and walked off.

It was the oddest encounter they'd ever had. And it was all her fault.

She'd wanted to disappear right then. Had begged the ground to open up and suck her down so she would never have to face him again. But when she'd gone to him days later asking to stay with him for the summer, he'd grabbed her face in his large hands and promised he would always be there for her—he would always take care of her.

Always.

Sam latched onto that promise. It was all the hope she really had of a future with Christian and, even if it was just a tiny thread of something that would never be what she wanted it to be, she had never let it go.

On the outside, she treated him like the annoying brother who constantly got in her way while, on the inside, she would be forever wishing that she was what he desired. That she fit the mold.

That she belonged with him.

So she lingered in the heat that came from his quick kiss to her temple in hopes that it would give her just enough courage to get through the rest of the hell she was currently in.

Chapter 1 - Sam

She wanted to scream in annoyance. It's not like they hadn't all been taking these tests for years. Hell, it was the second semester of junior year, so it wasn't like the other upperclassmen in the auditorium with her hadn't known it was coming. It was there in black and white on the syllabus they'd been given on day one.

Learn. Study. Prepare. Get the test. Answer the questions correctly. Rinse and repeat.

Yet, every single time, people panicked. Sam had learned not to panic about easily controllable things early on in life. It was one of the things that had helped her get this far. Helped her hone in on what she needed to do to keep up with the strategic plan she had in place.

Read. Devise. Calm.

That's what Mr. Clapps, her social worker, had taught her over the years. Read the situation, devise a plan, keep calm, and everything will be okay.

But it didn't seem like the majority of her cohorts had been taught the same message. If anything, most of their upbringings had probably been filled with nicely paved paths and people who reached out with a helping hand if ever a misstep occurred.

She rolled her eyes at the panic-stricken faces that surrounded her and wondered what their stories were. Where did they come from and how did they end up here?

Here being a dimly lit auditorium that smelled of musty air

and someone's leftover Chinese food they had stuffed into their bookbag for an after-exam snack. Sam managed not to gag and moved to sit a few rows back in hopes that the smell would stay near the front.

She was nothing like these people.

It couldn't be more obvious.

And yet, even though she fought hard to repress the feeling, she knew a small part of her was still so desperate to belong; to feel loved and accepted and wanted.

She had focused way too hard on that feeling in her younger years and had pretty much perfected the ideal of what others wanted from her. She became the student her teachers wanted, the sister her foster siblings wanted, the daughter her foster parents wanted, the girl Christian would hopefully one day want. She became the poster child for the system. The girl the agency put on the flier they sent out to local churches.

Twice, those fliers had resulted in couples coming to her foster home to meet her for a possible adoption. Which is rare once kids are out of the cute baby stage. But then, as soon as they'd come, she'd panicked.

What if it didn't work?

What if it was fake and they hurt her like the others did?

By the time she'd been old enough to realize she was in the system, she'd been old enough to know all the horrors of that system. Her only way to cope with this was to panic at the last second, act out, and make them not want her.

It was easier to say she hadn't been adopted because she didn't want to be than to consider the possibility of the couple not actually wanting her. By the time she'd learned how to cope, it was too late. She was too old and no longer cute or innocent enough.

The only consolation prize of the adoptions falling through was that she'd gotten to stay with Christian. They weren't siblings, and yet Mr. Clapps had tried his best to keep them together as if they were.

She'd left that last foster home the day after she graduated from highschool and promptly moved in with Sara, and only a week later, she'd moved into the motel with Christian. Then after a summer where she spent far too much time pretending things were more than they really were, with barely any money between them, and a trash bag full of barely fitting clothes and half broken belongings, they'd moved into the freshman dorms.

So here Sam was, sitting in Dr. Abram's neurology class, not panicking. She couldn't say the same for the girl to her left who kept wiping her hands on her jeans. And if the guy to her right didn't stop fidgeting with his pen soon, she might just throw it across the room. She wanted to scream at both of them to get them to stop moving.

This isn't rocket science, she yelled within her own mind, and then chuckled slightly at the thought. *Well, it is brain science, but still.*

She wondered how many would make the ultimate goal of medical school, and then how many would push through to the end. She had to. She had to break the cycle. She wouldn't end up as a statistic. She wouldn't end up on the streets or in a homeless shelter.

The day she'd gotten the acceptance letter to the University of South Carolina, she'd promised herself that she would make it. That she would be able to do this. That she wouldn't let anything—or anyone—distract her.

Chapter 2 - Sam

"Sam, hurry up! We're going to be late!" Kristin yelled from outside her room. Her voice barely noticeable over the loud music in the background.

After the most recent Giving Hearts luncheon she had spoken at, Sam had most definitely hit her quota for the month, or maybe even the year, of sitting at a fancy table and eating food she couldn't pronounce with rich people she didn't know. But this was Kristin's family, so she knew she had to go regardless.

Sometimes, the Hadleys had the entire neighborhood over for a dinner party. Sometimes, it was just another couple or two. Sam never quite knew what she was walking into until they arrived. She hated the fakeness of all the smiling faces that would be staring at her, curious about who she was and her parentage. Kristin hated it, too, for different reasons, but, sadly, they didn't have the luxury of saying no to her parents' monthly dinner parties. And, unfortunately, neither of them had a paper due tomorrow that they could use as an excuse to bail this time.

"I'm coming! Stop fussing," Sam said as she smoothed down the skirt of her dress and took one last look in the mirror. "What's on the menu for tonight?" she shouted down the stairs, knowing Kristin probably had no idea.

"God if I know, I'm just thankful you're coming so you can fake an illness halfway through and then we can leave early!" She leaned back to meet Sam's gaze, sending a pleading smile her way.

Sam rolled her eyes as she slowly made her way down the stairs and through the living room.

"I'm sorry, no. I'm not faking sick to get you away from your miserable family." She locked the door behind them as Kristin jumped the railing to go start her car. Her ebony curls bounced as she moved.

It was a small townhouse about a mile off campus in a neighborhood that was mostly inhabited by students.

Kristin could have lived anywhere she wanted. Her parents had enough money to afford the best. But Sam refused to let her pay for everything and this small two-bedroom, two-bath townhome with the chipped paint and half-functioning appliances was all Sam could afford. She had tried to talk Kristin into living with someone else—someone who could pay for the new luxury student apartments with the rooftop pool and bar. Kristin balked at the suggestion. They were practically sisters, she had said. And where Sam went, so did Kristin.

"Remember, my mom said they invited the Barkers over. Mr. Barker has been trying to get me together with their oldest son for, like, five years now. No one gets the hint that it's not happening. On either end," Kristin added with emphasis. "So, help a sister out. I would do it for you, you know." She pushed out her bottom lip, as if that would change Sam's mind.

"No way in hell. We've canceled every time she's invited the Barkers for, like, two years. I'll deal with them for three hours in order to get a free meal and some good booze." Sam wiggled her eyebrows.

"Whatever. See if I come to your rescue next time you are stuck on a sinking ship."

Sam started to laugh, but the sound was drowned out when Kristin turned the radio up so loud she couldn't even hear her own thoughts. She loved Kristin. Loved her with everything she had. Everything she knew. Outside of Christian, Kristin was her most trusted friend. She was her person.

Sam had been to Mr. and Mrs. Hadley's house multiple times over the past two years, but that still didn't lessen the awe that was certainly sprawled across her face as they drove up the drive. It was a three story mini mansion on the lake with a boat house larger than most homes Sam had stayed in during her childhood.

"I still can't believe you grew up here, I feel like I'm walking into the Biltmore House every time we come."

"Have you ever even been to the Biltmore?" Kristin asked and Sam shrugged in response. "Whatever. Let's get this shit show over with," Kristin continued, rolling her eyes, attitude on full display.

This was why they were best friends. The first time they'd met in Anatomy & Physiology 101, Sam had just *known* she would absolutely loathe Kristin. Typical rich girl with her fancy clothes, bag, and shoes that probably cost more than Sam's entire wardrobe. She'd known there was absolutely no way Kristin would actually get into med school, let alone attend. She'd had her pegged. Daughter of a surgeon—plastics, or maybe neuro—daddy's little prodigy who would breeze through classes in order to graduate and then marry the top pre-med student. She would be the dutiful housewife who popped out a couple of kids and had dinner ready and on the table by six every night.

But, by all accounts, Sam had been oh so wrong. She'd quickly learned not to mess with Kristin. Kristin may have come off cutesy and sweet, but that girl was full of fire. One group project and a semester where Kristin had pretty much bested the TA out of his knowledge base every time he opened his mouth and they'd become the best of friends. They'd finally moved in together in the fall semester of sophomore year and had never looked back.

"Girls, look how lovely you two are. We are just thrilled to have you!" Mrs. Hadley greeted them as she opened the door with an attempt to smile so big you could almost make it out under all the Botox.

Kristin almost always refused to use her house key. The only time she ever pulled it out was when her parents weren't home. It was another silly way she chose to rebel from them.

It was hard to even tell the mother-daughter pair were related. Except for the obvious similarities in bone structure, the two women looked nothing alike. In reality, Mrs. Hadley's skin tone was probably a shade lighter than Sam's, but no one would ever know due to the copious amounts of self tanner she used. Kristin looked like her father. Deep brown skin and bouncy curls. Kristin also possessed the most beautiful green eyes; a hue similar to Sam's. Kristin always said the eye was the window to the soul, hence they liked to joke that they were soul sisters deep at heart, even if they had only met the previous year and looked nothing alike.

"Now, Kristin, you won't believe who has joined us! Mr. Barker and his son and daughter from down the street! Isn't that wonderful?"

Though they had never actually met, Sam had heard the names cross Mrs. Hadley's lips on more than one occasion. She was the go-to for any and all gossip in the rich-people circles and Kristin absolutely hated it.

She knew The Barkers lived two houses down, and that they had three kids and were rich as hell. Connor, the doctor; Callum, the rebel; and Amelia, the apple of their eye.

Apparently, Mrs. Barker was off doing something far more important than neighborly dinner parties and there was no mention of Callum, who they didn't speak of much.

Kristin didn't even attempt to hide the eye roll she gave her mom. "Yes, you told me last week they were coming, then again on Wednesday, and reminded me with three texts last night. I'll have to tell Micah they said 'Hello!'" she said back with an equally big and fake smile. Sam tried to hide her smirk, but from the look Mrs. Hadley gave her, she'd failed.

Micah and Kristin had been together for a little over two years at that point, and as small a world as it was, he was best friends with Callum Barker. So it could get a bit awkward when her parents' constant hopes for the arranged relationship with the soon-to-be Dr. Connor Barker were constantly thrown in her face.

Sam tried to initiate a conversation with Connor more than once during dinner. He was a current resident in the local hospital's ER department and she was a pre-med student. She was sure they would have plenty to discuss. He was nice and concisely answered every question she asked, but seemed genuinely disinterested in actively taking part in any conversation at the table. Most of the night was spent with Connor sending what could only be referred to as absolute death glares to his father. Sam could tell he wanted to be here just as much as she and Kristin did.

That meant dinner was the same as always, boring conversation and gossip, but at least the food was delicious. And there was wine, which made any night tolerable.

Amelia Barker, the youngest Barker child whom Sam was also meeting for the first time that night, was surprisingly nice and asked lots of questions about Sam's dream of attending medical school. Apparently, she wanted to be a nurse and thus seemed genuinely interested in what Sam had to say. Amelia was a freshman in college and, for some reason, Sam had assumed she would be a stuck-up sorority girl with nothing much to add to the conversation.

She'd figured Amelia would be a product of her world, an exact replica of her mother, who Sam guessed was likely a carbon copy of Mrs. Hadley. But she wasn't at all like Kristin's mom. Mrs. Hadley was more concerned with the neighborhood gossip and the latest episode of The Real Housewives than having a real conversation with those around her.

One thing Sam knew for sure was that she never wanted to become the topic of Mrs. Hadley's gossip. She'd been to enough of these dinners by now to learn how to tiptoe around or all out avoid the questions about her past with precision. Not even Kristin's parents knew that she was a product of the system. To them, she was just someone who never spoke about her family. So, as far as awkward evenings with Kristin's parents went, this was probably the most enjoyable one they'd had.

****

"So, you want to come over to Micah's with me, or are you just going to chill here and study as always?"

Kristin knew Sam's answer before she even said it. Sam was fine with parties. She'd gone to plenty as a freshman trying to blend in with the masses, but she wasn't like Kristin. Sam had to actually study the material if she wanted to do well on the tests. Unfortunately, she had never been one for pure luck or ability to miraculously make perfect scores.

And besides, any screw up, no matter how small, and the funding she acquired from the Giving Hearts Foundation that paid for all this—the tuition, the books, the copious amounts of study guides and colorful pens for detailing out every function of every organ—would be stripped away.

But the foundation funds didn't cover everything, which meant, on top of that ridiculous course load and the extra community service hours she'd added in at the food pantry every week to seem well-rounded, Sam also had to have at least one part-time job. Sometimes those part-time jobs felt more like full-time aggravations. Over the last three years, she had shuffled between hours at a pet adoption center and waitressing. She normally had to have at least two jobs at once so she could afford the daily needs of someone in college: the food in the fridge, the rent, and the bus fare she used to go absolutely anywhere. Thankfully, since her applications to med school had all now been paid in full, she could step back from one. She chose to leave shoveling dog poop in the past and, just before the new year, she left the shit hole restaurant with the handsy owner for a ridiculously high end one on Main Street with supposedly amazing tips.

Kristin had, on more than one occasion, begged Sam to step back and take a break from it all, promising she would cover any expense needed. But Sam was far too prideful for that. It didn't matter if Kristin could have paid every bill and bought Sam every luxury with her shiny credit card, Sam had never been given a handout, and she wasn't about to start now.

"I'm going to call it a night. Your family wears me out. Is there a party going on or just the two of y'all hanging out?"

"Well, from the decibel level in the background, I'm assuming a party. Callum and Drew are officially back from Charleston, so I'm sure there are a good many people there. And I'll get to tell Callum all about seeing his perfect parents and even more perfect brother tonight," she said in a singsong voice as she grabbed her purse and headed out the door.

Kristin used to have to pack a small bag whenever she went over to Micah's. Now, she and Micah each had a supply of clothes and other random belongings stashed at the other's house. Sam was almost positive that if it wasn't for Kristin agreeing to live with her to help with rent and other expenses, the two love birds would already have a mortgage and maybe a car payment between them.

"Gotcha. Well then, I guess I'll see you Monday morning in Dr. Abram's class?"

"Yep, see ya!" She blew a kiss toward Sam as she disappeared through the door.

Hanging out with Kristin on girls night was one of her favorite things to do. However, getting the house all to herself for a few hours where she could spend the time quietly reading, studying, or just *being* was a luxury she would never turn down. People rarely thought about how loud foster homes and orphanages could be until they were trying to sleep, or study, or even just relax inside one. Most she'd lived in had been a chaotic surge of noise at all hours.

So, getting the night to herself was not a bad idea at all.

Chapter 3 - Sam

"Sazerac for me and a Negroni for her," the bald man said without even letting Sam introduce herself.

"I'm sorry, could you repeat that?" She wasn't familiar with those drinks at all, but still smiled back as he gave her an annoyed glance.

"Sazerac and a Negroni," he quickly answered, even more impatiently this time.

Fuck.

Her smile faltered. She wouldn't be able to repeat the names of these cocktails, let alone know how to spell them. This was going to be her table from hell tonight. There was always one.

"Yes, sir. I'll get that right now." She rushed off to the kiosk by the bar.

The audible groan she let out as she walked up caused Table 57 to quickly avert their eyes. Jess, the bartender who had saved her ass more times than she could count, was nowhere in sight.

Shit.

She looked around, trying to find someone who could help, but this place was packed, and everyone was running around in a chaotic mess, not bothering to pay attention to the waitress who looked very much like a lost puppy fumbling through the motions.

She couldn't afford to lose this job. She had been waiting tables at Topline for about three months at this point (a veteran if you asked Penelope, the mild-mannered hostess who had seen far too many souls come and go, many not even lasting more than a week) and she needed the money. It was *great* money. The tips were better than any other restaurant she had worked at, even if the clientele was a little on the *I come from a long line of Karens* side. She could deal with uptight know-it-alls who looked down on her. That had basically been her entire life up until this point anyway, so why not?

But with the long line of people that filled the entrance, and with how quickly the tables were being turned over with no consideration for what the kitchen was actually able to produce, she took slight solace in the thought that she wouldn't be the biggest screw-up of the night. The newbies had started just yesterday, so they were bound to have at least one meltdown in the group during their first official night on the floor.

On most nights, Sam loved working at Topline. But on weekends, this place could turn into a madhouse. It was a two-story restaurant right in the middle of downtown Columbia. It had a dark aesthetic with exposed brick and pipes, and instead of the standard light fixtures, it was filled with twinkling rows of what Sam referred to as fairy lights, and twisted vines running up the walls and across the ceiling. It was an absolutely magical building and there was at least one proposal made there every week. Sometimes, during a slow moment, Sam stared at the walls, trying to figure out where one vine ended and the next began.

The only negative to working there was the grouchy manager, Mr. Brimley. He was constantly wiping the sweat off his face and cursing under his breath. More than anything, he desperately needed to up his anxiety meds. He had been known to fly off the handle for any little thing that may upset a guest. Thankfully, she had not yet been on the receiving end of one of those tantrums.

But she had a small feeling that might change very soon.

Sam started to sweat as the kiosk became a blur of food and drinks and cocktails, and scanned every single page looking for something that looked similar to what that man had just ordered. She scanned over the drink menu to her side, but nothing popped out at her.

Negisa, Nimoni, something. Ugh.

She tried to remember exactly what they were called, but she wasn't a big drinker herself so she never really learned the names for the fancier cocktails.

Relief flooded through her when the bar door finally swung open from the back.

"Took you long enough, Je–" Her excitement was cut short when she promptly realized this person didn't have long wavy brown hair, but instead a mop of jet black locks that barely grazed the collar of his shirt. Nope, definitely not Jess.

But definitely new. One of the new hires for sure. She hadn't seen him before and, being as it was sink or swim night for the new crowd, she would put money on the fact that he was a blundering new crew member.

After far too many failed attempts at silently begging him to look her way, hoping that he would know what it was she was trying to ring up, the frustration got the better of her. She waved her hand a few times in the air, hoping to catch his attention but, as before, it didn't work.

One thing Mr. Brimley had instilled from day one on the job was that employees were to be seen and not heard. Most of Topline's customers were old school, upper class business men and their wives (or mistresses) who wanted to be waited on without having to listen to the lowly waiters and waitresses speak amongst themselves. So, Sam tried one more time to catch his eye as she waved across the wooden bar set between them to no avail. There was no way she was going to try to squeeze her way through the many patrons sitting at the bar, so she was stuck over at the side, waving her arm, and trying not to look ridiculous.

Fuck it.

"Hey, excuse me, could you come over here?" It was more of

a whisper-yell, causing one of the patrons at the bar to look up, but Newbie didn't turn her way. He paused for a mere second when Sam let out a grunt of annoyance, but continued on with his task.

It wasn't even nine o'clock, it had been a hell of a shift, she was already on edge, and she had an exam in advanced organic chemistry the next week, so the last thing she needed was some newbie asshole making her night more stressful than it already was.

"Hey! Excuse me!" she tried once more, a little more loudly than she'd intended. This time he paused, and she swore she heard a chuckle come from his direction. She knew she could see the hint of a smirk in between the dim lights that littered the glass backdrop behind him.

It was like he was hell bent on ignoring her, which was starting to seriously piss her off.

"Listen, I need your help with these drinks!" she yelled even louder this time. Loud enough that a few more guests popped their heads up in annoyance. She didn't care, though, as he finally stood up and turned in her direction.

Their eyes met for the first time.

Unkempt would be a kind term for what he looked like.

Nothing like the usual people Mr. Brimley typically hired.

They stared at each other for a second, Sam's eyes pleading for assistance, but also not so slyly taking in the way his hair fell just so across his eyes, the straight line of his jaw, the stubble that peppered his chin, the way his broad shoulders seemed to fit perfectly within the black button up shirt he wore, the twisted tattoo that snaked down his muscled arm, and the way his shirt met his black pants.

But there was also something oddly familiar in the way he looked. She knew his face, and yet she didn't. Sam tried to pinpoint if she had ever seen him before, but it was unlikely. He obviously wasn't in her cohort and she didn't remember him being one of the post-juvenile lock up kids getting their community service hours at the pet shop.

But he was definitely familiar. And easy to look at. Especially with the sultry way he was now staring her down.

She gulped before reality kicked in and she remembered this newbie was an ass that she definitely wanted absolutely nothing to do with.

He laughed at her embarrassment in being caught as he turned around and started organizing glasses. Her shock at his clear dismissal was written all over her face. Not really thinking through the consequences of her actions, she stalked to the back kitchen and then burst through the bar door.

The names of the drinks had long been forgotten, but she wasn't about to let Newbie-Asshole think he'd gotten the better of her. He was *not* going to ignore her and laugh at her and think he was better than her. Not tonight.

The foul words itched to be hurled at him as she slammed the door open and then promptly froze as all manner of noises—*Crash! Shatter! Bang!*—echoed through the building. Everyone stopped. Even the music seemed to pause, trying to take in what had just happened.

She'd definitely hit him.

With a feeling of nausea mixed with regret, she peeked around the corner.

Newbie-Asshole looked up at her with an expression reserved only for the vilest of creatures. To say he was pissed would be an understatement. He was crouched on the floor with a box of shattered glass sitting in his lap and three broken liquor bottles still rolling around on the floor. He slung his arms toward the ground, trying to shake off some of the shards of glass and liquor that had now soaked through his very tightly fitted shirt.

She opened her mouth, not sure whether an apology or snarky comment was about to exit, when Mr. Brimley turned the corner in search of the destruction. A look of utter shock and repulsion covered his features.

"Sam! *What are you doing?* Waitstaff do not come behind the bar!" He definitely wasn't a ray of sunshine, either.

Sam stammered out a quick apology for the sake of her job, trying to explain that she needed help, but was unaware the new employee was deaf and couldn't hear her.

Newbie-Asshole quickly slid his earbuds out with a bored expression.

"Really? Going there, are we? Ableist much? I was busy, if you couldn't tell, and by the time I noticed you, you were already stalking back here on a mission, and besides, I don't respond to random yelling across the bar." She guessed Newbie-With-An-Attitude finally decided to have a voice.

"Oh, you can hear me now. Good to know," she said back with as much bite as she could muster.

She was going to lose her job. She was going to have to ask Kristin to pay her half of the rent this month. She was going to stress until she couldn't think straight, and then she was going to fail a class and lose her funding and have to drop out of college, all before she even got into medical school.

She officially loathed Newbie-Asshole.

But she also knew that if he was working behind the bar on a Saturday night, then Mr. Brimley must have liked him, and that meant he would be around a lot. And she *had* to salvage this job. She absolutely couldn't afford to lose it. Not with how great the tips had been over the last few weeks.

"Listen, I'm sorry about your shirt, okay? I'll buy you a new one if that one is ruined. I'm dealing with the table from hell and I need your help. I'm sure they will be even more pissed now that it's taking three years to get their drinks."

Tired of the back and forth, and just wanting to move along with the night, she threw up a silent prayer that both men would let her off easy and that the plethora of patrons still staring them down would soon find something far more interesting to stare at.

"Just please help me get the drinks, and I promise you won't have to see me anymore," she urgently whispered in his direction.

Mr. Brimley began to speak in an awkward rush, "Sam. He

doesn't need to—"

"It's fine. I'll take care of it," Newbie-Asshole quickly cut in.

"I want a few words with you before you tip out tonight, Sam," Mr. Brimley said sternly as he reached down to lend a hand to Newbie-Asshole. But his offer for help was quickly brushed away as Newbie-Asshole stood by himself, further brushing off what he could. By the time he reached his full height, Sam was practically staring at the ceiling. He had to be at least a foot taller than her, maybe more.

"I'm so sorry about that. Sam's only been here a few weeks."

She jerked her head back toward Mr. Brimley.

A few weeks! More like going on four months, and she pulled in the best tips of anyone on her shift.

Sam almost came back with something snarky, but remembered how much she desperately needed this job and sealed her lips shut.

"Do you need anything?" Mr. Brimley questioned the newbie, but received a quick shake of his head in answer. Then, with a rather obvious look of disgust in Sam's direction, Mr. Brimley returned to the back.

"Just put them in under their tab and I'll make them," Newbie-Asshole said without even looking her way, but she could still see the obvious eye roll he made.

"That's the problem. I've never heard of them. They aren't on our specialty menu and I don't even know what to look under," Sam replied as she handed him the paper with the drinks written down. He gave her the side eye.

"What the hell are these?" His forehead creased in confusion. She was about to comment on their mutual unknown knowledge of the drinks when his face changed and a laugh bubbled out. "Wait, please tell me this isn't a sad excuse for trying to spell Negroni and Sazerac?"

"Well, yeah, I think that's what he said," she stammered back at him.

"Do me a favor and go back to first grade. Learn how to spell before your next shift." He laughed a little more at her expense, which cut deeper than it should. She started to make a rebuttal, but he cut her off while shoving the paper back toward her chest, "Don't get all pissy, okay? I'll make them." He headed over to the counter, and by the time she made her way back around to the kiosk, the drinks were waiting on the mat and he was nowhere in sight.

Chapter 4 - Sam

By the time Monday came around, Sam was exhausted. She had spent the better part of the weekend either with her face in a book or serving drinks. Newbie-Asshole hadn't been at work on Sunday, so at least she'd been able to avoid that miserable excuse of a human being. Still, with all the stress of the last few days, all she wanted to do now was sleep.

As she walked into her 8 a.m. lab, she found Stacy sitting in their usual spot giving her the customary look.

"Girl. You look like shit again. Don't get me wrong, most people do for Monday morning lab. But not for the same reasons as you."

"I know, I know. I just didn't feel prepared for the midterm next week so I stayed up studying and I had to work, too."

"Maybe this weekend you should just hang out and try not to work and study so much. You will survive if you don't make all A's. You know that, right?" Stacy laughed a little at herself. "And it's not like you have to work, anyway. Your tuition is basically covered by that scholarship, so can you start to chill?"

Sam cringed. No one outside of Kristin really knew about the Giving Hearts Foundation, but Stacy and Sam had pretty much circled through the same classes since fall of freshman year. They had formed a study group with a few others and on one drunken night last fall when they'd been trying to liven up the periodic table, Sam's tongue had become a little too loose and she'd explained that she had been awarded a scholarship that paid for school. As soon as the phrase had left her lips, she'd promptly sobered up and realized one too many shots too late that alcohol and keeping secrets didn't really mix very well. She'd never spoken another word about it, to avoid Stacy digging too deeply into her past, and let Stacy go on thinking she didn't have to pay a dime for anything. Which was, sadly, not the case.

"I know. But I have to keep my grades up in order to keep it. If I lose it and don't have enough saved up, then I will have to drop out. I can't afford this place on my own."

"Well, promise me you will at least relax a little this weekend. Even if it's just for a few hours. You are like the Energizer Bunny. You never stop, but one of these days you are going to completely burn out."

Sam laughed and rolled her eyes at Stacy just as the instructor walked in.

It was true, though. Sam never stopped. She probably should take more breaks, but she had a plan, and there was nothing that could cause her to deviate from it. If she lost this money, she was screwed. There was no way in hell she would be able to afford tuition on her own. And there were so many stipulations to maintaining the funding that literally any wrong move could cause it to be snatched away without a second thought.

She'd been eight when she and Christian had found out about the Giving Hearts Foundation. Basically, a bunch of rich wives got together and funded scholarships for underprivileged youth. Applicants had to jump through so many hoops to get it, though, that it seemed almost unattainable. Not only did the contenders need an almost perfect GPA, but also high SAT scores, and no bad marks of any kind on their record in order to even be considered. Oh, and, of course, a sob story for the ages.

Sam and Christian only knew of a couple people who had applied over the years, but one thing or another caused them not to be able to keep up with the requirements. Even Christian had been overlooked, which was more than odd, since he'd had better scores than Sam on almost everything. She was the lucky one. She'd been awarded the largest scholarship that had ever been given out by the foundation.

But with a check with that many zeros on it, she'd known there would be conditions that even the best would have a hard time achieving. The foundation's board checked up on her and the few other recipients across the state every semester to make sure they were doing well and cranking out the high scores.

She was sure it looked good on whatever pamphlet or flier they used to garner the *oohs* and *aahs* that their support had helped the less fortunate. She had only met with the new round of board members a couple of times since they'd taken over in August, both times at events designed to show off all the good work they were doing. Thankfully, while most of the new members seemed to fit the mold of past members, the new head of the board had been kind to Sam both times they'd met so far.

The luncheons she attended were a stipulation of the funds. Make a speech every couple months about how grateful you are, how much the money has helped you, garner some newsworthy achievements so the members could be fawned over for their kind hearts, and then you get to keep your funding.

She had skipped one luncheon freshman year because she'd been swamped with meetings and class and work, but that hadn't gone over well, and it had taken a lot of tears and even downright begging in order for the money not to be snatched away from her.

She hated those luncheons with every fiber of her being. She never wanted to go to them. She couldn't stomach it. She couldn't sit at a table for lunch with those men and women while they fawned over her like she was some enigma they couldn't figure out.

The girl with no home. No parents. No family. No money.

It was too much pity.

Most meetings left her breaking down in the back of an Uber before she'd even made it out of the drive. Even though he was sour about never getting the money, Christian had come as her date to all of the functions. He was the only one who had always been able to hold her together in those moments.

****

"Miss Williams, can I see you for a moment?" Stephen, their graduate instructor, asked as they all headed out the door.

"Yes?" Sam said as he handed her a paper that had her heart racing and her jaw dropping.

"We aren't giving these back until Wednesday as there are a few more to grade, but I wanted you to see." He paused for a moment, gauging her reaction. "What happened? You are the best student I've had since I started this lab. This isn't your typical work."

She could hear him speaking, but the sound of her heartbeat filling her ears took over, masking anything else that tried to enter.

"Now, this won't really affect your grade in the grand scheme of things, but I don't want this to become a habit."

Sam handed the paper back without a word, not sure what there was to say. She'd never failed an assignment before. She'd never even made a C, and rarely, if ever, had made a B on anything.

Her mouth opened in an attempt to verbalize an excuse, but no response came, and she silently walked out of the room, hot tears running down her face, before the panic attack took over.

Thankfully the bathroom was empty, and she could lock the door, spending a few minutes trying to calm herself down.

Don't panic.

It's one grade.

They can't pull the scholarship for one bad grade.

She repeated this mantra in her head for the rest of the day which, if she was being honest, went by in a blur. Kristin knew her all too well and hadn't for a second bought her excuse of being tired, so Sam knew she was going to have to explain later when she got home from her shift.

When she walked into Topline that afternoon, she couldn't focus on anything. She was too consumed by how she was going to correct this. She was supposed to inform the board at the Giving Hearts Foundation if she made anything less than a B on an assignment. She was going to have to tell them. Which also meant she would now be planted firmly on their radar.

"Move."

She was quickly jerked out of her thoughts by her favorite Newbie-Asshole.

"Seriously, move," he repeated. When she didn't even blink in response, he got even more frustrated. "You are staring at the screen, and I need to get there. Either do something productive or move out of my way."

"Asshole," Sam muttered under her breath. It came out before she'd even processed the thought. She didn't care, though. It was clear he thought the same of her.

She wasn't putting up with this tonight. She had too much on her plate already.

****

For as bad as she felt, the night went pretty okay. A few good tables and a decent amount of money from tips. Best of all, she hadn't had to interact with Newbie-Asshole since Jess was working the bar and handling all the drinks. Now that she thought of it, she hadn't even seen him since her shift started. Maybe he'd been clocking out earlier at the kiosk. That was the most welcome thought of the night.

At the end of her shift, Sam decided to order from the kitchen and sit with Jess to eat at the bar while they closed up. It seemed like it was always the two of them left for closing. She didn't mind. Jess was pretty cool and loyal. She knew because, during one ridiculously slow night a few weeks back, Sam had ended up spilling her whole life story while praying the rain would let up and someone willing to drop a massive tip would walk through the doors. She had never really told anyone except Kristin about her life, but something about Jess was so motherly and comforting, she couldn't help but confide in her.

"What's been up with you tonight? You're not your normal happy self."

"Am I normally a 'happy self?'" Sam asked with creased brows.

"No, I guess not." Jess laughed as she put away a few more bottles. "But you're still not yourself."

"Just a bad day in class. Things didn't go how I'd planned." Her answer was vague, but Jess wasn't the type to let something like this go. She just stared at Sam until she spilt the beans. "I failed this stupid lab assignment. It won't really affect my grade too much, but I'm pissed."

Jess cocked her head to the side before responding, "You're kidding me, right? You've been in a funk all night because of one stupid lab assignment? One that won't even affect your grade." Jess looked up then and motioned to a woman standing at the hostess stand, signaling that she would be out shortly.

"Who is that?" Sam questioned, but then went still in wide-eyed shock before Jess could reply. "Wait. Is that Gwen?" When Jess didn't say a word, Sam knew she had her answer. "Oh my God, Jess! She's gorgeous!" Sam added with a smile.

"I know. I know," Jess stated through gritted teeth as if she was worried Gwen would overhear them. "She is way too good for me, but hell if I'm planning on letting her slip away."

Sam then laughed as Jess sent Gwen a quick wink, causing the other woman to turn a bright shade of red.

"You didn't tell me y'all were officially a thing now."

"I don't know if we are," Jess said as she dried off the last few glasses in the rack. "But I'll tell you the details once they get juicy enough to tell." Jess wiggled her eyebrows and Sam laughed.

"Deal."

"Now. Back to more important matters." Jess cleared her throat as if she was about to state something poetic or profound. "You need to live a little, girl."

"Shut up." Sam rolled her eyes. "Jess, it's more than that. My entire college career is based on good grades and my scholarship. If I lose that, I'll be working in a restaurant when I'm thirty. I don't want that." Jess's eyebrows raised slightly at the statement. "Sorry. I didn't mean it like that. It's just not the plan I–"

"Little Miss Perfect is upset because something didn't go her way? I wish my life was that much of a fucking cake walk. Let me guess, you made a bad grade on your spelling test?" Newbie-Asshole said as he slid onto a stool a few spots down from them and dug into his own meal. He didn't even make eye contact.

Sam. Was. Done.

"Are you really this much of an ass, or is this some type of shitty, tough guy persona you're trying on? Maybe mind your own goddamn business and stay out of mine."

Jess became frozen with shock.

"Sam!" Jess whisper-yelled at her.

But Sam didn't care. Newbie-Asshole could go straight to hell for all she cared. They hadn't even really worked together, and she was already done with him. Her next thought was spent making a silent promise to never again interact with him.

"Jess, I'm out. Sorry, I don't feel like staying anymore. Are you good if I leave?" Jess nodded in understanding as Sam stood.

"Wait," Jess quickly stated as she reached into her pocket and pulled out a tube of the peppermint roll on Sam had let her borrow earlier.

"What's that?" Newbie-Asshole asked as he took another bite of the meal in front of him.

Sam wanted to roll her eyes. She almost didn't respond. She decided then that she would be perfectly fine if they never spoke again. Maybe it was just so she could have the chance to insult him again or maybe it was to feel the contentment of getting the last word in but for whatever reason, she turned toward him and answered. Her voice had lost its punch but her words still landed a lethal blow.

"It's a peppermint roll-on. It's my favorite scent. Bonus is

that it helps with calming and relaxation when you are stressed."
She opened it and rolled a generous amount on her wrists and neck
with a smile. "Which is something I'm going to need more of now
that I have to see *you* on a regular basis." She cocked her head to the
side, a smile filled to the brim with utter disdain plastered across her
freckled face.

Jess was wide-eyed and she not-so-subtly stifled her laugh
under a cough as Sam walked away and headed for the door, not
giving Newbie-Asshole the satisfaction of looking back his way.

Chapter 5 - Sam

"Could this be any more boring?" Kristin rolled her eyes as Dr. Jennings rambled on.

"Stop it, she's going to hear you!"

Kristin never paid attention. How the hell she maintained a 4.0 GPA was beyond questionable.

She nudged Sam once more. "Hey, listen, I need to stop by Micah's on the way back. I left my planner there last weekend."

Kristin was forever leaving things at his place. Sam figured it was her way of constantly having an excuse to see him. And since they had the same three classes today, she had ridden in Kristin's car instead of having to use the bus. She was thankful for the air conditioning and general lack of people bumping into her, but not so excited about the pit stop on the way home.

"Yeah, as long as you shut up and let me pay attention," Sam said with a humorous glimmer in her eye.

Kristin rolled her eyes, but didn't say another word for the rest of the lecture.

****

"Want to come in? I'll only be a minute and you haven't seen Micah in weeks!" Kristin was wearing the same smile that always tended to appear when she brought up Micah.

Sam knew that smile. She had kinda-sorta dated a few guys in college (if you can call meeting up at a bar or coffee shop one or two times and then being ghosted dating). She'd had one serious boyfriend in highschool, but she didn't talk, let alone think, about him anymore. Boys were off her radar. She told herself it was for the best. There was no way she would have time for a relationship with her current chaotic life. So she appreciated them from afar, and in her nighttime thoughts, and promised herself that one day Mr. Perfect would make himself known, or at least decide to stop seeing her as an annoying sister he loved to pick on.

She most certainly liked them, but at no time had she ever been what some would call boy-crazy. Well, unless you counted Christian. But they had never been a thing, and they never would be.

Sam was about as far from clingy as one could get. Kristin, though, was her absolute opposite. One might feel like that would normally push a guy away, but Micah was right there with her. They couldn't seem to stay away from each other for very long.

"Sure, why not. Only for a minute, though." She didn't really want to go in, but sitting out in the car during this random March heat wave might just have been a worse version of hell.

As they walked in, they quickly spotted Micah bent over and busy cleaning up what she was sure were the leftovers from last night's party. And, of course, the place reeked. Sam wasn't really sure how Kristin could stand to spend the weekends here, let alone random nights in the week, with the gag-worthy odor that seemed to be permanently burned into every piece of furniture. If there was ever a definition of bachelor pad in the dictionary, a picture of this living room would be right next to it.

"Sam! Long time no see!" Micah said as he walked over and gave her a hug. "You decided to step foot out of that library for a few minutes, huh?" He laughed a little at her expense.

"Yep, but I'm due back shortly, so we can't stay long." She smirked back.

"Seriously, though, you should come out of your dungeon and come over tonight. It's just going to be us, no big party or anything. We're going to grill out at the pool and then watch the games." Sam's nose scrunched in response, but he continued, "It's

March Madness. I promise, low key. I'll even order you a pizza from Dianne's. I know it's your favorite."

And there were the magic words.

"Kristin has divulged my greatest weakness, I see," Sam said with a hesitant smile. "Maybe. It's just not really my thing, and besides, I know nothing about March Madness."

"Me neither, I just pick the brackets based on the color jersey I like!" Kristin laughed as she walked downstairs to Micah's room. "And I even got to the final round last year picking that way, so I'm guessing it's a solid plan to stick to this time!"

"You would." Sam started to laugh, but was quickly cut off.

"It's fucking 10:30 in the morning. Why are y'all screaming down here?" growled a rather aggravated looking man as he walked down the stairs. She assumed that he must live there merely based on Micah's reaction to him, and how he stalked directly to the fridge and chugged milk straight from the container.

"Shut up, man. I'm cleaning up your shit from last night, so stop whining. Sam, this is Mr. Can't-Wake-Up-On-The-Right-Side-Of-The-Bed Drew. Drew, this is Kristin's roommate, Sam."

"Hi." Sam moved to reach out her hand, but Drew just did a weird head nod, then silently went to the coffee maker. His deep brown eyes seemed to match the hue of his skin and she became momentarily fascinated by the intricate design his shoulder-length dark hair was braided into.

It was an awkward few moments of silence as Micah took out the trash and Kristin was downstairs scouring what Sam assumed was a partially destroyed bedroom for her long lost planner, but she busied herself by staring at the hastily painted walls and shuffling on her feet. These kinds of uncomfortable situations just further solidified Sam's preference for solitude.

"Found it!" Kristin screamed and then quickly made her way back into the living room. "Hey, Drew." She waved toward Mr. Bad Mood. "So, Sam, does tonight sound good? We could hang for a few hours, nothing big."

Sam internally groaned then promised to ask her friend why she always had to put her on the spot. This conversation would be much better suited for the car where Sam could decline and not feel shitty about it. "Sure. Yeah. I don't see why not. I have to be at work by 10 a.m. tomorrow though, so I can't stay too late."

Kristin's face lit up. "Great! We will be back in a few hours!" Kristin said as she planted a kiss on Micah's lips and followed Sam out the door.

****

The drive back to Micah's that night was quiet. Sam's mind was noisily running through every excuse she could think of to get out of the party, as it had been doing since she agreed to go. She wasn't the most social person ever, and she had always been more of an introvert.

"We can leave anytime you want," Kristin said and Sam knew she could sense how tense she was. She gave Kristin a quick smile in response.

At least it was quiet when they pulled up, so Micah hadn't lied. Just the roommates and them, it seemed.

For a moment, she contemplated the reality that this could be a positive thing. She really did need to meet more people and start having an actual social life, but her world was so immersed in school that she tended to let the weekends fly by without a second thought. Jess and Stacy would be so proud of her.

As they walked up the steps to the porch, Kristin gave her a big comforting smile and opened the door without knocking. A complete one-eighty from what she did at her own family home.

Sam didn't make it three feet inside before she heard him.

"You've got to be fucking kidding me," Newbie-Asshole exclaimed in frustration without ever moving from his chair. His gaze was planted firmly on her.

Sam stood frozen.

She didn't move from the door frame.

It was Micah who broke the tension as he looked between the

two.

"Is there a history here we should know about?"

"This is the girl that spilled drinks on me last weekend," Newbie-Asshole said to no one in particular, keeping a definite glare planted in Sam's direction. "Let me guess. Sam, right? Kristin's roommate?"

Sam had never been in a situation in which she felt time stood still until this exact moment. It was obvious he was aggravated at having to see her again. She wasn't all that excited about seeing him again, either.

She scanned the room. She had already met Drew earlier that morning, and was well acquainted with Micah, so this must be Callum Barker, the tattoo shop owner and Barker boy screw up. Mrs. Hadley had made a few comments about him during their dinners. College dropout. Complete rebel of the family. She had never paid much attention to their neighborhood gossip, but it all made sense now. Callum fucking Barker was her most hated coworker.

"Yep. That's me. Sorry, we didn't get to exchange names during our first encounter. I was too busy trying to do my job and avoid assholes." Two could play this game. She tried to rein it in. That wasn't something she would normally say at all, but just seeing him again had evoked a level of anger she couldn't explain. It was bubbling up so close to the surface, ready to explode with just the smallest spark needed to set it ablaze.

"Um, do you want us to leave?" Kristin asked Sam as she gave her a panicked look. She was normally the hothead and Sam the cool one. This display might have been slightly out of character, but Sam didn't seem to care. She wasn't letting this guy run her off again.

"No, I'm fine. Let's get a drink. Micah, where is the pizza I was promised?" She smiled at the equally shocked Micah as she walked further into the home, fully planning to ignore Newbie-Asshole, now identified as Callum fucking Barker, for the rest of the night.

****

She absolutely and completely failed at her plan. When he wasn't yelling at the game or talking with Micah, Kristin, and Drew, Callum sat there at ease without even a single look her way. It was like she didn't even exist. He even responded to some of Kristin's comments, but nothing when Sam spoke. His purposeful ignoring filled her bones with a mixture of embarrassment and white-hot anger. She wanted to yell at him to look at her or answer her question. Hell, she would even take mockery at this point. She just wanted him to react to her in some way. And she hated that she wanted it so badly.

She had been stealing glances at him for the past two hours, unnoticed as she was sitting slightly behind him. Hence, she had absolutely no idea what was happening in the game whatsoever. It didn't help that, after looking him over, she was now debating whether or not his level of attractiveness outweighed some of the obvious character flaws.

She'd known he was easy to look at. She could tell that first night they'd met, even in the dimly lit bar. But if she was being honest with herself, now that she was able to fully assess the man before her in better light, she had to admit that he wasn't just attractive, he was fucking gorgeous, and she hated him for it.

Slightly wavy dark hair that desperately needed to be styled, or at the very least cut a little. Hell, she would settle for a run through with a comb. But then she thought, maybe not. Maybe that would take away some of the beauty. It fell to his shoulders and there was a fleeting moment in which she contemplated what it would feel like if she ran her hands through it. Then there was his shirt. She could tell by the way it fit across his broad shoulders that he was toned. Not built or particularly muscular, but she doubted there was an ounce of fat on his body. Why was it that guys could always look like they just rolled out of bed and yet were still somehow devastatingly handsome?

He also had the bluest eyes she had ever seen. She hadn't

noticed them during either of their previous encounters at Topline, but they were on full display now. The hue reminded her of what she assumed water in the Caribbean would look like. So enticing, but most likely hiding a deadly current underneath just waiting to suck you up, never to let you go.

Since he was wearing shorts, she was able to see that the design of vines trailing up his right arm was continued down his left leg from his calf up under the hem of his shorts. They were kind of mesmerizing in design, but she realized she needed to stop staring when she started to wonder if those vines connected somewhere in the middle. Kristin had caught her a few times, but thankfully no one else had. Everyone was too enthralled by the game to worry about where Sam's eyes were focused.

She sent up a prayer of thanks when the final buzzer sounded, and promptly decided some air on the back porch was much needed. She had been here a few times over the last year with Kristin while Callum and Drew had been off doing whatever it was they did in Charleston. Similarly to where she and Kristin lived, this neighborhood was technically considered a student townhouse community, even though it was a few miles from campus, and it was far enough away from the city lights that you could actually make out the stars in the sky.

That was one of the things she missed most about living in the country. She had spent most of her upbringing in the city, but a few foster homes had been out in more rural areas. She hadn't realized how much she loved staring up at the stillness of it all until it had been taken away.

So that's exactly what she was doing, counting the stars, while also trying to cool down, both emotionally and physically, when she heard the back door swing open and Callum fucking Barker walk out to lean back on the railing.

It was a small deck, barely large enough to fit a grill plus another five people comfortably, so she shifted a few inches over trying to get as far away as possible from Newbie-Asshole and the cigarette he lit up.

She kept her face turned forward, refusing to even acknowledge his presence. She wanted the upper hand here. She wanted him to break first. She needed him to be the one to say something. But he didn't say a word. The silence was absolutely deafening—maddening to the point that Sam felt as if her heart was going to beat out of her chest. She wanted to scream.

She broke.

"You know you're cutting ten years off your life with those. Lung cancer is a horrible way to go," she said without looking in his direction.

He gave a snide little laugh.

"Good thing I don't give a shit, huh?" He blew the smoke out in her direction, causing her to cough and that white-hot anger that had just barely cooled down while counting the stars began bubbling up to the surface once more.

"Could you at least not do it while I'm out here? I'd like to be able to breathe for the duration of my life."

He fully turned and looked her way for the first time, his face set in a permanent scowl so offensive it would give Mrs. Saunders a run for her money. For just a moment, she fought the urge to spit more venom-laced words in his direction. It took all her restraint to hold them back. She had never been this person. She had never been cruel or mean to anyone, and yet this man somehow provoked the worst out of her. Just his existence seemed to stoke the coals of a fire Sam didn't even realize she had brewing under the surface.

"This is my porch, not yours. So, if it's bothering you that much, please feel free to walk back inside. Or better yet, feel free to walk right the fuck out my front door," he said while giving her the most contemptuous *fuck you* smile she had ever seen.

Her shoulders were rapidly rising and falling along with the rollercoaster of emotions running through her. She bit her lips to refrain from spewing out the few choice words and phrases that seemed to be sitting on the tip of her tongue.

Then he licked his lips and her heart rate stumbled as she noticed how full those stupid lips were. And then he smiled slightly, causing them to pull up, and she noted how that stupid dimple on his left cheek seemed to fit in perfectly with the straight line of his stupid jaw.

He cleared his throat.

She startled when she realized he'd caught her admiring him. Again.

"Fuck you," she breathed out the words as she stalked the few feet back to the door, hoping he would stay out there for the duration of their time here. But he wasn't too far behind. She must not have been walking fast enough because, before she had even made it fully into the home, he all but pushed her to the side in order to get to the fridge.

She'd had enough.

Newbie-Asshole was a complete and total dick. It didn't matter how gorgeous he was, or how much she wanted to run her fingers through his hair, or how she suddenly wondered if his lips would feel as soft as they looked. He was a complete ass. An ass she had to work with. An ass that lived with her best friend's boyfriend. An ass that she would most likely be stuck with for an undetermined, but probably unbearably long time.

Ugh.

She let out a deep breath, willing it all to end.

"What the hell is your problem?" Her words had lost their fire and her resolve was beginning to falter. "I get that we didn't have the best introduction, but we are probably going to be around each other a good bit between work and then with Micah and Kristin dating. Could you at least not be so rude?" She held her hand out for him to shake, silently asking for a sort of truce. "Can we just start over?"

He stared at her for a second and there was something in the way he looked at her that she couldn't quite place. It caused her breath to hitch and her skin to pebble. She swallowed as she desperately tried not to let him see the mild trembling that had crept into her outstretched hand.

Then he burst out laughing.

He was laughing so hard he had to bend forward and hold his stomach. What was even more annoying was the fact that if it hadn't been at her expense, she would have been enthralled by how amazing his laughter sounded.

"Fine, then. Continue on being miserable and ruin your lungs in the process." She yanked her hand back and walked back into the living room only to find Drew flipping through channels and no Micah or Kristin in sight.

She had to hold in her groan of frustration when Callum parked himself opposite her on the couch and then Drew started toward his room upstairs.

She was stuck in this room, in this house, in this *world* with the one person she despised more than anyone else.

She pulled out her phone and sent Kristin a pleading text to come back up so they could leave immediately. As soon as she hit send, she heard a buzz coming from Callum's side of the couch. He dug the discarded phone out from between the cushions and read what was displayed on that blasted screen before his eyes cut back to Sam.

"Newbie-Asshole, huh?" he smirked back at her. "That's a new one. And for the record, I've lived here for over a year. This is the first time I've seen you here, so I think you are more the 'newbie' here, not me."

Why was he so damn annoying?

"Ugh," her audible groan seemed to reverberate through the townhouse. "That's from work, if you must know. We refer to all the new hires as newbies for a few weeks. The asshole part is just a reflection of your general character."

His facial expression made her pause. It actually looked like she may have hit a nerve. His eyes dropped to the ground, and he took a breath before they made eye contact again. But she had to stop it before it started. She didn't want to go back and forth tonight seeing who could throw more insults at the other. She just wanted to go home.

She reached out to yank the phone away from him before calmly asking, "Can you text Micah and see when they'll be coming up? I don't want to barge in on them in bed or anything, but I'm ready to go; it's past midnight."

Callum didn't say anything. Instead, he chose to take this moment to stare her down...again. It was as if she was a puzzle he just couldn't quite figure out. His eyes roamed from her head to her feet and she awkwardly shuffled on the couch as if the movement would lessen the feeling that stare gave her.

She was about to say *fuck it* and start mouthing off when he suddenly got up and headed downstairs without a word. Due to her knowledge of the townhome's layout, she knew his bedroom was across the hall from Micah's in the basement, and based on their interactions thus far, she assumed he was probably just ignoring her and had headed to bed.

She might be spending the night on this couch, and if so, Kristin was doing all of her laundry for the remainder of the week. Hell, maybe even the month.

She was more than surprised when Callum walked back in a few moments later followed by Kristin and Micah, the latter still awkwardly buttoning up his pants. She muttered out a quick "Thanks" and received a head nod in return before he disappeared back into the kitchen. Despite how brief it had been, this was their first interaction that wasn't openly hostile.

After a way too drawn out goodbye between Kristin and Micah, they finally started to leave. But when Sam looked back, she found Callum leaning against the door frame, watching her.

Chapter 6 - Callum

Callum had read through the same four pages of the catalog three times now without retaining a single ounce of information. His mind was too focused on the whiff of peppermint that had lingered in the air after Sam had walked away.

It had been two days since he'd seen her, and she was still stuck in his head. He hated that. He didn't want to think about the way her hair moved as she walked through the room, or the enticing curve of her neck just above the collar of her shirt. He didn't want to remember the way his chest had tightened when she burst out into a laugh at something one of the other waitresses had said, or the way her green eyes seemed to shine in the twinkling lights that were strung through the ceiling of the bar. He didn't want any of it. Mostly because it was perfect. It was all too damn perfect, and he would ruin it. That's what he did. Callum Barker ruined things.

"You figure out which ones we should order?" Drew waved a hand in front of Callum's face as he spoke.

"Um."

Shit.

He turned back to the front and looked through the first few pages once more. These chairs and tables were getting ridiculously expensive, but they needed at least three new sets for one shop alone.

"What's wrong?" Drew slid the book out of Callum's view and gave him a knowing look.

"Nothing," Callum spat out while he stood and walked over to the new cases of ink they needed to organize.

"Bullshit," Drew countered. "You're in a pissy mood, and

while you might physically be here, your mind is in a completely different place."

"I have a lot going on."

"No, you don't."

"I'm here fixing all this crap and dealing with the shit storm at Topline." He hoped Drew understood that said shit storm was the creep of a manager, Mason Brimley, whom Callum was still trying to figure out how to deal with, and not the girl who had lived in his every thought since he'd first laid eyes on her.

"You're thinking about her, aren't you?"

"Who?" Callum furrowed his brow as if he didn't know exactly who Drew was referring to.

"You know who." Drew stepped directly into Callum's line of sight.

Callum tried to lift up the crate to move somewhere else, but Drew quickly stopped him.

"Why were you so mean to her the other night?"

"I still have no idea who you're talking about," Callum lied.

"Cut the shit, Callum. You were an ass to her."

Callum reached for the chair behind him, making a very ungraceful plop as he sat. Drew promptly sat right beside him. It was a weekday and Inked was closed, so they were thankfully alone with no prying ears to listen in.

"I would fuck up her life."

"I don't think you would," Drew quickly countered.

"I know I would."

"Maybe try not insulting her or telling her to, I'm sorry, how did you phrase it? 'Walk right the fuck out my front door,'" Drew suggested with an incredulous look.

"If she hates me, then she won't become a problem."

Drew shook his head in frustration.

"Whatever, man." Drew stood up then and reached out a hand to pull Callum up as well. "Let's pick out these chairs and get home."

Chapter 7 -Sam

Sam's bus ride to Topline two mornings later was a combination of cursing at the horrible drivers on the road and praying Callum wouldn't be working. Fortunately, he was nowhere in sight, and her day was pleasantly mundane. Saturday lunches always were.

Between work and school, the remainder of the weekend and into Monday went by as normally as she could have hoped it would. After acting out a full conversation during her morning shower, she was even able to meet with her graduate instructor, Stephen, and get him to agree to let her do some extra credit in order to bump the grade of her failed lab assignment up to a B.

By the time she was walking into Topline on Tuesday morning, heading directly to the kiosk to clock in, Callum fucking Barker was the furthest thing from her mind. At least, until she almost walked straight into him.

"Well, look who's here," he said, blocking her way to the kiosk.

"Yep. Gotta pay my bills, so could you move out of the way?"

She crossed her arms in defiance and he rolled his eyes.

Thankfully, she didn't have to interact with him for the rest of the night. More than once, she questioned what kind of bartender he must be if he never actually made the drinks, but decided not to linger on the question—or other thoughts of him—for too long.

She was dragging, but had less than an hour left. She contemplated grabbing a quick coffee from the waitstaff coffee station at the back, but then remembered the lackluster selection with no whipped cream or caramel or cinnamon, and decided to just push through. Bitter coffee would almost be as bad as no coffee at all.

She was about to close out her last table and had already started to mentally tally up her tips when it happened. The woman at Table 42 didn't agree with the total on her bill, swearing she'd never ordered the cherry lime daiquiri, and promptly threw the ticket in Sam's face.

The lady was right; it was her friend who had ordered it, not her. And although mistakes did happen, they couldn't happen here. Not when the guest was always right and they would chew you up and spit you out for even the mildest offense.

She couldn't let it bother her, though. Never had before. All she could do was just nod politely, make amends, and fix the bill. Maybe she could even convince Mr. Brimley to take twenty percent off for the inconvenience. But then the lady started in on her. She chewed Sam out for the better part of forever, hitting every nerve she could in the process.

She was drunk. Sam knew this. It may not have been a daiquiri, but she'd had enough vodka tonics to cause the filter she should have possessed to fly away. But even though the insults were filled with more slurred ramblings than coherent words, they still hurt.

"Did your parents not teach you to read?"

"Did you even finish highschool?"

"Probably going to work here for the rest of your miserable life and never amount to anything."

"I bet you couldn't get into college if your life depended on it."

At first, she took it with a smile, but then her heart started to beat a little more rapidly and she felt the sweat gather on her neck.

Maybe it was because she was already on edge knowing Callum was there tonight. If he was anywhere in the vicinity, she was sure he would be loving the show.

So, she quickly corrected the woman, something Mr. Brimley would fuss at her about later. Sam told the woman she had a 4.0 GPA and was slated to go to med school after she graduated. She didn't mention that she hadn't yet heard back from a single school, or that her MCAT score was average. But then the woman cut in with a laugh and made her friends promise to never allow someone with such incompetence to treat her. She said that she would rather *die* than be left in the hands of someone as idiotic as Sam.

Eventually, Sam just walked away as the woman continued to rant. She would deal with whatever the fall out was later.

She didn't realize her vision had become blurred with unshed tears or that she was shaking until it took her three tries to enter her keycard into the kiosk. And then it took her four more times fumbling through codes before the correct check popped up on the screen. When she stopped to take a deep breath, hoping the increased oxygen would somehow make it to her brain and cause it to start working properly, the paper was yanked out of her hand. She jumped back, preparing to curse whoever was making her night even worse, only to see Callum deftly entering everything in the computer with record speed and fixing the checks without a word. She mouthed a quick "Thank you" and went to take the corrected bill back when he stopped her.

"Don't go back to that table. I'll handle it." He started to walk past her, but she grabbed his arm to stop his movement. She wasn't expecting the taut muscles underneath to feel as enticing as they did and quickly pulled her hand back.

"I have to check them out."

"I'll handle it," he repeated as he looked down at her.

"You're a bartender," she countered.

"I said I'll handle it."

Too stunned to really process anything, she turned toward

the bar to find Jess and asked if she could get a plate to go. She very rarely ordered after a shift. She considered it a luxury and only did it once a month or so. She had already eaten here last week, but she knew she was too physically and mentally drained to fix anything when she got home.

She hadn't even officially clocked out, but went straight to the already closed section of the bar and sat down. She didn't even notice that another person sat down beside her until the bill fold slid into view.

"The tip is in there. It's only a dollar, so don't worry about plugging it into the system. I went ahead and logged you out for the night." Callum's voice was surprisingly comforting. He took a deep breath before he pulled his hand back, leaving the billfold in front of her. "Don't worry about people like that. She was being a complete ass."

"Takes one to know one." She cringed, not having meant for the retort to come out as harshly as it did.

He flinched at her words.

"Dr. Sam, huh?"

She chose to ignore his remark and silently begged for him not to start now. She just wanted to walk out. She just wanted to go home and forget she'd let that woman get the better of her.

"Is that why I've never seen you with Kristin before? You're always tucked away somewhere studying?"
She couldn't tell whether this was an actual conversation with no ill will attached, or if he was about to live up to his nickname.

Sam decided to hope for the best.

"Yes, I am. Next year I'll be a senior, and then hopefully the year after that I'll be off to medical school. At least that's the plan." She still refused to meet his gaze.

"I didn't have you pegged as a med student. Actually, I kind of thought you might be a ditzy, entitled college girl just getting a degree to please mommy and daddy." He laughed a little and, while she could tell he hadn't meant it in a mean way, his words still stung.

Again, she didn't respond.

She gave Jess a quick smile as she passed over Sam's drink and plate. She had hoped Jess would stick around and maybe alleviate some of the tension. Sadly, Jess was gone before Sam even unrolled her silverware.

"What made you want to be a doctor?"

This time she turned toward him.

"Why all the sudden interest in my life?"

"Like you said, we are going to be around each other regularly now that Drew and I are back in town, so I figured–"

"Are y'all a couple?" she blurted out without thinking.

"What?" His brows creased in confusion.

"You and Drew? Are y'all a couple?" It was a perfectly logical question. They did almost everything together.
Callum rolled his eyes in annoyance. "Nope. He's just my best friend and we share the same passion."

"Don't get all fussy. It was an honest question." She started to dig into her dinner, hoping he would get the cue to leave her alone.

"We own a business together, hence why we travel together. Drew has a girlfriend and he mostly stays with her when we're in Charleston."

"What about you?" she asked between sips of her drink.

"What do you mean, 'what about me?'"

"Do you have a girlfriend?" Sam swallowed. She had *not* planned on asking that and it took all her self control not to curl into a ball and hurl herself outside to get away from him.

"Why do you want to know?"

"Like you said, we're going to be around each other more now that you and Drew are back." She cut him a not so convincing smile.

"No. I'm single."

She hummed in response, not wanting to admit what she'd

been looking for in his answer.

"What about you?"

She stalled, not sure if he was truly asking her relationship status or if it was something else she was missing. She didn't want to assume and then look weird.

"What about you?" he asked more pointedly this time. "Are you single, or is there a Mr. Uptight you hide down in the library."

"I'm not uptight."

"You're the most tightly wound person I have ever met."

"Ugh." She rolled her eyes and continued to eat her meal. She normally would have taken it home, and she wasn't quite sure why she hadn't just gotten up the second Jess had placed it in front of her, but here she was, sitting beside Newbie-Asshole Callum Barker, stuffing her face without a care in the world.

"You still haven't answered my question."

"I'm single," she blurted out with a mouthful of chicken.

"You also didn't answer my other question."

"What was that?"

"Why do you want to be a doctor?"

Her pause dragged on longer than she'd intended, but she wasn't sure whether to give some sarcastic half-assed answer or to tell him the truth. Her fight was almost gone and she was close to cleaning her plate.

She settled on the truth.

"I want to make a difference. I want to help people. Sara was a doctor, and she would let me come hang out at the hospital to get away. It was like an escape. So, I guess I just gravitated toward it." She hadn't meant to divulge that much information, but for some inexplicable reason it all just came rushing out.

"Is Sara your sister?"

She knew he was just trying to talk, but she didn't want to go there. Not with someone she found barely tolerable at best.

"No."

There was an awkward silence for a few minutes before she

decided to break the tension. If he was making an effort, she could at least match his energy.

"What about you? Master bartender by night and tattoo artist by day?"

He chuckled a little before responding, "I'm not a bartender."

She almost choked on her chicken.

"What?"

"Tattoo artist, yes. Though, not so much anymore. I spend most of my time on the business end of the shops now. But, no, I'm not a bartender. Or, at least, not in any official capacity."

Her brows creased in confusion and she fully turned in his direction for the first time. "That doesn't make sense. You were hired here and you made my drinks in the bar. You are wearing the black shirt and–"

"In case you haven't noticed, I always wear black shirts, and the dress pants are just because I want to at least look slightly professional while I'm here. I could wear another shirt if I wanted."

"I don't understand."

"I'm the owner."

She almost died right there. It was pure dumb luck she didn't choke on that last bite.

"I just took this on about a month ago. It kind of came out of nowhere. I'm here for the next few weeks to check in on the staff and patrons, and make sure everything is as it should be, and then I hope to take a step back once I know everything is up to par."

Owner?

She stumbled through each memory of every interaction they'd had, none of which could even begin to be described as pleasant.

Oh, God.

She'd spilled drinks on her boss.

She'd called her boss an asshole.

She'd said the words fuck you *to her boss.*

To.

Her.

Boss.

And now she wanted to vomit.

He must have seen it on her face, because the laugh he let out was completely genuine.

"Don't worry, Dr. Sam. You aren't getting fired."

"I spilled drinks on you," Sam stated in disbelief.

"You did." He nodded with the reply.

"Then I cussed you out at your house and basically told you to go fuck yourself."

"You did that as well." He started to laugh once more, and dammit if his smile wasn't ridiculously, jaw droppingly beautiful.

"Why are you not firing me?"

He swallowed and then shrugged his shoulders.

"Mason wanted to." He used Mr. Brimley's first name, which kind of made Sam's skin crawl and further confirmed to her that Mr. Brimley was his employee, which meant he really was no longer just Callum or Newbie-Asshole. He was *Mr. Barker*. "Actually, he planned to that night after the fiasco with the drinks."

"Should I call you Mr. Barker or sir from now on?" Her question was completely genuine.

His brows rose as he sucked in a breath.

"Let's not do that." His voice was too tight. "Yet," he added. He cleared his throat as he shifted slightly on the stool.

"Why didn't you let him?"

"What?" The question seemed to jolt him back to reality and he looked at her with a slightly stunned expression.

"Why didn't you let him fire me?"

"That's a tough question. Truthfully, I don't even know if I have an answer."

She quickly turned back around, facing the tower of liquor bottles in front of them, and finished her plate, taking care to slowly and thoroughly chew each bite in fear of any more revelations coming to light that might cause another near death scenario. She had thought he would get up then and leave, but he didn't move. He didn't speak another word. When one of the busboys came to grab her empty plate, she handed it over and turned back to face Callum.

She could have left right then.

There was nothing keeping her sitting in that barstool.

She could have told him thank you for not firing her and thus sending her down a road she was desperately trying to avoid.

She could have gotten up and gone home.

But something stopped her.

Something made her ask.

"What's your story?" She could tell by the look on his face that this, too, came out a little harsher than she'd intended.

"Why all the sudden interest in my life?" He smirked.

"I just mean–"

"I know what you mean. I was just...I was just..." He paused as he let out a deep breath. "I don't know. My story is rather boring. But I have a feeling you hide a much better one under that uptight, goody two shoes persona you put on."

Normally, she would have balked at his comment, but not now. There were too many questions circling through her brain to allow for halfwitted digs to surface.

"Why still do the tattoo thing if you own Topline?"

"Because it's what I'm passionate about."

She nodded in understanding.

"It's not bad revenue either, despite what others may think. We do well for ourselves. But if I could do anything all day, every day, I would draw, paint, create."

"You're not who I thought you were."

"You mean you saw the long, dark disheveled hair, tattoos, and party house, and assumed I was a lazy asshole bum with five dollars to my name and spent every cent I had on booze, drugs, and girls?"

The sheepish smile that crossed her face was a clear

giveaway. She couldn't hide it even if she wanted to.

"Would you hate me if I said that about hit the nail on the head?"

"You shouldn't judge a book by its cover." His words were quiet. Almost a whisper.

"I know. Trust me, I know." She nodded in agreement.

Well, that was a shocker. Definitely not what she'd been expecting. Especially since she'd met his dad and siblings. She thought his dad was a doctor of some kind, and she knew that his brother, Connor, was fresh out of med school. His family had been kind to her at the dinner where they'd met, but that was all she really knew about them. On the outside, they looked like a page torn out of a country club's monthly newsletter. Nothing like the image Callum portrayed. She wondered if that was why he was the way he was. Was he desperate to distance himself from the suffocating box that must have been his adolescence?

Her mouth continued to talk without her brain thinking through her next words. "So, are you the odd ball?" He looked a little confused by her question, so she clarified, "You and Connor are most definitely opposites." She didn't mean it as harshly as it sounded, and from the emotions that flashed through his eyes, she could tell her comment stung.

"How the fuck do you know Connor?" he spat out as he began to stand.

"I met him—"

"You know what? It doesn't matter. Just don't fucking compare us, okay? Don't do that."

And then he walked away, leaving her clueless as to what had just occurred.

Chapter 8 - Sam

Christian held the door as they walked in. They had spent the better part of the previous evening huddled together at a back table in the library and she was exhausted. He'd promised her that if she memorized the entirety of the muscle and nerve innervation chart by the time they left, he would buy her the largest cup of coffee she had ever seen.

She'd gladly taken the challenge.

"I can't believe junior year is almost over." She clasped her fingers around the hot cup, hoping some of the heat would soak in. It was still March and the last few days had found the famously hot city in a bit of a cold snap.

"One more year until you run off to do great things without me." Christian pushed out his bottom lip.

"Are you going to miss me?" Sam smiled broadly at that idea.

"About as much as I miss gum on the bottom of my shoe." His lips slipped up into a bright smile. He couldn't even be mean to her in a joke.

"Maybe I will stuff you in my suitcase and take you with me."

"Maybe you should," he added before he took another sip of his drink.

Sam smiled as she held in every emotion that threatened to burst out. Taking him with her was exactly what she wanted. Except, that's not really what he wanted.

Christian had one more year left of business classes, and

then was planning on becoming some big time financial advisor somewhere far away.

"What's that look for?" He reached out and laced their hands together as he spoke. She couldn't hide anything from him any more than she could hide it from Kristin.

"I do want to take you with me. I want to pack you up and stuff you in my carry-on so I can make you study with me every night while I bore you with minute details of the kidneys you don't need to know."

"I could never get bored of you." He squeezed her fingers. "What if we make a deal?"

"We just made one"—she lifted up the cup in her hands— "and I won."

Christian laughed.

"You go off and become Dr. Samantha Williams and, if you haven't been snagged by some hot shot med student by the time you graduate, then you and I can get married for the tax benefits." He laughed a little. "Then you can bore me with all the medical nonsense for the rest of our lives."

She used her laugh to cover up the tears that sprang from her eyes. He thought they were tears coming from a place of pure hysterics and absurdities. Little did he know, that one sentence had broken her and then pieced her back together only to break her once more.

Chapter 9 - Callum

He was supposed to be on the floor making sure everything was as it should be. That's what good owners did. Good owners finished with the boring office work and walked the floor. Except Callum couldn't do that. He had finished up that paperwork, made the new orders and confirmed the payroll and schedules for the following two weeks. He had also spent far too much time staring at her name on the lineup for that night.

Sam was in section eight. Mason had originally placed her in section fifteen, but those were small two-person tables near the back with no windows and he knew the tips would barely be anything to brag about. As soon as he was alone, and before the evening crew came bustling in, he grabbed the expo marker and switched her name with some guy named Kyle who he hadn't even met yet. He wanted to feel bad for the poor sucker who got stuck with the worst spot for the night, but he felt nothing but excitement at the thought of her smile when she saw where she had been placed.

By the time he finally dragged himself out of that office, he had worked himself up into a ball of stress. His palms were clammy and his shirt felt too tight. He had taken a shot to calm himself before he walked out. Okay, maybe the shot was really to help him muster up the courage to apologize for his shitty behavior.

The shot was not doing its intended job.

Maybe he should have had two.

Or maybe he just shouldn't worry about what Sam was

doing, or where she was at, or if her hair was pulled into a ponytail or a bun.

He let out a ragged breath.

He walked the floor as he should and happened to notice the section he had placed her in was completely full. She came bursting around the corner without even noticing him as she ran from table to table, passing out food and filling up drinks. She would most definitely go home with a bragworthy amount tonight.

He smiled.

And then he cringed at the notion that she was literally moving nonstop; so rushed that she barely had a second to breathe. He eyed the tables and took note of the drinks and then ran behind the bar to grab the water and sweet tea pitchers and exhaled a frustrated sigh. He didn't want her to be completely exhausted. *She might have class the next day, and if she was exhausted then maybe she wouldn't do well, and if she didn't do well then she would probably be upset and then....* He stopped that train of thought. There was absolutely no reason he needed to be worried about her class schedule, or her emotions, or anything else. He was her damn boss, not her boyfriend.

All night, he waited until she was back at the kiosk or inside the kitchen or kindly helping another section, and then quietly went up to each table, making sure their drinks were filled to the brim. He then checked her orders and put a rush on the ones he could tell were meant for the fussier tables.

He spent the entirety of the night making sure her section had everything they could need or want. When he overheard a table asking her for extra vinaigrette, he quickly grabbed one out of the kitchen and placed it at the waitress station before she even made it around the corner

He wanted to laugh when she abruptly halted as it came into view. He was sure she knew it hadn't been there a minute ago, but he knew she would have no explanation for how it had suddenly appeared.

Chapter 10 - Sam

By the time the weekend came, Sam hadn't spent nearly enough time studying. Most of her free time had been consumed with replaying her conversation with Callum in her head, and she was somehow still utterly confused. He'd seemed nice and surprisingly interesting while talking about school and work, but had gone nuts at the mention of his family. She had worked with him once since then, and they hadn't spoken a single word. Hadn't even made eye contact. She'd tried to smile a few times when he walked by, but he'd never so much as looked her way.

Still, on Friday night when Kristin asked if Sam wanted to head to Micah's for a party, Sam surprised them both when she immediately accepted the invitation. She hadn't yet told Kristin that Callum fucking Barker was her boss, and she didn't know if she would. That would add to the already awkward—though, admittedly, slightly intriguing—scenario she kept playing in her head.

Although she had never been to an actual party at Micah's, she had been there enough with Kristin over the last year to try and convince herself that she would be perfectly fine. If Callum was there, then maybe she could smooth things over with him again.

A part of her kept questioning why she even cared enough to want him not to hate her.

Why did his opinion of her matter so much?

Why had it consumed most of her thoughts over the last week?

She kept telling herself it was because he was her boss and the last thing she needed was a boss who hated her. But even she knew that wasn't the full story.

When they arrived, she suddenly felt like perhaps this was a bad idea. She could hear the music from all the way across the parking lot.

Walking into the townhouse felt like a punch to her gut. She wasn't sure whether she wanted to run or if she would just vomit right there on the tattered welcome mat. There was a small sense of relief when she realized there were not nearly as many people as she had assumed would be here. For as loud as it was, she had definitely expected a larger crowd.

There were maybe ten people in the living room, but there was enough alcohol for fifty. That, she'd expected.

Then the smell hit her. It wasn't the usual repugnant odor that screamed of far too many late night parties.

It was sharp, but enticing. It made her take a deep breath, and she felt the tension in her shoulders release as she exhaled.

It was peppermint.

"What is that smell?" Sam asked, knowing full well what it was but wondering the source.

"Some type of peppermint spray thing Callum came home with the other day. Said we needed to stop smelling like pigs." Micah laughed. "And then he placed one of those in almost every room." He pointed to a teardrop shaped container with a seemingly timed emission of fragrance. "It's about to be summer, and he chooses a scent that is literally the definition of Christmas," Micah said, shaking his head.

Sam couldn't wipe the smile off her face.

Micah began introducing her to the others in the room while Kristin headed to the kitchen. By the fifth person, she realized she wasn't taking in a word anyone was saying. She was pretty sure she had nodded appropriately during each introduction, but she couldn't recall a single person's name. She was too busy focusing on the fact that Callum fucking Barker had bought and filled their home with the exact scent she liked to wear.

Maybe it was just a coincidence.

Maybe it meant absolutely nothing.

Maybe it meant absolutely *everything*.

She snapped out of it when they finally reached the kitchen, and made a promise to herself to try to remember the names of the next few people Micah brought her over to. Travis and Megan. They seemed okay. At least they spoke when they were introduced and she remembered the conversation. She was making progress. Then there was the blonde dude whose name Sam had already forgotten, and the girl wearing...*was that a bathing suit?*...didn't even bother to look up at her. The rest just nodded in greeting and got back to whatever it was they'd been talking about.

"Well, shit. I didn't think you would show. No textbooks need reading?" Callum called out as he approached from behind, his words coming out just a tad bit slurred.

"Not tonight," she replied, trying to keep her tone even. She had hoped to somehow ease the tension between them, but now that he was in front of her, she didn't even know what to say. She tried to come up with a comment about how nice the house smelled, but then realized she would sound completely insane if she voiced that aloud. She turned to head off into the kitchen just as bikini girl sat on Callum's lap.

That sight caused a flutter of unfamiliar emotions she refused to acknowledge to rush through her.

****

Sam ended up spending most of the evening sitting on the back porch (thankfully, the smell of Christmas didn't make it through the back door), drinking beers and tossing stories back and forth with Kristin, Travis, and Megan. Most of their tales consisted of happenings she had missed out on while basically living in that dungeon of a library. Some caused her to double over, clasping her stomach when all the laughing started to hurt.

"I didn't know you would be here!" she heard Christian's scream as he came from behind and jumped the deck railing to wrap his arms around her.

"What are you doing here?" she asked as she returned the hug.

Normally, they saw each other multiple times a week; whether it be for a study group, a quick lunch, coffee date, dinner, or just to sit on the couch and watch mindless TV to decompress from all the stress of life. But it had been almost a week since the last time they'd grabbed coffee. One of the longest times they had ever gone without seeing each other, save for that one time he'd been sent to a different foster home when they were seventeen. She'd cried for three days when he went away. Christian had stayed there for close to six months before returning to her town. In the time since, he hadn't once spoken about his time at the other foster home, and she'd always assumed it had been one of the dreaded types of placements.

They'd never known what would await them from home to home. The horrors that some adults would inflict upon their foster kids; monsters only opening their homes in order to get that measly check in the mail once a month. So, after that first despondent week when he'd barely spoken and had outright refused to answer her questions, she'd decided to leave it alone.

"Technically, I'm not *here*," he said, laughing. "I'm hanging out next door, but saw you over here and had to jump the fence to come say hi."

"I'm glad you did! You should stay!"

"No, he shouldn't," Callum seethed, leaning against the back door frame. "Get the fuck off my property before I call the cops."

"Callum?" Sam questioned in utter shock. Her confusion was echoed in everyone's eyes.

"I said get the fuck off my property!" Callum shouted, standing a bit taller, the taut muscles under his shirt rippling. She was sure he would fight somebody by the end of the night; she just wasn't sure if that fight would be with Christian, or with her, or with some unsuspecting person unlucky enough to get in his way.

"Don't talk to him like that!" Sam practically yelled as she placed herself between the two men. She was half the size of both, and definitely wouldn't be able to do a thing to stop them, but she sure as hell wasn't going to let Callum talk to Christian in that way.

"No. It's okay, Sam. I'm heading back next door. Come hang out over there when you get bored of this shit show."

"Don't fucking test me." Callum spit at the ground by Christian's feet before he turned and walked back into his house.

Her anger continued to build, but she wasn't sure where she should go or what she should do. A quick glance in Kristin's direction was proof enough that they were all a bit more than shocked by Callum's outburst.

"I'm so sorry, Christian," Sam yelled across the yard just as he started to jump the fence. He didn't say anything, but gave her a little wave and a nod before disappearing in the neighboring yard.

Without thinking, she burst through the back door into the kitchen. She caught sight of Callum's black shirt heading down the stairs and all but pushed the others out of her way in an effort to get to him.

"You can't just treat everyone you don't like as if they're pieces of shit," she screamed at him as she descended the stairs two steps at a time.

She saw him loop behind and under the stairs and assumed that was the way to his room, but she didn't make it that far. He was there the second her feet hit the bottom step, forcing her to move with her back to the wall to put some space between them.

"Sam. Don't. Just don't."

She wasn't sure how he'd made it back to the bottom of the staircase so quickly or why his body was all of a sudden pressed so tightly against hers that she could feel the inlaid grooves in the wall at her back.

"Fuck you, Callum." She pushed against his chest. He didn't

move a muscle. "Boss or no boss, you're a real dick. You know that, right?"

"Stay away from him," Callum said, bringing his face to her level to meet her gaze. Their breath swirled between them.

"You don't even know him!" She pushed him away a second time. He still refused to budge.

"Trust me, I know him, and he is a fucking asshole. The worst kind of human there is. Stay the fuck away from him, okay?"

"He is one of my best friends!" Sam's words caused Callum to recoil.

"He's one of...You have got to be kidding me."

"What do you have against him?"

"Maybe you aren't who I thought you were, either. Maybe judging a book by its cover sometimes turns into exactly what you suspected it would."

"What the hell is that supposed to mean?"

He turned away from her as she spoke, but she grabbed his chin, forcing his gaze to find hers once again.

"Go back to the party, Sam." He yanked her hand down away from his face and she jumped slightly when the wall reverberated with the slamming of his door.

Chapter 11 - Sam

As Sam was walking into Topline the next morning, she was greeted by a familiar face. Christian was seated in her section, waiting with a smile.

"What are you doing here? You hate this place."

"I was at the record store across the street and got hungry. Decided I might as well stop in and say hey. I miss you." He stood up and gave her the biggest bear hug she had ever had. "I remembered just how much I missed you when I saw you last night."

"Okay, okay. I can't breathe," she said through the laughter, and he tightened his hold. Even when he set her back down, he still didn't quite let her go. "I'm sorry about last night. Callum Barker is an ass." She leaned her head against his broad chest.

"Trust me. I know."

"How?"

"We've run into each other a few times. He's a prick and pretty much fucks anything with legs."

"Sounds about like him."

Although, it really didn't. It didn't sound like him at all. At least, not the Callum she'd sat with after her shift. That Callum was a strict contrast to the one who had made himself known the previous night.

"Are you really planning on eating here?" Sam questioned as she looked around and into the other sections.

"Yeah." Christian furrowed his brows in confusion. Her words came out in a rush. "Then do me a favor and stay over here in the back of my section."

"Are you embarrassed by me?" Christian's tone was clipped and full of anger.

"No. No. Absolutely not," Sam quickly replied, trying to calm him.

"Why are you hiding me?"

"I'm not hiding you." She groaned, knowing where this was headed. "Well, I kinda am, but only because Callum works here, too." She wasn't about to add that he was her boss.

"Callum? Callum Barker works here?"

"Yeah."

Christian took a deep breath as he looked around. His voice was filled with frustration. "Don't worry Sam, I promise not to kick his ass where you make your money."

"How about we just don't kick any ass whatsoever and go on with our day?" She gave him a cheesy smile, but the previously happy Christian was now in a foul mood.

"Don't be mad," she pleaded.

"Why do you think I'm mad?" He crossed his arms as he spoke.

She tilted her head and rolled her eyes. "Because you're doing the thing."

"What thing?" he asked.

"Getting all upset and moody and this." She gestured to his crossed arms and clenched fists.

"I don't want you working here anymore."

She threw her hands up in the air. "See, I knew you would get like this."

"I'm being honest. Quit. Come work with me at Papa Peet's."

"Christian, don't be ridiculous. You barely even get on the schedule. They're so slow I don't even know how they stay in business. You say so almost every time you work."

Christian rolled his eyes. "I'll grab you an application when I go by tonight."

"I don't want an application. I'm staying here."
She didn't want to admit that she might have been staying there because stupid Callum fucking Barker had made his house smell like her. And, for some reason, that made every nerve ending on her body stand up.

"I'll drop it off on my way to class tomorrow. You should be able to be on the schedule by the weekend."

"Christian, I'm not–"

"So"—he quickly cut her off—"do I get a discount for being their best girl's best friend?"

Sam took a breath. She knew that smile plastered on his face was just a façade, and that deep down he was seething. Christian didn't get angry often, but, when he did, it was a sight to behold. She, of course, had never been on the receiving end of that short temper, but she had witnessed enough school fights to know the struggle that bristled under the surface.

She decided to just go with it today. She had seen Callum's truck in the parking lot, which meant he was somewhere mulling around the restaurant, and there was not enough energy in the world to deal with both Callum and Christian at the same time.

She put on a smile almost as fake as Christian's and said, "I wish! Mr. Brimley is such a stickler, though. He barely even allows *us* to get a discount."

"No worries. A fancy high-priced meal is worth it if it comes with seeing your pretty face." He bent down and placed a kiss on her forehead.

Sam rolled her eyes. "You are such a heartbreaker. Is that the line you use on all the girls?"

"Only the endgame one."

Her heart nearly stopped. She wasn't quite sure how she was able to hold herself together at that moment, but she gave the customary swat of his arm and walked off, promising to be back as soon as she clocked in. The amount of emotions she had just gone through all but caused a wave of nausea to burst forth.

"You win the lottery last night or something?" Callum said as he leaned against the bar beside her.

She jumped at the noise. "What?"

"You have the biggest shit-eating grin going on here." He pointed to her lips.

"I'm not talking to you." She quickly turned back to the kiosk and refused to look in his direction.

He laughed. "You just did."

"Fuck you." She braced her hands on the table beside her as she desperately tried to rein in the punch she wanted to throw at him.

"That's not very appropriate work language." He threw a cherry into the air and caught it in his mouth.

"Well, I guess it's a good thing I don't give a fuck anymore." She knew he could fire her right there on the spot. She almost welcomed it. At least now she would have another job lined up by the weekend.

"Have a fun shift...not giving a fuck," he added, tossing up another cherry and leaning his head back in preparation for the catch.

It was pure dumb luck the bar had been built a few feet lower than the floor of the kiosk she currently stood on. She had never understood why it had been designed that way. Now, she decided it was just for this very moment. She reached out just before the cherry reached his lips and clasped it in her hand. Then she squeezed it, letting the sticky juice fall onto his stupid, annoyingly beautiful face.

He sputtered as he quickly wiped off the sticky residue. "Back at you."

She gave him a smirk and promptly walked away.

The rest of her day shift went by pretty fast. Christian being there had definitely made it easier than it would have been otherwise. She didn't see Callum again, and when she was ready to clock out, Mr. Brimley was there waiting for her.

"Don't forget we have the employee luncheon slash dinner thing tomorrow to raise money for our charity. I don't want to lose again this year. Not with higher management here." She internally groaned, knowing who he meant. "Since you're working day shift, I expect you to be there sometime tomorrow night to show support." She nodded and then headed out.

They had these events every year. Local restaurants competed for different charities by attendance, and planned lame activities and contests for attendees. Most of Topline's wait staff were in their fifties and sixties, so they probably wouldn't win any of the competition type stuff. Nonetheless, employees were required to at least show their faces to add participation points to the board. She had been working at a different restaurant this time last year, and had been able to get out of going.

Somehow, she knew she wouldn't be so lucky this time.

Chapter 12 - Sam

The next day was the same as always. Sam hadn't seen Callum around the restaurant, and assumed he was spending the day at the charity events.

Mostly, his absence felt like a weight off her shoulders. She didn't want to see him. But then there was that small, annoying part of her that felt a pang of remorse that he wasn't there.

About midday, when she still hadn't seen him and had the sudden revelation that this meant he was definitely at the event and she would absolutely see him that night, she had to sit down. A quick rush of excitement ran through her and nothing she did caused it to lessen.

Her reaction didn't make sense.

She thought she hated him.

She was supposed to hate him.

But, still, there was something she couldn't quite figure out: why had he been able to cause so much confusion and anger and...she didn't actually know what the other feeling she had for him would be called.

It definitely wasn't lust.

That wouldn't make any sense when she had already decided she would loathe him for all eternity. *Would it?*

Originally, she had planned just to head straight to the event from work. But something made her go home and change. Not only change, but also take a shower and put on a little make-up. She even teased her curls a little.

She got there at eight. The event was almost over. A small part of her had hoped he would already be gone. Another part of her was desperately hoping he was still there. She decided she would stay for thirty minutes and then head straight to the library for a few hours to get a start on her upcoming assignments.

The tally count was right at the entrance to the park. One look at the board and she knew for sure they were going to lose. The other restaurants had too many young—and present—employees for Topline to compete with.

She kept a close eye on her watch, and quickly signed herself in. Thankfully, she found a seat in the back row and sat, refusing to look around. Refusing to look for him.

She had been there all of twenty-seven minutes, debating whether to hold out for the next three when Callum plopped down beside her.

"Are these events always this lame? I mean, I wasn't expecting much, but from the way Mason built it up, you would have thought it was a mini Olympics," he casually observed, keeping his gaze on the crowd.

She slowly turned toward him, not sure what to say or do. Of course, her mouth promptly betrayed everything her brain instructed.

"Why are you gross and sweaty?"

"Relay race. Second place," he said with a smile. It must have just happened. He was still slightly out of breath.

She nodded, but couldn't help the urge to admire the way the sweat was formed on his brow. There was some stupid taunt forming on the tip of her tongue, but she lost it the second he threw his head back and ran a hand through his long dark hair. She turned back, not sure how to proceed.

God, this man was fucking beautiful.

She looked down at her watch and realized it had now hit forty minutes since she arrived. She could leave. She had plenty of work she should get done in the library.

But...she didn't.

"Mr. Brimley gets a little extra with stuff like this. I think he's desperate to win your approval."

"I can tell." Callum's reply was quick, as if he'd been waiting for it the entire time.

"Can I ask a personal question?" she blurted out, immediately regretting it.

"Maybe? Depends on what it is," he responded, still keeping his eyes trained on the crowd.

Just as she opened her mouth to reply, she noticed Mason—Mr. Brimley—headed their way.

"Hey, Sam, you haven't done an event yet and we need two more people."

"No thanks, Mr. Brimley, I think I'm going to sit this one out. I'm exhausted and it's late." She began shuffling with her phone, suddenly overcome with an itch to leave.

"Not a chance. The three legged race is next and you two are in it."

"I'm sorry, no, I don't think so. I'm about to head out anyway," she countered and began to stand to leave just as Callum spoke.

"Live a little," he said to her before he stood and asked Mr. Brimley where they needed to be. After they were directed to the starting line, Callum looked down at her with a smile. "Come on. It's one event. It isn't going to kill you."

"Being tied to you just might," she replied as the woman began tying their legs together.

It wouldn't take a genius to realize this was never going to work. He had to be at least a foot taller than her, if not more. When the girl finished securing their legs and walked away, Sam looked directly up to find Callum about to burst into a fit of laughter.

"I may actually die. You know that, right? We are going to trip, and you are going to fall on me, and then I'll have brain damage."

"Jesus. Way to go off into left field on that one. I was just going to suggest a few broken bones." He smiled, then burst out laughing again at her reaction.

"Ahh, that's so much better," she said with as much sarcasm as she could muster.

"Ready. Set. Go!" one of the hostesses shouted, and they took off.

Not even two steps in, they were on the ground. Callum rolled on top of her as they burst into an all-out fit of laughter.

"Dammit, Sam! Why do you have to be so short?" he said in jest while his short bursts of air flowed through her hair.

"I can't help my genetics! Now get off of me!" She playfully pushed him away.

"Come on. We are *not* going to be left at the starting line." He jumped to his feet, ripping the tie and picking her up in the process.

"What are you doing?" she asked as he threw her over his shoulder and started to run toward the finish line.

When he put her down, they were both still bursting with laughter.

Laughter which she used to hide the fact that she was about to burst at the seams. Callum Barker had just had his hands all over her. Her skin was on fire and her mouth suddenly became dry.

"Never again. I am *never* doing one of these again," she said while trying to catch her breath.

****

Sam and Callum humbly accepted their last-place finish and walked back toward their abandoned seats. It was then that she noticed his scent firmly planted in her hair. She tried not to be too obvious when she looped a strand in her fingers and brought it closer to her face.

"Sam? Hello? Are you listening to me?" He tapped her nose.

"What?" She quickly dropped the strand of hair and silently prayed he didn't clue in on what she was doing.

"I asked you a question and you completely zoned out."

"Sorry. What were you saying?"

"You had been wanting to ask a question right before Mason interrupted us?"

"Oh, right!" She had to take a moment to remember what that exact question was. Her brain was currently just trying to function following what had just occurred. "What was your first tattoo?" she finally blurted out as the thought came to her.

He turned away from her, but didn't say a word. He scooted his chair out and pulled down the neck of his shirt to show the top of his right shoulder blade. It took her a second to make out the design, but once she did, she had to forcefully hold in the gasp threatening to escape her lips.

It was beautiful. It looked like a geometric compass intertwined with a navigational compass, except it wasn't pointing North, and the glass was shattered.

Before she was even aware of the movement, she felt her finger tips brush along the outer edges of the design. Her hand jerked back as he tensed and she cleared her throat.

"I'm going to assume there is some significance to that?"

He wasn't looking at her and yet she could still tell he was wound far too tight by his tone alone.

"You would assume correctly." He turned back but didn't look at her.

She wanted to scream at her stupid idiotic brain.

And hand.

And self.

Callum was probably merely tolerating her, and here she had to go and reach out and touch him. Okay, technically he'd touched her first during the race, and he'd fallen on top of her, and picked her up, and carried her to the finish line. But that was all for a set activity they'd been pretty much forced to participate in. Well, kind of. He was the one who'd actually told her to live a little and basically forced them to do the race to begin with. But that didn't mean anything other than the fact that he wanted his business to win and get bumped up in the standings.

Maybe he did want to touch her.

Maybe he didn't.

Maybe he was just...

"That is actually my first professional one I had done," Callum said, pulling her from the rampant tornado of questions her brain was currently spiraling within. "Drew and I messed around with tattoos on each other before this, but I had those covered with better ones over time. We weren't the best when we first started." He laughed a little and took a swig of his beer.

Oh, god...

Why was that laugh the most beautiful melody she had ever heard?

"What's the story behind it?" Sam quickly inquired. She wasn't sure if she wanted him to laugh again or not. It would be so very torturous to hear it again, but then again, the torture of not hearing it again might be even worse.

He didn't answer, but instead shook his head in a definite no while smirking.

"Oh, come on. You just showed me a massive tattoo and you won't tell me what it means?"

"I'll tell you one day when I'm too drunk to care. How about that?"

"Whatever." Sam rolled her eyes.

"My turn," he said as he cocked his head her way. "Why are you so goddamn stressed all the time?" She started to argue, but he cut in again, "Don't take that the wrong way, okay? But you are so wound up all the time. Even before I walked over here, you looked like you had every muscle in your body tensed. What gives?"

She opened and closed her mouth multiple times, trying to find the right words to say. In the end, she settled on the truth.

"I have this scholarship, and there are a lot of stipulations in place that I have to live up to if I want to keep it. I basically can't get anything below a B for a single assignment, and I have to keep a 4.0 GPA. It hasn't been that hard to keep up with until this past year when classes started getting a lot tougher. I'm not sure how I will fare in medical school. So, anyway. I'm just stressed about the possibility of losing my scholarship and not being able to afford my last year of college. I would have to drop out until I could save up."

"What about your parents? Or grandparents? They didn't give you any money to help out with school?"

"Nope. It's all on me." Her heart tightened at the words.

"Well, that's shitty, but not completely impossible. I'm sure you will do fine."

"Let's hope I do," she responded with a smile that didn't quite reach her eyes.

He sat quiet for a moment before asking, "Would you like to come with me to Social for a while? I'm going to hear my friend's band tonight."

For a moment, she was a little clueless as to how she should respond. She checked her phone to find it was somehow already after nine. Had they really been talking for over an hour already? She wouldn't get much studying done tonight even if she did leave now.

So far, they had only interacted at work and then at Micah's. And very few of those interactions were what one would call positive. This would be the first time they would purposefully plan to meet up somewhere.

Would that make them friends?

She knew she should decline and head home to get some rest. She opened her mouth to say just that, but for some reason the exact opposite came out.

"Um...yeah, sure. Where is it?"

"Social? It's right downtown. You can follow me and then head out for home whenever."

"Okay, yeah. When do you want to go? Now?"

"If that's okay with you, yeah. His band starts at ten. I

promised I would at least make an appearance."

"Alright, lead the way, Newbie." She smiled as they got up and said a prayer of thanks that she had driven Kristin's car tonight instead of taking the bus as she normally would have done. That was a conversation she didn't want to have.

"What happened to the *asshole* part of that name?"

"I've since decided that may have been a misjudgment of character on my part. Don't get me wrong, the jury's still out, but I'll wait a little longer before I make the official decision," she responded, smirking.

He started laughing, and it was the same perfect sound he'd made earlier.

Chapter 13 - Callum

Callum was gripping the steering wheel so tight he could feel the leather crunch under his grip. He had just invited her to see a band, and...

She.

Said.

Yes.

That was not how it was supposed to go.

It was supposed to go something like this: do the three-legged race and piss her off (not have to hide the raging erection that came after he'd landed on top of her), say stupid shit while they spoke that made her mad (not almost stop breathing as she brushed her fingers across the skin of his tattoo), and then leave her sitting alone and frustrated (not ask her to meet up with him to hear a band).

He had royally fucked up.

Now he would have to spend the next hour acting like he wasn't about to burst at the fucking seams. He watched as she circled the lot a few times in her rather expensive Mercedes-Benz and he wanted to throw up even more. She came from the same circles as he did. Normally, that would make someone more compatible. But after the life he led, he knew they would be nothing but an absolute disaster together. She most likely came from money and perfectly polished parents who would faint at the idea of their perfect pre-med daughter being seen with a tattoo-covered disappointment.

He pushed those thoughts from his head.

They weren't there as a couple.

This was not a date.

They were just going to see a band.

He repeated those three phrases over and over again in his head as walked to meet her at the entrance.

Chapter 14 - Sam

It was obvious that Callum knew a lot of people at Social; she had been introduced to at least ten people just trying to make their way through the door. The band was good. It wasn't her kind of music. She was more of a Swifty, but it wasn't bad at all.

After about thirty minutes of standing and slowly being pushed further and further back, the place became packed and they ended up nearly pressed up next to each other. She tensed when the side of her arm brushed the side of his, but he didn't seem to acknowledge the touch.

It took an immense amount of self-control to keep from constantly turning to look at him. Thankfully, he only caught her gaze a few times. She still blushed whenever his eyes met hers.

"I'm sorry for bringing up your brother the other day. I didn't realize it was a sore subject and I'm sorry. I'm...I'm just sorry I upset you," she said the apology so quickly she wasn't exactly sure if he heard it all.

Callum smiled as he took another swig of his drink.

"It's okay. It's not really a sore subject. I don't know. Maybe it is? We just don't get along great and it's just a big family drama situation you don't want to hear about. But yeah, it's okay. Sorry I just bolted when you brought it up." *Well, thank fuck.* She was hoping maybe he wouldn't hate her forever for that. "And...I would like to say sorry about the thing with...Christian the other night, but I would be lying. I hate him, and he is never welcome on my property." Callum forced out Christian's name with the most obvious disdain.

She wasn't really sure how to respond to that. There was definitely no malice in his words. Just straight facts.

"Why do you hate him so much?"

"I can't talk about that now."

Sam let out a frustrated breath. "Will you ever talk about it?"

"Probably not."

"So I'm just supposed to forget the fact that y'all know each other?"

Callum cut his eyes down toward her with a smirk.

"How do you know him, anyway?" he asked, tilting his head further her way.

Panic immediately started to set in. Surprisingly, anyone who didn't already know her past had never asked her who Christian was to her. But she was prepared. As always. She had a story made up in her mind; childhood best friends, blah blah blah. But...for some reason, she didn't want to lie. Nor did she want to tell the truth.

"Um, Christian and I–"

"No, not him. I don't want to hear about him ever again. I was asking about my brother, Connor." Relief flooded her system. In one respect, she wanted answers. In another, she knew those answers may lead to more questions about her and she most definitely did not want that.

"I went to dinner at Kristin's parent's house a few weeks ago and your dad, Connor, and Amelia were there. I think your dad and Mrs. Hadley are hoping for Kristin and Connor to get together." Callum burst out laughing at that statement. "But it's not happening."

"No, it's definitely not. She's not really his type," he said.

"Why not? I mean, not that I'm hoping they get together, because she and Micah are perfect, but she's a great catch. I'm sure she's almost anyone's type," Sam countered. She might be able to slightly forget the mishap with Christian (even though she wouldn't fully admit as to why), but she sure as hell wasn't going to let Callum speak negatively about Kristin.

Callum shook his head and amended, "No, I don't mean it that way. She's great. But Connor's gay."

Well, then. She guessed Mrs. Hadley would be sorely disappointed when she discovered that news. Sam couldn't stop the laughter from bubbling out. She wasn't sure if it was the alcohol running through her veins or...she abruptly stopped when she noted Callum was giving her that death glare again.

"What the fuck? Are you seriously about to–"

"No, no, no. Sorry, I'm not laughing at your brother. I'm just laughing at the fact that Kristin's mom is dead set on him and Kristin getting together, and I'm picturing how sad she'll be when she finds out. Nothing against him or his love life, just thinking about Mrs. Hadley," she quickly clarified.

Sometimes she hated herself and her stupid reactions. This was one of those times.

In that moment, she realized whatever had happened between Callum and Connor couldn't have been that bad if he became so defensive over him so quickly.

Callum took a relief filled breath.

"Yeah, I've heard. Don't tell Kristin, but I don't think my mom is very fond of Mrs. Hadley at all. She tolerated her since our dads are friends, but I don't think they really get along too well."

Sam was shocked when she suddenly realized they were actually having a decent conversation.

Sam nodded. "Sounds about right. Kristin's mom is very fake. And you don't have to hide that thought from Kristin, she'll agree. I sat with your sister at dinner. She was really sweet. We talked for a while about my wanting to go for my MD and her wanting to be a nurse."

She smiled at the memory.

"Can I ask another question?" she questioned as she looked

over to him again.

He nodded, imploring her to continue.

"I tried to talk with Connor at dinner, but I could tell he wanted nothing to do with the conversation."

He eyes her suspiciously. "That's not really a question."

"I don't know. I was just wondering why he was there in the first place if he wasn't going to even interact with anyone."

Callum looked down at his beer as he started peeling back the label. She could tell he was looking for the right words, and she immediately regretted letting her stupid mouth get her in a situation with him again.

She was about to change the subject when he spoke.

"Sam, no matter what it looks like on the outside, not everyone grew up in perfect cookie cutter families. Trust me when I say all three of us Barker kids have some serious trauma we are working through."

Callum stopped fidgeting with the label and took another swig of the beer in his hand. He looked sad. For a moment, she wished she had never even brought it up.

"I didn't mean to—"

"No, it's fine. It had probably been a bad day with my dad that led up to that night. Connor is normally very outgoing and talkative. Well, at least he was. He and I used to be closer. In any other normal situation that didn't involve my father sitting feet away, I'm sure he would have loved to talk about all things medical."

Used to be.

"I'm sorry, you don't have to say any more."

He gave her a shy smile.

"Since we're apologizing," he ran his hands through his hair and took another sip as if he was building himself up for whatever he was about to say, "I guess I should apologize for being a dick that first night at Topline, and then at March Madness, and then the next two shifts at work."

She tried to hold in the grin at the idea of him apologizing and waited for far too long for the words to leave his beautiful mouth. When none came she nudged him in the side.

"I'm waiting." She smiled his way and he returned it with an eye roll and a groan.

"I'm...sorry," he dragged out the words.

She laughed.

"It's okay. I was kind of a bitch too. And while we're at it, I'm sorry about your shirt."

He nodded in response.

She wasn't sure how long they stood there not really listening to the music before she spoke again.

"How did you and Micah become friends? No offense, but y'all are complete opposites."

"Yeah. That's a story. Um...He came into the shop one time because he lost a bet. He had to get some stupid tattoo, and he was scared shitless. Not only about the tattoo, but I think he would have peed himself if I had actually started to use the needle on him. So, I made a deal that I would paint it on him in the back room so his friends would leave him alone about it. I'm not about to do something to someone's body that they will carry forever if they don't want it. So, I painted a skunk on his thigh, covered it with Vaseline and a wrap and called it a day."

Her smile was so broad it made her cheeks hurt.

"Are you serious?" She looked at him to see if he was messing with her, and he nodded while laughing a little. "That's hilarious."

"The best part is that I used the wrong kind of paint, by accident. It stayed on his leg for about a month before it finally all came off. He came back the next day when it wouldn't wash off and he was supposed to meet up with Kristin's family for the first time. He was in a panic. He ended up wearing long pants...on a boat...on what was probably the hottest day that spring." Callum started laughing at the memory and for some reason the sound made her stomach feel as though she had just fallen from the top of a coaster.

She wanted nothing more than to hear it again. "We started hanging out after that. What about you and Kristin?"

"Nothing special or anywhere near as interesting as your story. We just met in class and were both looking for a new roommate."

He nodded in understanding, then asked, "Where are you from?"

She took a deep breath unsure of how to get out of that one. "A lot of places?" This was not a conversation she felt like having tonight.

"Are you an army brat?"
She turned to face him. "What's that?"

"When your mom or dad are in the military and you travel to different bases to live."

"Oh, no. Not that. I guess I have lived all of my life here in South Carolina. Just hopped around the state every few years."

"Was it for your parents' jobs?"

"No. Not really." She was debating on how to switch to a different topic when they were abruptly pushed further back, causing her drink to suddenly spill on the floor, splashing on them in the process. There was no way they could make it to the bar for napkins, and really, the floor had already been a disgusting mess even before the spill. She had a fleeting moment of concern for their property insurance, wondering if the building was at max capacity, and how many people would end up slipping and falling over the course of the night.

"Sorry!" She turned toward him and began attempting to wipe off the liquid that had landed on his shirt.

He smiled, leaning down a little closer so she could hear him. The bass was so loud it began drowning out all the other voices. "It's okay. Not the first time you've spilled drinks on me."

A rush of heat ran across her skin at their closeness. She quickly turned back to face the front, hoping not staring directly at his face would cause the fire building within her to smolder. Instead, she found his body directly behind hers in this position, she wasn't sure if that was any better.

He bent down a few more times, each time remarking on the song or the aesthetic of the room. But, in this new position, all she could focus on was the way his hair brushed against her cheek, and the way his breath tickled her neck causing goosebumps to stretch down her body, and the way his hand, which had been against the wall, had now somehow made its way to her hip.

Every time he bent down, it was as if his scent engulfed her. Despite how sweaty the man had already been when she'd joined him in the three-legged race, he smelled *so good*. He smelled of mint and cherry and something else she couldn't quite place. And she might have been imagining it, but it felt like he lingered a little longer every time he leaned in. At one point, his nose rubbed against her neck and she involuntarily leaned back and further into him. The hand that had at some point wrapped itself around her hip tightened its grip slightly.

They stood like that long after he had made his last statement, both pretending to watch the band in front of them. She couldn't even begin to tell what it was he'd said. She was sure that, to the strangers who stood next to them, they looked like a couple who couldn't get close enough. The thought caused a surge of excitement mixed with dread to work its way through her. She was about to pull away when she felt the arm that was wrapped around her tighten and twist her slightly to face him.

"You smell like Christmas," he said, and the fluttering in her stomach caused her core to tighten.

She wanted to laugh. She felt as if that was such a silly reaction to a silly statement and yet his words had her heartbeat racing. "Christmas, huh?"

"I think it's the peppermint." His lips were so close to hers she could almost taste him.

"It seems to have become a favorite scent of yours, given that you filled your home with it."

She watched his flushed cheeks turn a shade darker and his embarrassment at being caught caused that fluttering deep within her to turn into a consistent throbbing.

He shrugged his shoulders. "It's my new favorite."

She had been watching his lips and his cheeks and his nose and his hair...and then they caught each other's eyes for just a split second. That deep azure that seemed to flow through them was churning. She had called it that first night at his house. She'd known his eyes would pull her in and she was right. Only now she wasn't sure if that was such a bad thing.

She meant to pull away. Meant to playfully swat him across the chest and then turn back so she was facing the band and not him. That was her quickly-made and ill-conceived plan. Because, maybe if she wasn't facing him, or if she wasn't staring into his blue eyes that had somehow now turned a shade darker, or if she put a little separation between them, then this feeling that was beginning to stir deep within her would dissipate and she could go back to feigning hatred for him.

But then he was grasping her waist and pulling her closer.

And then his mouth was on hers.

She was kissing him.

Callum. Fucking. Barker.

In the middle of a group of strangers.

She even thought she heard some guy howl out a whoop at them, but wasn't really too sure. Her senses were already flooded, overtaken by everything this kiss was doing to her.

His lips were warm and, yes, she had been correct in her initial assessment; they were surprisingly soft. They melted against her own. And then she melted against him. If he hadn't had his arm wrapped around her middle holding her up, she was sure she would fall straight to the ground. But then the other hand was gripping onto her waist and sliding upward.

Her breath hitched when he grazed the side of her breast and then she all but lost consciousness when he cupped the side of her throat, tilted her sideways in the most deliciously demanding way he could, and deepened the kiss.

It was a war of tongues and lips and teeth. He would sneak in a nibble of her lip just for her to whimper in response. Then a quick swipe of his tongue surged across the area, soothing the ache. She had never been kissed like this. Like he was drowning within her. As if she was his sole source of air and he would never let her go.

A break in the music and the stumbling crowd around them was what finally caused them to part. She wasn't sure how long she'd spent letting him devour her, but by the time she leaned her head on his strong chest and took a breath, she knew her lips were swollen and pink. She focused on the rapid beating of his heart as she tried to steady her own and he wrapped his strong arms around her.

After a minute, he leaned down to speak. He ran his right hand over her hair and tilted her head back slightly.

"Come back to my place tonight." It wasn't a question. And, god, she wanted to. His lust-filled eyes were damn near begging her.

"Callum." She hesitated for a split-second, debating if she should do just that. She averted her eyes, knowing that staring into his for another moment would cause any resolve she had left to buckle. She would get caught within that deadly azure current and she would gladly let it take her away. "I can't. I want to, but I can't." She looked up at him and he nodded.

Her brain was too foggy and she was far too close to giving in and telling him yes. But she knew that wasn't like her and she would regret it in the morning. She looked back up at him once more. He hadn't taken his arms from around her and she was *not* going to be the first to let go.

When the band started up again, she twisted back to face the front, but leaned back further into him. His right arm stayed planted across her collar bones while his left hand snaked around her side, pushing the hem of her shirt up slightly so he could draw lazy circles on her stomach.

Over time, she noticed that people must have started to leave, the push of the crowd starting to recede. She had no idea how long they stood there wrapped up in each other, but eventually the room thinned out. She could still feel his heartbeat and, when he suddenly stepped away, she was a little shocked at the amount of disappointment she felt. She could have stood like that for hours.

Before she had the chance to further sulk at his detachment, she felt an arm pulling her back down and onto his lap. She mustered a small amount of courage to look him in the eye. They still hadn't really spoken since what would now be forever known as *the kiss* and she felt as though her heart was going to explode out of her chest from sheer tension.

No one had ever made her so nervous and yet so comfortable at the same time. He went to brush some of her hair back and she wrapped her arms around his neck, running her fingers into his hair. He closed his eyes, a dreamy, almost drunk hint of a smile stretched across his face. She could tell he wanted to kiss her again, but he was waiting for her to make the first move. He opened his eyes, reached up and rubbed the pad of his thumb across her bottom lip, popping it from the firm hold of her teeth.

"Stop thinking so hard."

"What?"

"You think too much," he said as he shifted her to the side and leaned his forehead against hers. A trail of goosebumps followed his hand as it snaked up her back to pause at the nape of her neck. It took considerable effort to hold in her moan as he gently massaged the muscles on the back of her neck. He had ignited a fire in her with just a simple touch. A touch like none she'd felt before. She shifted slightly, tentatively brushing her lips against his. His hands, which had made their way to her waist, slowly slid up her back and to her neck again. A continuous movement she never wanted to end.

They were so close she could breathe him in. She smiled against his lips and then let go of her restraint. She kissed him as if he was the only thing left in this world. And in that moment, he truly was. It was them and no one else. When his teeth scraped against her bottom lip, wanting and needy, she let out another whimper which seemed to invigorate him even further. He shifted her slightly, pulling her in closer, and she felt him hard and ready under her.

"Dude. You're supposed to be listening to us, not sucking face with your girl the entire time."

They quickly broke apart, both looking rather guilty and extremely flushed. Callum looked her way, not correcting the stranger.

Your girl.

Chapter 15 - Sam

"Well, maybe if you sounded a little better I wouldn't need a distraction," Callum said to his friend, smirking. "Sam, this is Keiser. Keiser, this is Sam."

They exchanged hellos, and then she realized she had actually met him the previous week at Micah's house. Sam would normally have mentioned their having met before, but her brain was on autopilot.

She couldn't think straight. Not when she was acutely aware of the fact that she was still planted firmly in Callum's lap.

Her brain and muscles started to debate whether she should get off of him or stay put. She had never been one for public displays of affection, and here she was practically dry humping a guy she had sworn to hate. And every moment of it in full view of a crowd of strangers.

Sam thought Callum could sense her slight shifting because he reached around to hold her to him tighter. His small motion made her smile. Sam had never been boy crazy. She honestly thought those girls were insane. They would get all giggly and giddy because some guy looked at them the right way. Yet, here she was trying to figure out why she couldn't take the damn smile off her face.

Callum and Keiser talked about music for the duration of the break, leaving her to overanalyze the fact that she was sitting there like it was the most normal thing between them. He continued drawing little circles against her skin, but this time he let his fingers linger on her hips. He was so close to the apex of her thigh that, if there hadn't been a thread of fabric between them, he would have certainly felt the evidence of her desire.

After a few minutes of conversation, Keiser excused himself to return to the stage and Sam tried to come up with the right thing to say. The buzz of her phone was her saving grace.

> **Kristin**: ARE YOU
> ALIVE!?

Sam didn't have time to respond before the next text came through.

> **Kristin**: I just checked
> your location. You ARE
> NOT at the library. You
> are at SOCIAL! Have
> you been kidnapped?!

Callum buried his face in Sam's neck as he unsuccessfully tried to hold in the laugh that erupted.

> **Sam**: Yes. Be home
> shortly!

Then she quickly realized what she had typed and rushed to fix it before Kristin called in the National Guard.

> **Sam**: Yes, I'm alive.
> Not, yes, I've been
> kidnapped, haha. See
> you in a few...Mom.

"I need to head back. I have an 8 a.m. lab and it's after midnight."

"Nothing I can do to convince you to stay, huh?" Callum said, more to himself than to her. She shuddered. She swore she felt his lips graze her neck as he spoke.

But she silently shook her head. She needed to stand up. That would be the first move in walking away. But his head was planted on her shoulder and his arms were still holding her tightly to him.

"You are going to have to let me go," she whispered in his ear. She hoped he could tell by the reluctance in her voice that leaving was the very last thing she wanted to do.

"Never," he whispered back.

Her heart rate spiked and she wanted nothing more than to lean back into him and let him take her home. She wanted it more than she had ever wanted anything in the world.

"Are you going to kidnap me?"

"Yes. Kristin can come visit you at my house." His answer was immediate.

She burst out laughing at that.

"I don't think you want her there every day."

"What if I want *you* there...every day?"

Her hand had somehow made it to his cheek.

"You don't even know me."

"I would like to," he said, gently leaning into her touch.

"You don't even like me."

"Oh, Sam." He smiled and shook his head at her words. "You have absolutely no idea how much I do, in fact, like you."

"You're my boss." She rubbed the stubble across his jaw and swore she felt his entire body tense.

His words were a whisper in her ear. "You're fired. There. Problem averted."

She burst out laughing again and then took a steadying breath.

"There is still one tiny problem."

He brought his lips right next to hers. "And what is that?"

She let her lips graze his cheek as she moved to his ear. "I have sworn to loathe you for all eternity," she whispered, letting her lips tickle his skin as she spoke. He tensed further and she knew he was holding in the moan that threatened to escape.

"As long as you are loathing me while still perched on my lap, I'll take it," he offered.

She swatted his arm at that. He quickly grasped it, bringing her fingers to his lips, and placed a kiss on the pad of each one.

"You have no idea what effect you have on me, do you?" he asked.

She wasn't sure how to respond to that statement other than a shy smile. He made her so nervous, yet excited, mad, and then scared all at once. It was like her brain couldn't figure out which emotion it wanted or needed to feel.

"I've got to go," she said one last time.

If he didn't let her go this time, she knew her resolve would falter and she would follow him anywhere.

"I'll see you at work then," he said as he dropped his hands from around her.

"Bye, Callum."

"Bye, Sam."

Chapter 16 - Sam

Sam didn't even remember driving home. She was on autopilot the entire time.

Before Sam made it fully into the house, Kristin all but ran out into the living room, clutching a bowl of ice cream and pointing her spoon into the air, using its movement to punctuate her every word.

"I'm mostly mad because you didn't invite me. I get that you have your own study group and y'all do God knows what in the wee hours of the morning in the library, but going to Social and not–"

"I kissed Callum," Sam blurted out, quickly burying her face in her hands. She was still trying to debate if that had actually happened or if it had all been some massive hallucination.

"What?" The spoon was frozen; stuck in the air as if Kristin was about to use it to cast a spell.

"I kissed Callum," Sam admitted again. This time at almost a whisper.

"Callum? *Callum Barker?* Mr. Newbie-Asshole that you can't stand?" Kristin stared at her in confusion, the spoon still suspended in the air.

"I don't know what happened. He was at the work event tonight and then...and then he invited me to hear a band, and I don't know. We were just standing there and then he had his arms around me and then he said something about how he liked the way I smelled and then he kissed me," Sam explained in a rush and then promptly started to cry.

"Oh, shit." Kristin discarded the bowl of ice cream and makeshift wand and rushed toward Sam.

"Did he hurt you?" Kristin's hands cupped Sam's face, forcing her to lift her gaze as Kristin promptly assessed everything she could see.

"No. No, it wasn't like that at all. It was... It was... It was *perfect*."

That caused Kristin to pause, a confused look etched across her face.

"Okay. Then why are you crying? These don't look like happy tears." Kristin's finger brushed away a droplet as it raced down Sam's face.

"This isn't my plan, Kristin. He isn't my plan." Sam reached for the tissue box, embarrassed that this was what one kiss had reduced her to.

"Sam, it was just a kiss. He didn't propose, he didn't even ask you to hang out with him at a later date, did he?" Sam shook her head in answer. "Okay. Look. You have to know that plans rarely go the way we want them to," Kristin countered, still not having let go of Sam's face.

"But my plan has to."

Kristin deflated, then took a deep breath and let the words flow.

"Sam. I love you. I have loved you since the day we met. You are my best friend. You are the kindest and most genuine hearted person I know. You are also a smartass, and you will one day be a fucking amazing doctor who will cure all sorts of diseases and save millions of lives. But–"

"I don't think it's a good sign if 'but' comes after all of that," Sam said the words through the lingering hiccups that now plagued her.

"But," Kristin continued, not letting Sam deter her, "I need to lay down a truth for you that might be hard to take."

Kristin paused for a moment, waiting for Sam to shut her down.

When there was nothing but acceptance in Sam's eyes, Kristin continued, "You force yourself to have this unmeasurable amount of control over everything in your life because your childhood was the definition of chaos. You crave stability and consistency and routine because it is *safe*. But life doesn't care what you want, Sam. Life will throw you seventeen different curveballs all before you finish your morning coffee." Kristin wiped away another lone tear. "And Callum Barker may be a curveball. A beautiful, sexy, annoying curveball. He is not a part of your plan. Micah wasn't a part of mine either, and here I am looking at wedding dresses every night."

That caused a burst of laughter to come from Sam.

"But just because he isn't a part of your plan doesn't mean he can't *become* part of it. Let life happen, Sam. Let it throw you a curveball or three or seven. *Let yourself live.* Because if you don't, then one day, when you are old and gray and covered in wrinkles–"

"I'll find a cure for wrinkles," Sam quickly interjected and Kristin laughed.

"One day, when you get to the end, I want you to know that it was worth it."

Sam stared at her friend for a moment as she took in her words. They were the complete truth and she knew it. She had spent the last twenty-one years of her life building up a wall around herself. A barricade meant to keep out anything and anyone that might even hint at the chance of causing a detour. She knew somehow that Callum Barker could shatter that barricade in a matter of moments. He could somehow weave himself past every single defense she had in place and bury his roots deep within her. She hated him for it. She also never wanted it to end. She contemplated what this path would look like if she made room for something unplanned. That thought scared her more than she was willing to outright admit.

"What if I regret letting him in?" Her words were a whisper.

"What if you regret keeping him out?" Kristin countered.

Sam closed her eyes and tried to picture every future path she could. Except, no matter how hard she tried, not even she could predict her future.

"Okay," she conceded.

"Okay?" Kristin looked at her as if that answer came as a complete shock.

"Yeah. Okay." Sam wiped her eyes just as Kristin pulled her in for a massive hug.

"Now," Kristin said as she pulled back, fixed Sam's tousled hair, and handed her the wand and bowl of discarded ice cream. "Spill. Every. Single. Detail. From start to finish."

Sam spent the next thirty minutes explaining how everything had happened. She couldn't even believe what she was saying. She worked with him. He was Micah's best friend. He was her boss. She was going to have to see him again. She couldn't wrap her head around this. It was too much to take in.

"This is so messed up," she went on, unable to even look Kristin in the eyes. "I mean, we work together and then there's you and Micah. Kristin, I'm so sorry. I didn't want to cause it to be awkward or anything. I don't even like him, you know. He is so aggravating and full of himself. He's honestly just an ass. Right? I don't even like him," Sam whispered the last words.

Kristin laughed. "Sam, you can try and lie to yourself all you want. But you can't lie to me. I knew you had something going on in that head of yours when you couldn't keep your eyes off of him the first night we saw him at their house. And by the way, he looked you up and down every chance he got as well. This has been brewing for a while. I mean, I didn't think it would happen this fast, but I figured it was coming at some point. You two are like ice and fire. You are complete opposites, but for some reason it could work. Micah could even tell something was up and he is as blind as a bat when it comes to shit like this, okay?"

Sam gave her a wide-eyed glare. "How could Micah tell something was up? Am I completely that obvious? I didn't even realize it until tonight."

"No. Not you, you idiot. Callum. Apparently, he's been talking about you."

"Talking about me? Now it's your turn to explain." Kristin laughed again and rolled her eyes at Sam.

"Come on, we could see this coming a mile away. You remember the night you spilled the drinks on him?" Sam nodded. "Well, I guess the next day he wouldn't stop bitching about the girl who did it, and then he wouldn't stop talking about her in general. Micah and Drew started messing with him about his new 'work crush.' I walked upstairs for part of the conversation, but I didn't know he worked at Topline."

"Wait," Sam quickly interjected.

"What?"

"He doesn't just work at Topline. He owns Topline."

"*Owns?* Callum Barker owns a business that's not a tattoo shop?" Kristin toyed with the idea and then a wave of shock came across her face. "He is your boss!"

"Yeah..."

Kristin's shock quickly turned devious. "Oh. That could get kinky. Maybe a quickie on the desk between shifts."

"Kristin!" Sam pushed her friend's hand away. "All we did was kiss, okay? I'm not about to jump into bed with him."

"You kind of are, though. At least, I'm kind of hoping you are." Kristin gave her the side eye and then continued, "Anyway, that's a whole other issue I am now far too excited about."

"Stop!" Sam admonished her while shoving the last bite of rocky road into her mouth.

"I just read a book that had this entire boss-employee trope going on and let me tell you–"

"Stop!" Sam repeated with a mouth still full of the chocolatey, nutty, marshmallowy deliciousness.

"I'll lend you the book. Might give you some ideas."

"You are horrible," Sam said with a smile.

"But as I was saying, I was too hungover to care about his drama. So, anyway. Then we show up for the game and it's you, the girl from work. After that, he wouldn't leave it alone. Micah said he hasn't stopped asking him questions about you since that night. Micah even asked me last week if something was going on between y'all. But, of course, I said no and that, as far as I knew, y'all couldn't stand each other. I guess my answer has changed now."

"Maybe."

"This is good! We can go on a double date!"

"We are not dating. One kiss, remember? One. Kiss."

"That's okay. Tonight when I can't sleep and I'm knee deep in all things wedding, I'll make sure to look up some dresses that would look amazing on you," Kristin said with a smile.

Sam shook her head in feigned annoyance.

"You two aren't even engaged. I thought you didn't want to get married till after med school?"

"Oh, I don't. But I want a big ole diamond ring on my finger so when I'm crying through exams and bored out of my mind in class lectures I'll be reminded of what I have waiting for me at home." Kristin winked.

"You're ridiculous." Sam started to laugh and then threw her head back on the couch before abruptly standing up. "Okay, I'm done. I have a lab in six hours, which means I have to be up in four."

"You could be up in five and still make it," Kristin countered as she placed the now completely empty bowl in the sink.

"I'm going to bed, you dork. I love you, goodnight!" Sam called from the top of the stairwell.

"I love you, too. Sweet dreams," Kristin teased, and Sam let out a groan before shutting her door.

Her sleep that night was fitful, filled with dreams of long dark hair, tattooed arms, and blue eyes.

Chapter 17 - Callum

Callum didn't say a word as he rushed through the living room and passed by a very confused Micah and Drew. By the time he was able to gather his thoughts, he felt the sting of the cold water against his back.

"What the fuck are you doing?" he whispered to the icy droplets that raced down his face as he tried to steady his breathing. "What the fuck are you doing?" he repeated as he let his head fall against the wall.

He had kissed far too many women in his life.

He liked kissing women.

He wanted to kiss women.

But he had never once *needed* to kiss someone as desperately as he had that night.

He had tried to resist. He had tried so damn hard. And then, somehow his hand had landed on her waist and she hadn't pushed him away. If anything, he was almost positive she'd leaned further into him. And then there was the way her freckles had lit up in the lights coming from the stage, and the way her hair had looked as if it were set ablaze as she moved. It was the way her smell seemed to permeate every pore of his skin until he wanted to soak her in and never let her go.

"Fuck!" He punched the wall and felt the vibrations move through him.

It was only then that he realized this cold shower, the one

that he so desperately needed, was also washing *her* off of him. He almost tripped as he jumped out, dripping water all over the tile floor.

****

He was still trying to process what exactly had happened that night when he walked back upstairs and rummaged through the fridge. When he stood up to his full height and slammed the door, he found both Micah and Drew now sitting at the bar, each with a shit-eating grin plastered on their faces.

"What?" he said in between gulps of milk.

"I just got a call from a very excited Kristin," Micah stated.

"Uh, huh." Callum tried to act indifferent. In reality, he was desperate to know what she'd said.

"Apparently, Sam went to Social tonight and made out with some guy."

"Hmmm?" Callum responded, still not wanting to give in to where he knew this conversation would lead.

"Have anything to add?" Drew piped up.

Callum rolled his eyes as he looked between his two best friends. Both had rather ridiculous looking expressions.

"Kristin said she hoped the guy knew that if he ever broke Sam's heart then she would cut his balls off."

Callums eyebrows peeked.

"I'm sure she would." His voice was flat.

Micah groaned. "Dude, come on. Talk to us."

"Why do you two look like fucking rainbows and sunshine?"

"Because," Drew answered, "you're finally showing interest in someone. The same someone you acted as if you couldn't stand two weeks ago."

"I feel like this is progress," Micah chimed in.

"Progress toward what?" Callum genuinely asked. He decided complete avoidance of Drew's previous statement was probably for the best.

"Progress toward not acting like you are a block of ice who

doesn't feel a damn thing so you don't have to deal with your past."

Callum leaned back against the counter as he ran his hands through his dripping wet hair. "It'll never go anywhere."

"Why not?" Drew furrowed his brow.

"Because I'm not good for her." He started toward the stairs. "You both know that." He was halfway to his room. "Don't hype me up about something that will never even happen," he called out just before he slammed the door.

Chapter 18 - Sam

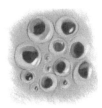

By the next morning, Sam was absolutely dragging. She was exhausted enough that she even contemplated skipping class. Stacy just kind of gave her a knowing look as she walked in.

"I know, I had a long night at work and didn't sleep well," Sam stated and then let the lab continue on, as if she was actually able to think through mole mass conversions when all that was consuming her mind was what Callum's hands would have felt like had she not had on any clothes. What they would have felt like trailing over her bare skin.

The rest of the week was uneventful. She had a shift Tuesday night, but Callum wasn't there. She guessed that made the minor panic attack she'd had in Kristin's car on the drive over seem a little silly. By Friday night, it seemed like everything was back to normal.

When she walked into Topline for her shift, she didn't see Callum anywhere and promptly breathed a sigh of relief. But then she felt immediate disappointment. She needed to get him out of her head. It had been a week since she'd last seen him. He hadn't reached out, or stopped by, or attempted any contact at all.

Well, in all fairness, neither had she. But that was beside the point.

He had initiated the trip to Social. And the kiss. And the sitting on his lap. And all the wonderful things that had been said between them. She'd never voiced it out loud, least of all to Kristin, but a small part of her had hoped that he would get her number from Micah and text, or call, or maybe show up at her door. She wasn't expecting flowers or anything, but just maybe a *Hi, I wanted to see you*, or *We should get lunch one day*, or maybe even a *Sorry for completely turning your world upside down* would have been nice.

All those thoughts came crashing to a sudden halt as soon as she turned the corner and ran straight into him.

"Long time no see, huh?" he said as he leaned against the wall. Her brain and mouth didn't seem to be connecting, and all she could do was shake her head and laugh. "What's the final decision?"

"On what?"

"My name. Am I still Newbie-Asshole? You left before I was able to figure out my standing."

She could tell he was toying with her and she knew he could see her embarrassment.

"Jury's still out. We'll have to see how my night goes and whether or not I'm fired, and then I may be able to make that decision."

She liked this.

She liked *him*.

"Alright. Well, I guess I should head back, I wouldn't want to be too much of a distraction for you. Wouldn't bode well for you if your boss caught you being all googly-eyed over some guy during your shift."

"You're such an ass." Even though she was trying to appear stern, she started to laugh. He walked away without another word, but with a smile plastered across his face. To her growing frustration, they didn't get to speak again the whole shift. It was so busy, they were able to do nothing but share a few glances.

When she clocked out for the night, Callum was nowhere in sight. She paused a moment before heading out the door, and debated whether or not to wait for him at an empty table. There was no way in hell she would head to the back to try and find him. For all she knew, he was in Mr. Brimley's office doing whatever it was owners did. And she didn't want to come across as clingy or obsessed.

So, she slowly walked out the door and caught the bus home.

Chapter 19 - Sam

When she got out of the shower Saturday afternoon, she had a text waiting for her.

> **Christian**: Rain check
> makeup tomorrow?
> Lunch?

She debated on how to respond for far longer than she normally would. Lunch dates with Christian were her normal. They generally happened every week like clockwork. She knew the only thing stopping her from an immediate reply was Callum's face plastered in her mind.

Callum and Christian hated each other for reasons she still had no knowledge of.

But she and Callum were not a thing, and Christian was her lifelong friend. The worst thing she could do was lose him because of a stupid boy.

> **Sam**: That sounds
> good to me. Dianne's?
> See you then.

She hit send, but then a sinking feeling in her belly made her second guess her decision.

"We're leaving in thirty minutes!" Kristin shouted from the living room, and then before Sam could even formulate a response, she burst through her bedroom door, finger pointed directly at Sam. "Don't play coy with me. I'm heading over to Micah's for a party tonight and you are coming. I'm not asking. I'm telling you. You spent last weekend on Callum's lap. No way in hell are you turning down the party tonight."

Sam knew there was a party, there was always a party, but she had kind of hoped Kristin would just head out without any pressure. It seemed that would not be the case.

Sam wasn't nervous until they parked. Kristin could plainly see her hesitation to so much as get out of the car.

"I know I've talked a lot of shit about Callum and Drew over the last year, but they honestly aren't bad guys. Just different from Micah. Callum is also gorgeous. And the tattoos, well, they add this mysterious factor, right?" Kristin wiggled her eyebrows as she spoke.

"No, he's not so bad. But I don't even think he will care or probably even acknowledge me. Besides, I'm having lunch with Christian tomorrow. Not Callum, remember?"

"Do you have any idea why they hate each other?" Kristin questioned as they made their way through the parking lot.

"None. And I'm scared to ask. It might set Callum off."

They had to park further away than usual. Apparently, there were a good many parties going on in this complex tonight.

"Lucky, lucky me! I get to see you here again. Twice in one week!" Christian startled them as he walked over from a neighboring yard. "You know you can come next door anytime," he offered.

"Who lives there?"

"A few of my friends from freshman year. I'm thinking of moving in here next semester."

Sam startled. *Oh, that would not be good.* Callum and Christian living next door to each other sounded about as enticing as chocolate covered worms.

"Can't convince you to join us, can I?" Christian had on his winning smile. His blonde hair was cut short and neatly styled. He had always been a very good looking guy.

In many ways, he was the exact opposite of Callum. Christian was everything she'd ever wanted in a guy. Clean cut, appropriate, nice, stable, routine. Safe.

But maybe not anymore.

Maybe it was time to break the mold.

Maybe it was time to veer off the path she had set forth and take a chance on something new and scary and exciting. Something that made her hair stand on end and her heartbeat increase and her stomach twist into the most delicious knot.

She truly loved Christian. She did. But, maybe that love wasn't what she needed. Sure, he would always be there. He was her constant. He was her past and her present, and she knew he would always have a role to play in her future. But, maybe she had convinced herself that the warm feeling that trickled through her body whenever he was around was more than what it truly was. Because that warm trickle turned to a damn near flood whenever Callum crossed her mind. It was all-encompassing and uncontrollable. It made her want to shatter every single plan she had ever made if only to see him smile or hear him laugh. And Christian had never made her feel like that.

"I'm sorry, I wish I could. I should probably stay with Kristin, though. Don't have too much fun." She smiled back while he reached in for another hug. Just as her arms wrapped around his neck, she caught sight of Callum leaning against the railing on their front porch. She caught the hint of that beautiful smile she was so desperate to see turn downward as Callum saw her arms move to encompass Christian.

Christian saw it, too. She knew because when he pulled back, a devious smile played on his features. And, for just a moment, she felt as if she didn't really know him. He started to walk away and had made it almost into the neighboring home when she heard him call out.

"We never decided on a time for our date tomorrow. Is eleven still good? I'll pick you up." Christian's smile was far too large. He didn't wait for an answer, because he already had one. And she knew that his little display was only for one person's benefit, and it wasn't hers.

"Yeah, that's fine. I'll see you then." He was inside before she even finished her reply.

She shot a quick glance in Callum's direction only to see his back as he disappeared into the home. Her mind raced as she tried to figure this out, but Kristin was pulling her forward and, before she even had a chance to replay what had just happened, she was inside Callum's home and had a straight shot view of the back of a girl sitting on his lap. His hand rubbed up and down the girl's side just like he had done to her at Social.

Their eyes locked on each other. It was a battle as to who would look away first. She felt her heartbeat spike and she wanted nothing more than to slap that stupid grin off his stupid face. He wasn't supposed to have been able to get under her skin.

She blinked away the tears, hoping he didn't notice how flushed her face had just become. Then internally scolded herself for having allowed her mind to spend the last few days spiraling down a path she knew wasn't where she needed to go anyway. She had almost convinced herself not to care, but then he whispered something into the girl's ear and she burst into a fit of giggles and leaned further into him. Sam's chest felt as if it was about to explode. She felt her lips drop into a frown.

With a quick tug on her arm, Kristin had Sam turned away from the sight. Sam feigned oblivion as to what was happening just feet away as she desperately tried to loop herself back into the conversation with Kristin and Micah. It didn't work. All she could think about was what Callum's hand was doing behind her.

Was he telling that other girl the same things he had told her?

Was he causing a trail of goosebumps to snake across her skin?

Micah wouldn't stop talking.

He was completely unaware as to what was going on just feet away, but Kristin had figured it out. When Sam's breathing continued to increase, Kristin looped her arm around Sam and abruptly announced the need for a bathroom trip. They made it through the kitchen and then downstairs to Micah's bedroom before she asked if Sam was okay.

"I'm fine," Sam lied. "It's really not a big deal. We only kissed that once, and I'd rather spend the night forgetting about it then rehashing it."

Kristin waited a moment before she spoke. Sam could tell that pause was because Kristin didn't believe a damn word that came out of her mouth. Thankfully, Kristin didn't call her out this time. Maybe they could rehash this later. Later meaning after she indulged in some much needed alcohol, that way she could blame the tears on the haze that was surging through her body and not on her true feelings.

"Good. Just wanted to make sure. But I think we can both agree that Callum is just doing that because he is jealous of the fact that you and Christian are seeing each other tomorrow."

"Christian is just my friend."

"Callum doesn't know that. From his point of view, I bet it looks like you are fraternizing with the enemy, and maybe even doing it on purpose."

"I honestly don't care either way. How about we just go upstairs and have a good night? I want to forget about all the drama for a while."

Thankfully, there was no more discussion, and after a much needed hug, they both silently walked back upstairs. Sam tried not to look at the half-opened door that she knew led to Callum's room. She tried not to note the table with the paint set and the half-completed artwork strewn around the room. And she sure as hell tried not to acknowledge the pang of sadness that had slowly crept in.

The party was relatively entertaining. There were a few more girls there than there had been the last time, and at some point they all ended up in chairs on the back lawn. She hadn't seen Callum since that first encounter and, for all she knew, he could have already taken that girl to his room. She let the image consume her thoughts while tossing back drink after drink and, before she knew it, the ground wasn't as stable as she had thought. The one beer had somehow turned into three...or maybe four?

She got close enough to Micah's door to grasp the handle, hoping for a quick bathroom break to empty her now full bladder, before she heard Kristin's moans and promptly turned herself around. She was already in the other downstairs bathroom and buttoning up her pants before she fully clued in to where exactly she was.

There was a moment of sobering hesitation, and then everything came back into focus. She was in Callum's room. Callum's bathroom, to be exact. Callum's bed was just on the other side of that door. She would have to walk back through it to get out. For all she knew, he was currently in that bed with that girl and she hadn't been any the wiser when she'd walked in. If she was caught, he would think she was certifiably insane.

She tentatively opened the bathroom door, praying that no one was around, and by some miracle, the room was empty. She quickly made it to his bedroom door when she noticed the paints again and, despite her better judgment, walked back in to get a better look. Her heart was beating so fast she couldn't process exactly how wrong this decision would be.

Her breath caught at the beauty before her. Various scenes and random people she didn't know. A man in a three-piece suit sitting on a bus seat. A woman pushing a small child on a swing. The sunset. The lake. A seagull soaring high above.

Her.

The black and white drawing placed directly under the last was stunning, and for a moment, she wasn't exactly sure if she fully breathed. As if the exhale would shatter the moment. The girl in the picture was her. But it didn't completely look like Sam. This girl with her untamed curls, face full of freckles and wide smile was much too beautiful. She was laughing at something far off and there was an immense happiness in her eyes.

"What are you doing?" Callum's voice cut through her thoughts.

"You drew me." Her answer was immediate as she stayed frozen in place, the drawing of the far too beautiful girl shaking in her hands.

Sam couldn't tell if it came out as more of a question or statement. She waited for a response, but nothing came. And now she was afraid to turn around.

He hadn't said a word.

Or, maybe he had.

Maybe her ears were ringing so loud she didn't hear him.

"Yeah, I did," he responded, voice so low she almost didn't catch it.

"Why?" This time, and without full control of her limbs, she somehow twisted her body to face him and found a pink glow covering his cheeks. Callum shuffled on his feet before he finally made eye contact.

"I can't get you out of my head." He sighed, then turned to shut the door before making his way toward her, stopping just short of where she stood.

"Is that what you told that girl upstairs too?"

Callum grimaced. "That was not one of my finer moments. I'm sorry." He paused and took a deep breath. "I got irrationally jealous and used her to get back at you. I regretted it as soon as I saw your face. *You* are the only one I've drawn. *You* are the only one who I just can't seem to kick out of my thoughts."

Sam still wasn't sure how to feel about that, but would think more on it later. Right now, all she could focus on was how close they were. They were barely more than a foot apart. Their breath mingled and his fingertips grazed the side of her palm. He was so close she could make out the length of his eyelashes and the way his stubble was just slightly thicker across his chin than the rest of his face. There was an entire world going on upstairs that had no idea of what was transpiring down below.

"Do you want to?" Sam asked and he looked at her with a surprised and yet confused expression.

"Want to what?" His brow creased.

"Do you want to get me out of your head?" He visibly relaxed at the question. And then, without notice, a small burst of laughter erupted from him. She reveled in the sound.

"No. Not really. But it wouldn't matter if I did. I've tried. You're still there."

They stood in silence, neither knowing quite what to say, or do, or think, or feel.

Finally, he closed the gap between them and slowly removed the drawing from her hand.

"I'm going to set this over here." He placed it on a side table out of reach. "It's one of my favorites and I don't want to ruin it."

She thought she might have smiled, but she wasn't sure because, as soon as her lips started to tilt upward, he shifted his hands to graze the barely visible skin at her hips. Sam sucked in a breath with the touch. And there was the flood. That trickle that she thought was all she would ever feel from someone turned ravenous. The dam burst and with it her resolve. A soothing warmth spread through her body.

Without an ounce of effort, he lifted her onto his desk and stood between her legs.

She expected him to lean down and kiss her just like he had at the bar, but he didn't move anything other than his eyes. They scoured over every inch of her face. It was as if he was memorizing every detail he could take in. It was agonizingly torturous in the most delicious way.

Unable to take the inspection further, Sam finally parted her lips. She wasn't sure what was going to come out of her mouth, but she wasn't surprised when the one worded plea did.

"Please."

It didn't sound like her at all. It was all breathy and was definitely a plea for something. She just wasn't sure yet what that something was.

He made eye contact one more time. His lips tilted upward and then that damn dimple popped back into place. Through no voluntary motion of her own, somehow her fingers found themselves tracing the small dot and then the curve of his lips.

He sucked in a ragged breath as his grip on her tightened.

"What do you want, Sam?" His voice was deep and commanding.

"You."

He didn't hesitate. His lips were on hers before she could finish the word.

This was what she wanted.

What she needed.

Him.

He felt so good, and kissed her so thoroughly she was sure her lips would be bruised by the time he finished. He threaded his hands into her hair and yanked back slightly, making a whimper escape her lips. She'd never been one to make noises, but he brought out a side of her she wasn't sure she'd ever seen. With him she wanted to scream, and cry out, and let him know without a doubt all the ways he made her feel.

When he took her bottom lip between his teeth, the tension in her body coiled up. Her hands were frantic, running up to his face then back down across his torso then grabbing his hips to bring him closer. He had barely touched her, but she swore she was already primed to burst.

He ran a trail of kisses across her jaw and gently dragged his teeth down her neck. She couldn't talk if she wanted to. Her mind had gone blank and she was selfishly enjoying everything he was doing to her. When he finally pulled away to catch his breath, she unexpectedly whimpered at the loss of contact.

He laughed a little while picking her up, carrying her to the bed and deftly laying her down.

"Don't worry, Sam. I'm nowhere near done with you."

Chapter 20 - Sam

She moaned when he cupped her breasts through her shirt.

"Fuck, I love your little noises," he said through gritted teeth, and she knew he was holding back.

If she told him to, he would have had her fully naked and writhing underneath him in seconds. And she would have loved it. But he was still new. This was still so new. She wanted to enjoy it.

When his lips started to suck on that spot where her neck met her jaw, the rest of the world went silent. In her head, she knew there were other people on the other side of his door and throughout the house. The house was now packed. It didn't matter. Nothing mattered more than what he was doing to her right then. Nothing mattered more than the feel of his lips, and his tongue, and his teeth.

His hands were like fire, leaving a burning sensation in their wake. Going up and down her thighs and then, with each pass upward, ever so slowly pushing away her shirt.

He was a drug.

Plain and simple.

This man and everything he was...*he was her drug.*

He stalled before pushing her shirt up the rest of the way.

"Is this okay?" he asked.

She swallowed, not sure how to tell him.

"Yes. I'll...I'll let you know when it's too much." And with that, her shirt found its way onto his floor and her bra followed soon after.

"God, you're so beautiful," he said as his eyes raked down her body following the trails his hands had already taken. "You can't imagine the things I want to do to you right now."

Her body turned to jello in his hands. Her brain wasn't working other than to reach up and pull him back down to her. He was so good at this. She could get lost in him and never look back.

He leaned back once more and looked at her with a wicked grin. "I want to kiss every single freckle on your body."

Sam burst out laughing.

"We might be here for a while then."

He licked his lips. "I'm okay with that."

In a moment of pure bravery, probably fueled by the copious amount of alcohol she had previously consumed and the drug that was Callum currently racing through her veins, she tugged on the hem of his shirt and lifted it over his head.

Seconds later, his mouth was on her neck and then her breast and then her stomach. He was alternating between soft kisses and gentle sucking. She let out a whimper as his teeth took each nipple, but the noise soon turned to a relief-filled moan as he used his tongue to soothe the ache.

Then he laid down a gentle assault on her left hip bone before trailing his lips over to the right. She thought she might combust right then and there. Her body was warm—far too warm— and that previous fluttering sensation at her core that she had managed to ignore had now turned into a violent, persistent throb that begged for attention.

Her hands fisted into his hair and she could feel the smile he placed against her skin. When his hand reached between her legs and lightly pressed in, she involuntarily bucked up against him and all but screamed out.

"You are so responsive," he murmured against her, licking the skin directly above her pant line. "I can't wait to see what you do when it's my tongue and my cock here instead." He pressed in again and this time the moan she let out filled the room.

He reached up and popped open the button on her pants. And that small noise was what finally brought her back down and into reality.

"Callum, wait."

He immediately stopped and brought himself back up to face her.

"Not yet. I...I just need–"

"You don't have to explain, Sam. We can stop anytime you want."

Was that what she wanted? No, most definitely not.

But she barely knew him, and as much as she was enjoying this, she didn't want their first time to be at a random college party. She wasn't sure why that mattered. She'd also never chosen to cross that final threshold before, and when she did, she wanted it to be *real.*

"I just don't know you well enough yet, and I want–"

"My favorite color is orange," he quickly interrupted her.

"What?" Her brows furrowed in confusion.

"I like chicken and pineapple on my pizza. My favorite movie is anything in the Marvel universe, though I'm partial to Thor." He looked away in concentration and then looked back at her. "Actually, it's Guardians of the Galaxy. That's my favorite." She started to laugh. "I absolutely love to ski, both water and snow," he quickly clarified. "I have a fear of spiders. In fourth grade I tried to impress a girl by opening her can of beanie weenies and got this scar on my left thumb. Needed seven stitches." He proudly lifted his hand to show her the pale, indented line that cut through his fingerprint and Sam laughed even harder. "I am allergic to peanuts. I have a temper, and I easily get jealous and make rash decisions when I find out a girl I'm interested in has a date the next day with someone I hate."

She cupped his face in her hands, irrationally wanting to tell him she would never lay eyes on another man again for as long as she lived, but he shushed her and kept talking.

"I had a dog named Spots as a kid. One year I ate both mine, Connor's, *and* Amelia's Halloween candy in one sitting and was sick for almost three days. And I will never ever live up to my family's expectations of what I should be."

"Callum..." Her voice broke. She wasn't sure why the idea of his pain was so tortuous for her, but in that moment she wanted nothing more than to take it all away.

"I'm not saying all that so you'll let me have you tonight. I don't want you to think that at all. I just...I just want you to know me, to see me. The real me. Not the me I let everyone think is there. Not the me my family sees. Just me."

"I see you."

Chapter 21 - Sam

They lay there for a few minutes just staring at each other before he gave her a surprisingly gentle kiss. The movement startled her from the quiet reprieve they had somehow settled into. She felt her cheeks heat as she buried her face into his chest. She had never felt this instantly comfortable with someone. Especially someone she had previously decided was nothing more than a bump in the road.

But now, instead of worrying about important stuff like papers, and upcoming exams, and money, her mind was consumed with the sound of his heartbeat under her ear, and if the placement of her hand across his lower abdomen was okay, and whether or not she should have pulled back her hair and not let it fan out across his sheets.

"Do you want to head back upstairs?" Callum reached down and passed over her discarded shirt and bra as he spoke.

Thankfully, he left his off.

She didn't want to move, but somehow the observation of her half naked body on top of his made her blush run deeper. She tossed on her clothes, but quickly noted his arm still propped open as if ready for her to lay back down against him. She didn't hesitate before she nuzzled into his side.

"No. I'm good right here." She smiled and then quickly paused her movements, nervous that maybe the question was his way of telling her he was ready to go without wanting to embarrass her. "Unless you want to leave." She started to shift.

"No, that party was kinda lame anyway. You are much better company." He rubbed the small of her back and she sunk further into him.

"You're such a bad liar," she said into the bare skin of his chest.

He gave her a small laugh then tilted her head upward to press a gentle kiss against her lips.

"Not about this. This is exactly where I want to be."

They stared at each other as they let the moment linger on. He pulled her head down to lean against his chest and she snuggled into him. Then he reached for a blanket and covered them up. Her body was lulled into sleep by the small circles he now drew across her hips.

****

The rapid banging against his door caused them both to rouse.

"Callum! Get out here." The voice was familiar and yet strange. The haze of sleep still tugged at them both, but then the incessant banging came barreling in once more.

"Go away," Callum yelled without opening his eyes and then turned to bury his face in Sam's hair. He wrapped his arm around her middle and pulled her in.

"Callum, stop being lame and get out here." The voice came out as a whine this time and Sam felt Callum go still behind her.

"Fuck," he whispered into her neck as he detached himself and walked to the door. He barely had it open before the obviously drunk girl barged her way in and reached up to pull his lips down to hers. In his sleepy state, it took him a second to realize what was occurring before he pulled back.

"What the fuck are you doing?" Callum promptly pushed her away, putting ample distance between them. A look of confusion and hurt crossed the girl's face before her eyes caught sight of the now fully awake Sam cuddled up in Callum's bed.

"Who the fuck are you?" She inclined her head toward Sam.

"None of your business," Callum answered before Sam could get a word in. "Lynn, get out. I'm tired and going to bed." With a face filled with pure shock, she backed up a couple steps into the hallway and he slammed the door in her face.

A loud bang hit the door with a "Fuck You" screamed after it before Sam heard Lynn's heels stalk back up the stairs.

"Are you and her...a thing?"

"What?" Callum rubbed his eyes as he climbed back into bed behind Sam.

"Was she your girlfriend or maybe a–"

"I don't date." It came out fast and almost bitter, and for some reason, hit Sam directly in the chest.

"Who is she? She obviously didn't like me being here."

"Lynn doesn't like most people." His head fell back on the pillow as he draped an arm across his face.

"You've slept with her?" Her hand flew to her mouth the second the words were stated. "I'm sorry. That's none of my business. You can–"

"Yes. I slept with her, and now she is attached, and I am not."

She wasn't sure whether that information was comforting or infuriating.

"So you two aren't together? In any way?"

"No." Callum twisted to face her.

"Okay," Sam conceded. She wanted to turn back over and go back to sleep in his arms. She wanted to go back to ten minutes prior when she was still in a bliss-induced haze. One caused by his smell and taste and the way his body so perfectly molded against hers.

"What about you and Christian?" The question pulled her from her thoughts, and she turned to meet his gaze as he played with the ends of her hair.

"What about us?"

"Are you still going on a date with him tomorrow?" He froze

with the question, as if speaking it aloud had caused the anger and hurt that the idea brought to come bubbling to the surface.

"It's not a date," Sam corrected with a hesitant smile.

"It sounded like a date."

She noted the hint of jealousy and maybe betrayal in his features. She turned to more fully face him and ran a hand across his cheek. A flash of frustration barreled through her. She didn't want to have this conversation. Not now. Not after the last hour had been damn near perfect. Why couldn't he just understand that her friendship with Christian wasn't just going to go away because she met someone who didn't like him?

"We get coffee or lunch at least once a week. I told you, we are just friends," she stated a little more pointedly this time. She tried to hide the exasperation in her tone, but by the wide eyed look he was now giving her, she knew she had failed.

"Why?"

"Why coffee or why friends?" she asked incredulously, not sure how to convince Callum that there was nothing to worry about.

Maybe a few years ago, hell even a few months or weeks ago, there might have been. But now, having spent time in Callum's arms and with his lips on hers, she knew that nothing she ever felt for Christian could compare to what she was feeling right now. She would always love Christian, he'd been there for her when no one else was. Maybe he was just the safest option; the only option she had really ever had. But things were different now.

"Friends," he clarified.

"Because we've known each other for years and..." She paused as he once again fell back to stare up at the ceiling. She quickly shifted his chin, bringing his gaze back to her. "Look, he's like a brother to me. That's all." She wanted to say more. She wanted to tell him that no matter what Christian used to be to her (even if it had only ever been one sided) those feelings were slowly slipping away, and in their place was a new fluttering that only Callum seemed to cause. That sensation then caused an unfamiliar feeling of confusion to settle deep within her. She wanted to tell him that there was nothing for him to worry about or fret over. But then, maybe that would be a little presumptuous on her part.

Maybe he wasn't worrying at all.

Maybe she was making this all up in her head.

Callum huffed. The new waves of anger rolled off him faster than her muddled brain could decipher the situation. Then he abruptly shot up to sit on the edge of the bed, his back facing her.

"I don't want you to see him anymore." It was nothing less than a blatant command.

"What?" Sam shot up behind him. The disbelieving tone did nothing to hide the anger that began bubbling up within her at his statement.

"I want you." He turned back to face her. "I want you in more ways than you could ever imagine." He looked her up and down as if he was drinking her in. "I want to do so many things to you. I want to make you scream out my name. I want to make you smile and laugh. I want it *all*. But I can never be with you if I know you are still friends with him."

Sam tried to swallow down the frustration.

On one hand, he had just blatantly admitted to wanting her, to wanting to do things *to* her. Her core tightened and she couldn't tell if it was another PVC, or if her heart was about to give out. On the other hand, he just pulled the most annoyingly misogynistic shit she had ever heard.

"You can't just control who I hang out with."

Callum quickly shook his head. "Just him. You can hang out with *anyone* but him."

She wanted to scream.

"No," she quickly replied.

"Please, Sam."

"No. He is my best friend. I don't even know you." She stood up from the bed and slipped back on her shoes.

"He's an ass. Trust me, you don't know *him*."

"I've known him since we were kids. I know him better than you ever will. He may be overprotective and sometimes jealous, and he may not want me hanging out with you, but that's only because he wants what's best for me. He is trying to keep me safe." She felt her heartbeat increase. But, this time it wasn't from nervous excitement, it was from the heat of anger that surged through her.

"No, he isn't. Trust me."

She threw her hands in the air, knowing there was no way she was going to get through to Callum. "Why would I give up someone who has been there for me for years, who has taken care of me and loved me like family, just because you might want to fuck me?" Her words came out more harshly than she'd intended, and a flash of pain registered on his face.

"Sam. That's not what this is and you know it." His words were pained.

"Really? What is this then?" She gestured between the two of them. "Because you just said, 'I don't date,' and from where I stand, it's starting to look like you and him have some stupid beef and I'm your way to get back at him."

"That is not what—"

"Why? Why do you hate him so much?" The plea found its way back into her voice and she hated herself for it.

"It's complicated."

"Uncomplicate it for me." She wanted to stomp her foot on the ground like a petulant child. She wanted to scream and hurl something across the room at his beautiful face. He was ruining it all.

He was ruining it all because of some jealousy and ridiculous revenge.

"It's not that easy. Just know he isn't a good guy."

Sam laughed at that.

"And how do I know you are?"

He stood and reached toward her.

"Sam." The sound of her name was laced with something she couldn't quite detect.

She shook her head, feeling as though her world was somehow shattering into a million pieces. "I think I'm done here."

He took a step toward her and she took a step back. He immediately froze.

"I'm not about to allow some guy to dictate who I can and can't hang out with just so I can keep his attention. I may be a lot of things, but I'm not that desperate."

Sam made it up the stairs and out the front door before she had even registered that she'd left his room.

By the time it finally did register, she was halfway across the parking lot waving down an Uber driver who was parked at the entrance, and the rain had soaked through her clothes and hair.

She jumped in and slammed the door shut just as she heard Callum shouting her name.

Chapter 22 - Callum

His leg muscles finally kicked in moments after she left the room. But by that point she was already out of the house. And by the time he made it to the front porch and was somehow involuntarily calling out her name, she was shutting the door of a car and riding off.

He refused to acknowledge the questioning looks of concern he got from Drew and Keiser (and pretty much everyone else) as he walked back into the house and down to his room.

He let out a grunt of frustration as he slammed his bedroom door.

Why was he so surprised? It's not like he didn't already know he was going to fuck it up. He always fucked everything up.

He'd fucked up school and his career path.

He'd fucked up Rebecca's plan.

He'd fucked up his family.

Why was he so surprised that he fucked it up with Sam?

******

He couldn't find the drawing. He had walked right back to his room and straight to the table where he knew it was. But it wasn't there. A momentary panic set in before he saw it sitting off to the side. Sitting right on the table he'd placed it on before he kissed her. Right before he'd damn near fallen into oblivion and never looked back.

A breath of relief escaped. His fingers were shaking as he lifted the drawing from the table and then carefully placed it inside his bedside drawer. He knew that drawing was all he would have left of her, and damn if he was going to let it go.

He would keep it safe.

Even if he couldn't keep *her* safe.

When he lay back on the bed, he couldn't ignore the smell of peppermint. It could have been coming from the diffuser he had placed in the corner, but he knew it wasn't. It was too authentic to be anything but her, and when he turned over to bury his head into the pillow where her fiery red curls had only moments ago been, that scent surged. It slammed into him so hard he knew it would never leave.

This was it.

There was no turning back from here on out.

If he were a better person, he would leave it alone. If he were a better person, he would decide that the momentary high he experienced when her lips were on his, and her moans filled his ears, and her hands roamed his body was all he would get.

But he was not a better person.

He was selfish and greedy, and he was poisonous.

Chapter 23 - Sam

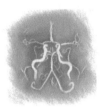

Sam was patiently waiting for Christian to pull up on Saturday morning. Even she was surprised at how well put together she appeared. The makeup was doing a good job of hiding the bags caused by her lack of sleep over the still crowned Newbie-Asshole.

Last night had been perfect, and then it had become her worst version of hell. She had never felt so alive before Callum. His touch, his mouth, his eyes, his...everything. He was a drug and she was an addict. And then he had to go and act like a complete and total ass and ruin it.

She had experienced enough misogynistic assholes in her life at this point. Growing up in the system, she'd dealt with plenty. Now, they were nearly impossible to escape in a male-dominated major. And she knew her chosen career would be filled with assholes who got off on being the ones with the answers, the ones in power, the ones who made the decisions.

She didn't take Callum for that kind of guy. And deep down she knew he probably wasn't. But that still didn't lessen the sting of what he had said, what he had demanded. Christian was her best friend and if Callum couldn't give her a reason as to why that shouldn't be the case then the entire situation was moot. Callum wasn't worth it.

He wasn't worth it.

He wasn't worth it.

He wasn't worth it.

She repeated that phrase over and over again as she brushed her teeth and waited to hear the familiar honk of the car horn when Christian pulled up.

She expected to feel excitement when that sound rang out, that was her normal emotion whenever Christian was around. But she was somehow not at all shocked that all she felt was a slight disappointment it wasn't Callum stepping out of the car instead.

"I hope you're hungry!" Christian said with his winning smile in full force.

"I'm starving," she lied, but he didn't seem to catch it as he politely opened the door and helped her in.

She gazed over in his direction when he finally turned on the car. Christian was a gentleman. He was handsome and kind and had a literal heart of gold. He was her best friend. And in that moment, as he was non-stop ranting about how much he hated his roommate for roping him into yoga as an elective, causing a burst of laughter to erupt from her lips at his explanation of his recent poses, she promised herself never to let anyone tear them apart.

******

Lunch was nice and uneventful, which pretty much described most of their interactions. Christian was safe. She had realized that while she watched him devour the plate of pasta in front of him.

He was safe.

He was her routine.

He was also rather boring, and she hated herself for thinking so. She had once thought they'd make a perfect match. She had once thought she would one day marry him.

But now, after knowing how Callum could make her feel, everything else just felt cold and empty.

That didn't mean that he was a bad person. It didn't mean she needed to stay away from him. Christian was safe and sweet. He was her best friend, and there was no way anyone, even the magnetic Callum fucking Barker, could ever come between them.

He cleared his throat as he shoved over a stack of papers.

"What's this?" Sam questioned.

"Your application for Peet's. I filled it out already; just need your signature. I was going to go ahead and do that, too, but..." he shrugged his shoulders.

"We already talked about this. I'm not working at Peet's." Sam furrowed her brows.

"Stop fighting me on this. I already talked to the night shift manager. He has a spot for you lined up. You start next week. This paperwork is just for formality purposes."

"Christian, I'm not working at Peet's." She bored her eyes into him, hoping he got the message.

"Sam. Stop being ridiculous. I did this for you. Don't make me look like an—"

"Hey, Sam!"

Sam looked up to see Cassy headed toward her.

They had shared a lab freshman year and, even though Cassy had changed her major to childhood education, they had sporadically kept in touch. She liked her and they had even contemplated sharing an apartment for sophomore year. Sam jumped up to give her a quick hug, thankful for the interruption, and hoping that it would cause Christian to forget about that stupid job she didn't want.

It was only after she had asked Cassy the same question twice about how she was doing that she realized Cassy wasn't paying a damn bit of attention to her. She caught Cassy's eyes and followed their trail to Christian.

The two were in a downright death match of a stare. Christian had the oddest expression glued to his face. Sam couldn't tell if he was going to punch something or vomit. And then Cassy turned back to Sam squeezed her shoulders and promptly turned to walk away. She was out of the restaurant before Sam could even contemplate what the hell just happened.

"Are you just going to stand there and stare at the door, or are you going to sit back down and sign this?"

"What?" Sam shook her head as she tried to piece that interaction together.

Christian rolled his eyes. "I need you to sign this."

Sam plopped down into the seat and then internally groaned when she realized exactly what Christian was referring to.

"I'm not signing it." She pushed it back toward him.

"You're being stubborn." He grabbed the pen and signed her name in the open spot.

"Christian!" She looked at him with wide-eyed frustration. "You know that's a federal crime, right?"

He laughed. "Turn me in."

She looked back down at her plate, deciding to leave it be. She wasn't planning on working at Peet's anyway, so it wasn't a problem. She would deal with his frustration later. Right now, she just wanted to figure out why Cassy had pretty much done a one-eighty within a matter of seconds.

"What do you think that was about?" Sam asked, more to herself than to Christian.

"What what was about?" he asked as he shoveled more food into his mouth.

"Cass. She just...I don't know. That was just weird, right? She didn't even answer me."

"Maybe she's just weird." He shrugged his shoulders. "Or maybe you smell." Christian pretended to sniff the air and then made a disgusted looking face. "Yeah, you definitely smell."

Sam laughed.

"I do not smell." She kicked him under the table and he flicked a small piece of garlic bread at her.

"Alright, enough talking about jobs or weirdos who smell." He winked. "I made an executive decision the other day."

"And what was that?" She peeked up at him with a little bit of concern as to where this was going.

"You need an Instagram."

"No, I do not."

"Yes, you do. You are the only person I know under the age of fifty-six without one."

"I don't even really take pictures. It would be pointless." She moved the food around on her plate, hoping it at least looked like she was enjoying the meal. She would, of course, get a to-go plate for later, and hoped to at least have gained her appetite back by that evening. Her bank account would literally scream at her if she were to pass up a fully paid for meal.

"Make a page filled with all your notes and study materials. I'm sure people would pay good money for–"

"Shut up." Sam rolled her eyes, then jumped when Christian reached across the table to swipe her phone from beside her. "What are you doing?"

"I'm making you an Instagram. You honestly can't continue on without one. Trust me," he said with a wink. "Come sit over here," he added as he patted the booth beside him, "and I'll walk you through it."

She begrudgingly shifted to his side and he placed an arm around her shoulders as he ran through the basics. There had been a time when she would have reveled in his touch. Now, it just felt like a dead weight she desperately wanted to remove.

"You realize I won't remember any of this?" she said as she watched him tap away.

"You can remember the intricacies of the Circle of Willis and yet you can't recall how to use an app?"

She cut him a sideways glance. "I *like* the Circle of Willis."

He ignored her and instead focused on going through the app once more.

"Last thing is to add a photo. Let's take a selfie for your first official internet footprint." He put his arm further around her and pulled her in close. For just a second, she felt her body tense, but then he reached around to pinch her side, making her laugh out loud as he snapped the picture.

He set it as her profile picture and quickly handed the phone back while paying for the bill.

By the time they exited the restaurant and were back in his car, she realized she had done nothing all afternoon but be frustrated by Christian and think of Callum.

****

"Any plans for the rest of the evening?" Christian asked as they drove back toward the city.

"If I told you I was reviewing the Circle of Willis, would you believe me?"

"Probably." Christian laughed and then shook his head as he pulled the car over onto a dirt road.

"What are you doing?" she questioned as he let the car slow to a stop.

"Come hang out with us."

"Who is 'us?'" Sam's eyes narrowed in question.

"Some of my friends you don't yet know because you are always stuck inside a book."

Her shoulders sank. "I don't know. We've already been gone for two hours and—"

"You have gone to two parties at *that* house in the last two weeks and you have never once come out with me. This isn't even a party. It's the middle of the day. We are going to play disc golf at The Cardinal."

"The Cardinal?" That was directly beside Callum's townhouse complex and she wanted to be anywhere but near there.

"Yes. It's about to be our last year before you are shipped off to med school and then I'll only get to annoy you via text and during holidays. Please stop saying no to everything."

"I might not get into med school."

Christian threw off his seat belt and leaned over the console until he was directly in her face. He cupped her cheeks with two hands. She wanted to pull back, but she was stuck within the confines of the car.

"Samantha Adelaide Williams–"

"You know I don't have a middle name."

"It's the name we came up with when we were kids."

"It's not legal."

He ignored her. "Samantha Adelaide Williams, I am going to need you to stop shit talking yourself and go ahead and accept that you are going to be an amazing doctor. You are going to save lives."

She gave him a tentative smile. "You think so?"

"I know so." He kissed her temple and she felt a chill race through her.

"If that's the case then I should get back home and–"

"Nonsense." Christian threw his hands up in the air and then put the car in drive. "You have already memorized everything there is to know in every textbook ever written. I'm not letting you say no to this."

She stared his way and then off into the trees beside them. He had spent the better part of three years asking her to hang out with his friends and she had spent the better part of those same three years feigning a too busy schedule just so she wouldn't have to see him get handsy with some girl who wasn't her.

"I can only stay an hour, okay?" she relented and turned back to face the window, still not ready to be anywhere near where Callum might be.

The walk from the parking lot to the field was almost more than Sam could bear. She could just make out the row of townhomes where Callum lived and she knew once they turned the corner she would have a perfect view of the community pool and their back porch.

She breathed a sigh of relief when she noted their porch was empty, but then promptly felt the urge to vomit when she spotted them lounging by the pool. It wasn't a particularly hot day, yet Sam felt a flush cover her skin as she took in Callum's chiseled physique. Neither him nor Drew, nor any of the plethora of other people who seemed to always surround them noticed her and she sent up a prayer of thanks at that realization.

She was thankful she'd remembered her sunglasses as it allowed her to covertly stare.

God, he was beautiful.

Not in a traditional way. More in a *I will kill anyone who crosses me but would also lay on the floor and pet puppies all day* kind of way. His dark hair was pulled up into a bun. She had never once considered man buns to be attractive. Actually, she had never considered them at all. But now she decided it was one of her most favorite things. His broad shoulders seemed to take over the entire width of the chair he was lounging in and his tattoos rippled across the expanse of his muscular chest and abdomen.

But his arms.

That man had the arms of a god. For a moment, she conjured up an image of him easily holding her up against a wall as he whispered all manner of wicked things into her ear and had her screaming out his name. She was quite enjoying the image when it shattered at the sound of hers and Christian's names being yelled from across the field.

She didn't know why, but her immediate (and idiotic) response was to look straight to Callum. Who, of course, was now looking straight at her. Even at this distance, it was hard for him to hide the rollercoaster of emotions that crossed his face.

Shock. Anger. Jealousy. Indignation.

She didn't care.

That's what she told herself in order to remain calm. She didn't care that he was possibly the most beautiful man she had ever laid eyes upon. She didn't care that he was somehow also the most annoying and yet intriguing man she had ever met. She didn't care that he made her entire body ignite as if it had turned to pure flame. She didn't care that he'd drawn her. She didn't care that he was currently surrounded by a number of beautiful women who were not her. And she definitely didn't care that every time she thought of him, a rush of goosebumps washed over her skin.

She. Didn't. Care.

But she did.

She most definitely, certainly, absolutely *did* care. Which is why it took more than a moment to reply when the two girls standing before her kindly introduced themselves.

"Hey, I'm Amanda and this is Maddie," the taller of the two said as she reached out her hand.

"Sorry." Sam shook her head. "I'm Sam. Nice to meet you."

"I'll be right back. We are going to set up the targets," Christian whispered a little too close to her ear before he walked away.

"So, he finally got you to come out with us, huh?" the other girl, Maddie, questioned. A rather large smile was plastered on her face.

She tilted her head in confusion. "What?"

"Christian talks about you all the time. Says you two grew up together?" Sam's heart rate spiked in fear that they knew who she was and where she came from. She knew she shouldn't have been ashamed of where she came from, but it was hard to wash away the stigma of being an orphan. It was a stain that had bled through onto every aspect of her adolescence, and she wanted to make damn sure it didn't get a chance to alter her future.

She figured that most people, in one way or another, were trying to run away from something that had occurred in their past. Whether it be a person, or an action, or even themselves. But the problem for her was that she was trying to run away from her entire past and everything in it. Every minuscule detail of that time before she had left that last foster home was littered with feelings of inadequacy, loneliness, hatred, and loathing. She didn't want that to also become her future.

"Yeah, we did." She gave off a smile she hoped hid the fear bubbling up underneath. It was a vague enough reply, and she prayed there wouldn't be a follow-up question. Thankfully, there wasn't.

"Has he made a move yet?" Amanda wiggled her eyebrows with the question.

"What?" Sam said at the same time Maddie's look shot virtual daggers at her friend.

"Amanda! You can't just ask her that. We literally just met her."

"What? It's a valid question. He is obviously totally in love with her, and I'm just glad he finally got her to come out so we can stop just hearing about her and actually get to know her." Amanda smiled as she tossed her arm around Sam and started walking toward the group of guys.

"We aren't like that. I love him, but like a brother. Nothing more," Sam quickly interjected with words she'd never thought she would say.

She wasn't sure why the idea of Christian wanting something more now seemed like the most repulsive thought she could have ever come up with. This was what she'd always wanted. This was what she'd spent far too many nights dreaming about. Even though she wouldn't admit it to the girls, she had to admit to herself that Christian was different today. He had constantly found an excuse to touch her, or compliment her, or just be near her. Normally, they played their brother-sister role perfectly with just the right amount of teasing and aggravation, but also just enough mild flirtation to let others know they weren't really related. That tiny little tease of more was what used to drive her crazy. It's what had kept her up until the wee hours of the morning, replaying their conversations over and over again as she tried to figure out if there could ever be something more.

Today was the complete opposite. Today, it was obvious what he wanted, and the very thought made her skin crawl.

Maybe she was sick?

Fever?

Meningitis?

Ebola?

Something that snuck its way in and altered her mind making her see, think, and want things that would never have lined up with who she truly was. That was it. She had meningitis. It was the only explanation as to why Christian now seemed like the last person she wanted to be around and Callum was all she could think about.

"Ready to lose?" Christian wrapped his arms around her from behind and Maddie winked at her.

"What makes you think I'm not a world class disc golf champion?" Sam said as she twisted slightly, moving her body away from his and stepping further away with the guise of grabbing a disk from the bag.

He laughed a little as he tried to wrap his arm back around her waist. She quickly tried to dodge the movement, hoping the others couldn't tell, but he was too strong. He had his right arm around her before she had the chance to move.

At first, she laughed, acting as if it was just a bit of playing. It was. She knew it was. This was Christian, and he was just playing with her. But for some reason it now felt far too intrusive, and she wanted the contact to end. She patted his arm and looked back to give him a smile as she attempted to step away. But then he leaned his head onto her shoulder and tightened his grip.

"You're mine," he whispered as he kissed the side of her brow.

There was no way to hide the amount of shock that came across her face at that moment.

"I'm nobody's," she whispered back as she tried to step away, but this time his left hand came up across her collar bones, holding her shoulders tightly against his chest.

He chuckled as he whispered in her ear, "I'm talking about teams, silly girl. You're on *my* team." Then he winked. "You're funny."

And then he abruptly released her as he walked off. She stared at the disc in her hand for a moment, trying to figure out what exactly had just happened.

****

By the time she got home, thanks to Maddie and not half-drunk Christian, she was sore and completely worn out. The soreness was partly from the game, and partly from her constant need to stay vigilant and not allow Christian within a few feet of where she stood. He had somehow managed to wrap his arms around her each time he had gotten close enough and she had hated it.

She groaned when she stepped out of the shower and heard the ding from her phone.

Christian: Had a great
time tonight.
Can't wait for the next
one.

Chapter 24 - Sam

For once, Sam was in a good mood when she walked into work the next day. That ended abruptly when Mr. Brimley caught her heading to her section.

"Sam, come see me in the back room after you clock in!" he yelled as he headed toward the storage room.

She dreaded the walk through the kitchen, already knowing what Mason wanted. There was a festival going on downtown, which meant it would be a slow night. On rare occasions, that meant he would send a few of them home. She had made it clear on one of those previous nights that she would stay and help in any manner if it meant getting paid. She hadn't realized that would mean washing the bathrooms and spending far too many hours rolling silverware.

When she saw her normal section hadn't even been set up, she said a quick prayer that it would be a silverware night and not a bathroom night. When he turned left into the small back storage room, she smiled, remembering she had at least brought her headphones tonight and could listen to music while she worked.

That excitement turned sour when she found Callum standing directly to her right.

"Sam, Mr. Barker here has offered to help with some of the back stock tonight. I told him you could handle it, but he insisted. Please, no more blunders." Mr. Brimley's eyes bored into Sam's, pleading with her not to mess this up. "So, we need the silverware rolled. Our to-go bags aren't made up either. And we got in a new shipment of menus that need to be placed into the bindings. I need them all organized and put together. Let me know if you need anything."

"Mr. Brimley, I'm sure—"

"Do the silverware first, okay? People can't eat our food with their hands," he said with a smirk as he walked out the door and headed back to the front, leaving her alone and behind a closed door with Callum.

They stood there silently for a moment, each waiting for the other to say something.

Neither budged.

Sam took a deep breath to gather herself, then took off her apron and threw it in the corner. If she was going to be stuck in here with him, she was going to make sure the task was completed as quickly as possible.

She was halfway through rolling her third set of silverware when she realized Callum still hadn't moved from his spot against the wall. Although she couldn't see him from where she stood, she was certain she hadn't heard the door open and close. He was most likely standing behind her not doing a damn thing but being a creep, and she made a promise to herself not to be the first to crack. She continued with the task until it became mindless and rote—until she had no clue how many sets of silverware she had rolled.

"You should make sure they're all facing the same direction."

"I'm sorry, what?" she asked, tone full of attitude.

"The fork. Every now and then you turn it backward compared to the spoon and knife." His voice was timid and shy.

She turned back to finally make eye contact. Did he really just criticize her while he was standing there doing absolutely nothing? Her palms began to sweat and it took more self control than she knew she had not to scream in his face right then and there. She had to get out of here. She would tell Mr. Brimley she was sick and then go home.

"Fine, you do it." She threw down the fork and spoon she was holding and made it almost all the way to the door when he caught her arm.

"I'm sorry. That's not what I meant." His voice was barely a whisper in her ear.

"Really?" She may not have been able to throw a few choice words in his direction now that she knew he was her boss, but she could at least spit out the words she did state with as much venom-laced sarcasm as she could muster. "And what is it that you meant, *sir*?" She swore he shuddered.

"Sam. Don't call me that."

"What is it you meant, sir?" She dragged the last word out, making it a tad more breathy than the rest, and began to yank her arm from his, but he quickly twisted them around so her body was pressed firmly between him and the wall. Her two hands were held directly above her head with his one. She looked up to catch his gaze just as his eyes swept across his lips.

Her every curve lined up perfectly with every hard line of him.

"What are you doing?" She wanted to appear stern, but their proximity and stance made her breathless.

"I want to talk."

"And you thought criticism was a good intro?" Her voice was too breathy, but this time it wasn't on purpose. She couldn't focus when all she could think about was how good he smelled and how much she wanted him to push further into her. How much she wanted to taste him and devour him. How much she wanted him to devour her.

That throbbing that always seemed to make itself known when he was around surged forward, and it took all the will she could muster not to press her hips further into him. But then he exhaled, his breath tickling the skin of her neck, and her hips shot forward, desperate to find friction and relief.

He moaned at her movement and then he was pressing harder into her. And, god, it felt so damn good. He pushed forward again, but this time he used his free hand to reach down and shift her hips just slightly to the side. She let out a small whimper as that throbbing became a persistent ache that blossomed and spread through every inch of her.

His lips hovered slightly over the skin of her jaw as he whispered. "I can't help that being around you makes me forget how to fucking function."

This time, he pressed his head against the wall closest to her ear and she could hear his ragged exhale. He stood there for too long. She felt her hands start to tingle from the position he had her in, but she wouldn't dare move an inch in fear that he would pull away. She would let every part of her body go numb if it meant getting to touch him.

When the seconds turned to minutes, she became anxious. She needed him to say or do *something*. She couldn't take this wonderfully tortuous hell any longer, and hoped that his choice would be to lean in closer instead of pushing further away.

"Talking requires the parties to open their mouths for sound to come out. You should try it."

He laughed a little as his nose brushed against her cheek. "You are so fucking annoying. You know that, right?" His breath tickled her ear, and she knew he meant it in the best possible way. But then he shifted just slightly so his face was damn near pressed up to hers. "You drive me absolutely insane."

"I could say the same for you." She felt the slight stubble on his chin against her lips as she spoke.

He huffed out another laugh. "I wish that was the case."

"I can't stop thinking about you," Sam confessed. Her eyes met his and his grip on her loosened, but he didn't let go.

"Even while you were on your date?"

"Even while I was out to lunch with a friend," Sam quickly corrected.

His eyes closed and, before she could lean in further and brush her lips against his, he pulled away, placing a few inches between them. Her hands dropped to her sides.

"Tonight is my last night here at Topline."

"What?" Her voice cracked and she felt an immediate pang of sadness at the idea he wouldn't be here at her next shift.

She shouldn't feel that way. But she couldn't fathom a world in which he wasn't there the next time.

"I thought I could be around you, but I can't."

"Why can't you?"

"Because. You are quicksand." He closed his eyes.

"You think I'm trying to trap you?"

"I'm already trapped. And that's the problem. I like it. I want you to ensnare me and take everything I have to give. I want you to take everything I am," he explained.

"You are giving me whiplash." She deadpanned and he laughed. The sound was quickly cut off with her next words.

"Are you refusing to see me because I'm friends with Christian?"

"Don't say his name."

"Tell me why."

"I'm supposed to be at a birthday party right now."

She furrowed her brows at his words. "What?"

"It's my father's sixtieth birthday. He rented a boat. Whole family, well, most of the family, and a shitload of people my father barely tolerates are cruising around on the lake getting drunk."

Sam wasn't sure exactly why he brought that up.

"Why aren't you there?"

"Because my father and I don't particularly get along."

"And what does this have to do with Christi–" She immediately closed her mouth when he eyed her at the name. "What does this have to do with you not wanting me to hang out with a friend?" Sam amended.

"It doesn't," he answered, growing visibly despondent.

"Callum." She buried her face in her hands as she heard him take a step closer to bring his body back next to hers once more.

She wanted to push him away, even if only to feel his sculpted muscles under her hands once more. But before she could finish the thought, he reached out and dragged her hands from her face.

"I don't even know how to talk to you," she confessed as traitorous tears started to cloud her vision. "You don't make any sense. One minute you're yelling at me, then you're kissing me senseless, the next we're fighting, the next I find your drawing of me, and then you're undressing me in your room and then the next minute you are yelling at me again and critiquing my silverware rolling skills." He laughed at her words, but she continued, "I don't know how to react to this. I don't know what you want me to–"

His lips crashed against hers. Then his hands cupped her face and it was all she could do to stay upright in his arms.

He pulled back and she reached out to pull him toward her again without thinking, but paused as he said, "I don't know either. I need to figure that out. But what I do know is that I don't want to stop doing this." He looked back down at her lips once more.

"Me neither." Her breath tickled his lips as she spoke.

And then he was on her once more.

A wave of heat rippled down her body as his tongue swept across her lips, begging for entry. His hands made their way to her hips. He squeezed as he pushed his body further into hers. The moan that escaped her lips was far too loud.
Callum jumped back at the noise.

Somehow, they managed to both be rolling sets of silverware by the time a line cook peeked through the peephole window in the door.

Neither could hold in the fit of laughter that burst free when they were once again alone.

They didn't say another word. Instead they each spent the rest of her shift stealing glances at the other and then quickly turning away when caught. She didn't stop him as his hands suspiciously grabbed onto her hips when he shifted to get something from beside her, or when his lips brushed against her cheek when he reached around her. By the time they finished each task Mr. Brimley had lined out for them, it was well past closing and she was about as tightly wound as a brand new spring.

"Where did you park?" Callum questioned as they walked out the front door. It was the first utterance either of them had made over the last two hours.

"I don't have a car. I took the bus."

"It's 11 p.m." His voice was incredulous and full of shock.

"Well, aren't you just a little Sherlock Holmes?" she replied, her voice full of sarcasm.

Callum wasn't amused. He stared at her for a few moments, letting what she'd said sink in.

"You ride the bus to and from every shift?"

"Yes."

"What about class?"

"It depends. If mine and Kristin's schedules line up, we ride together. If she has other stuff to do, then I take the bus."

"What about that night when you met me at Social?"

"I drove Kristin's car that night." She wasn't sure where this conversation was headed.

"The bus isn't safe."

"It's perfectly safe. I've been taking it for years."

Years meaning since she was twelve. She had to admit that back then it had been a little questionable, and there were a few times that she'd been frightened, but she'd always had a can of pepper spray and a carving knife hidden in her bag.

"Here." He reached out to hand her his phone. "Put your number in my phone and just let me know your schedule and I'll be there."

"Absolutely not."

"It's better than riding the bus and getting kidnapped."

She rolled her eyes at his concern. "I'm not going to get kidnapped. If I wasn't kidnapped while riding it at twelve and thirteen, I think I'm safe now."

"You rode the bus alone at *twelve years old?*"

She mentally cringed. She didn't mean to divulge that, but it just came out.

"Yes, and it was perfectly safe."

"Your parents let you ride at twelve? What were they doing that they couldn't take you to and from places?"

She swallowed, not sure how to respond, so she abruptly changed the subject.

"Can I ask you a question?" she blurted out.

"You just did."

"Are we going to just continue to toy back and forth with each other?" She shuffled on her feet, not sure how to act when voicing such a direct question.

"I don't want that," he admitted.

"Me neither." She wanted to wait for a second before continuing, but she couldn't help it. "What *do* you want?"

His answer was immediate. "Something I can't have."

"Why can't you have it?"

"Because it's too good for me. I would ruin it."

She stood still for a moment as she leaned against the truck she hoped was his.

"Do you honestly think that's the truth? Or are you telling yourself that so you don't have to deal with the potential disappointment of that thing, whatever it is," she asked, despite knowing damn well he most likely meant her, "not wanting you back in the end?" At that, he stilled then ran his hands through his hair.

"It doesn't matter what the reason is."

She put her bag on the hood of the truck and took a step toward him.

"It absolutely matters what the reason is. If it's the latter, then you should know I've been through that more times than I could count. And most of the time, the disappointment you end up feeling is your own doing, not because of anything or anyone else."

She was standing directly in front of him now. They were separated by mere inches. "Most of the time, the disappointment comes from never taking the chance on something that could have been wonderful, all because you were too scared to fuck it up."

Chapter 25 -Callum

He watched her walk to the bus stop at the corner as he sat in the cab of his truck and waited. Then, he followed behind that bus for the entire forty-five minute drive it took to get her home. There were three stops between Topline and her place. He could have gotten her home in under ten minutes.

He watched as the lights in her townhouse turned on, and then, when he finally decided she was safe, he pulled away.

He made it two blocks over before he pulled off the road, turned off the truck, and ran his hand through his hair.

She took the bus.

She didn't have a car.

The fancy car she drove to Social was Kristin's.

Her parents let her take the bus at fucking twelve years old.

Her parents were fucking shitty.

Her parents were...

And then his head shot up in realization.

Sam and Christian had been friends forever. That was what she had said. They were lifelong best friends and nothing more.

Christian was an orphan and had grown up in foster care. He knew this because he knew Christian.

Sam didn't have anyone to help her with school or money or anything else because she was a foster kid.

"Fuck!" He slammed his fist against the steering wheel.

She was so damn independent and driven because she was all she'd ever had.

She had made something of herself without help from literally anyone. She was strong, and fierce, and witty, and, god dammit, he wanted to take away any pain she ever had.

He wanted to help her and to be there for her.

He wanted to love...

He swallowed as the thought tore through him.

****

It was well past midnight when he walked into his house and found Drew and Micah doing absolutely nothing while they chilled in the living room.

"What are you two still doing up?"

"I don't know," Micah stated, still scrolling through his phone. Drew didn't even answer as he stared blankly at some sports recap on the TV. Callum grabbed a beer for himself, and another two that he passed between the guys before taking a seat. He had downed half of the bottle when he finally decided to speak.

"Can you send me Sam's number?"

That caused both Micah and Drew to pop their heads up in unison.

"And why would you need her number?" Micah challenged.

Callum gave him a rather annoyed look. "Just send it to me."

"You like her," Drew cut in. "Just admit it. You fucking like her."

Callum looked between the two busybodies he called friends and then threw his head back against the chair in exasperation as he spoke.

"Fine. I like her. I fucking like her, and I want her number. I admitted it. Now, can I have her number?" He lifted his head and eyed Micah. He didn't even acknowledge Drew and the laugh he was very obviously trying to keep from bubbling to the surface.

"Why do you think I have it?" Micah countered, and for a split second Callum's shoulders sagged. "I'm kidding. I've got it. Damn, man, you looked like a sad fucking puppy when I said that," Micah added as he joined Drew in trying not to smile.

"Stop being a dick," Callum stated as he downed the last of the beer.

"You see her tonight?" Micah questioned.

"Yeah." Callum rolled his eyes. "Should I go get face masks, finger nail polish, and glasses of wine so we can all sit around and chat about my feelings?" Callum said with about as much sarcasm as he could muster.

Drew let out a huff. "Stop. We are happy for you. But, if you got a face mask that can take away this breakout shit on my chin," he pointed to the deep brown skin of his face. "I would *not* turn it down."

They all three laughed.

"Do me a favor," Micah stated just as Callum heard the ping on his phone and looked down to find Sam's contact info.

A smile crept over his face. "What's that?"

"I don't know the history, but I think Sam has been through some shit, okay? I just know that Kristin is ridiculously protective over her and...I don't know, man. I don't want my girlfriend going to prison for murdering my best friend."

Callum laughed and then that smile turned down. He had a feeling he now knew exactly what that history had entailed.

"I'm not going to hurt her. At least...at least, I'm going to try not to." He leaned forward as he clasped his hands together and stared at the carpet. "I don't know. She's different. Everything about her is just so..." He paused and took a breath as he continued to stare at the floor between his legs. "She's so smart, and her laugh is the best sound I've ever heard. She just doesn't give a fuck what other people think about her, you know? She is so damn strong and independent and brave. And she always makes sure to play with the kids at the tables, and whenever there is someone who has a disability or any special needs she is, like, hands down the best person, and makes sure everything works for them. She is just so kind and caring and..." He stopped when he looked up to find both guys giving him the biggest shit-eating grins of their lives.

"Go on," Drew said with a laugh.

Callum's face grew hot as he muttered a very disingenuous

"Fuck you" to both and then threw a pillow at Drew's head.

Micah was practically rolling on the ground with laughter. Drew was trying hard not to join him.

"Dude, you got it bad. Like bad bad," Micah said in bouts while he caught his breath as Callum made his way toward the stairs.

"Shut up," Callum called out as he tried to hide the embarrassment that currently flooded his features.

"Like head over heels, in love and wife her up kind of bad," Drew added just as Callum made it to the bottom stair.

He closed the door and then promptly fell on top of his bed.

They were right.

Fuck.

He tried to envision what exactly that meant. He had really only ever dated one girl. He'd spent his highschool years with the mentality of *get with as many girls as possible before you get to college,* and then had spent the first two years of undergrad continuing the tradition by sleeping with every girl who let him. Then, when he'd finally given it a try and then his only relationship had ended in disaster, he'd decided to swear off relationships altogether.

There had been a good many who'd tried to get him to date them, but he didn't think relationships were for him. He would ruin whoever he was with. They were better off if he just cut ties and let them go off and meet their Mr. Perfect.

He was the guy before Mr. Perfect came around. He was the *greatest lay of their life* who they would discuss with their friends over a glass of wine ten years from now. But he wasn't dating or marriage material.

Except, with Sam he felt different.

He realized then that he wanted those things now. Instead of envisioning his life as a cycle of running businesses and fucking around, he somehow had now moved on to eating dinner with Sam, watching a movie with Sam, cleaning the dishes with Sam, going on vacation with Sam, having a life with Sam...

Fuck.

Fuck.

Fuck.

He was a goner.

Chapter 26 - Sam

Sam had read the same paragraph four times over and had hardly retained any of the information. All she could focus on was what had transpired the previous week with Callum.

She had walked away to the bus stop after she left Callum standing at the truck. She'd pretended not to notice how that same truck had followed right behind the bus until she'd gotten off at her stop. And then she'd pretended not to notice how it had stayed close behind her as she walked the hundred yards to her apartment complex.

He hadn't driven off until she'd turned on her bedroom light, and even then it had lingered for a moment as she peeked out from her window.

She hadn't seen him since, mostly because she was working through two projects and she hadn't been to Topline or to Micah's in a few days.

But she had been thinking about that night all week. Had barely slept more than an hour or two at a time.

She had hoped a review of the material for her upcoming exam would help take her mind away from the man that now plagued every one of her dreams, but nothing took him from her thoughts.

Sam was just about to call it quits for the day when she saw her phone flash with a new message.

Unknown: Come
outside.

It wasn't a number she recognized, so she sneakily peeked out the blinds from her second-floor bedroom before responding. She didn't see anyone familiar and was planning on texting back *wrong number* just as a second message arrived.

Unknown: I'm not the
boogie man, Sam. You
can open the blinds all
the way and check.
Sam: Who is this?

Unknown: Who do
you think it is?

Sam: Someone who is
annoying me.

Unknown: I got your
number from Micah.

Sam: That tells me
nothing. Micah is
friends with far too
many people.

Unknown: It's
Callum. Will you come
outside?

Sam: Why?

> **Callum**: Because I
> want to see you.

She took a deep breath and looked down at her SpongeBob pajamas. It was supposed to be a *stay at home and do nothing but study* day. She hadn't even fixed her hair. She wasn't even certain if she'd brushed her teeth now that she thought about it. Her hand came up to her face as she blew out a puff of air and then cringed at the odor that erupted from her mouth.

> **Sam**: Give me 5
> minutes.

It was a rush of trying not to look like an absolute slob. She quickly ran her fingers through her hair and made sure her breath smelled of mint. She reached for the shorts and tank, but then the tags from that flowy summer dress Kristin had given her the previous year shimmered in the light of her closet.

The dress was brand new. It was a gorgeous deep blue that reminded her of the ocean and a perfect blend of comfortability and sexiness wrapped into one. Something girls would wear when they want to look effortless and yet impress someone. Kristin had found it during a shopping trip and Sam hadn't yet had a chance to wear it during her weekly lunch or coffee visits with Christian.

With a deep breath, she yanked the tags off and threw it on over her head. She hadn't even tried it on before, but when she stood before the mirror even she was a little taken aback by how well it fit. And it was casual enough that maybe he would think she'd had it on all along. She felt a small sense of betrayal knowing that who she'd intended to wear it for and who she was actually wearing it for were two completely different people.

When she saw him sitting on the front porch steps facing the street, she contemplated running back upstairs and blocking the number. But then he turned, lifting his hand up to cover his eyes so he could make out her form from the other side of the storm door.

"What are you doing here?" she asked as she opened the door. He looked up, a relaxed smile on his face like none she'd seen on him before. His eyes took her in from head to toe.

"You're beautiful, Sam."

She rolled her eyes. "Stop." She wanted to curl in on herself. She had never been good at taking compliments.

"Would you rather I told you a lie?"

"What are you doing here?" she questioned once more, hoping to steer the conversation away from his statement.

"I wanted to see you. You haven't been at work at all this week."

"I thought you didn't work there anymore?"

"Yeah, well. Seems I just can't stay away for long."

"Did you miss me, Mr. Barker?" She tried to sound strong and confident, but instead it came out as more of a sincere question than she meant it to.

"I told you not to call me that."

"You also said not to call you 'sir.'"

"Sam." Her name was a warning. She wasn't sure why addressing him in such a way seemed to dismantle every wall he'd built up between them, but she liked it.

"Do you miss me, sir?"

He shook his head as he ran his hands across his face. "You are going to be the death of me."

"You didn't answer my question."

He looked down at the ground to his shuffling feet.

"Yeah, I did miss you." When he looked back up to meet her gaze, she was sure his eyes had darkened by at least three shades. "Are you going to invite me in or not?"

"Why would I do that?" she inquired.

"Because, even if you won't admit it, I know you missed me, too, and it's hot as hell out here."

She did refuse to admit it and rolled her eyes once more.

Then without her own volition, her feet moved to the side to allow him room to pass. "Well, come on in then."

"No, thanks," he said with a shit-eating grin.

"What the hell? You just asked to come inside."

"No, I asked if you were going to invite me inside. Those are two completely different things."

She felt her skin turn hot. This man aggravated her more than anyone else she had ever been around. She had never known someone she both wanted to slap and kiss in the same moment.

"You are insane. You know that, right? Completely and totally insane."

"So I've been told. Anyway, I'm headed down to the river and since there's an entrance to the Riverwalk near here, I thought I would see if you wanted to come."

Her arms crossed over her chest as she surveyed him in question.

"There are about fifty different entrances to it. Why come to this one?"

"Because I felt like it." He shrugged his shoulders. "So, go get some shoes on and come with me."

"I can't."

"Why not?" Callum mirrored her pose and leaned against the door frame.

"I have two projects I'm working through and an exam next week."

"What have you been doing all morning?"

"Studying."

He smirked. "Exactly. Take a break, get your shoes, and meet me outside. Please."

"Callum," she dragged out his name.

"Yes, that's me," he replied with a smirk and she groaned in annoyance.

But she knew there was no more fight left in her, and in truth she really did want to spend time with him. She took a deep breath and stepped behind the door to slip on some shoes. "So, where's the entrance?"

"How do you not know? Haven't y'all lived here for a while?"

"Well, yeah. But I haven't ever been down to it."

"Jesus." He furrowed his brow. "You live right by the river and you've never had the urge to just go down there and relax?"

"I don't really have time for relaxing," she said as they made their way off the porch.

He turned to the right. "It's got to be this way. I came from the other direction and didn't see it back there."

Sam promptly reached in her pocket to pull out her phone. Callum abruptly stopped her.

"No fucking way are you going to look up a map."

Her eyebrows peaked with a mixture of confusion and surprise. "How did you know I was going to look for a map?"

"Because you're you and that is the exact opposite of spontaneous."

"What if we don't find it and then we wander around all day?"

"Has anyone ever told you that it's not always about the destination but the journey?"

"That sounds oddly poetic."

Callum smiled.

They walked in comfortable silence, only making it another block before the entrance came into view.

Within another few steps, they were surrounded by trees. The rustling of leaves above them drowned out the noises of the city and the canopy above provided a gentle shade from the afternoon sun. She turned when she noticed Callum no longer in step beside her and found him intently examining a bird's nest with a few eggs resting inside.

"Don't touch it. Your scent will scare the mom away," she whispered as she wrapped her fingers around his arm and pulled him forward.

"I won't," he promised, smiling. She started to let go, but he quickly shifted his hand to clasp hers.

She stalled for just a moment as her eyes took in their joined hands.

"Sorry." He let go of her. "I didn't mean to—"

"No." She quickly reached back out and intertwined her fingers within his. "It's okay."

She had held a few guys' hands before. That she was sure of. But they'd meant nothing; teenage boys she had used to try to make Christian jealous. This was something much more than that. She swore she felt her fingertips tingle each time he squeezed just a little bit.

It wasn't a long walk. They could still make out the entrance to the path by the time they made it to the river. She wasn't sure why she had never come here before, especially when it took all of five minutes to get here.

"It's crazy to think this is just outside the city. I feel like we are in a completely different state."

"Come on. There should be a dock over the water at some point with a bench." He pulled her along, causing their steps to fall back into line.

She realized then how easy it was to fall into step beside him. How easy it would be to fall into this chaotic rhythm they had somehow developed. It was a punch to the gut when she realized she wanted that more than she was willing to fully admit.

It was only a short walk before the dock he was talking about came into view.

The patio-like structure started on the end of the walking path and extended a few feet over the river allowing visitors to lean out and watch the water flow. Sam's feet seemed to move before she could think and she let go of Callum's hand and found herself perched on the edge. In front of her was the most beautiful view she had ever seen. She internally chastised herself again for the fact that she'd never taken the time to come down here.

"Are you going to draw this?" Sam asked when she finally looked back toward Callum, who was sitting casually on the bench a few feet behind her.

"Yes." But he wasn't staring at the view before them, he was staring at her.

She leaned back, letting her elbows rest against the railing and tossed her head back to soak in the sun raining down on her face. It was far too hot for April, or maybe it was just the fact that she was near him that caused a flush and sheen of sweat to begin to move across her body, but within moments, a cool misty breeze from the water covered her.

When she looked back to Callum, he still wasn't looking at the water or the sun, or even the beautiful trees. His eyes were focused directly on her. It was the same look he had given her when he perched her up on his desk. He seemed to be memorizing this. Memorizing every detail to later put to paper. He finally took a breath and ran his fingers through his hair, severing the trance they were stuck in.

"So, what exam is on the schedule for this week?"

"It's on nephrology."

Callum's eyebrows peaked. "That sounds like a Harry Potter class."

Sam laughed. "No, it's just the kidneys."

Callum's nose scrunched up. "That sounds incredibly disgusting and boring."

"It actually kind of is." Sam nodded her head in agreement. "I'm dying to get it over with. We'll go back to cardiology next week and that's what I like the most." She had always leaned toward cardiology. Something about the heart and all its intricacies fascinated her. Without the heart, no one could function.

"So, you want to be a heart doctor?" Callum questioned.

"No. There are so many different specialties. I don't know, maybe. I haven't even gotten into med school. I could end up being a waitress for the rest of my life." She made her way over to him and when she sat down there were only a few inches between them.

"No. You'll get in and I'm sure you will make an amazing doctor. Heart doctor, that is...cardiologist," he quickly corrected himself.

Sam couldn't hold in the smile that erupted on her face. For some reason the idea of his belief in her meant so much. It was then she realized she wanted him to be proud of her. Which was silly. She didn't really even know him and he barely knew her. But that small little profession of his faith in her brought forth an uncontrollable happiness.

"Is Sara a heart doctor?" His question surprised her. Sam had let Sara's name slip during their first *normal* conversation, but she never thought he would remember it.

"No, she wasn't."

"And she isn't your sister?" She was the closest thing Sam ever had to a sister—to any family, really. Christian was always there, but...

"No, she was not my sister."

"Okay. So. What kind of doctor is 'not your sister' Sara?"

"She was a pediatrician."

"She isn't anymore?"

Callum was clearly not going to let up.

"No. She isn't anymore."

He reached over to her legs, lifting them and laying them across his lap.

"Is this okay?" he questioned.

She nodded a yes, then he began drawing lazy circles on the exposed skin of her thigh.

"What does she do now?"

"Can we talk about something else?"

"Yeah. Okay." They entered a comfortable silence for a moment and she closed her eyes, soaking in the feeling of his hands on her.

"Tell me about the tattoo shops." She was desperate to

change the subject without losing the momentum of the previous conversation.

"They're pretty straight forward. You come in and pick out what you want and then one of our artists puts it on you."

She shook her head with a laugh. "I know the general idea. I mean, how did they come to be. You and Drew are really lucky to be so young and have so much success, right? How many shops do y'all have?" It was truly amazing how well they had done in such a short time and while so young. "Wait, how old are you?" Sam quickly cut in before he could answer.

"I'm twenty-five. I told you about how we would tattoo each other in high-school. Well, it just kind of evolved from there. When I first took a break from college, I didn't really have anything going for me, so I worked at Topline and was living with Drew."

It was the first time he had ever mentioned college. She wanted to ask more on the subject, but she let him continue.

"We were low on cash and started doing tattoos again on the side for money. Eventually, word spread about how good we were, and more and more people came to us. We started in a small little basement shop down in Five Points. I swear there were rats living under the floors and it smelled like vomit. But it was a start. Then we just got busier and busier and ended up with two real licensed shops downtown within a year. By the next year, we had one in Charleston as well. And we just opened up a second one in Charleston last summer. That's why we were gone so much during that time. But anyway, it's all about word of mouth. People want a good artist, and thankfully, Drew and I are really good. So, it just kind of took off. I bought Topline a little over a month ago on a whim. Honestly, I had been thinking about selling it. Even if the money is insanely good, it's more work than I had realized. But then I wouldn't have met you."

"I'm glad you didn't sell it, too." She smiled up at him. "Your drawings are amazing. I would love to see some of your other artwork." He was a great artist. She could attest to that after seeing some of his work.

He squeezed her leg at the compliment, giving her a sheepish smile.

"Thank you."

"How long have you been drawing?"

"All my life."

"Are you going to draw me again?" she asked in a moment of bravery.

"Yeah," he said as he stared out toward the water.

"Why?"

"I already told you that."

"So, what? I'm just stuck in your head. What does that even mean?"

"It means...I don't know what it means other than the fact that you drive me absolutely fucking insane."

"But–" Sam began to argue, but he cut her off.

"No, stop. I don't mean that in a bad way. I just mean...I can't stop thinking about you."

"There is a part of me that is convinced you hate me."

He chuckled and shook his head at her words.

"No. I could never hate you. If I hated you, I wouldn't have had you in my bed like I did, and you know it." A blush started to creep its way across her skin at his words.

"Callum." Sam turned away, not sure if she could voice the truth while staring into his eyes. "Honestly, I don't know anything. I mean, no offense, but you confuse the shit out of me. And we got interrupted when I wanted to talk about it at Topline. I feel like we have this thing going on between us. It's more than obvious. But it's just out of reach somehow. I don't know. Does that even make sense?" Saying it out loud made it more real by the second.

"Yeah, it does."

"So, where does that leave us?" She looked up at him.

"Where do you want it to leave us?"

"I want you. You know that. I'm about as obvious as they

come."

"Not really. Not when you go out on dates with other guys."

She sighed, exasperated. "I'm not sure how many more times we can rehash this. I told you that wasn't a date. Just lunch with a lifelong friend."

Callum sat there silently for a while with his hands clasped on top of her legs fidgeting with his thumbs.

"You could ask me out." The words came out in a rush. She wasn't sure where this brazen woman was coming from. Kristin would be shocked at what trouble Sam was letting her mouth get her into. But when no response came she continued. "But that's not something you're going to do, right? You aren't going to ask me out because you 'don't date.'"

"It's not that. If I was going to date someone, it would most definitely be you. It's just that I would hurt you. And I don't want to hurt you."

"No, you wouldn't."

"Yes, I would. I hurt everyone I'm close to."

"Try me." She sat up further, closing the distance between their faces.

"What?"

"Try me. I'm a big girl. I can handle myself." She watched as he leaned back against the bench, closed his eyes and ran his fingers through his long hair again.

"You realize people would talk right? I mean, I'm covered in tattoos, and I'm seen as a failure by my entire family."

"You are most definitely not a failure by any means," she countered, but he didn't stop.

"And you look like a fucking ray of sunshine and have all these plans for med school. We aren't exactly a typical pairing, are we?"

"I'm going to take that as a compliment," Sam said, rolling her eyes. "Why do we have to be typical? There isn't some perfect mold we have to adhere to. If everyone lived a cookie-cutter life, the world would be pretty boring, right?"

"I would fuck up your world," he said as he finally made eye contact with her again. This time he turned more fully toward her, letting his arm rest across her legs.

"No, you don't know what would happen if we were together because you haven't given it a chance. You can't base life on the what ifs," she said just as a gentle mist started to fall.

Callum looked up at the sky at the same time she did and then lifted her legs off of him. "Come on. Let's head back. It'll be a downpour before too long."

The walk back was silent. The tree canopy shielded them from the mist that had started to fall, and they seemed to use that as an excuse to slow the walk; to stay in their own little world before something came crashing in to tear them apart again. It wasn't until they began to break through the tree line and onto the main road of her complex that the rain really started coming down. Callum grabbed her hand as they made a dash for her house. By the time they made it to the front porch, they were both soaked and freezing. They stood there in silence staring at each other, not sure where to go from there. This was something they seemed to have perfected over the past few weeks. This was the invisible pull that surrounded them.

A loud crash of thunder broke the silence and made them both jump.

"Did you kiss him?" Callum asked abruptly.

"What?"

"Last week, when you were with Christian. Did you kiss him?"

"No."

"Good."

Within seconds, Sam's legs were wrapped around his waist and his mouth was once again on the soft spot of her neck. Her heart was racing so fast she knew Callum could feel each beat as he licked the rain from the skin on her neck.

They stumbled through the door and he had her up against the wall. When his mouth finally found hers, she felt it all the way to her toes. She lost track of time when he kissed her.

The world went silent.

"Where is your room?" His words came in between pants. He was already out of breath from the attack he had levied on her neck.

"Upstairs. Second door on the right."

He lifted her higher and headed for the stairs without another word. They didn't break apart again until he kicked her bedroom door open and laid her down on the bed. His hands once again tortured her by slowly trailing their way around her body. He touched every piece of exposed skin he could reach.

She could tell he was holding back again, but today she wanted none of that. Her body was ignited and she didn't want this feeling to end. She wasn't sure how to voice the words, so she let her actions do the talking as she quickly lifted his shirt over his head. Her movement caught him off guard and his eyes bored deep into hers in question.

"Sam. Don't do this for me, okay?"

"I'm doing this for me."

He stalled for a split second before he could no longer fight it.

It became a push and pull. Sam fought to get him undressed just as fast as he was fighting for her. The wet clothes sticking to their bodies and Sam's constant need to reattach her lips to his made reaching the goal a little more difficult. When he at last lowered the straps of her dress and threw it to the floor, he stopped and placed her onto his lap. She was stuck under his gaze in just her bra and underwear now. There was little to hide the evident need he possessed for her and she could feel him straining against the fabric of his boxers.

She leaned in again, desperate for another kiss, when he stopped her.

"Let me look at you." The way his eyes slowly trailed down

her body made her feel so beautiful. She had never had someone look at her like this. Like she was the last drink of water and they were about to enter the Sahara Desert. She had never been so bare before someone and yet, the way he stared at her made her feel more brave than she had in any other time in her life.

"Fuck," he said as he laid back and covered his eyes with his hands.

"What's wrong?"

"I can't do this."

"You what?" She leaned across him, letting her wet hair drag over his chest.

"I can't do this to you."

She wanted to laugh at the absurdity. "Callum, I promise I am a perfectly willing participant. We are doing this together." She leaned down to pepper his exposed chest with kisses and trailed her lips along the vines that covered his body. His breathing was now ragged and he reached down to grip her thighs. As her kisses continued, that grasp became so tight it teetered on the precipice of pain and pleasure. She decided to go with the latter. Her lips made their way to the patch of hair that trailed down his stomach before she felt his hand grip her chin and lift her face to meet his.

"Sam. Wait. Come here." He pulled her up to meet eye to eye. "You would regret this later. You would hate me."

"No, I wouldn't."

"I can't give you what you need right now, and the last thing I want is for you to regret this...regret me."

She was so damn tired of the back and forth, and yet here they were again. She didn't think she could handle it. She pushed off his body, reaching for her shirt.

"No." He tried to stop her as he grabbed her wrist. "I'm not letting you go. I...damnit." He fisted his black hair. "I want you so bad I can't think straight, okay? You have consumed my every thought since you spilled all those drinks on me. You are literally all I think about. I have tried so damn hard to forget you and stop this.

But I can't. I want it to be real for you. I would never allow myself to be in a relationship and you deserve someone who can give you that."

"So I don't get a say in this? What if this is what I want?"

"I don't want you to hate me."

"So we just go back to what we've been doing. Fool around, fight, make-up, fool around again, fight. It's an endless cycle, and honestly, it's driving me insane."

"I don't want that," he agreed. "Maybe you should stay away from me?" He quickly stood and she could tell by the look on his face he meant the exact opposite of what he was saying.

"You are the one who showed up here," she all but screamed at him, her frustration getting the better of her. "And now you're saying that you don't want to be near me?"

"No. That's not what I mean." He paced the room for a moment. "You are like a drug I just can't get off of. And I don't want to, but I just don't know how to be what you need."

"Just leave." Sam threw his clothes at him. "I can't deal with the back and forth any more. I'm done." The tears were starting to blur her vision. "I'm done with you deciding what I do and do not need. I'm a grown woman and can make my own damn decisions. And I chose this. I chose you. You." She paused as she felt a sob begin to erupt. She tried to hold it in. There was no way she would let him see the extent of the turmoil he had caused within her. She steadied her breathing and looked him straight in the eyes. "But if that's not enough for you then so be it and get the fuck out of my house."

He looked at her with a shock filled expression. But she was done. She was tired of the constant cycle and him thinking he knew better.

"Leave." Her voice was quiet but demanding.

"Damnit, Sam. I don't want to leave." He made his way toward her. She stepped back. "I don't want to leave. I just want to be near you." His voice finally broke with the words. "I feel okay when I'm near you."

She watched as a war raged on within him, evident in his features. She wanted to pull him in and wrap him up in her arms. She wanted to take away this pain. But she knew that momentary solace would only last for a few hours—days at best. And then they would be right back to this place. Right back to being half dressed and screaming at each other.

"I want the world for you." His voice was barely a whisper.

"What?" Her eyes creased in confusion as to where this was leading.

Callum looked at her and she felt the weight of the pain in his eyes. "You deserve the world. You deserve someone who can love you and put you first. You deserve someone who will take care of you and—"

"I can take care of myself," she quickly interjected. Her emotions were flying in every direction. In one moment she wanted to punch him, and the next she wanted to kiss him.

He smiled sadly then as he nodded.

"I know." His words were a whisper. "Believe me, I know. But that doesn't mean you don't deserve the best. And that's not me. I'm far from the best. I fuck—"

"Yeah. I know," she quickly cut him off again. "You remind me all the time. You fuck up people. You ruin people. Right? That's what you were going to say?"

He silently stared at her as she spoke.

"Look around, Callum. I'm already fucked up. You think my life is so damn perfect because of my major or my funding? Are you serious? There are a million people in the world that make good grades, and I promise you at least half of them have a fucked up past and a closet full of skeletons they are hiding."

He swallowed, his body was practically frozen as she spoke.

"You aren't pushing me away because you are afraid you would fuck me up. You are pushing me away because of what you feel for me and that scares you. You are scared."

He deflated with her words.

"Sam?"

"Admit it!" she screamed as she picked up a pillow and threw it at him.

He didn't move. He didn't say a word. He let the pillow fall to the floor at his feet.

"Admit it!" The scream had lessened, but now the words were punctuated by the sobs she could no longer keep at bay.

He seemed to break as he watched the tears fall down her cheeks. "I'm just trying to do the right thing here. I don't want to shatter your ideal and turn this into something that causes you to hate me."

"I already hate you." Her voice was so quiet she wasn't sure if he even heard her.

"No, you don't, Sam. Don't say that."

"If you don't leave now, I'm calling the police."

He stared at her silently. An unimaginable hurt covered his features.

"Seriously?" he questioned.

He went to take another step toward her, but her sudden backward movement caught him off guard and he finally relinquished.

"Fine, I'm leaving." He grabbed his clothes and quickly threw them on. "I'm sorry again that I can't be what you need."

She huffed in frustration, then stared at the wall, refusing to look upon that stupidly beautiful face as she broke.

He paused for only a moment at what she assumed was her doorway and though she wasn't looking at him, she felt his stare cover her. She didn't move.

With that, he slammed the door shut and she heard his footsteps echoing down the stairs as she collapsed onto her bed and let the tears flow.

Chapter 27 - Sam

Sam couldn't focus on anything to do with school for the rest of that night or the next day. She even ended up calling out of her Monday and Tuesday night shifts at Topline. If she was going to completely get over him, then she most certainly couldn't be around him again. Just being in the same room as him seemed to impede her ability to think straight and made her emotions go all haywire.

She was just so angry.

And sad.

And frustrated.

And confused.

She spent most of what would have been her Tuesday shift searching the Help Wanted papers for a new job. She knew she technically had one at Peet's, but for some reason, she just couldn't bring herself to call them up.

When she sat beside Kristin for Dr. Cho's nephrology exam, Kristin didn't even have to ask.

"Callum might be in an even worse mood than you right now," Kristin said as they were readying their IDs and making sure they had enough pencils and scratch paper.

"You know I don't want to talk about him. Can we just act like I never met him?"

"Well, he is acting like a sourpuss and it's pissing Drew and Micah off. I have been tasked with asking you to fix whatever caused this mood he has stumbled into."

Sam groaned in frustration. "I'm not fixing anything. He caused this *mood* himself. He can wallow in it."

"Like you're wallowing in yours?" Kristin countered.

Sam rolled her eyes. "Stop. I want nothing more to do with him. Besides, I don't ever plan on laying eyes on the man again so it's not my problem to fix."

Kristin grabbed Sam's shoulder and twisted her so they could finally face each other.

"What about hanging out at Micah's? And work? Are you just never going to go back? We had so much fun out at their pool last year. You can't tell me you aren't going to want to go back out there this summer."

"Well, if *he* opens up another tattoo shop somewhere far away and is gone for most of the summer again then I will come and hang out with y'all at the pool. If not, I think I'll stick with getting a tan on our back deck." She turned back to face the front.

"Sam. Stop this. I don't know what happened other than seeing him rush out the door and then finding you a complete mess in just your underwear, but something is up."

"Kristin. Please stop."

"Listen. I've left you alone about it like you asked, but it's been days now, you need to talk to me. You aren't yourself. You haven't even been to work. After this exam is over, you and I are having a girl's night. Okay? We can get wasted and you can tell me all the reasons Callum Barker is worse than a piece of dirt."

Sam smiled at her friend. "I think I need that."

"That's why I'm here," Kristin whispered back to her just as the exam started.

******

Sam was a nervous wreck as she walked out of the auditorium. Her mind was mush, and she didn't know what half of the questions were asking, let alone what the right answers were. This was the first time she could recall not being confident about a grade. When she opened the doors to the outside hallway, she found

Kristin waiting on a bench.

"Please tell me you thought that came out of left field in there?" Kristin asked and Sam was somewhat relieved that it wasn't just her who felt completely blindsided.

"I have no idea what that was. Did we even study that? I mean, what was his plan? Try and fail half the class?" Sam asked as they passed by a girl currently vomiting into a trashcan.

"Well, if I didn't before, I definitely need alcohol now."

"Same," Sam agreed.

They ended up parking in between the liquor store and gas station.

"I think tonight calls for something a little stronger than wine," Kristin announced as she headed in the opposite direction.

"We have class tomorrow. We can't get completely wasted." Sam attempted to redirect her to the gas station.

"Who cares? Besides, even if you get hungover, you can miss one class. It's not the end of the world if you miss one class."

Sam had no fight left within her and, for the first time in her life, she truly didn't care.

"Fine."

Kristin squealed so loudly that the attendant inside the store jumped in surprise.

"Tequila or vodka?" Kristin lifted up the two bottles in the air.

"Is that a real question?"

"Tequila it is!" Kristin agreed.

"This is not going to end well," Sam said as Kristin wiggled her eyebrows and headed for the checkout.

******

"Oh my god. You have got to stay still. I'm going to pee myself," Sam exclaimed when she couldn't stop laughing at Kristin's inability to successfully walk across the living room floor.

"I'm making another drink. You want one?" Kristin yelled out from the kitchen.

"Yes, please!" Sam screamed as she stumbled toward the bathroom.

She needed this. They hadn't had a girl's night like this in weeks. And, she had to admit the tequila was the right choice. This was the first time in...she couldn't actually remember how long it had been, that she was not stressed and on edge.

Sam washed her hands and then stared down at her phone sitting on the counter.

10:58 p.m.

She wondered what *he* was doing right then. It had been five days since he'd walked out of her room...well, since she'd kicked him out of her room. Knowing he had her number, she'd immediately blocked it after hearing his car drive off. A part of her desperately wanted to unblock it now. Now that she had alcohol running through her veins and thoughts of him began to creep further and further in, it started to seem like a good idea.

She hovered over that unblock button four times. The only thing that kept her from hitting it was the possibility of seeing his name pop up without a single notification. She so desperately wanted him to have tried to call her, text her...anything. But she couldn't handle the further rejection and didn't know what it would do to her if she found out that he hadn't attempted at all.

"What's taking you so long?" Kristin slurred as she burst through the door. Privacy had apparently gone out the window along with her common sense. Kristin walked over to the counter and looked down at the name Sam hadn't uttered since last week. "Are you sure you want to do that?"

"No." Sam's reply was immediate.

"Then what are you waiting for?" Kristin cocked her head toward Sam and slid the phone back in her direction. Her drunken response didn't make any logical sense, and then again, it did.

It felt like forever before notifications started scrolling down the screen. But then they didn't stop. One after the next, after the next.

"Holy shit. There are a ton," Kristin said with her mouth wide open.

"Nine text messages and four missed calls," Sam whispered to the static air between them.

"Are you going to just stare at the envelope, or are you going to open them?"

Sam's fingers hovered over the envelope but then, after a much needed deep breath, she pressed it.

Callum: I'm sorry. That's not how I wanted today to end.

Callum: Let me know when it's a good time so we can talk.

Callum: I told you I would fuck it up. I promise I was only trying to do the right thing.

Callum: Please don't hate me.

Callum: Sam. Please answer the phone.

Callum: Can we talk after work tomorrow? I can have Hunter cover your last hour or so.

Callum: Are you okay?
You missed two separate
shifts. Please call me.

Callum: You aren't the
only one confused by all
this.

Callum: I'm sorry.

"Are you going to call him?"

"Why should I?" Sam said as tears filled her eyes.

"Oh, god. Sam! Please don't cry. I'm so sorry. Please. He isn't worth this."

"I know," she said as she tried to hold back the emotion threatening to spill over. "We aren't even together. Why does he have this hold on me? Jesus, Kristin. I've known Callum for all of three, no...four weeks now. Why am I being like this?"

"I don't know, Sam. Sometimes people just make an impression on us and I guess you two made one hell of an impression on each other. Maybe you should call him?" At that statement, Sam jerked up to look at Kristin through the mirror. "I mean, I feel like in one messed up sense y'all work. I don't understand it, and I don't think y'all do either, but I think we can both agree that you have to figure it out one way or another. You are both absolutely miserable like this."

"It would be pointless. We would apologize, then end up making out again, someone would end up partially undressed and then one of us would come to our senses, piss the other off, and we would be back to where we are now. It's basically the same cycle every single time. He's probably blocked me by now and he won't even answer." The latter would be worse.

"Well, that's your decision to make. I just don't like seeing you so upset. I wish I could make this all go away."

"Yeah, me too."

****

She hit end before she ever even heard the first ring. She was normally not this impulsive, but she was drunk at this point. Nothing about this would turn out well.

"Why don't we just head to bed and we can take turns vomiting in the toilet in the morning?" Kristin slurred as she plopped down on the couch.

"Your bed is this way, you know," Sam pointed up, trying to redirect her upstairs.

"I know. But I'm so comfy here. I'll see you in the morning."

Kristin already had her eyes closed and was asleep by the time Sam made it to her room. Sam didn't even bother changing out of her clothes. She just curled up on top of the covers and tried to drown out her racing thoughts.

******

She was awoken by a loud banging from the front door. For a second, she couldn't decide if it was in her head or truly happening. She decided the latter when she heard the front door open and shut and Kristin's incoherent mumbling.

It was 12:05 a.m.

She hadn't even been asleep for an hour, and she wasn't quite sure how Kristin was able to function enough to call Micah and tell him to come over, let alone get up and open the front door. She reached down to cover herself with the blanket just as her door swung open.

She had drunk far too much.

Her tolerance level had definitely gone down since the last time she and Kristin had spent the night drowning out their worries. Because there was absolutely no way in hell Callum fucking Barker was standing in her doorway right now.

"I'm never drinking tequila again," she said as she reached over to turn the lamp on. She let out a groan when she realized the man standing in front of her was, in fact, not a hallucination. "What are you doing here? It's after midnight."

"You called me and then blocked my number. Again."

"No. The tequila called you and I intervened and blocked your number." She tried to sound assertive, but it came out slurred. She threw her head back against the pillow, hoping this was all a dream she would soon wake from.

"Are you drunk?"

She couldn't tell if he was concerned or pissed.

"Maybe. Why does it matter?"

"Why?"

"Why what?" Sam countered. Her words were less coherent than she'd initially thought.

"Why are you drunk?" *Concerned.* He was definitely concerned.

"Because boys are idiots."

He raised his eyebrows. "You're drunk because I'm an idiot?"

"No. Wait. Actually, yes you are an idiot. But I'm drunk because my life is shit right now and I hate nephrology."

"You're not making any sense."

"I think I failed my exam." She closed her eyes and pulled up the blanket over her shoulders.

"So, you got wasted and called me?"

"I already told you that was not me." She tried to sound coherent, but her words continued to come out slurred.

"Sam. You have been ignoring me all week."

"I'm still ignoring you." She gave him a lazy smile.

"You're talking to me."

"You just broke into my house. I should call the cops."

"I'm here because I'm worried about you."

His voice was so sad, and so distant, and she wanted nothing more than to walk straight up to him, wrap him in her arms and hold him until the end of time. She quickly shook her head. That was the tequila talking, not her.

"Did you steal Micah's key?" she quickly questioned before

her mind could venture down any other paths.

"What?" Callum furrowed his brow.

"How did you get in?"

"Kristin let me in."

Ugh. She and Kristin would be having words in the morning.

"Well, tell her to let you out." Sam turned back over and pulled the blanket up over her head.

"Sam. Can we please talk?"

"I'm drunk right now. I don't think that would be smart." Her muffled slur was barely audible. She creased her eyes at him, hoping he could see the frustration building, but then realized her head was still under the blanket. *Ugh.*

"But you will ignore me again when you're sober and can remember why you hate me," he said as he came over and she felt the bed shift with his weight.

She wanted to hate him. She wanted to hate him for making her feel something she had never once felt before. She wanted to hate him for causing her stomach to twist into knots and her heart to sputter whenever he was near. She wanted to hate him...but she didn't. Not even a little bit. She, in fact, *didn't* hate him so much she couldn't think straight.

"I don't hate you. You frustrate me."

"Well, at least there is something we have in common." He reached over, grabbed her hand that was poking out from the blanket, and started drawing little designs on her palm with his fingers.

"That feels so good." Her sleepy mumble caused him to smile.

She was basically drooling. And she was so glad he couldn't see her face. Sam had been craving his touch so much the past few days, this felt like she was getting a hit of the drug she was trying to stay far away from.

"I promise we can talk in the morning," she said with a yawn and buried her face into the pillow more.

"If you truly want me to leave, I will. But we both know you won't let me back in in the morning."

Sam peeked out from underneath the covers and found a solemn expression on Callum's face. "I don't really want you to leave."

"Are you sure?"

Sam nodded. "Stay," she whispered just before she drifted off to sleep while holding onto his hand.

Chapter 28 - Sam

When Sam awoke, her first thought was how damn bright the sun was. It was streaming in through the window, and causing her ever-growing headache to steadily intensify. While trying to decide if the amount she drank last night was worth it, she finally sat up and prayed she wouldn't vomit.

"Here, I found it in your bathroom."

Sam bolted up in shock at the sound of Callum's voice.

"What the fuck? Why are you...what...?"

Then it all came rushing back. The text messages, missed calls, and then her poorly executed attempt at not contacting him.

"Please take the aspirin."

She looked down to Callum's waiting hands to find two white pills and a bottle of water. She hesitated, but the throbbing in her head continued and she reluctantly reached out for the items.

"You stayed?" she questioned as she swallowed the pills, hoping the lingering nausea wouldn't cause them to resurface anytime soon.

"Of course I stayed. You asked me to."

She quickly looked around the room and then beside where she slept. The spot next to hers was completely undisturbed. "Where did you sleep?"

He gestured toward her small futon across the room. It had one of the decorative pillows from her bed on the left side and a small blanket pushed to the other end.

"Did you sleep on my futon?" she asked and he gave her a quick nod. "You are like twice the size of it."

"Trust me, I know," he agreed with a smile and then made a dramatic display of stretching out his sore muscles. She wanted to laugh, but then she remembered she wasn't supposed to like him at the moment. And despite how much she wanted to kick him out, her body craved his touch.

"You could have just stayed in the bed beside me."

"And risk facing your wrath if you woke up next to me and didn't remember how I got in? I don't think so." He shook his head with a smirk.

"Thank you." She ran her hands across her face. She wasn't completely sure what she was thanking him for, or what she looked like right now, but if it was anywhere close to how she felt, it was bound to be terrible.

"Can we get coffee?" Callum asked.

"I need a shower."

"I can wait downstairs. Take all the time you need."

She took a deep breath and lingered on the view of him standing there in her room. Even just after waking up he looked like absolute perfection, and she still hated him for it.

"What are you thinking about?" he questioned hopefully after her gaze lingered on him just a moment too long.

"That it's not fair."

"What isn't?"

"The fact that you can make me so mad and yet I still want to kiss you." He smiled at her words. "But mostly because you slept on a futon half your size and still woke up looking like that." She waved a hand toward him with a grunt.

He laughed and tentatively took the three steps toward her.

"You are absolutely breathtaking. Don't ever believe otherwise." He kissed her on the cheek.

Even though her emotions were still a jumbled mess when it came to Callum, that compliment and his touch that followed sent butterflies straight to her stomach. As much as she'd like to, her traitorous heart wouldn't let her forget that she loved being around him.

"I'll be downstairs. If you don't want to go with me, just have Kristin kick me out." He headed out her bedroom door.

He peeked back in briefly before completely exiting with a smirk on his face.

"For the record. You talk in your sleep." And with that, he went downstairs and Sam was left with the ever-mounting feeling of needing to vomit; this time more from nerves than from tequila.

****

When Sam finally made it downstairs, fully showered, dressed, and not about to vomit, she found Callum sitting at the kitchen table and Kristin standing not too far away from him with an absolutely murderous scowl etched on her face.

"You ready?" Sam asked and grabbed her purse.

"Are you sure?" Kristin interjected before Callum could speak. Kristin's eyes were pleading.

"Callum just wants to go get coffee and talk. I'll be back after class."

Kristin swallowed and took a deep breath. She still had her body somewhat placed between Sam and Callum, as if she was the barrier to any hurt and would protect Sam with her life.

"Kristin, I promise it's okay. I'll be back soon."

"Call me if you need me. For anything." She put an extra emphasis on the last words and quickly turned her head to face Callum. Sam couldn't see the face Kristin made toward him, but from the awkward smile he gave her and the way he threw his hands up in mock surrender, Sam was sure it was nothing but deadly.

The car ride to the coffee shop down the street was silent. Sam wasn't sure what to say, so instead, she methodically picked at her newly painted nails. In her defense, she was sure Kristin wouldn't be too upset with Sam for ruining the design since it was hideously painted during their previous night's drunken escapade.

The first utterance either of them made was the order. True to character, Callum ordered black coffee. Sam ordered a frap with extra whipped cream and caramel drizzle.

She tried to balk when he paid for both, but he swiped his card before she could even get her wallet out.

"You realize that's not really coffee?" Callum observed as they made their way toward a table by the window.

"What? Yes, it is. You just heard me order it."

"It's mostly cream and sugar with a splash of coffee. It's basically a milkshake," he teased with a tentative smile.

Sam playfully sent a glare his way.

They sat in surprisingly comfortable silence for a few minutes while each let the coffee fill them with some courage to speak. Sam was shocked that it was his voice that broke the silence.

"You want something to eat?" Callum asked as they stared out the window. It was past ten in the morning, which meant she'd definitely missed her lab. She would have to text Stacy for the notes later.

"No. I'm not really hungry at the moment." She gave him a smile and quickly looked away when their eyes met.

She wasn't sure why, but she felt so small and shy in front of him at that moment. He was a complete contradiction to her initial assumptions. She wanted to hate him, but she didn't. She didn't hate the way he'd left her all those texts and calls. She didn't hate the way he'd come to check on her the previous night. She didn't hate the way he'd stayed. She didn't hate the way he'd had water and aspirin waiting for her when she awoke.

It wasn't supposed to be him. Not him. Not the college dropout with the long hair and the tattoos. That hadn't been her plan. She had fought so hard to make sure her future was pristine. She wanted the white picket fence with two and a half kids, a yellow lab and a husband who was home every night for dinner. That was supposed to be the ideal life, right? The perfect life that had been shoved down her throat for so many years. She tried to picture it. She tried to picture that house and yard and perfectly clean-cut husband, but now all she saw was him.

Now, all she saw was how much of a hypocrite she had been.

She had spent the last few years basing her life choices on what she thought was right, what was supposed to be right. She was judging every book by its cover while desperately hoping no one judged her by her past. She was a hypocrite, and in that moment she hated herself for it.

She looked him over once more. He'd dropped out of college and built a business from the ground up that now had four separate locations in less than five years. He was a business owner who worked his ass off practically every day to make sure everything was perfect. He was kind. She knew that from watching him with the various patrons at Topline. He was honest. He hadn't led her on, but instead had been truthful about what he could give her from the start. He was...

"Are you okay?" Callum's voice barreled into her thoughts as he reached out to interlace his fingers within hers.

"What?"

"You have tears running down your face."

She quickly reached up, face hot with embarrassment and wiped away the dampness she found.

"Can I ask you a favor?" She desperately needed to change the subject.

Callum looked up quizzically and then nodded his head.

"Can you please get a new playlist for Topline? We listen to the same fifty songs every single night."

Callum laughed. She could tell he wanted to inquire further about why she was suddenly crying in the middle of a packed coffee shop but he left it alone.

"Yeah. What would you like to hear?"

Sam smiled. "I don't think my taste aligns with that of most of our clientele."

"What's your taste?"

"Taylor Swift."

Callum had to wipe away the coffee that burst from his mouth at the laugh. "For some reason, I just don't see fifty-year-old socialites wanting to hear Shake It Off as they dine with their mistresses."

Sam laughed. "Actually, now that I'm thinking about it, she would be perfect. Her music literally *transcends* generations. That's what they said during her montage at the music awards ceremony last year. You should definitely use her Evermore and Folklore albums."

"I'll take it into consideration." He smirked and then sipped on his coffee. It was another minute of silence before he spoke again. "Can I ask you a question?"

"You just did."

She'd thought he would have smiled at her dig, but his face held a pensive and stressed look.

"What exactly would an *us* entail?"

His question caught her off guard. "What?"

"If we got together, for real, what would that look like?"

"Um, I guess just like any other relationship. You get out of it what you put into it."

She couldn't believe they were having this conversation. She wouldn't let herself get too excited, but the fact that he was even asking must have meant that he had been thinking about it. *Right?* Maybe he had been stressing and crying and raging as much as she had since their big argument. Maybe he'd finally come to the decision to take that leap and let her in. Her guard was still up, but a little bubble of hope started to build inside her.

"So, we get dressed up and go out to eat every weekend or something?" he asked and Sam rolled her eyes playfully.

"Think about the relationships you've seen. Your parents are married and you have been a firsthand witness to Micah and Kristin. It's whatever we make it. And, no, we don't have to get dressed up and go out. That's not me, and I know that's definitely not you."

"So, basically, we just do what we've been doing now."

"Kind of," Sam said and then quickly added, "But without any other girls in the picture."

"And without Christian in the picture."

"Callum." His name was a warning. This was a line she refused to cross.

"I'm serious. I don't want you hanging around him. Even if *us* never happens, I still wouldn't want you near him."

"That's too bad. He is one of my best friends. If that is a requirement, then this," she motioned between two of them, "will never happen." It had nothing to do with the fact that Christian was Christian and Callum was acting like an insecure little boy, but everything to do with the fact that she would never allow a man to tell her who she could and couldn't be friends with. She was an adult, and only she was in control of her life. She started feeling that little bubble of hope fading away. "I've told you a thousand times, there are no romantic feelings there whatsoever. He isn't your competition."

"It's not that," Callum quickly amended.

"Then what is it?"

"He isn't a good guy."

Even though Sam felt frustration at Christian's recent behavior around her, she wasn't going to let someone speak ill of him when she knew him better than anyone else.

"You keep hinting at that, and yet you refuse to back it up with actual facts." She downed the rest of her drink. The familiar buzz of the caffeine now flooded her system making her want to jump out of the chair.

"I want to. Trust me, I do. But I can't."

"That's ridiculous. And controlling."

This time Callum became more stern. "He is a piece of shit," he all but snarled.

She stood up and chucked her empty cup in the bin behind

her. She was done. The nausea had now returned. Maybe she shouldn't have drunk an entire milkshake-coffee after a night spent tossing back shot after shot of tequila.

But it gave her just enough bravery to quickly say her piece and finally end this before it ever really started.

"Callum, I like you alot. But I think this entire back and forth thing is not good for me. I'm sorry, but I think it's best if we just remain friends. I really mean that. I'm not going to stay away just because we don't work romantically. But we have different priorities and opinions that will only cause problems in the future."

"Sam." Her name was a plea. His eyes begged her not to leave.

She swung her purse over her shoulder and shot Kristin a quick text to come pick her up.

"Thank you for the coffee. I'm sorry I missed work this week." Her tone was different. She was no longer speaking to Callum. She was apologizing to her boss and, by the look on his face, she could tell it killed him. "I promise to be there for my shift tomorrow. And I promise not to let what happened between us affect my work or Kristin and Micah."

"Sam. Please sit back down."

"Goodbye, Callum."

Chapter 29 - Callum

Two days.

Two fucking days since he'd watched her walk out of that coffee shop.

He stared at the design in front of him as he worked at shading in the sunrise of the tattoo on the man's arm. It was a great design, the customer loved it, and Callum was proud.

And yet he couldn't take the scowl off his face.

The orange they had chosen for the perfect hue of the sunset reminded him too much of her hair. Then there was the tattoo he did the day prior of a forest. The green matched her eyes. The blue in the ocean of a design later that afternoon matched the little sundress she had worn on their walk.

Everything reminded him of her. He knew he should just break down and tell her how he knew Christian. It was the right thing to do. But telling her would mean breaking someone else's trust and the promise he had made to them. He knew she deserved to know, but he also knew that knowing would crush her. Knowing would shatter her world, and he would not be the cause of any more pain or...

"Ow!"

The customer jerked away and Callum stilled as he saw a streak of red trickle down the man's arm.

"Shit. I'm so sorry man." Callum wiped away the evidence of his mistake as he apologized.

"Went kind of deep there."

"Won't happen again," Callum promised and went back to working through the design that perfectly matched the hue of Sam's hair.

****

By the time he walked in the door, he was a shell of a person. His entire afternoon had been spent staring at things that reminded him of her.

Drew slid a beer over his way as he plopped down at the kitchen table.

"I have a proposal."

"What's that?"

Drew took a deep breath and Callum knew this was something big.

"I'm going to ask Mel to marry me."

Callum sat straight up, smiling more broadly than he had in weeks.

"Oh, shit. That's like a proposal-proposal."

Drew rolled his eyes, smiling. "I know."

"Congrats, man!" Callum reached out to shake his best friend's hand, then stood and chose to bring Drew in for a massive hug. It wasn't every day that your best friend decided to pop the question. He quickly pulled back to find Drew's face practically beaming with excitement. "I get to plan the bachelor party right?"

Drew laughed. "You and Micah can fight over it."

"Duly noted." Callum nodded his head in mock seriousness as he sat back in the chair.

"There is something else to add to that." Drew stated with a concerned look.

Callum furrowed his brow. "Okay."

"You're miserable."

Callum eyed him as he downed half the beer, wondering where this was leading.

"Thanks."

"I'm serious. The semester is almost over and our lease is up in a few weeks. What if we let Micah know we aren't coming back for next year and we move down to Charleston?"

"That's quite a suggestion."

"I'll move in with Mel, and you can stay with us until you find somewhere to rent. She and I have been talking about moving in together anyway. And if you didn't want to stay with us, you could stay at the house in Mount Pleasant if needed."

Callum groaned at the suggestion.

"Don't get all fussy. We both know you love that place, even if you feign hatred for it."

Callum decided not to acknowledge the statement about his parents' beloved beach house. "What about Topline and Inked?"

Drew shrugged his shoulders. "Inked practically runs itself, and we could check in here just like we are currently doing for the shops in Charleston. And Topline is doing great. They don't need you there checking in every single day. Step back from it all. Spend a little of that money you keep shoving in the bank. Go surfing. Have some great summer sex with girls you don't have to worry about seeing again."

"You mean have great summer sex with someone who's not her."

"Exactly."

"For some reason, I don't think that will make it go away."

Drew shrugged. "It probably won't. But I can't stand to see you like this. You mope around here day in and day out. The only time you even get a tad bit excited about anything anymore is when you know she's on the schedule."

"I want her. But...but there is this thing between us that would never go away. It would be like a constant stitch in my side."

"Is she worth letting it go?"

"What?" Callum tossed the empty bottle in the trash.

"Whatever it is that is coming between y'all, is she worth enough to you to just let that thing go?"

Callum mulled over Drew's question but didn't answer. He also didn't acknowledge the fact that he had to blink a few times to clear the vision that had barely begun to blur. He'd never before let emotions overtake him, and he damn sure wasn't about to start now. He turned his head and wiped the offending eyes, just to be sure his emotions knew who was in control before he walked down the stairs toward his bedroom.

Just before he shut the door to start getting dressed for work, he cleared his throat and called back up, "I can stay at the Mount Pleasant house until I find somewhere else to rent."

And then he shut the door to his room and to all thoughts of a future with Sam. She wanted to just be friends, and friends is what he would be.

Chapter 30 - Sam

She was surprised how calm she felt walking into Topline the next day. There was no promise he would be there, but there was always a chance.

When she'd walked out of the coffee shop two days earlier, she had started to block his number, and then remembered that friends didn't do that. She wasn't going to hate him anymore. She was just going to live her life and realize that she may still see him due to circumstances she couldn't control. She would most likely see him at work and at his townhome, and even smiled at the thought that she might have to endure being in a wedding party with him one day, should Micah and Kristin ever decide to make it official.

Then she cringed at the idea of him bringing a date that wasn't her, and promptly shut that train of thought down. There was going to be no more thinking of Callum Barker.

That was, until she recognized the song playing in the background.

The Lakes by Taylor Swift flowed through the air and she had to stop for a moment to listen to the words. A small smile crept across her face.

"You were right. She's pretty good," Callum said from behind her.

When Sam turned, she found him leaning against a post separating two sections.

"This is one of my favorites," Sam said.

"I spent most of the last twenty-four hours going through her musical catalog."

Her eyebrows peaked in surprise. "And what did you think?"

"It wasn't too bad."

"That's all?"

A flush of crimson embarrassment covered his features. "It was really good. I downloaded all of her albums."

"Oh no!" Sam exclaimed.

"What? I thought you would like that."

"I should have warned you. We only buy the newer albums that she owns or the older ones that are part of TV."

Callum furrowed his brows in confusion. "What does that mean?"

Sam chuckled. "It's a long story."

"Well, I picked out a few that I think would work here. You can let me know if any don't fit the bill." He started to laugh. "Mason about damn near had a heart attack when I uploaded the new playlist though, so I can't promise he plays it on nights I'm not here."

"Thanks," Sam said with a shy smile.

"No problem. You were right. This place definitely needed a change." He stood up more fully then and turned to walk away as he smiled kindly at her. "Hope you have a good shift."

******

Her shift went well. At least, until she took her designated fifteen minute break outside and decided to check her email, desperate to see if there were any responses to her recently sent off med school applications.

What she saw caused her heart to begin to race.

The email was from the Giving Hearts Foundation. *Mandatory Meeting* was sitting in the subject line below.

That was never a good sign.

She had only ever received one other similar email and it was the time when she'd missed her luncheon freshman year and had to

practically beg them not to take away her scholarship. She raced
through her memory as she tried to mentally decipher why they
would be wanting to meet with her.

By the time she opened the message she only had three minutes left
before she was supposed to be back on the floor.

"Miss. Williams,

*Per our regulations, the university
has sent notice of unsatisfactory
performance in recent weeks across multiple
classes. Per the Foundation's regulations, we
must schedule a meeting to discuss where
this change in performance may lead. Please
see the below dates of availability and let us
know within 24 hours as to which time suits
your schedule best.*

*Regards,
Ms. Clemmings, Giving
Hearts Chair*

She couldn't breathe. She stared at the screen. Her palms
began to sweat, which caused the phone to slip from her grasp and
shatter when it hit the cement sidewalk below.

"Sam?"

She jerked her head up, but the man standing before her was
too blurred. It was only then that she realized she was crying.

"What happened?" Callum was there brushing away her
tears before he finished the question. She stepped back and out of
his reach, shaking her head in the process. "Do you need me to call
Kristin?"

"No. No. No." She repeated it as if saying that word over and
over again would somehow make this go away. She looked down at
her watch and realized she had been standing out there for an extra
ten minutes past when she was supposed to be inside.

"Are you sure?"

"I'm sorry. I didn't mean to take this long of a break."

"Sam, I don't care about the break. What happened?"

"Nothing. I need to get back inside." She rushed past him, making it all the way to her section before she could hear him utter another word.

The rest of the night was a complete disaster. She spilled drinks on two separate tables and forgot to enter appetizers for another three. Mr. Brimley was forced to comp three full meals, and he made it known he was not happy with her.

Just when she was about to clock out, Mr. Brimley came around the corner stating he needed to see her in his office ASAP.

She knew this was coming. He had always been an ass, but for the most part she was able to avoid the wrath that he put down on some of the other wait staff. She took a deep breath as she entered his office, but then completely froze when she found Callum sitting at the desk staring diligently at something on the laptop, his back to her. He probably had no idea she had walked in. Mr. Brimley didn't even acknowledge him.

"Samantha Williams." Her name was a curse as it passed Mr. Brimley's lips and she noticed Callum freeze his movements. "I'm not sure what happened recently, but if you can't come to work prepared to work then don't come to work at all." It was practically a yell, and Callum turned abruptly to focus solely on the man in front of her. "I'm not sure if this is school or personal life related, but tonight you cost us more money than you brought in."

She wanted to die right there. She wasn't used to not excelling in everything she did, so being admonished was not something that happened frequently. And it definitely didn't happen directly in front of the one person who had currently turned her life upside down.

"I'm so sorry. It was an off night."

"You're on probation for the next week–"

"Mr. Brimley, please. I promise–"

"Seven days." Mr. Brimley was more than upset.

She could tell he was absolutely pissed at how much of a disaster the night had been. Sam stole a quick look in Callum's direction and in that moment realized that no matter what Mr. Brimley felt, he didn't hold a candle to the amount of fury contorting Callum's features just then.

"All your shifts are covered, and *if* I decide to let you come back, make sure you at least look like you're trying." Callum was breathing so hard she thought the buttons of his shirt might just burst open. "You looked like shit tonight–"

"That's enough, Mason," Callum interjected as he stood to step between them.

Mr. Brimely looked up to Callum. "I'm sorry Mr. Barker, I should not have come in while you were working. I'll take this to another room."

Mr. Brimley stepped forward and forcibly grabbed Sam by the arm to yank her out of the office.

"Get your hands off her." Callum all but threw the man backward as he pulled his hand from Sam's arm. Mr. Brimley stumbled into the file cabinet behind him.

"Callum. Stop." Sam reached up to place her hands on his chest, forcing him backward.

"Don't ever fucking touch her again," Callum seethed. His hands were already balled into fists, ready for the fight.

"Mr. Barker?" Mr. Brimley looked between them and then realization hit his features. Callum had pulled her into his arms, burying her face against his chest.

She couldn't stop her chin from shaking. She wasn't crying, thank God, but she felt as though her entire body was somehow detached from its current form.

"Go home, Mason. I'll let you know when you can come back—*if* I decide not to fire you."

Mr. Brimley stood in that moment, shock and anger strewn across his face. "I didn't take you for someone who slept with their employees," he spat toward Callum and Sam knew that if he didn't have her in his arms right then, Callum would have thrown Mr. Brimley to the ground.

"Get out!" Callum threw the venom-laced words at the man as he hurried from the room.

Callum clutched her tighter to his chest as if she was his anchor. She felt him lean down and bury his face within her curls and deeply breathe her in.

She didn't know how long they stood there holding onto one another, but as the minutes ticked by, she felt a calmness encompass her. Even the email was momentarily forgotten as he rubbed her back.

"Did you just fire your main manager?" Sam asked incredulously as she finally pulled back to look up at him.

"I think so." He raised his eyebrows.

"Callum! You can't do that!" Sam gently pushed off of him and rubbed her hands across her face. They were friends and friends didn't hold each other like that. "What are you going to do now?"

He shrugged. "I guess I'll be here a hell of a lot more until I find someone to replace him."

"I can't believe you just did that." Sam stared at him in absolute shock.

"It was a long time coming." He shook his head as he stepped closer to her and reached out a hand to brush away the curls that had fallen down from her bun. "I'm sorry if I scared you." Callum rubbed a hand over his face, obviously distraught at the idea of causing her fear. "But when he put his hand on your arm, I just snapped."

"You didn't scare me."

Callum swallowed and gave her a sad smile.

"You don't have to tell me what happened, but I know something is up."

"It's nothing," she lied.

He eyed her more directly. "You don't have to tell me what

happened," he quickly repeated, "but I'm here for you if you need me."

She buried her face in her hands then. Her muscles were tense as she tried to hold back the tears that were threatening to overflow. When he wrapped his arms around her and pulled her in tight, the dam broke free.

Sam sobbed into his chest. This was now the second time she caused his shirt to become soaked at work. Third if you count their trip to Social. She couldn't explain it, but in that moment, she felt nothing but safe and accepted in his arms. It took a few minutes for the tears to dry up, and by that point she had somehow ended up on his lap with her head on his shoulder. She peered over to the clock on the wall. It was now past 11 p.m., an hour after closing, and she assumed they were most likely the only ones left inside.

"I'm sorry."

"Don't be. Mason is a creep. I'm sorry I didn't fire–"

"That's not why I'm crying," Sam corrected him.

"Why are you crying, Sam?" Callum had his hands cupping her cheeks and she knew he could feel the slight tremble in her chin.

She contemplated not answering. That's what she would normally do. She would either change the subject altogether or walk away. But she knew she couldn't do that. Not with him.

Fuck it.

"Remember how I told you I have a scholarship that pays for school?"

He nodded his head. "Yeah."

"I think I just lost it." Her voice broke. She was a mess. A snotty, bubbling mess. The hiccups seemed to mingle between every other word. "I'll have to postpone my senior year and then I may lose my shot at getting into med school. My entire life is about to fall apart."

"Sam," he whispered her name as he brought their foreheads together. "What can I do? What do you need?"

She laughed. It was an absurd moment to laugh. Especially

when she could barely string two words together. But what she needed was absurd in itself. What she needed was twenty grand to pay for her next two semesters and she doubted he would have that to freely hand out.

"Something you can't give me."

"How much money was the scholarship?"

She eyed him before she wiped the leftover tears from her face.

"Callum." She shook her head.

"I have more money than you would think." She could not believe he was going there. She wouldn't even let Kristin help her with rent and Callum was trying to offer her tens of thousands of dollars. Why did he have to be so damn perfect and nice and kind? Why did he have to hate the one other man in her life that she truly loved like family? "I wasn't kidding when I said we did well from the shops, and this restaurant was a phenomenal business decision. I have just been stuffing cash into my savings for months."

"No." She jumped off his lap. This was something she couldn't accept.

"I want to help you." He stood to face her.

"Not like *that*. Please. Don't offer *that*."

"Sam."

"We are just friends." She started to walk toward the door.

He stepped in front of her. "Friends help each other out when they need it."

"Not with twenty grand, they don't." Her voice was too high and her heart was pounding. She couldn't let him offer her anything. Because if she took something from him, she would no longer be just Sam, she would be his new charity case. She would get nothing but pity from him, and that was something she would never be able to stomach.

"Is that how much it is?"

"No. Yes, but *no*. Absolutely not." She was speaking too fast in desperation to get away.

"What's the name of the scholarship? My mom works with the university now, maybe she can help?"

She shook her head. There was no way she would give him that information. If he knew the name then he could look them up and find out they only funded orphans with no families. Then their entire dynamic would change. Then he would truly pity her.

The room had begun to close in on them. She took a deep breath and tried to slow her breathing, but nothing worked. This didn't make sense. She didn't panic. She was able to control herself. She could control this.

But she couldn't. Not now. She couldn't control her scholarship, and she couldn't control all the feelings for Callum that kept making themselves known despite the fact that it would never go anywhere. She couldn't control the way just looking at him made her happy, or the way his smile caused something in her stomach to flip upside down. She couldn't control that his laugh was damn near perfect, or how he commanded attention whenever he walked into a room. She couldn't control how he was in her every dream, her every thought. She couldn't control his hatred toward Christain. She couldn't control it.

"I need to leave." She turned toward the door. Sam had to get away from here. Between her scholarship possibly falling through and everything that had happened with Callum, she was about to break. She needed to get home to Kristin. She needed to leave Topline and go work at Peet's with Christian. She needed to get away from all these stupid feelings, because all they caused was heartache and pain.

"You are not taking the bus this late." Callum grabbed his keys and ran after her.

"I don't have another option, Callum!" she screamed as she turned around to face him. "I don't have a car or money for an Uber. I can barely afford my bus fare. I don't have another option." The last sentence was barely a whisper.

"You have me."

"No, I don't!" She pulled at her hair as the words came barreling out of her. "You don't seem to get it. Everything was fine in my life. Everything was going according to plan and then you show up and everything gets fucked up. You fucked it up! You kiss me and my brain turns to mush and I can't think straight and then I can't study. I can't study and I fail assignments. I have never failed an assignment in my life and since meeting you I have failed two, possibly more from the way that email sounded. I can't deviate from my plan. I can't have distractions. And you, Callum Barker, are the biggest fucking distraction I have ever known."

He stood still, frozen in shock at her outburst, and then took a step back, his face so full of pain that she momentarily wanted to take the three steps to him and melt her body into his as she profusely apologized.

She hated herself for the words that she just spoke. She hated herself more than she had ever hated anyone or anything. She hated the look of pain that now races across his features that she had caused.

He wasn't the massive fuck-up he thought he was.

It was her.

She was the fuck-up.

She watched as his face all but crumpled in front of her and she knew no other escape than to run far away. To run away from him and everything that knowing him brought with it.

But she didn't want that. She didn't want to run away from him. She wanted to run to him.

Fuck!

"I'm sorry." His voice broke, and with it her heart.

She nodded her head as she felt a tear fall down her cheek.

Her feet were leaden. Her heart was screaming at her to take it all back, but she just couldn't move.

"I'm taking the bus." Her voice was barely a whisper and her chin trembled with the words. "Please don't follow me home this time."

"Okay."

Chapter 31 - Sam

Sam made it all the way into her room before she made the call. With how long the bus took to get her home , she wasn't sure if he would be asleep or awake. But she knew he would answer.

"Hello?" Christian's voice was muffled as if he still had his face buried in his pillow.

"Christian?"

"Sam? You okay?"

"I'm going to lose my scholarship." Her voice broke with the words.

"What are you talking about?" His voice sounded much louder now, but still just as groggy.

"I just forwarded you the email I got tonight."

"Okay. Hold on. Let me read it."

He paused for a moment, and she heard the familiar clicking noise as he searched through his phone for the email. Then there was silence for far too long and she knew he had read it over at least twice.

"What date did you pick?" This time she could tell he was wide awake.

"Next Wednesday. Will you–"

"I'll be there. I promise," Christian quickly cut in.

"They can't take it away, can they?" Her voice quivered.

"They are a bunch of wealthy, uptight pricks and we are their puppets. They can do just about anything they want."

"Christian, I can't lose this. I won't be able to pay for next year."

"Sam. Calm down. If worst comes to worst, you can do what

the rest of us do and take out a loan."

"I don't want to take out a loan. I don't want to be saddled with debt for the rest of my life."

She could tell from the exasperated sigh that just escaped his lips that it was most likely followed by a massive roll of his eyes. "I get that. I really do. But, in all honesty, it's not that big of a deal."

"It is to me."

"Babe, it will be fine, and you will make more than enough to cover all your loans once you start making all that doctor money."

"That's not the point." Her voice shook. She was furious. Christian had been there for her every step of the way. They'd spent countless hours together in high school prepping for the scholarship and he knew how important it was to her. "Why are you acting like this isn't a big deal?"

"I'm sorry, Sam. You're right. I didn't mean to upset you. It's just the middle of the night and I'm not thinking straight. I will help you in any way that I can." When Sam didn't say a word, he continued, "I have a break around two o'clock tomorrow. Why don't we grab a late lunch and chat?"

"Fine."

"I'll text you later."

And then he hung up and Sam was left even more frustrated than when she had first called him hoping he would calm her down.

****

She wasn't sure if she slept at all. It was a night filled with tossing and turning and staring at the alarm clock waiting for it to go off.

By the time she walked into the campus plaza, she could barely keep her head up.

"You look like shit," Christian said as he handed her a coffee.

"You are oh so charming." Sam rolled her eyes and then started to sip on the steaming concoction in front of her.

She wasn't sure what exactly he had ordered for her, but it definitely didn't have whipped cream and cinnamon on top and tasted terribly bitter.

"This is so good," she lied and started to stand. "But I'm going to add a little—"

"Sit back down," he said in a playful but serious tone. "You are not ruining perfectly great coffee with cream and sugar and whatever else nonsense you can think of."

She slowly lowered herself to the chair and forced the liquid down her throat while he smiled at her.

"Alright. How are we going to fight this? What is it they've found?" he casually asked as if he hadn't just pissed her off.

Maybe it wasn't him, and it was just the fact that she was already on edge. She knew Christian liked his coffee a certain way and couldn't stand when people ruined it. Adding all that extra stuff couldn't be healthy either, and she knew he was just trying to help her. She needed to rein in her anger, she knew it was directed at Callum and there was no reason to take it out on Christian.

"I'm not completely sure. I know I failed a lab assignment a few weeks back, but I'm certain I brought that grade up. We had a nephrology exam last week and I definitely bombed that one. There was an advanced level chem midterm that I made a B on, but I don't know. I just didn't think all that together would impact my grade so much. I've kept a 4.0 this entire time."

"Do you think you have been too distracted by Callum Barker?"

Her eyes, which had been planted on the scenery outside, quickly shot up to him.

"What?"

"Come on, Sam. I've known you longer than anyone else. I know y'all have been hanging out, and I know he isn't the best guy out there. Maybe he's a bad influence on you and it's carrying over into your schoolwork."

"You two don't seem to get along," she said cautiously, hoping to get more information out of Christian than she had out of Callum.

Christian took a deep breath and refused to meet her gaze. "No, we don't. But whatever he has told you is probably a lie. You should stay far away from him."

"Funny. He said the same about you." She waited for him to elaborate, but he kept his mouth in a thin line as he looked around the shop. "Christian?" He peeked over toward her and she decided to just come out and ask. "What happened between you two?"

"If I tell you, you might not like it."

"Just tell me," Sam pleaded as she reached over and grabbed his hand.

"His sister and I were together for a short while a few years back. He took the big bad older brother role a little too seriously and beat the shit out of me. Normally I would have just taken him down, but I didn't want to get in trouble and lose the scholarship. Jokes on me though, 'cause I ended up losing it for grades anyway. Maybe I should have just given it back to him."

"Oh my god. Christian. Why didn't you ever tell me?" She squeezed his hand.

Christian shrugged. "It was years ago. It's over now, and I want nothing to do with anyone in his family ever again."

"Honestly, that surprises me. He can be very...protective at times. But I just don't see him as the type of person who would do that."

Christian blew away the steam that bellowed from his cup. "People aren't always who they portray themselves to be. You are probably only seeing one side of him because he wants to get in your pants. He's a prick."

She tilted her head, a mask of confusion playing on her face.

"Stop." She didn't want to believe him, but then again he had no reason to lie to her either. And she had seen Callum practically throw Mr. Brimley to the ground the previous night.

"Stop what?" Christian looked at her with a hint of anger in his eyes.

She bristled. "Nothing. Just–" She looked back down at the

bitter concoction in front of her. "I just don't know that side of him. That's all."

Christian laughed and then shook his head. "Well that's what you get for not listening to me in the first place. You always do this. If you would just listen and not try to be so damn independent all the time, you wouldn't end up in these situations you put yourself in."

She seemed to cower at his words. She hated when he got like this. But in truth, he was just trying to protect her and she knew that. "I know."

"Do me a favor?" Christian questioned.

"Anything." Sam quickly nodded her head.

"I don't want him to know I told you. That's in the past, and I would rather not bring it up."

"Of course. I won't say a word."

He squeezed her hand back. "Thanks. Now, let's talk about what to say at your disciplinary meeting."

Chapter 32 - Callum

Callum was standing at the staff coffee station way before Topline opened for the lunch crowd when he realized that for a restaurant as large as Topline, they had a good many staff perks, one of those being that they had free rein of the coffee bar the previous owner had installed. It especially helped when someone pulled a double and needed an extra kick to get through the last few hours. His eyes scanned over the selection.

Black forest roast.

Italian roast.

French roast.

Bold roast.

It all worked for his taste, and he downed at least one cup every time he was there. But there wasn't a single thing that had any sweetness to it in the least. He wanted to slap himself.

He rushed out the door as soon as the main cooks started walking in.

"I'll be back in a few!" he called out.

He didn't wait for their reply as he jumped in his truck and drove the two blocks to the nearest grocery store.

When he walked back in an hour later, he had three full shopping bags in his hands and a smile plastered on his face. He was going to friend the shit out of Sam to make up for the tears he had caused the night before.

He may have gone a little overboard.

There were the various whipped creams; the caramel, vanilla, and hazelnut drizzles; the powered cinnamon and brown sugar; and then the various types of sweet creams (he'd chosen almond, hazelnut, soy, white chocolate, french vanilla, etc).

But he was most excited about the peppermint flakes he'd found on the baking aisle. He had no idea if that was a coffee thing or not, but there was no way he was passing them up.

Chapter 33 - Sam

Somehow, getting to Wednesday felt like it took a million years, but still it seemed to strike without warning. She had barely slept at all the last few nights. Normally, her meetings with the board were for various luncheons and events.

This was a disciplinary meeting.

Her second.

And that did not bode well for her mental health.

To make matters worse, this was an entirely new committee since her other disciplinary meeting, so she had no idea what to expect from them. She tried to calm herself with the thought that absolutely no one could be worse than the dreaded Mrs. Saunders, but Sam had learned a long time ago not to count your chickens before they hatched. For all she knew, the next board would make the previous one look like child's play. At least the new head of the board had seemed nice the couple of times she'd met her before, so all she could do was hope.

"Take a deep breath. It will all work out," Christian said from beside her on the bench, a soothing hand rubbing her knee. They were in one of the university's newer buildings and the light from the crystal chandelier above them was making her sweat.

"I know." But she didn't know. And when a small man who couldn't have been taller than Sam poked his head from behind the door and called her name, she was sure she was going to vomit.

"Good luck, I'll be out here for you the whole time," Christian said as she stood.

****

The auditorium was so bright. Sam was sitting in a lone chair before a half circle table set on a platform about five feet higher than her. It made her feel as though she were a small child getting ready to be admonished for stealing a treat from the kitchen.

The air was stifling and, for a split second, she thought she couldn't breathe. Her throat tightened and she shifted in her chair, desperate to suck in as much air as possible into her lungs. She heard a slight tapping echo through the room and then realized it was the sole of her shoe rapidly banging on the marble floor below her.

There were seven of them sitting before her. Four men and three women. And they held the keys to her future. Sam recognized the woman in the middle as the new committee head, Ms. Clemmings, and she felt a moment of relief at the thought. Ms. Clemmings seemed more down to earth than any of the other committee members she'd met to date. She wasn't covered in diamonds, nor did she appear to have spent thousands of dollars on plastic surgery. She looked as if she could be anyone's mom.

"Miss Williams," Ms. Clemmings said and Sam shot her eyes upward to meet her gaze. "As you know, my name is Ashlyn Clemmings, and I will be presiding over this hearing. Is there anything you would like to say or ask before we get started?"

"No, ma'am." Sam tried to smile, but couldn't hide the worry in her eyes.

"If at any time you do not understand what is being stated, please raise your hand so we can further clarify," Ms. Clemmings continued and Sam nodded. This was a good sign. Mrs. Saunders had never given any of the recipients a chance to speak or ask questions at previous meetings. "It has come to our attention that there have been some recent developments in your academic standing. Are you aware of these changes?"

"Not completely," Sam responded.

"As you know, Giving Hearts is funded by many individuals in the community, but also from a large stipend provided by the university. Due to the large sum awarded to our various recipients, we have high standards that each has to meet and maintain. It seems as though your nearly perfect track record will have a few blemishes this year."

Sam swallowed, but the woman wasn't admonishing her. If anything, she felt as though Ms. Clemmings had a large amount of sympathy for her and was just reciting an obligatory script.

"This does not bode well for our community. As I am sure you are aware, numbers matter, and right now the amount that we are allowed to give to various orphaned students is dependent on how well our current cohort performs. Hence, if you make high scores then the university sees our program as a success and they award increased funds for other upcoming students once you have graduated. If our current recipients do not do well, then the university may see fit to shift our funding to other, more successful programs." She stopped talking then and waited for a response.

"I understand," Sam replied.

"We don't hold you to such high standards as a punishment, but more to ensure that we will be able to provide for others down the line. It seems you have encountered some recent hurdles in your classes this semester. At this time, you are welcome to provide some information as to why this may be."

At least this woman seemed kinder, and even a little sad at all that the rules required. The previous committee head had seemed to bask in the terror she'd imposed upon others.

Sam took a deep breath and, with a shaky voice said, "I'm aware that I scored poorly on a lab assignment earlier in the semester, however I completed an extra assignment later that same week to bring that grade up. I am also aware that I may not have performed well on a chemistry midterm. I'm not sure of my exact scores on either assignment at this time. I am unaware of any other poor grades."

"Thank you, Miss Williams. However, we are not concerned

about two small individual grades. We are concerned about your current overall failing grade in Advanced Biological Sciences 428."

Sam froze.

Her brows furrowed and she felt a weight settle in the pit of her stomach. But then the weight lifted and she felt a momentary relief. This was all a misunderstanding. She wasn't in Bio 428. She had thought about signing up for it as an advanced elective and even worked her schedule around it at one point, but never officially added it in.

"I'm not in Bio 428," Sam countered, finally feeling the edges of her lips tilt upward as she felt a surge of hope. She ran through her list of classes in her head. Advanced Chem 412 for three credits, Advanced Calc 513 for three credits, Neurology 314 for three credits, Biological Functions of the Body 489 for three credits, and her elective of Astronomy 215 for two credits. Those were all her classes.

She was not in Bio 428.

"I am looking at your current course list and it is listed on here. Class is every Tuesday and Thursday at 8 a.m.," Ms. Clemmings corrected.

"I think there must be a misunderstanding. I am not in that class."

"If you're not in that class, then you do not have the required number of fifteen credits to hold your full-time student standing and thus your scholarship."

She froze in shock, the small smile that had begun to creep upward still plastered across her face.

"That's impossible." She began to count the credits in her head. Chem was three, plus calc for three which equaled six. Then she added in neurology for another three to equal nine. Biological functions for three which equaled twelve, and astronomy for two which equaled fourteen.

Fourteen credits.

Fourteen credits.

Fourteen credits.

She was only taking fourteen credits.

"I'm only taking fourteen credits?" Sam whispered in disbelief.

There was no way she would have made that error. She was meticulous in every moment of her life, especially with regards to her school work.

She could not have missed that.

How could she have missed that?

She counted her class credits over again in her head and then she started to hyperventilate.

"It seems we have a situation here," Ms. Clemmings stated. "You are technically signed up for seventeen credits because you are signed up for Biological Sciences 428, and since you have yet to attend a single class, turn in a single assignment, or take a single exam, you are currently failing that class. However, it seems you were unaware of this."

"I honestly didn't know." Sam's voice was barely a whisper. She felt her heart sink. Her hands began to shake and she had to grip the edges of her chair to try to remain steady.

"The drop period has already passed, so this grade will remain on your permanent record. However, it wouldn't matter if you had the ability to drop it, because then you would lose the scholarship as you would not be meeting the requirement of being a full-time student."

Sam knew what Ms. Clemmings was saying. She had worked it all out in her head only a moment ago. Still, the words felt hollow when they hit her ears. A deep, muffled sound and her rapidly beating heart were now all she could hear.

She had royally screwed up. She racked her brain for the day she'd signed up for classes. She'd been sitting alone in her apartment over Christmas break and spent two days scheduling everything out to perfection. She'd been exhausted due to the fact that she had picked up extra shifts at Topline every day in order to pad her savings account to pay for her med school applications.

"Miss Williams?" Sam's head snapped up when she heard the man's deep voice. He was in a fitted suit with a well trimmed beard and did not appear to be as kind as the woman who had previously spoken.

"I'm sorry." Tears were starting to fall from her eyes and she hated the amount of pity that came from each person facing her. She cleared her throat in order to let go of some of the emotion that continued to build. "What were you saying?"

"We asked that you step out for a moment so we can discuss where to take this."

"Of course." Sam nodded.

"It shouldn't take long, as the violations are straight forward," the man said.

Sam knew he had told her his name at some point, but it didn't stick. All she could currently process was how quickly her life was falling apart

"I understand," Sam said as she stood and made her way back to the double doors at the front of the room.

She jumped when the large wooden door slammed behind her. Her eyes searched the bench only to find it empty and Christian nowhere in sight. He'd promised to always be there for her. That he would be sitting right there waiting. The pain of his abandonment just piled onto the mounting stress and fear she was currently feeling. She was completely alone on a sinking ship.

She sat down and stared at the floor below, letting her vision swim unfocused with the curved designs in the marbled grooves under her feet. It could have been five minutes or five hours by the time they called her in. She wouldn't have known either way.

******

When she sat down in the chair once more and looked up, she was shocked to find only the woman, Ms. Clemmings, standing before her.

"Samantha?" Ms. Clemming questioned.

"Where is everyone else?"

"I dismissed them. Sometimes, it can be a little overwhelming when you are being stared down by a room full of people you do not know."

Sam nodded her head in agreement, thankful to not have to sit in the spotlight with all those peering eyes. Ms. Clemmings slowly dragged over another chair and sat beside her.

"Your record is impressive. You've made it to the last semester of your junior year juggling a 4.0 GPA, multiple jobs, and volunteer work. I personally believe you will one day make a fine doctor."

"Thank you." That was only if Sam actually made it into med school.

"However, mistakes were made and there are consequences to that."

Sam nodded in agreement.

"But I didn't run for this position in order to take away someone's funding at the first offense. So, I have a proposition. I don't want you to lose all your funding for the next year. It took some back and forth and not everyone on the board agreed, but I have the final say in the matter at hand."

Sam's heart was racing.

"You will lose your funding for the upcoming fall semester. *But*, if you sign up for Biological Sciences 428 in the fall and can finish the class with an A, I will reinstate your funds for the spring semester. I will also write an addendum to any med school of your choosing, helping to explain the pressures placed on you at the time, your full course load, part-time job, and community service hours. I don't think this will be an issue in the long run, but I will do what I can if it becomes one."

"Thank you." Sam started crying. "I'm so very sorry. I have never messed up like this before."

"Samantha. You are human, and you are allowed to make mistakes." There was nothing but kindness in Ms. Clemmings voice.

"Can I tell you a little secret?" She reached out to place a comforting hand on Sam's shaking fingers and, in that moment, Sam was almost positive the woman was a mother herself.

"Of course."

"I was in foster care as a young child."

That revelation made Sam sit up a little straighter.

"Really?"

"Yes. I was very fortunate that I was adopted by my foster family, but I was a preteen by that point. So, I know firsthand some of what you have gone through." She gave Sam a knowing smile. "They didn't have this program when I was your age, but, to be honest, despite the good it does, I still don't think it's everything it could be. I know the stipulations are rigorous, almost too much so. But I plan to change that."

"How?"

"Well, between you and me, I don't think we should have the mandatory 4.0 GPA and job and community service hours. It's too much. How are you supposed to let loose at least one night a month if all you ever do is study?" She gave Sam a wink and laughed.

"I don't think I have ever truly let loose."

"Maybe it's time to live a little, then. People make more mistakes when they don't take time for themselves. Consider this me telling you to take a little time for yourself, okay?"

Ms. Clemmings patted Sam's shoulder and stood up.

"Go do great things, Sam. And when I see you for our follow-up mid-fall, I know you will have wonderful things to show me."

Chapter 34 - Sam

She was practically a zombie as she walked into work two days later. She hadn't yet told Kristin, or anyone else for that matter, what the decision from the board had been. In all honesty, she was still trying to process it herself.

So it came as a complete shock when she went to hang her bag up that she noticed all the new items placed on top of the coffee station. She was so deep within her own thoughts that it took a second to reconcile with what she was looking at.

"What the hell is all this?" she questioned no one in particular.

"Mr. Barker did it," Jess chimed in and then nudged her side with a knowing look.

She wanted to laugh.

Mr. Barker.

That's how everyone here saw him.

But not her.

Their Mr. Barker was her Callum.

Her Callum.

The Callum who'd filled his home with her scent. The Callum who filled her ears with her favorite music. The Callum who now had stocked the coffee station with her favorite flavors and then some.

Her Callum.

Even if the last time they'd seen each other she had made it abundantly clear they were only friends. It didn't matter. Somewhere deep inside of her, she knew he was hers, and she was his, and that was frightening. If she was being completely honest, it was absolutely terrifying. Mostly because the feeling was new and unknown and she wasn't sure how to reconcile that with the knowledge that they were now, because of her, just friends.

Only friends.

He was a friend who put together an entire coffee bar with all of her favorite things.

She smiled when she saw the peppermint flakes. She had never added that to coffee before, but she figured she might as well try it. It sounded amazing.

She could not believe how boggled, yet totally clear her mind was right then.

Callum.

Callum.

Callum.

This tiny, amazing gesture just summed him up so perfectly. He was so considerate. He always listened to her. He had never pushed her about anything that made her uncomfortable. He had followed her home and made sure she was safe. He was there for her at the drop of a hat, as soon as he thought she might need him.

Sam knew that she wanted him in her life, but she wasn't sure what exactly that might look like. She stared at the new additions as she tried to picture that friendship.

She burst out into a laugh at the thought. There was absolutely no way in hell she could just be this man's friend. She felt like a ridiculous idiot. She laughed so hard at the notion that she was bent over and holding onto her stomach when she felt a hand grip her shoulder.

When she looked back, she found Callum's face tilted in confusion as to her outburst.

"What's so funny?"

"You." She looked at him pointedly.

"Me?" he asked, rather shocked.

"Yes. You." She rolled her eyes as she smiled. "You and your peppermint diffusers, and your new playlist, and your *improved* coffee bar."

His cheeks went red.

"Is it working?" He ran a hand through his hair.

She looked around to find them standing alone without another soul in sight and leaned forward to whisper in his ear.

"Yeah. I kinda hate you for it," she said with sarcasm and a smile. "But it's working. You are a really, *really* good friend." She blushed as she spoke.

And as she walked by him she reached out to squeeze his hand. He hooked his finger around hers and as she stepped further away, she found both their arms stretched out toward the other. She stopped just as she moved out of reach and turned to look back at his devastatingly beautiful face just as his hand dropped from hers.

"Good luck out there tonight," Callum said, his voice low and wanting with a devious yet jaw dropping smile on display.

****

She was surprised when they spent the next few hours working alongside each other. He was somehow constantly at her side. She could tell he was trying not to make it so obvious but, in truth, he was miserably failing at that. Even Jess kept giving her a wide-eyed expression whenever he came near.

He'd started out helping all three waitresses in Sam's section. He filled drinks, helped run the food, and even turned the tables over. But as the night went on, she realized he was spending more and more time near her. At her tables. With her guests.

And she couldn't stop the smile that spread every time they passed each other and his hand not so slyly brushed against her hip, or arm, or back.

And she loved every second of it. She just loved being near him.

Chapter 35 - Sam

"What do you say we get out of here for the weekend?" Kristin asked as she leaned against Sam's bedroom door.

Sam had spent the first two days after that meeting in an obvious funk. Then, after their night at Topline together, she spent the next two days unable to wipe the smile off her face. She finally confessed to Kristin what exactly caused that smile and then promptly walked straight upstairs with the notion of needing to study so she didn't have to answer the millions of questions she was sure Kristin was dying to ask her.

The only time in which that smile turned down was when she thought of Christian and how he had bailed on her when she'd needed him most. The lone apologetic text she had received later that night had been promptly deleted before it had even been fully read.

She wasn't sure what could have caused him to leave so quickly, but she wasn't yet ready to forgive him for it.

"And where do you suggest we go?"

"Charleston." Kristin looked way too happy about this.

"Okay. I can tell by the devilish smile on your face that you have something planned. Where would we stay? And, what are we doing? Where would we get food? How are we–"

"We would stay at a nice big house on the water," Kristin promptly cut her off.

Sam eyed her skeptically at the notion of 'big house on the

water.'

"For free," Kristin quickly added with a massive smile and then the rest came out in a rush, "And we would get free food and free drinks, and there is a pool. Oh, and I could take you shopping on King Street. I have barely spent any money this month, so my mom will think something is wrong if I don't drop some serious cash. You could finally see Rainbow Row and The Battery and The Charleston Market. Oh, Sam! I'm so excited for you! I know you've wanted to go for a while."

Sam waited a moment to let Kristin catch her breath.

"Just us two? A girls weekend?"

Kristin scrunched up her nose and admitted, "Not really. But while the guys are away, we can go to the pool and then burn through my stupidly large inheritace."

Sam sat up more fully at that and set down the novel she was reading. She wasn't sure she wanted to know the answer to the question she was about to ask.

"Which guys?"

"Okay. So, hear me out."

"Kristin..." Sam dragged out her name as a warning. "Are you suggesting we spend the weekend with Micah and Callum?"

"And Drew," Kristin added as she placed her hands in a pleading gesture.

"I don't know." But she did know. She knew exactly what she wanted. She wanted to go to Charleston with Callum and spend all weekend teasing each other like they had at work. She had never wanted anything more in her life.

But she was scared to see him again. She needed to apologize. The last time they had really talked, the night when she'd been a complete ass and told him he ruined her, she had broken a piece of him and she was slowly drowning in embarrassment. She had to apologize for what she had insinuated. She couldn't hide behind a busy schedule, a coffee bar and a plethora of Topline guests if they were on a beach. She would have to face the awful things she'd said. And that was terrifying.

"You haven't even heard what the deal is," Kristin said in an exasperated tone.

She gave Kristin a look, imploring her to continue.

"Okay." Kristin sucked in a deep breath and Sam knew Kristin was about to spit everything out in rapid fire before Sam could turn her down. "So, there is this festival going on this weekend and Callum and Drew have a booth or something for the tattoo shops. Micah is going to help them set up and do some of the behind the scenes stuff while they are working with customers. Actually, he's probably really going because it's free, and it's Charleston, and there's alcohol, but that's beside the point. So, he told me I could come, and I said I would only go if you went, too."

Kristin took another deep breath, causing Sam to laugh.

"This weekend?" Sam gave her a side eye.

"Yes. We would have to miss Calculus tomorrow."

"Calculus is at 8 a.m. We would leave before eight in the morning?" That didn't sound very logical. "Wait...no, I can't. I'm working a double shift this weekend. All day Saturday and one shift Sunday."

"No, you're not," Kristin countered.

"Yes, I am." Sam reached out to grab her calendar sitting on her desk. She needed to make sure she was correct, especially after that fiasco with her course schedule. The exact fiasco she had yet to tell Kristin about.

"Sam." Kristin placed her hand on top of Sam's, halting her from picking up the calendar. "You don't have to work this weekend. I know because your boss said you didn't have to."

"What?"

"Callum said he could get your shifts covered if you wanted to go."

"Kristin." The name was a warning on her lips.

She wasn't sure how she felt about them planning this behind her back.

"Please come with us. I don't want to leave you here all weekend by yourself."

Sam thought about it for a moment. She didn't want to be alone. Not after everything that recently happened.

"Can we at least leave *after* Calculus tomorrow?"

"No. We will have to miss calc tomorrow because we are leaving tonight."

"Tonight?" Sam looked at her clock. "It's already almost 5 p.m. When would we leave?"

"In an hour? Maybe thirty minutes?"

Sam wanted to scream. Instead, she started to laugh. "You have got to be kidding me, right? I can't pack and get ready to leave in thirty minutes."

"Yes, you can. I have already packed my bag and you know I packed enough for both of us, anyway. Shove your toiletries in a bag, grab some underwear and a bathing suit, and you'll be ready well before they get here to pick us up." Kristin paused to look Sam up and down. "Unless you keep stalling."

"You already told them we were coming, didn't you?"

"Maybe," Kristin said as she got up from Sam's bed and walked over to her closet.

"Fuck. Fine. Throw me that bag." Sam pointed to the top shelf. "Start pulling out whatever you think I need to take." Kristin jumped up and down in excitement like a child going to an amusement park.

They spent most of the next half hour deciding what Sam should and should not take. Most of Kristin's picks left little to the imagination and Sam quickly shot her down.

Sam had just made it downstairs and slung her bag onto the couch when she was startled by loud banging on the front door. She took a deep breath, knowing who was most likely on the other side, and slowly opened the door. Callum and Micah were both leaning on opposite posts on the front porch.

Micah's face was the picture of excitement, Callum just

looked apprehensive. She could tell he wasn't sure if she had agreed to go or not.

She took a deep breath, building up the anticipation. "I hear we're going to Charleston for the weekend?"

Callum's eyebrows peaked and his aggravatingly beautiful smile suddenly covered his entire face, but before he could say a word, Micah jumped in.

"Are you telling me Samantha Williams has agreed to join us?"

"Apparently, my boss is letting me take the weekend off, so why not?" Her gaze drifted to Callum, whose excitement was on full display.

"You must have an amazing boss," Callum observed.

"He thinks he's pretty cool. I have yet to make a final decision on the matter." Sam shrugged her shoulders in indifference and Callum shook his head knowingly. "Where's Drew?" she asked while she guided them inside.

"Filling up his bike," Micah answered. "Where's Kristin?"

"I'm here!" Kristin called out, practically out of breath, as she lugged two full suitcases down the stairs.

Callum tilted his head in confusion. "We are going for three days. You need a swimsuit and two outfits."

"Listen here, Callum Barker. A girl must have choices." Kristin's finger was inches from Callum's face. "What if we go to dinner? Or brunch? What if we go to the theater or a dance club? And I will need good shoes for strolling all up and down King Street. And then sandals for the pool and I'll need heels for dinner," Kristin exasperatedly explained.

"Point taken," Callum conceded as he stepped back to watch Micah throw her bags in the back of his truck. "What about you? Where are your bags?" Callum gestured toward Sam.

"Just this," Sam said as she threw her backpack over her shoulders.

Packing light was something she'd learned from childhood.

She'd never known when she might have to move from place to place, and being afforded time and space to pack was a luxury she had never been given.

"Two outfits and toiletries."

Callum grinned.

"I didn't know Drew had a bike?" Sam questioned as they walked outside and locked the front door behind them.

"Yeah. He should be here in just a moment. Micah and I already filled the trucks last night."

"Why are all three of you driving?"

"We both have single cab trucks," Callum said as if that explained everything.

Sam widened her eyes in question.

"Since you and Kristin are both coming, we all needed to drive to make room."

Sam knew where he was going with that.

"Who am I riding with?"

His answer was a shy smile.

She took a deep breath. "Sounds about right."

Sam wasn't sure how she felt about this. She still hadn't apologized for her outburst the night she'd gotten the email. She had made him believe it was all his fault and she hated herself for it. There'd been so many times she'd almost stopped him that night they'd worked together. Once, she'd almost blurted it out at a table as she was filling drinks and he was passing plates. She knew she would have to say something at some point, but the words just wouldn't come.

In her mind, she was teetering on the line between him being just a friend she desperately needed to apologize to for implying he'd fucked up her life, and he was just a friend she desperately needed to stay away from because every thought of him ended in barely clothed daydreams.

Chapter 36 - Sam

The short ride from their house to the interstate was silent.

Sam sent Kristin a short and concise text letting her know how much she owed Sam for what she was being made to endure. It wasn't necessarily bad, but he was inches from her.

Inches.

She could smell him. She could see the defined lines of his bicep. She could reach out and touch him if she wanted to. She could lean over and kiss him at any moment. But she wouldn't, and it was absolutely torturous.

They each spent the better part of the first hour stealing glances at the other and waiting for the other to break the uncomfortable silence. At some point along the way, Sam placed her earbuds in her ears and leaned her head against the window, hoping to drown out the tension that seemed to always surround them.

She hadn't meant to fall asleep, but was woken up sometime later by a nudge to her shoulder. After sliding the earbuds out and readjusting her eyes, she found a beautiful sunset coming through the window.

"Do you need anything?" Callum asked.

"Huh?" she asked groggily, wondering what in the world she was doing in this truck with him.

"I'm going inside to grab something." Sam looked up, finding the blinding lights of a gas station above them. "Do you need me to get you anything?"

It was then that the last hour came rushing back. She looked him over to find the same sweet hint of a smile gracing his features and the slight stubble she desperately wanted to brush her thumb against. She blinked rapidly, forcing herself back into the reality where they were only friends and she had no reason to touch him like that.

"Oh. No, I'm good."

As he began to step away, she noticed the street lights flickering to life.

They were definitely not on schedule.

"Wait? Where are we?"

He popped his head back into the cab. "North Charleston. There was a bad wreck on 26 and we were in standstill traffic for over an hour." And then she was left watching him walk inside while she contemplated how she was going to spend the next three days being just friends with this man.

Sam played with the radio, not sure what else to do while waiting for him to return. A small part of her wanted to snoop around the small cab of the truck, hoping to find an inkling of the man he truly was. She immediately froze when he opened up the door and began rummaging through a bag. He grabbed a blue Gatorade and tossed it onto her lap.

"What's this?"

"You're always drinking one of those." Callum shrugged his shoulders and turned the key.

"Oh. Thanks."

Sam took a few sips and pondered how much more he had noticed about her. Then she realized she didn't need to search through his truck to discover who he was. He showed her every time he did something like this.

"So, where exactly is this place? Did y'all rent it?"

"It's in Mount Pleasant. It's my parents' house."

The revelation gave her pause. He hadn't spoken much about his family, but from what he had said before, she had drawn the conclusion that they didn't mix well.

"We're going to your parents' house? I didn't think you got along too well with your family?"

"I get along with them fine as long as we don't see each other very often."

"Oh. I'm sorry to hear that."

"Don't be. I'm not." He paused and then, just as they pulled back onto the highway, added, "Just because someone is blood related to you doesn't necessarily mean that they are your family."

"You have no idea how true that statement is." Sam took a deep breath. "Can I ask you a question?"

"Sam, you could ask me a thousand questions and I would never tire of it."

She smiled and tried to ignore the flutters those words caused. "What exactly are y'all doing in Charleston? Kristin said it was for your work or something."

"There is an arts festival downtown and they're having an exhibition for body artists. Piercers, tattoo artists, etc. We reserved a booth and are going to showcase some work. Just trying to expand more."

"I bet your parents are proud of you."

"One would think so. But sometimes it's hard for parents to be proud of their kids, despite how successful they are, when they go down a completely different path than what they had planned for them."

Sam could tell by the look on Callum's face that there was nothing funny about what he'd said, but she still had to hold in a laugh just thinking about the irony of the paths they'd chosen. There were such obvious discrepancies in how society's expectations of them were affected by their very different upbringings, and it was almost as if each had chosen to take the other's path.

He had deliberately veered off the path his parents had set for him. She assumed based on the fact that his dad was a doctor as was his brother, that they had planned the same for him.

At the same time, Sam had never once had someone to lay out a path for her. She was surging forward down a carefully and meticulously designed path of her own making. One she was desperate not to veer off of.

But who was she worried about letting down? Christian? The foundation? Herself? That was a little too deep of a thought to contemplate during what was supposed to be a weekend getaway.

She cleared her throat. "They're crazy. You're not even close to thirty yet and you own a business that's doing really well. Actually, you own multiple businesses."

"My mom is proud of me, I think. Millie is as well. Maybe Connor is, too, although we don't speak very often, so I wouldn't really know. My father and I don't speak at all."

"Do you want to talk about it?"

"You're rather nosy at the moment," he said with a laugh and Sam rolled her eyes.

"You are the one who said you would never tire of answering any questions I had."

"Touché." He gave her a solemn smile. "But no, I don't really want to talk about it."

"Okay. How much longer till we get there?" She shifted the conversation to get away from the tension that had started to build again.

"About twenty minutes. We're about to cross the bridge now." Callum pointed over to the largest bridge she had ever seen in person.

"Oh my god. Callum!" Sam called out as he drove up onto the ramp. It was as if her head was on a swivel and she couldn't seem to look everywhere she wanted. From this vantage point, she could see most of Charleston, the surrounding towns, and the harbor. "This is gorgeous!"

"Have you never been to Charleston?" Callum asked.

"No."

Callum looked a little shocked, but then spent the next few

minutes pointing out different landmarks, churches, and other buildings. She gladly let him talk and she pulled out her phone and started snapping photos. She decided she most definitely wanted to remember this place.

The rest of the ride to his house was quiet. It was in a gated community, which meant they had to stop at the gate so Callum could tell the guard to allow in Drew's bike and Micah's truck. Sam was in shock as they drove through the neighborhood. She had spent countless dinners and days by the pool at Kristin's parents' home, but even that monstrosity was nothing compared to the houses before her now.

In the middle of her frenzied exploration of the scenes before her, she realized the rest of their group was no longer behind them.

"Where are Drew, Micah, and Kristin?"

"They stopped at the store to get some stuff for the weekend."

Sam nodded in understanding and then deeply inhaled when Callum rolled down the windows. She knew they were on the marsh, but this was the first time she had ever had the chance to smell the salty ocean air. She removed her seatbelt and leaned out the window, taking it all in.

Callum laughed a little at her reaction.

"If this is all it took to make you happy I would have brought you down here weeks ago."

She turned back toward him, not even trying to contain the huge smile plastered across her face.

Chapter 37 - Sam

This wasn't what she had expected at all.

"*This* is your house?"

"It's my parents' house," Callum quickly corrected.

"Holy shit. What kind of doctor is your dad?"

"He's not a doctor, he's an architect. He designed it."

She had only assumed doctor because she knew he was friends with Kristin's dad.

"Wow."

Sam stood outside for a moment, mentally patting herself on the back. There was no way Micah wasn't going to break a sweat carrying Kristin's two bags up the massive structure that masqueraded as front porch steps.

She headed for the large stairwell, but Callum diverted them under the house. She assumed he was going to grab a hide-a-key but, instead, he pushed a button that caused a set of elevator doors to open.

"You have an elevator...in your house?" She looked at him with a wide-eyed expression. Callum shrugged in response.

The elevator was smaller than most, probably only meant for one person or a set of luggage at a time.

Throwing caution to the wind, she stepped forward and they crammed in, front to back, with her standing so close to him she could feel his breath shifting the lightest of her curls. For a fleeting moment, she recalled their trip to Social. Her mouth became dry and her heart began to race. She counted the seconds until she heard the ding indicating they were finally at their destination.

When the door slid open, she quickly stepped out first, desperate to get away from the feelings his exhale had caused. She only made it a few steps before she had to stop in awe at the sight before her.

The back of the room was a wall of floor to ceiling windows overlooking the marsh. The pool below was lit up with surrounding lights and there were palmetto trees scattered about the yard.

It was paradise.

By this point, the sun had set, making it difficult to see much beyond the yard in the dark, but she was sure the view tomorrow would stun her even more.

The living room itself was larger than the entire home she shared with Kristin, and was furnished as if it was suited for the cover of a magazine instead of somewhere people actually lived. But then the small details started to creep in. A finger painting obviously completed by a toddler hung on a far wall. There was a set of ceramic vases sitting on the coffee table that looked more like they were completed in an art class than bought at a fine arts store. The wall between the massive kitchen and what she assumed was a pantry had height marks scaling up the walls.

She stood there for a moment, taking it all in and wondering what his childhood was like if he was able to frequent places such as this.

What kind of memories did he hold of this place? Had it been his fingers and hands that had crafted the artwork all around? Or Connor's or Amelia's? She also wondered what could have happened to cause such strife between him and his family.

Then there was a moment of mounting frustration she had to reign in. He obviously had any and everything he could have ever needed and then some. She wanted to scream at him that he should be grateful for what all he had been given. She turned back to find Callum leaning against the kitchen counter, looking her way.

"You're doing it again." He started to walk toward her.

"Doing what?"

"Thinking too hard." He reached up and popped her bottom lip free from the grasp of her teeth. The spot where he touched seemed to buzz even after he let go.

"I was just thinking about how amazing it would have been to grow up here. You are truly blessed."

"One person's perception is another person's reality."

"What?" Her brow furrowed.

"I just mean, my life wasn't always what it might have appeared to be."

"How did it appear?" she leaned against the table beside her.

"Perfect."

"And it wasn't?"

"It was in the beginning, I think," he clarified with a raised brow. "But time moved on and things happened and then it wasn't so perfect anymore. Or maybe it never was in the first place, I just lived with the rose-colored glasses of a child who was only able to see what he wanted to see."

She thought about her own childhood then. She had never had the luxury of rose-colored glasses. Her situation had never been anything she'd particularly wanted. Sure, there had been good families along the way. But, for the most part, she never had a home. Not a real one, at least.

"What about your parents?" He interrupted her thoughts. "I mean, you're in college and planning to go to med school. Most would be cheering their kids on for going into a field like that," he observed, an expectant look in his eyes.

"Most probably would." She crossed her arms over her chest just as they were interrupted by Drew coming through the back door and Callum's shoulders fell.

"They're here with food," Drew called out. "Kristin said she bought stuff for this chicken roll thing and to preheat the oven," he added as he made his way up the stairs to where Sam assumed the bedrooms were located.

"Why are we cooking?" Callum questioned as he turned to walk back into the massive, white and gold kitchen.

Sam quickly corrected him, "Y'all aren't. That's my secret recipe and Kristin loves it. So, I guess I'm Chef Sam tonight."

Callum turned to give her a smile.

"I'm good with whatever you fix. Come on," he motioned toward the stairs. "I'll show you where the bedrooms are while they bring everything inside."

The first door they passed was a bedroom where Drew was now laid out on the bed working on a laptop. The next room was empty and Callum indicated Micah and Kristin would be in there. Then there was a large media room, another bathroom, the master bedroom with a massive porch overlooking the water, and lastly, another bedroom.

"You can stay here." He opened the door to the final room.

As soon as the room filled with light, she knew it was his. There was a large table in the corner with drawing supplies neatly placed in various containers and the walls were filled with artwork representing varying degrees of skill.

"Where are you staying?" She turned to ask him.

"What?"

"This is obviously your room. If I'm in here, then where would you stay?"

"There is a second master bedroom downstairs. You can stay in it if you would be more comfortable there and I can sleep on the couch."

"Why don't you want to sleep in your room?"

"I just don't, but I'll do whatever makes you most comfortable." He ran his hands through his hair and she decided to drop her line of questioning.

"This is fine. Thank you."

"I'm going to go help them bring stuff in," Callum said as he walked backward toward the door. For some reason, he now seemed awkward, as if he was tiptoeing around her. "I'm looking forward to your chicken roll thing." His lips quirked upward in a devilish smirk.

"You say that now. I have no clue how to work that fancy contraption you call an oven. I could burn it all up."

"Eh, once the firefighters get the blaze under control I'll just order pizza. Probably won't be as good as Dianne's, though."

"Nothing is as good as Dianne's," she agreed with a laugh as he walked out of the room.

The sun may have set, but it was still significantly hotter on the coast than it was inland, or maybe that was just the rush of heat caused by being so near him for the last few hours.

Sam was desperate to cool off so she quickly changed into a tank top and some yoga pants. She'd contemplated a sexier outfit more than once, but finally settled on the fact that friends didn't worry this much about what they wore in front of the other.

When she made it back downstairs, this time in much more comfortable attire, she found that Callum had made himself busy by putting away all of the groceries.

"Where are the others?" she asked while looking around the empty room.

"Drew went to grab some supplies from one of our guys so we don't have to worry about it in the morning. Micah and Kristin headed upstairs a few minutes ago. I don't think they'll be back down for a while." Callum looked up and smirked.

"They can't seem to keep their hands off each other," Sam agreed with a shake of her head.

"What do you need me to do?" He asked.

"Have you ever actually cooked a meal?" Sam's brows furrowed.

"Excuse me," he feigned offense, "I own a restaurant."

"Let me rephrase. Have you ever cooked without using the microwave?"

He scrunched up his nose.

"Let's just say I have a feeling we'll end up having to order pizza if you try to help me."

"Fine." He threw his hands up in mock annoyance. "I offered once. Isn't happening again. I'll just sit here and make you do all the work."

With that, he planted himself on the counter opposite Sam and leaned back against the cabinets with a smile.

Chapter 38 - Callum

It had taken more restraint than he'd even known he possessed not to touch her on the ride down to Charleston, and then even more to quietly walk out of the bedroom he'd told her she would be sleeping in, and then even more still now as he sat quietly against the cabinets and watched her cook.

He would never tell a soul, but, god, he was thankful for that traffic jam. It had allowed him to sit and silently watch her for so long. It still hadn't been long enough, though. He'd memorized the way her lips moved as she breathed, and the sounds and noises she made as she slept. He'd memorized the curve of her fingers and the freckles that dotted her skin. He'd memorized the way her hair fell in wild ringlets, and the way the cabin of his truck started to fill with the essence of peppermint. She was a goddamn masterpiece of her own, and he knew he would never lay eyes on anything as beautiful.

He had initially cringed when she had started asking him about his family. That was a hard subject to work through. But it had given him an opening to ask her about hers in hopes she would tell him the truth. He'd contemplated just coming out and asking her about her past outright, but then thought that might embarrass her, which was exactly what he didn't want. He wanted her to tell him, but he wanted her to tell him because she felt safe and comfortable confiding in him, not because he'd forced the truth out of her.

So he'd reached out just slightly with his comment on her

being a med student and how most parents would be proud. When she hadn't taken the bait, he'd reeled back and decided to let it go. Hopefully, one day they would get there. He just hoped that day came sooner rather than later. Because, now that he knew the little noises she made as she slept, he didn't think he could go another night without her by his side. That wasn't how one normally thought about a friend, but he couldn't help it.

He also knew that in order for her to open up, he probably needed to do the same. He needed to tell her about his asshole father, and the falling out he'd had with his brother. He needed to tell her about how he'd fucked up his parents' marriage and broken up their family. He needed to tell her about Rebecca. He needed to explain again that he ruined things, but that he thought maybe he wouldn't ruin her.

Chapter 39 - Sam

Sam spent the next fifteen minutes prepping and cooking while trying desperately to forget Callum was watching her from the counter behind her. She was proud of herself for not looking back at him. And for only once asking for an item that then immediately slid up beside her. It wasn't until she'd placed the dish in the oven and was washing her hands that she felt him come up behind her. From her position at the sink, she could see his reflection in the glass wall feet away. He was mere inches, if that, from her. Just as she turned the water off, she felt him slide his hands across her hips as he leaned down close to her ear.

"Do you have any idea how torturous it is watching you move and not touching you?" His arms wrapped tighter around her. When his head dipped down by her neck, she could feel his stubble tickling her sensitive skin.

"I never said you couldn't touch me." She was already breathless.

"Good." He twisted her around, picked her up, and placed her on the counter, separating her legs to step between them.

Sam swallowed as she let her arms drape across his shoulders.

"I don't think we can be just friends," Callum whispered, his voice deep and full of need.

Her heart was beating too fast as she inhaled, tasting the minty tang of his breath. She heard herself let out a throaty chuckle, but she couldn't make her mouth move to form words. Thankfully, Callum spoke again.

"I'm sorry I woke you up earlier in the truck, but I wanted to make sure you didn't need anything."

She exhaled with his change of subject.

"It's fine. I wasn't mad about it."

"I was."

"Mad you woke me up? Why?"

"You are so beautiful when you sleep." His finger traced her jaw, and then her nose, and then her lips. Her eyes fluttered closed. "When you're awake, you're always so tense. It's like you're waiting for the floor to fall out from under you. But when you sleep, you have this little smile you do. I like you like that. Relaxed. Not thinking so hard about everything." He reached up at his last statement to once again pull her lip from the grasp of her teeth. "And you tend to mumble and talk in your sleep. That's always entertaining."

"Do I even want to know what I said?"

"Nothing too bad. Just how I'm the most handsome man you have ever laid eyes on."

"I did not!" She swatted at his shoulder and buried her face in his chest while laughing.

He pulled her in a little tighter. "No, you didn't."

"Not that it wouldn't be true or anything." She looked back up to him and wrapped her arms around his neck, sweeping his hair out of his face. "You need a hair-cut."

"I know." He didn't acknowledge her initial statement. "Callum?"

"Yes?" His hands were once again rubbing up and down her thighs, inching their way higher with each pass. Her barely there yoga pants did nothing to ward off the sting his touch brought.

"We've been here a million times now. I don't want this cycle to keep going."

"I know." He slid his hands up to her hips and then to her

stomach when he pulled back a little and cocked his head to the side in confusion. "What the hell is this?" He lifted her shirt slightly to see the top of her pants.

"What? They're yoga pants?"

"I know that. Why the hell are they so high up your stomach?"

She laughed a little at his shock. "They're high waisted. Very comfortable. And they have pockets." She showed him exuberantly.

"Well, I liked them a lot, until now. Way too much fabric up here." He pinched the top band, and for some reason the notion caused Sam to burst out laughing.

"You're ridiculous."

"I never said I was anything else." He paused for a brief second then continued, "I don't want you to stay in my old room tonight."

"Okay. I told you I didn't care where I stayed. But I can sleep on the couch. I don't want you to—"

"No. That's not what I mean. I want you to stay down here. In the guest room. With me."

"Callum."

"I'm not asking for sex. But there is no fucking way I'm getting an ounce of sleep tonight if I know you are just above me in the house. I need you with me."

"I don't think that's a good idea." She wasn't sure why those words were what came out. She felt the exact opposite.

"I promise I'll behave myself." He held up three fingers.

"Scout's honor."

"Oh, god. Were you a Boy Scout?"

"Yes. Eagle Scout, actually," he clarified. "I can tie any knot you want or need." Her mouth went dry. "I'm a little out of practice now, although lately I've been dreaming about tying knots. Funny thing, isn't it?" She tightened her lips, hoping he didn't see the quiver that had started. There was a momentary flash of a vision of him tying her to the bed while doing all manner of deliciously horrible things to her body. Her legs tightened around him, her body desperate for some type of friction at her core. From the way his eyes darkened, she knew his mind had gone there, too. "I'm serious, Sam. Stay with me."

"Maybe."

"I can work with that," he said as he once again started rubbing her thighs and then nuzzled his face into the crook of her neck. "But you are definitely changing into some regular waisted pants." He leaned back to meet her eyes with a smile, causing her to laugh a little again. But there was no humor in his features. "I need to be able to touch your skin."

"I could just go with no pants?" she bravely countered.

His eyes widened slightly at the offer, "I think that's a very good decision." He leaned in, and for the first time in days, she felt his lips on hers.

One would think for two people who fought and bickered as much as they did that this would get old. But every time he touched her, she felt more alive than the time before.

His touch was slow and torturous this time. He started with just a few tentative kisses to her closed lips and then he made his way along her jaw to her ear before turning his attention back to her mouth once more. Every sensitive spot he hit along the way caused her to involuntarily thrust her hips forward, begging for relief.

When their lips met again she was ready and met each of his movements with her own. They had kissed enough times by this point that she knew the way he liked to tilt her head to the side, the feel of his stubble as it grazed her chin, the way his tongue would sweep out begging for entrance. It still felt new and raw and as if it was everything she had been waiting for.

They only got to enjoy the feel of each other for a few moments before a throat clearing from behind Callum caused Sam to jump back with a start.

"Pay up," Micah said and reached a hand over to Drew who handed him some wadded-up cash. Kristin couldn't hide the smirk on her face. When Callum and Sam both gave them questioning looks, Micah explained, "I bet him twenty bucks y'all would be all over each other when we got down here. He doubted me." And then all three onlookers started to laugh.

They didn't get any more alone time after that, as all five of them spent the next few hours laughing and drinking, pausing only to eat Sam's famous chicken roll.

Drew explained the plans for the next day, stating that they needed to be there by seven to set up for the festival starting at nine. Callum grunted in frustration at that and Micah questioned when he was truly needed.

Kristin and Sam made plans to sleep in and lay out by the pool for a while before meeting up to bring the boys lunch. By the time the leftover food was put away and the dishes were cleaned, Drew had detailed out most of the next three days. Saturday would look a lot like Friday, except Kristin planned for more shopping than sunbathing. There was apparently a great bar and dance club they wanted to go to Saturday night and then they would leave shortly after lunch on Sunday.

Sam and Kristin eyed each other frequently. Apparently, Sam was not the only meticulously scheduled person in the room.

Sam hadn't spent very much time with Drew before that night and she had wrongly assumed he was just a lazy college drop out. The same title she'd once given Callum. She was quickly learning not to judge people so unfairly when she didn't really know them. Now she could see Drew was half the brain behind their business. She was sure his artistic skills were wonderful as well, but didn't think she would ever find any artwork as stunning as what Callum could do.

It was after ten when they decided to call it quits for the night. Sam made her way upstairs, brushed her teeth, and quickly got ready for bed. More than once, she had to physically stop herself from running down to Callum. She wanted nothing more than to curl up in his arms and fall asleep with his lips on hers. This weekend was supposed to be stress free. That was what she had promised herself on the way down and she knew what would happen if she were to give in to him.

Sam closed her eyes and tried to steady her breathing. She would get through this weekend without giving in. As she opened her eyes back up, she jumped with a start.

"Hey," Callum said shyly. His reflection in the mirror gave away that he was standing directly behind her.

"How long have you been standing there?"

"Not long at all."

Sam nodded her head before turning around to fully face him.

"You make a decision yet?"

"I think it's best if I stay up here and you stay down there."

"You're slowly killing me." He leaned back to rest his head against the wall.

"At least you'll die with a full belly," Sam noted and he laughed.

Then, by some miracle, she gained an absurd amount of courage and hooked her finger on the collar of his shirt, pulling his face down to meet hers. She noted a quick moment of shock that crossed his features before she tilted her head upward, closed her eyes, and planted a simple kiss on his lips. Callum lingered for a moment with his eyes closed after she pulled away.

"Don't make me beg. Please come downstairs with me."

Sam shook her head while slowly pushing him back and out of the room.

"I'll see you for lunch."

"Sam?" Callum pleaded one more time as his feet backed over the threshold.

"Goodnight, Callum," Sam stated with a smile as she shut the door.

Chapter 40 - Sam

"What time do you think we should head their way?" Kristin asked as she turned over to sun her back.

"I don't know. Have you been texting Micah to see what they want?"

Kristin laughed. "Yeah. They don't care as long as it's seafood and fried."

Sam laughed as well, then stretched out further on the chair, trying to relax. The hot sun felt good as it warmed up her skin, turning it a slight shade of pink in the process. It didn't, however, do a damn thing to take her thoughts away from Callum.

She had debated heading down to his room the previous night for longer than she wanted to admit. But in the end, she'd convinced herself it was better to stay where she was. Once she'd finally made her way to bed, sleep had come easier than she had anticipated. She had worried she would still toss and turn all night, consumed with thoughts of him.

A small, and admittedly selfish part of her, had hoped he had done the same.

If she was being completely honest, she hadn't been on her best behavior last night. She had had a secondary reason for staying upstairs. She'd wanted to explore his room. To try and get a sense of what trauma happened in his youth to make him grow up into the guarded man she knew today. She definitely remembered him mentioning there was something they'd all endured, but he'd never opened up about what that was. The walls, covered with brightly-colored artwork from his youth, were a bright teal color, his bed a typical teenage boy dark bedspread, and flowing gauzy curtains matched. On the art table, she found supplies fit for sketching, painting, modeling, and even...drafting? He had said his father was an architect, so she wondered if he had tried his hand at it as well.

There had also been a few photos pinned to a bulletin board. Callum holding a fish about the length of his arm. A very young Callum smiling at the camera from over a woman's shoulder. Sam assumed perhaps it was his mother, but she was facing away from the camera, so she couldn't get a glimpse of her features other than her dark, wavy hair. Callum, Connor, and Amelia dressed in matching outfits for family photos. He and his brother looked almost exactly the same. She wouldn't have been able to tell them apart except for Connor being slightly taller. Amelia had her same long, dark, wild hair. A photograph of an older Callum with his arm draped around a beautiful young woman Sam had never heard of, but she presumed was probably an ex-girlfriend. Sam was embarrassed to admit, even if only to herself, that she was a bit jealous of that photo and what it indicated.

"—are a few good ones on King, but we should start with The Market," Kristin said in complete oblivion of where Sam's mind had gone. She smiled at Kristin, hoping that satisfied whatever statement she had previously made. "It's almost noon already. Let's go get ready and head their way."

She gathered her towel and headed for the door.

****

"Here you go." Kristin smiled as she laid a white sundress on the bed.

Sam furrowed her brow.

"I was just going to wear some shorts and a t-shirt."

"No, you are wearing that dress and these sandals. I brought them down just for you."

Sam eyed the outfit. It was very pretty, but nothing at all like what she would usually wear. When Sam wasn't in her work uniform, she typically stuck with jeans or shorts paired with a tank or t-shirt. She had exactly one sundress. Which just so happened to be the one Callum had taken off of her.

"Why?"

"Because I think you'll look pretty in it," Kristin pleaded.

"Seriously? I've known you too long, Kristin. You are always scheming. What's your plan here?" Kristin visibly deflated with the knowledge that Sam had figured her out.

"I think Callum will go crazy when he sees you wearing that."

"Why? It's not sexy or anything."

"That's the point." Kristin threw her hands up in the air.

"I don't get it. It looks like something I would wear to meet up with your grandma."

"Exactly. You will look innocent as hell in that. And I'm pretty sure that will drive him insane."

"And that's what I want? To drive him insane?"

"Yeah. It is."

Sam ran the cotton fabric between her fingers and deeply exhaled.

"Kristin, to be honest. I don't know if I want to continue this back and forth thing he and I keep doing."

"But you like him, right?"

Sam hesitated a moment before answering.

"Yes, I do." It was barely a whisper, as if she wasn't sure she wanted to finally voice the truth out loud. "I really do. I feel more for him than I ever felt for Christian or anyone else. It's like he understands me better than anyone." Then she cut her eyes over to Kristin. "No offense."

"None taken."

"But I can tell there's something holding him back, you know? He is so damn closed off. It's like he has this wall built up to keep everyone out. I mean, we are so good together and we have fun, and...and..." Sam trailed off, trying to figure out how to explain it better, but Kristin always understood what she was trying to say, even when Sam didn't.

"It's okay. I get it." Kristin placed her hands on Sam's shoulders and gave her a knowing look. "Have y'all had sex yet?"

Sam rolled her eyes in response.

"If we had, you would've been the first to know."

Kristin nodded. "I figured. But you've come close right?"

"Yeah. A few times. He wanted me to stay with him in his room last night, but I told him no. Now I'm worried he'll be upset or think I don't want him anymore when we show up."

"I doubt it. From the way Micah was talking last night, Callum basically thinks you walk on water."

Sam scoffed.

"Have you told him about your past?"

"I haven't brought it up yet."

"Sam. How do you expect to get to know someone if you don't share things about yourself as well?"
Sam turned toward the window and tried to tame her unruly hair.

"He isn't going to judge you and run."

But that was exactly Sam's fear.

Sam had only had one real boyfriend in her life. His name was Jackson. It was during sophomore year of high school and they'd been young, but they had also been good together. Really good. He was the first boy who had managed to get her to forget about Christian, even if only for a few moments at a time.

Sam had spent the better part of that year with him, avoiding her past and distracting him with other means whenever he brought it up. She had usually been successful. Until one night around Christmas when Sam and Jackson had snuck one too many beers out of his father's garage fridge. He'd wanted to get a gift for her parents for Christmas, the parents she'd never let him meet, and had been badgering her about what they would like.

She had ended up spilling it all out for him then. Her entire past.

The good foster homes.

The bad foster homes.

The people that were supposed to have taken care of her.

The abuse.

The days when she'd slept through class so she would be rested enough to remain awake at night to fight off a drunk foster dad.

Everything.

She'd let it all out.

At first, he'd been understanding and said it didn't matter. Then, he'd started acting funny if Sam tried to pay for something or if she bought him a gift. He had fully stopped accepting the things she gave him. Then, he'd told his friends. The ones who had never liked her. The ones who always said she was stealing him away. The ones who, after finding out, convinced him she was only with him for the free dates, food, movie tickets, and rides. That she was using him as a way to experience the things she hadn't gotten to before. It became hell. Their relationship had turned into Sam walking on eggshells and never knowing when the floor would cave in. They hadn't even lasted three weeks after she told him. Thankfully, a month later she'd been transferred to another foster home and thus a different highschool, never to see him again.

"But what if he does?"

"He's not Jackson. I promise. You were practically a kid when that happened, and you and Callum are definitely *not* kids now. Besides, if he did, I would personally kill him."

"That's why I love you," Sam said as she grabbed the dress and shoes and headed for the bathroom.

After finishing her hair and makeup, she threw on the outfit and stared at herself in the mirror. From the front, she definitely looked the picture of perfect southern innocence. It had a straight neckline that barely hinted at her collar bones with wide base shoulder straps. It was fitted in the bodice, but flared just slightly from her waist to where it ended at her upper thigh. It was beyond short and she would definitely not be able to bend over.

Or maybe she would.

The back was not nearly as innocent and sweet. It was completely backless, the front wrapping around to the back just above the curve of her bottom. It was a perfect fit.

"See, I told you. You look amazing in that," Kristin said as she stood in the doorway, congratulating herself with a wide, devilish grin.

"It does fit really well and it's super light and comfy. At least I won't be a sweating mess."

"Come on. It's already noon. At this point, we will barely get any shopping in after we take them lunch."

Sam rolled her eyes. "We still have Saturday to shop, you know?"

"You have no idea what it's like shopping in Charleston. We need at least a week to hit every store I want," Kristin yelled as she made her way out of the room and back downstairs.

Sam grabbed her bag and followed her out. She stopped at the landing of the stairwell when she noticed a bookshelf filled with photographs that she hadn't paid attention to prior. There were a few from when Callum and his siblings were younger. There were a few with them on the beach and one of them on a skiing trip. The biggest difference from the Callum in these photos compared to the Callum she now knew was his expression. He had a big smile plastered on his face in all of them.

"You coming? I've got the truck running," Kristin yelled from downstairs.

"Yeah, I'll be right there," Sam replied.

What happened to that happy little boy with the infectious smile?

Chapter 41 - Sam

The ride over to the festival was uneventful until they tried to find somewhere to park and Kristin had loudly cursed out each of the full lots they passed. Sam buried her face in her hands as she laughed at the expressions of the people on the street who'd heard the outbursts.

The abundance of one-way streets had Sam completely turned around and she knew she wouldn't be able to get out of the city if her life depended on it. After far too many right turns and a parking garage that cost more than Sam could fathom, they began to stroll quickly by the market on their way to grab lunch.

She was so transfixed by the sights and sounds that she couldn't keep up with a thing that came out of Kristin's mouth. The smells alone could keep her occupied for hours. Every turn down another street brought in a barrage of fragrances, a combination of jasmine, fresh cut lawns, salt water, and fresh cooking. The cobblestone streets took her back to a time long before she'd been born. There were horse drawn carriages and people dressed as if they lived in another century.

It was like nowhere she had been before. And nothing like what she had imagined. Just as their destination came into sight, a chorus of church bells rang in the next hour. Now she knew what Callum had been talking about as they'd crossed the bridge the previous night. She could have spent hours here taking it all in.

When Kristin walked inside the restaurant to grab the

orders, Sam decided to park herself on a bench outside to people watch. She drank it all in and decided that she really needed to double check and make sure her application to MUSC was on point. She could definitely get used to life down here.

The festival was taking place in Marion Square. On their walk to the next destination, Kristin pointed out different shops and places she wanted to visit either today or tomorrow. Sam barely heard half of what she said. She loved Kristin, but that girl could talk for hours if Sam let it go on, and sometimes she just had to drown her out. It was normally with a good book. Today it was with the bustling city around them.

When they reached the festival, Sam guessed there must be at least a thousand people milling around, probably more. Booths and tents were set up in all directions, hosting things from handmade paintings, piercing booths, ceramics, tattoos, and anything else a creative mind could dream up. She got especially caught up looking at a booth filled with ladies weaving together what looked like dried grass into the most beautiful baskets, bowls, and art. The movement of their fingers had her transfixed. When Sam was just about to reach out to grasp the leaves, Kristin reached out to pull her back in the correct direction.

"Come on. We can look through all the booths later. We are so late, and they are probably starving."

Sam rolled her eyes. If she knew Micah at all, then she knew he had stashed a plethora of snacks in his truck that they had most likely been devouring all morning. They made their way through a maze of booths and people, trying to find the guys' spot. When Sam finally laid eyes on Callum, she felt the familiar tightness in her belly and the quick increase of her heart rate. He was not quite facing away from her, but he was so focused on his current design that she didn't think she would have been able to distract him even if she walked straight up to him completely naked.

She stood back for a few minutes to observe him while just making out the design he was tattooing onto his client. It was a weeping willow tree that spread across her ribs. It looked as though she had a streak of scars over the area he was skillfully covering up. Sam was so consumed by watching his hands work, she didn't even register when Kristin walked over and took the boxes of food from her grasp.

He was so deliberate and precise with each movement, placing the needle in just the right spot and turning the scarred skin into a beautiful masterpiece. Sam wondered what his hands would feel like if they paid her that level of attention. He was already well versed in the art of making her squirm and he hadn't even touched her bare skin where she desired it most. If she wasn't before, now she was sure he would have her moaning out his name within seconds.

When he finally finished the tattoo, he had its new owner examine the work, then covered it with a salve and bandage. It wasn't until the woman had paid and walked off that he realized Kristin was sitting beside Micah and eating. He quickly turned his head, searching the area. When his eyes finally found their intended mark, he stilled and let out a sigh of relief as Sam walked up.

"You're really good. That was beautiful," she told him. They were only a few feet apart, but that invisible string that constantly pulled them together was doing its best to draw her in.

"Thanks."

He rubbed the back of his head, giving off the same air of shyness he had last night. His eyes then took her in from head to toe and she silently reminded herself to say a thank you to Kristin. She thought this was probably the first time she had ever seen him speechless. She mercifully decided to end his torture.

"I brought your lunch. It's on the table." She took another step closer to him.

"Thanks," he said again and Sam laughed a little at his current state. It seemed as though this was the only statement he knew how to make today. For once in this insane push and pull they had created, Sam was the one who felt in charge.

"I'll fix us a plate," Sam said as she walked past him and toward the table only to hear him whisper a quiet "fuck" to himself when he noticed the back of her dress.

When Sam looked up to Kristin, she couldn't help but smirk. Kristin gave her a quick wink before turning back to talk with Micah.

"Do you want to stand and eat, or can we sit over there?" Sam gestured to some picnic tables off to the side. He still didn't voice a thing, but quickly nodded his head in a *yes* motion.. She took that as an okay for the tables and headed off in their direction.

"I like that dress," he said as he came up beside her.

"Thanks," Sam copied his simple reply from earlier as she began to dig into her meal.

"How long were you watching me?"

"Just a few minutes. Not long at all."

Callum nodded his head and Sam decided she liked having the upper hand for once. She wanted to toy with him a little more.

"Maybe you could give me one later."

His head snapped up and he choked a little on his shrimp. "What?"

"I think I want a tattoo," she said with an obvious pout on her face.

He looked her up and down. "Are you sure? That's a lifelong commitment. Maybe think about it for a few days. Don't just get caught up in the hype of the festival."

"Maybe Drew will do it. Actually, I saw another artist up front that had some good work. I could ask him to do it." She looked back up to him to realize her mission had been successful. His face was the picture of complete shock.

He turned more fully toward her. "First of all, if you ever do get a tattoo, it would be me and only me that's allowed to touch your skin. No one else. Got it?" He made eye contact with her again.

She chose to ignore his statement and the obvious flush of heat his words had caused. "This one girl had a big dolphin across her hip. Maybe I should do that?"

"A dolphin?" He stopped eating at her statement, looking utterly distraught. "You're playing me, right?"

"I don't know. What if I really want one?" His eyes widened just slightly as if telling her to cut it out. But she couldn't stop just yet. This was too much fun. "Fine. I won't get a dolphin. Maybe a turtle."

"Jesus Christ." He dropped the shrimp on the plate and shook his head back and forth. She decided to take away his misery.

"I'm kidding. I'm kidding. I honestly don't think I would ever get a tattoo. But if I ever did, I guess I would let you be the one who did it."

He visibly relaxed, slightly. "I kinda don't want you to get one."

"Why? You must have over fifty."

"I like your skin the way it is," he said, then added as an afterthought, "I don't want to cover up your freckles."

"Okay." She let him win the argument at that. It surprised her how much her stomach flipped when he made statements like that. She tried to ignore the mounting butterflies that were becoming a constant when around him, but it seemed like nothing could drown out the way he made her feel.

He paused then and turned to more fully face her. "Sam. If you really want a tattoo then get one. It's your body. You are beautiful no matter what. But let me be the one to do it, okay? I don't want anyone else touching you and messing up."

"I promise if I ever get one, I'll let you do it."

"And it won't be some gaudy dolphin on your hip," he urged.

She laughed. "And it won't be some gaudy dolphin on my hip."

He smirked and then leaned forward to kiss her cheek.

Sam wasn't sure what was more frozen. The permanent smile that always seemed to be etched on her face when he was around or her entire body from pure shock. He had just kissed her cheek in a very public place with far too many witnesses.

****

"You ready to head out?" Kristin asked, sliding onto the bench across from them and, thankfully, breaking the trance Sam was in.

"Where are y'all going?" Callum asked as he finished off the remainder of the fries.

"Around. She has never been to Charleston or seen the ocean, so I'm—"

"I'm sorry, what did you just say?" he asked Kristin, but then directed his gaze toward Sam. "You've never been to the beach?"

"No." For some reason, his question made her nervous. His utter amazement at the fact just intensified how different their lives had truly been. She had never once been on a vacation before. She guessed this trip would be considered her first.

Callum stared at her a little longer, probably debating if she was being serious or not. Sam was sure this was something he just couldn't fathom.

"I knew you had never been down here to Charleston, but I didn't realize you meant you'd never been to any beach *ever*." He shook his head a little, as if in utter disbelief. "Wait here." He jumped up and headed back over to the booth to speak with Drew and Micah.

Kristin turned to Sam. "You know, if he knew more about your past, he might not seem so shocked when you drop bombs like that."

"I know. I'll tell him. And for the record, you dropped that bomb. Not me," Sam corrected just before Callum walked back toward them.

"You care if I steal you for a while?" Callum looked at Sam and then back to Kristin. "I'm sure you are perfectly fine spending money solo for a few hours."

"Yeah. I don't care. As long as it's okay with you?" Kristin eyed Sam in question. "We can pick back up shopping tomorrow."

"Yeah. Yeah, I'll meet up with you later," Sam answered, not sure where this was leading, then looked back toward Callum. "What's the plan?"

"I want to show you something."

"What about the booth?"

"I've been doing most of the work so far. Micah and Drew are going to take over for the afternoon. Besides, two of our artists from the shops here are headed down, so they can help out if needed."

"Okay." Sam nodded, still not sure what he was planning.

"Alright. Let's go." He grabbed her hand and pulled her toward the street.

She expected him to let go at some point, but he never did, and they walked hand in hand all the way down King Street.

"Where are we going?"

"I have an Uber meeting us at The Market in a few minutes." Sam tried to keep her face as neutral as possible, not betraying the true level of excitement she was feeling. As they passed by a stand on the edge of the market and waited for the light to change, she saw another woman making those baskets out of grass and yanked on Callum's arm.

"I saw someone doing that earlier. They're making those things out of grass," she said in disbelief.

"It's called sweetgrass. They're all over Charleston." Sam let go of his hand to make her way toward the woman and her beautiful creations. She examined a few before picking up a gorgeous bowl with a ribbon-style wrap. She gasped in shock when she flipped it over and saw the price.

"Oh my god. Callum. That's, like, three hundred dollars," she whispered in shock.

"Yeah, they can get expensive." He chuckled at her reaction.

"They're really beautiful, though. Maybe I'll get one someday."

"Maybe so." He then grasped her hand again and leaned down to speak more closely to her ear. "Come on. The car should be here soon."

Chapter 42 - Sam

"Are you Callum?" the driver asked, and Callum nodded. "Headed to Folly Beach Pier?"

Callum tensed, then nodded once more just before they slid in. He then looked at Sam and flipped over her hand to start his finger drawings on her palm.

"We're going to the beach?" Sam asked with more excitement than she had intended.

"Yeah. I wanted it to be a surprise, but..." He shrugged his shoulders and indicated to the driver in the front. "It's about a thirty minute drive to Folly, but I didn't think you would mind."

"No, that's fine," she assured him.

The ride was comfortably silent, except for the few times Callum pointed out a special location or told her a story about some mischief he'd gotten into when he was younger. He held her hand in his the entire time, drawing small circles and designs with his thumb. When they finally pulled up to the pier, he thanked the driver and they headed off in the opposite direction of the water.

"This way," Callum tried to direct her to a shop across the street.

"What about the ocean?"

"As much as I would love to see you get into the ocean in that dress, I think we should find something more suitable." He winked.

"What? I was just going to wet my feet. I don't have any money to get anything, anyway."

"It's fine. I've got you. You can't go to the beach for the first time and expect to not actually get in." He pulled her across the street before she could argue.

She paused in the shop as she looked through the price tags on all the swimsuits. They were outrageously expensive.

"Callum. I can't let you pay for this. I promise, I just want to get my feet wet."

"What if I promise to let you pay me back. Will that make you feel better?"

Sam sighed. She wasn't going to win this argument. She also knew Callum would never let her pay him back.

They each grabbed a suit and one towel to share and then changed in the dressing room before heading for the register with tags in hand. He grabbed a bottle of sunscreen from beside the register while she fidgeted with the hem of her dress. Something about knowing he was going to see her in what basically amounted to socially acceptable underwear made her stomach turn to knots. The last time she'd been this undressed around him, he had turned her down.

Callum grabbed a bag to throw all their stuff in and they were on the other side of the street in a matter of minutes. He took her hand again just as they made their way across the dunes and the ocean came into view.

She didn't mean to, but she inadvertently froze at the sight. Something about seeing the ocean for the first time made her think about all the other things she had missed out on growing up. When she turned his way, he was looking down at her in what she could only describe as awe.

He rubbed his thumb across her bottom lip.

"Your cheeks are going to get pink. We'll stop and apply some sunscreen before we get in. You'll get blistered if you don't, and I intend to let you fully enjoy the beach."

He shook his head.

"Come on, let's find a spot." They made it a short way to the water before he dropped the bag and pulled off his shirt.

Sam stopped when they started to walk toward the water. "You're just going to leave it all there? What if someone takes it?" she asked as she looked around to survey the small groups of people spread across the sand.

"Sam, look around. Everyone's stuff is just strewn about. No one is worried about our extra clothes. I promise it will be fine." She looked back at the ocean and then back to him. "Go ahead. I can tell you are about to burst. Run on into the water."

"Come with me." She reached back out to him with a smile.

"Should we count to three or something?" he joked as she hesitated.

"Shut up." She rolled her eyes and yanked him with her.

It was much colder than she would have assumed, and she stopped running when it hit her knees.

"We aren't stopping yet, are we?"

Sam quickly turned to face him. "Are there sharks?"

He cocked his head to the side a little. "Well, it *is* the ocean."

"I mean, will they come this far in?"

"Sam, you'll be fine. If a shark comes, I'll let it take me first, okay? That way you get a running start," he said and then burst out laughing at her horrified expression. "Calm down. I promise you won't get attacked by a shark."

"What about jellyfish or sting rays?" All of a sudden, she began to think this wasn't the best idea.

"Oh dear lord," he said in exasperation and quickly picked her up as he ran further into the surf.

"Callum! Wait! What are you doing?" The water made its way up to his chest before he stopped.

"Can you swim?

"Yeah. But I think–"

"Good." He hadn't finished the word before he threw her in.

When she popped back up, he was standing still a few feet away with water up to his shoulders, trying to contain a laugh. She tried but couldn't quite touch the bottom so she frantically swam to him, wrapping her body around his under the pretense of keeping her afloat.

"You are such an ass." She swatted his shoulder with her free hand.

He looked back at her, grinning. "How was your first underwater ocean experience?"

"Sucky. It tasted like shit and I got thrown in, so I swallowed some."

"Sounds pretty normal to me."

"Ugh," Sam groaned.

She should unwrap herself from him. She knew how to float and swim, but her arms wouldn't release their hold. They bobbed up and down with the current for a minute.

"We should have bought a couple floats in that little shop." She finally made herself drop her arms in an attempt to swim away.

"No. I like holding onto you." He reached out to her before she could get too far away and brought them back together again. "It feels good, right?" he questioned and she nodded her agreement, not knowing if he meant the water or the feel of his body so close to hers.

"Do you remember your first time in the ocean?"

"God, no. I was probably a baby. We would come throughout the year. And we basically lived here during the summer. But I do have some early memories of riding a boogie board with my dad, and Connor getting in trouble for knocking me off one." He laughed a little to himself. "He was always the golden child, until Millie came along, so it was nice whenever he ended up getting in trouble instead of me. To tell you the truth, I think she was a surprise."

Sam smiled at his statement.

They took turns splashing and dunking each other and then jumping a little with each passing wave that crashed right before it reached them.

"Come on, let's go a little further past where they crest." At this, they both swam a few feet out. They were only separated for a moment before Callum brought them back together again.

She was in heaven. And it was all because of him. She leaned her head back letting the water thoroughly soak her hair and when she lifted back up she found that dizzy drunk smile on his face.

"What?" Sam asked with a nervous laugh.

"Just..." He paused and looked her over once more.

"Just...you."

"Me?" She wrapped her arms tighter around him.

He nodded his head before he bent down and brushed his nose against hers.

"I want you." His whisper tickled her skin.

"I want you." She brushed her lips against his.

"We should probably stop fighting this." His fingers brushed up her arm and cupped the back of her neck.

"Hmmm," she hummed in appreciation of all his little touches. "You've finally come to your senses."

"I think I've lost all my senses. That's the real problem." He smiled and she completely lost every ounce of self control she possessed.

She didn't even have to think before she crashed her lips against his. She just knew she needed to feel him—taste him. She needed him.

It wasn't sweet or gentle like when he'd kissed her the night before. This was rough and demanding, and from the moan that escaped his lips, she knew he was enjoying it. She felt his hands cup her ass and she lost her breath when he pulled her in tighter and she felt the evidence of exactly how much he was enjoying this. She involuntarily ground herself against him. The instant surge of electricity that moved through her was like nothing she had felt before. She bit down on his lip as she tightened her legs around him.

He quickly jerked back, his eyes glassy and his breaths coming in pants.

"I'm sorry," an absurd amount of embarrassment flooded her

system.

"No." He was still panting between each word. "Don't apologize. But"—he took another breath—"if we don't slow down, I'll end up in jail for taking you on a public beach."

She bit her own lip at the thought.

"I wouldn't hate it if you did." She smirked, then quickly clarified as she buried her flushed face in her hands, "Not the jail thing. I don't want you to go to jail. I just meant—"

"I know what you meant." He rubbed his cock between her legs and she let out a ragged moan as she laid her head on his shoulder.

They floated for a few minutes as each desperately tried to calm down. When she finally felt as if she could look at him again without completely losing her restraint, she tilted back and gave him a devious smile.

"Thank you for bringing me here." She'd expected something similar in return, yet all she got was a sad and confused expression.

"You've lived in South Carolina most of your life?" he questioned.

"Yeah."

"And you never visited the beach before?"

"No."

"I'm going to ask you this, but please don't take it the wrong way, okay?" Sam nodded as her heart rate picked up.

"You've never been to the beach despite living here most of your life. You work your ass off to make good money, but, from what Kristin says, you never spend it, and you have a scholarship that helps you pay for school. One that you're scared to death of losing if you make bad grades."

"That wasn't a question. That was more a list of observations."

He rolled his eyes as if to say *I'm getting there.*

"Did you grow up really poor or something?" *Oof.* Not exactly what she'd been expecting.

"Um, you could say that," she answered as honestly as she could.

"You know, you never give me a solid answer to anything I ask."

"I'm a very private person. You already know more about me than most everyone else."

"That's sad, Sam. I mean, don't get me wrong, I'm about as private as they get as well, but you still know more about me. I don't know if your parents are married or divorced. I don't even know your middle name."

"I don't know your middle name either."

"Franklin," he said a little shyly.

"No!" Sam laughed out loud. "Callum Franklin Barker. Sounds pretty fancy to me."

"Don't ever repeat that." He eyed her sternly and then laughed. "What's yours?"

"I don't have a middle name."

He looked at her like that was the oddest thing he had ever heard, and Sam knew there was another upcoming question. She continued before he could further pry, "Callum, listen. The life I had before I came here to college and met Kristin is very different from the life I'm now living. There are only a few people that know my past. If I told you, your entire view of me would change. I don't want that."

"Try me. I'm a big boy. I can handle it." Callum smirked and Sam recalled having once used that same line on him.

"That was my line."

"Well, now it's mine."

"Can I tell you later? I just want to enjoy the water without all that shit lingering over us."

"You promise to tell me later?" He pulled her into his chest with a pleading look.

"I promise." Sam nodded, knowing her little bubble would soon come crashing down, most likely followed by him wanting nothing further to do with her.

"Alright, let's see how far out you will go." He wiggled his eyebrows and let the current lead the way.

They spent most of the afternoon wading in the water. That was, until he was conned by two six year olds into giving them twenty dollars for their shovels and buckets. He then spent the next fifteen minutes building Sam her very first sand castle. She was still bursting out in laughter when he yanked out his phone and snagged a picture of her beside the half fallen down structure.

Chapter 43 - Callum

She fell asleep in the car.

Again.

And he loved it.

The only problem was that she hadn't fallen asleep until they were fifteen minutes into the drive, which meant he had only maybe another fifteen to watch her before they arrived back at the market.

He realized at that moment that he never wanted to stop watching her. He wanted to watch her as she slept and as she cooked. He wanted to be there when she studied and when she worked. He wanted to celebrate with her when she got into medical school and he wanted to be the person she called when she had a bad day. He wanted her to get mad at him for not folding the towels correctly and then he wanted to kiss her until she forgot exactly what it was he had done to make her mad in the first place. He wanted to bring her lunch and make her breakfast. He wanted to eat ice cream with her after dinner and walk along the beach with her at sunset.

He wanted every moment, every tear, every laugh, every smile. He wanted it all. And he would do whatever it took. He wanted nothing more than to be able to experience all of that with her.

Chapter 44 - Sam

Sam was awoken by a kiss to her forehead just as they pulled up next to The Market. She must have fallen asleep against his shoulder on the way back from the beach.

"We're here," Callum said as Sam tried to adjust her eyes to her surroundings.

The sun had now fully set, and Sam thought that night-time Charleston might have been an even better experience than day-time Charleston.

They made their way through the maze of streets she realized she would never fully know, but she didn't feel lost or nervous. She was holding Callum's hand and, for some reason, that small touch calmed everything in her. They hadn't had this much consistent physical contact yet and she felt as though she was being spoiled by his touch. Even if there was a small part of her that recognized it wouldn't last forever.

Being around Callum Barker was a constant flurry of trying to remain calm and enjoy the moment, but also waiting for the rug to be yanked from right beneath her feet. It took her a few minutes of dazed inner thoughts before she realized they were not, in fact, heading toward the festival.

"Where are we going?"

"I'm starving. I figured you might be, too." Callum squeezed her hand.

"What about the rest of the group? Should we see what they

want to do?"

"I spoke to them on the drive back while you were sleeping. The festival is closed for the day and they've all headed back to the house. They had to use my truck for equipment, so we'll have to Uber back later." Sam nodded in understanding. "Do you have any preference for dinner?"

"I don't even know what they have down here. So, I'm going to let you decide that one."

"Good, I already made a reservation at my favorite spot, anyway."

"Why did you ask, then?" Sam laughed, stopping to look at him in question.

He shrugged his shoulders before answering, "I don't know. I would have canceled the reservation if you wanted something different."

They continued to make their way down cobblestone streets lit only by street lamps and moonlight in comfortable silence until he slowed and then stopped near the water.

"This looks like a boat," Sam observed as they entered a restaurant called Fleet Landing.

He laughed a little at her statement. "That's kind of the point. Let's sit out by the water." Callum squeezed her hand as the hostess took them to an outside booth.

Sam looked over the menu, not really sure what to get. She could count on one hand the number of times she had ordered at a sit down restaurant that wasn't her place of employment. She felt a moment of tense anxiety flood her system at the thought of how much of an outsider she was.

"What do you want to eat?" he asked as the waitress walked up to get their order.

"Um, what you normally get is fine."

He furrowed his brow but didn't push the question. "We'll each get the shecrab soup to start, and then a bowl of shrimp and grits to share."

"Grits?" she questioned his order just as the waitress walked off. "That's breakfast food. It's almost nine at night."

"Trust me. It's delicious."

She turned back to watch the water and then felt his hand slide across the table and grab hers. He quickly started his finger drawings she had now come to expect. She stared at her hand and then back at him. She had come to love this feeling, and was beginning to realize it had now become a habit of his.

"Why do you do that?"

"Do what?" Callum asked.

"That." Sam looked between them to where his thumb was pressing into the center of her palm.

"Oh. I don't really know." He pulled back for a moment before Sam reached back out to grasp his hand.

"I didn't mean for you to stop. It feels good. It's just, it seems to be a habit of yours, so I figured there was a story behind it."

He shrugged his shoulders once more. "My mom used to do this whenever I was scared or had a nightmare. It had a calming effect, I guess."

"Do I look like I need to calm down?" Sam laughed at his insinuation.

Callum shook his head and smiled. "No. Well, actually, yes you do. You are way too stressed and stuck in your own little world most of the time. But that's not why I do it."

"Then why do you do it?"

"I like touching you." He cut his eyes back toward her again and they once again fell into a comfortable silence while they waited for their food to arrive.

The food was good. It was better than good. She had initially scrunched up her nose when the waitress placed the grits between them, but one bite later and she was officially hooked.

She stuffed herself beyond belief and, just when she thought it was over, Callum ordered a slice of the most perfect looking chocolate cake.

"I'm going to be sick." She shook her head as if she was going to be able to resist a bite.

Callum shrugged his shoulders, sliding the plate all the way over to his side of the table.

"That's fine. More for me." He scooped up a huge portion and exaggeratedly moaned in delight when he placed it in his mouth.

Sam hid her face with embarrassment when the two tables nearest to them jerked their heads upward in horror at the noise.

"Oh god! Sam! It's soooooo good!" he was practically screaming, and she knew exactly what he was doing. Now, at least five tables were looking in their direction.

"Callum!" she whisper-yelled across the table. "People are staring at us. Be quiet," she tried to admonish him, but her words came out in fits of laughter.

"I guess you are going to have to come over here and take it away from me." He patted the seat beside him.

He was good at this. Far too good at this. She quickly slipped from her side of the booth onto his and yanked the spoon out of his hand. She scooped up a portion just as large as he had and stuffed it in her mouth. It was so large she could barely chew it, and it was pure dumb luck that she didn't choke when they both burst out laughing.

"You're right, it is definitely delicious," Sam said once she was finally able to swallow. She looked up at him with a smile.

Callum paused and then looked down to her lips.

"You know. I bet it tastes even better when eaten off of you instead of a spoon." He smirked and then leaned down and kissed the edge of her lips. A slight suckle and lick later and she had turned to molten lava.

She let out a moan that had absolutely nothing to do with the deliciousness of the chocolate cake.

Onlookers be damned.

"Oh, yes. Definitely much better."

It was then that the waitress came over with the check. Still flustered, Sam jumped up and reached into her purse to grab her wallet.

"Don't. This one's on me." Callum leaned over the table and reached out to stop her movement, pushing her wallet back into her bag.

"Callum. You've already spent so much money on me today between the Uber and the swimsuit, and now dinner. Please let me pay for something."

"No. I got it."

Sam gave him a frown in response.

"You can buy my drinks later."

"Are we going for drinks?"

"Why not? It's not too late, and we're already downtown. Might as well get the full Charleston experience while you're here."

******

"You know, this is about the best non-date I think I've ever been on," Sam said as they began to criss-cross through the downtown streets of Charleston.

"Would you rather it be a date-date?" he questioned with a shy smile as they stepped up onto the sidewalk.

Sam stopped walking then and looked up at him. "I don't need a label. I just...I just need you."

Callum looked at Sam and stared into her eyes. "Maybe we can talk seriously about those labels later."

Before Sam could process what he'd just said, Callum quickly jerked his head back and forth and then pushed her backward into a wonderfully placed alcove.

"What are you doing?" She started to laugh.

"I'm going to kiss you. But I can't make any promises as to where my hands might end up, and I don't feel like sharing the sight of you with anyone else," Callum explained as he pushed her up against a brick wall.

It was too dark without the moonlight shining over them,

and she couldn't quite see his face. But she could feel every place where he touched her skin.

He was mapping out her body in agonizingly slow strokes. His fingertips trailed from her hands up her arms and then across her collar bones. They then made their way to her breasts and she stifled the moan that threatened to erupt. At some point, the purse that held their recently purchased swimsuits and towel became discarded on the ground.

He growled in delight when his hands wrapped around her to feel the smooth skin of her back. "I fucking love this dress." And then she felt his teeth scrape across her neck. "I can't wait to rip it off you."

Her breathing became ragged and he had yet to even kiss her.

"Tell me to stop," he breathed against her neck as his hands cupped her ass and pulled her closer.

"No."

"Sam...Once I have you, there is no going back." Their lips were so close she felt his statement as she heard it.

"I know. I don't want to go back. Take me home."

Chapter 45 - Sam

Sam was absolutely sure they would be kicked out of the Uber at any moment. They were a mess of hands and lips and fits of laughter. There was no way their driver didn't know exactly what they were up to.

With the cut of her dress, Callum had limited access to her breasts and she could tell it aggravated him beyond reason. At one point, she burst into a giggle when he slid his hand into the backless portion of her dress only to reach his fingers around to the front, desperate to touch her.

"You're going to rip it!"

"Kristin won't miss it," he said between peppering kisses to her neck.

"Mmhmm," she moaned out when his other hand slid further up her dress to cup her ass.

They were jolted apart by the rapid stop of the car. It was only then that Sam noticed they had made it all the way back to his home.

"You two have a great night!" the driver called out with a laugh as they ran up the front porch steps.

She could hear the others laughing from inside as Callum unlocked the front door. The laughter quickly turned to hushed whispers as they made their way through the foyer and toward the hall that held the guest suite. Kristin, Drew, and Micah all sat around the kitchen table, each with a drink in hand.

Sam chose not to look Kristin in the eye as they passed her. They could talk tomorrow about whatever happened in that room tonight.

But once they were inside and the door was shut and locked and a lamp flickered to life, she promptly lost her bravery.

"I need pajamas." She wanted to slap herself. It was the first thing that came to mind.

"Sam. I promise, you most definitely will not be needing pajamas," Callum said as he stalked toward her.

Her breathing increased and her heart felt as though it was about to flutter away.

"You're shaking." Callum reached out to intertwine his fingers with hers.

"I'm sorry."

"Don't apologize." His other hand reached up to pull her lip from her teeth. She had never realized she had that nervous tic until he'd pointed it out. "If you ever want me to stop, at any point whatsoever, just tell me, okay? Just say the word and we can stop. We can literally stop right now if you want to."

"I don't want to stop."

Callum smiled as he pulled her toward him. His legs hit the bed and then she was straddling him.

"I like this dress," he said, taking her in as he touched her bare back.

"You've said that a few times now," she said as she smirked at him.

"I just want to make sure you know. Because it's about to be in two pieces on the floor, so I'll never be able to compliment you in it again."

Sam laughed just as Callum's lips crashed into hers.

They were a tangle of frantic movement. First their shoes, then his shirt. She stopped then to admire his muscled abdomen. He sucked in a breath as she ran her fingers across the inked swirls that curved around his ribs. His belt and pants were next and then her dress somehow made it over her head, still in one piece.

"Do me a favor?"

"Anything."

"Don't give that back to Kristin. I have plans for it."

Her answer came out an octave lower than before. "Whatever you say, Mr. Barker."

His eyes shot to hers then, and before she could take her next breath, he had her flipped onto her back and under him.

"I have dreamed up so many fantasies of you. One of them definitely involves you calling me that while I fuck you on the office desk at Topline."

"Do you prefer Mr. Barker or sir?"

He growled in response as he freed her from the confines of her bra. He froze when her chest was finally bared to him.

"You are going to be the death of me."

And then he attacked.

Teeth and lips and swipes of his tongue were all that she could focus on. It was painful in the most delicious way. She had never had someone touch her—taste her—the way Callum did, and she hadn't known how sensitive she could be. She arched her back and muffled her scream in the decorative pillow when he bit down on her pebbled nipple.

"So damn responsive," Callum murmured against her skin.

Sam wasn't quite sure what to do other than let him take the lead. She moved when he moved and, as his hands explored a part of her, she let her hands explore that part of him.

"Fuck." His throaty whisper tickled her ear. "I've never wanted someone so badly before." He pulled back to look at her with a shy smile. "Don't hate me if I don't last very long the first time. I promise this will be an all night event." He laughed at his own embarrassment.

"Stop worrying and kiss me." She tried to pull him down to her. But he stayed rigid in his stance.

"I want this to be perfect for you. I want it to be the best sex you've ever had."

That caused her to smirk. She had a feeling any sex with him would most definitely be the best sex she *would* ever have.

"I promise it definitely will be." Then her nerves settled in her stomach.

What if she didn't make it good for him?

What if all this build up led to complete disappointment on his end?

"I might be bad at it," Sam quickly added.

Callum looked at her incredulously. "What?"

"I want it to be good for you, too, but I might be bad at it." Callum laughed.

"Sam, you could flop around like a fish out of water and it would still be the best sex of my life."

She wanted to laugh, but she was shaking again. Her whole body trembled under him. She just hoped he took that as excitement instead of nervous energy.

"Tell me what you like." He nuzzled her neck and his hands slipped down to cup her breasts and then her ass.

She was breathless at his touch. "This. You."

He laughed. "Good. I like you too. Very much. But tell me how you like to be touched." His hand slid down to the apex of her thigh and skimmed over the front of her thong.

She froze.

"Sam?"

"Um...I don't know."

Fuck. He was going to ask.

Callum stopped his movements, pulling back to look her in the eye and then scanned her entire body.

She initially felt nervous under his stare and turned her head to the side in order to avert his gaze. She instead found herself reflected in a nearby mirror hanging on the wall beside the bed. Her red curls were fanned out behind her, lit up in the light as if a golden crown laid atop her head. Her face was flushed and she could feel that her heartbeat was far too erratic. Her skin was a contradiction of goosebumps and shimmering sweat that had started to form. She was still mildly shaking.

Any other man might have assumed those were just the telltale signs of excited energy from being about to get laid. But, as usual, Callum somehow knew her far too well.

He slid back on his elbows to give her some space.

"Have you ever done this before?" he asked in a gentle voice.

She couldn't answer.

"Sam?" He kissed her cheek then ran his thumb across her jaw. "Have you ever touched yourself?"

She rolled her eyes. "Of course I have."

He smiled at her momentary frustration, then added, "Has anyone else ever touched you?"

"You're touching me now."

He cocked his head to the side in question. For just a second, he studied her face and she was desperate to know what thoughts were swirling through that head of his.

"Are you a virgin?"

She paused at his question. Mostly because she wasn't exactly sure what the correct answer was.

She cringed as she said, "I hate that word."

"What?" He furrowed his brow.

"Virginity isn't some magical line that has to be crossed. It's just a made-up word used to oppress women and make men feel like they're winning some coveted prize."

His eyes widened. "I didn't mean it like that." He quickly clarified. "I just wanted to know if you had done this before."

"Does it matter?"

"No." His answer was immediate.

She accepted his answer, then ran her hands along his muscled torso, "Please don't stop."

He tilted his head. "I'm not going to stop. But I need to know you absolutely want this."

"I want this." Her reply was urgent. "Please don't make it a thing."

"I'm not. I'm just...I just don't want to hurt you."

"You won't. I want this." Her hands cupped his face. "I have had plenty of experience with myself, and I know that I want this. Please don't stop."

"Are you on birth control?"

She frantically nodded. "Yes. And I take it religiously. Everyday at five o'clock."

He laughed and kissed her cheek again. "I wouldn't expect anything else."

His eyes moved from her swollen lips to his hand that now lingered over her chest to the apex of her thigh and then back to her eyes once more.

"Promise me that if you change your mind at any moment, or that if it's painful or...or, well, for anything, that you'll tell me to stop."

"I'm not changing my mind."

"Promise me," he implored.

"I promise."

"Okay. Can I borrow this?" He fingered the hair band on her wrist.

She slipped it off and handed it to him. "Yeah. Why?"

"I need to pull my hair back for what I'm going to do to you."

And then there was no more talking.

He brushed his lips against hers and then molded the hard lines of his body to the soft curves of hers. Only two very measly strips of fabric separated them now. He spent his time kissing and sucking and licking every part of her he could reach. Sam went from trembling in nervousness to practically shaking with desire.

He spent what felt like hours toying with her chest, and each time he bit down on her nipple she screamed out a muffled curse. When his mouth finally made it down her stomach, he paused to widen her legs and then she lost her breath when he ran his finger down the fabric of her thong.

"So wet," he murmured against her thigh.

And then his finger slipped under the fabric, and it was all she could do to keep her body from convulsing in release right then.

She had expected him to remove the thong, but he had her keep it on while he simultaneously tortured her over and under it, and for some reason, that was exactly what she needed. That small barrier somehow eased her into his touch without the crippling embarrassment she was afraid she would feel.

It wasn't until she was whimpering into the pillow that he leaned back and fully removed the last remaining piece of her clothing. He looked up at her then, a devilishly handsome, greedy smile plastered on his face, and she had to turn her head back into the pillow with a laugh.

And then his mouth was on her.

He lazily dragged his tongue upward once as if he wanted that first taste to last. His eyes met hers and then he was all over her, kissing and licking and sucking and sending her to the goddamn moon.

Her fingers became buried in his hair. She practically screamed with pleasure then, no longer concerned about what anyone else in the house could hear. They could go sleep out on the dock for all she cared.

He was truly devouring her.

And then he paused.

She was staring at the ceiling, chest heaving and not sure if she could manage the head tilt needed to look down at him.

"Sam?" he questioned as she felt his fingers tease her entrance.

"Please." She wasn't even sure if he heard it at first. It was a barely audible plea. But then his mouth was back on her and she felt his finger slowly sliding inside.

"Fuck," Callum breathed against her clit, causing her to buck up toward his chin. "You are so goddamn tight," he whispered.

She was panting now as she felt him slowly fucking her with his hands and mouth. She wasn't sure why she had waited so long to try this. It was absolutely amazing. She didn't think anything would ever feel better than this.

But then she lost all damn sense of self when he hooked his finger upward and found that sensitive spot she hadn't even known existed. A stream of unintelligible cries rang from her lips just as her world shattered around her.

"Good. Fucking. Girl."

******

She wasn't sure how much time had passed, but at some point she had gone from soaring through the sky to laying in Callum's arms.

Her heart was still racing, and she still wasn't quite sure what to do with her hands.

"Was that okay?" he whispered into her ear as he kissed her neck.

Still unable to form words, she nodded in response. It's not like she hadn't ever had an orgasm, she most definitely had. But that was on a completely new level.

His lips made a path across her jaw until they came up to her lips that were still parted in effort to suck in as much oxygen as she could.

She stalled when he finally kissed her.

"Is that what I taste like?" She scrunched up her nose.

Callum licked his lips. "Tastes like heaven to me."

"We aren't done yet, right?" She exhaled, realizing just how difficult it was to form words at that moment.

Callum laughed.

"Sam. I'll never be done with you." He leaned fully over her, then began to pepper her face with gentle kisses. "Do you want me to use a condom?"

She wanted to feel all of him. But getting pregnant was most definitely not in her plan. For a split second, she tried to calculate the chance of using one form or both. And then promptly shook her head, not believing she was about to try to figure out a math problem while the most gorgeous man alive was currently laying on top of her naked body.

"Sam?"

"Yes. Is that okay? I know I'm on the pill, but sometimes things don't work, and I want to–"

"Sam, it's fine," he said with a smile as he reached over to pull a strip out of the drawer beside them. Then he paused. "If at any time you want me to–"

"Callum," she quickly cut him off. "If you don't stop fucking talking and start fucking me, we are going to have a problem."

His grin was so large it covered his entire face. "Yes, ma'am."

He was somehow able to manage kissing her, feeling her up, and taking off his boxers all at the same time. When he finally pulled back, she knew there was nothing separating them.

Her hand snaked between them then. She wanted to feel him. She wanted to make him feel as much pleasure as he had given her. He let out a groan and her eyes shot downward when her hand wrapped around him.

There was absolutely no way this would work.

"Callum?" She wasn't sure what there was to say. But he saw her question in her wide-eyed expression.

"Don't worry. You expand, too." He rubbed his nose against hers and then pulled back. "But we can stop here."

"Absolutely not!" She leaned up, her face was less than an inch from his. "If you don't fuck me right now I will riot."

"Riot?" Callum laughed.

"Yes. And I will let someone that's *not* you give me an obnoxiously large dolphin tattoo." She raised her eyebrows in challenge.

"Well, that does it," he feigned frustration. "I didn't want to, but now I'm going to *have* to fuck you."

Sam shook her head in mock sadness. "It's a hard life."

"A very, very hard life, Sam," he said as he rubbed his cock against her clit.

She moaned at the contact.

He kissed her temple, put on the condom, and then whispered against her lips. "Spread your legs for me."

And she did.

For some reason, she had assumed she would be shaking with nerves at this part, but Callum had somehow eased away every fear and feeling of embarrassment she could have had.

"It might hurt in the beginning. Just let me know."

"Callum." She kissed him then. "Stop talking."

He smiled against her lips.

She felt him nudge her entrance and she inhaled in relief. She had never felt so empty before now.

He worked his way into her so very slowly, and she could tell the restraint he had was stretched almost to its breaking point.

"Relax, baby," he cooed into her ear.

She wanted to tell him to relax as well. He was the one tensed up and barely moving.

He then reached behind to lift her hips and that small movement was all it took. She sucked in a breath of air as he slid all the way in.

"Callum." His name was a prayer on her lips.

"Are you okay?" He was panting now. There was a dull ache, but it in no way lessened how full and amazing this sensation was.

"Yes. More than okay."

"You are going to have to give me a minute." He was frozen on top of her.

She felt a moment of fear that she had done something wrong. "Callum?"

"If I move right now, I'll come. I need to calm down."

She laughed and that little jolt of movement caused her to tense around him.

"Jesus fucking Christ, Sam!" He buried his face in the curve of her neck. "You feel so goddamn good, baby."

That was the second time he'd called her that. She decided she liked it very much.

"Tell me what to do?" She asked.

"Just...nothing. You are perfect. Absolutely perfect." He lifted his head then and slowly slid out of her.

He started slow.

Agonizingly slow.

Slow to the point that she could no longer take it. She reached behind him to grab his ass and pull him into her faster.

"You want more?" He pulled back from kissing her with excitement in his eyes.

"Please." She wasn't sure how she was even able to form the word at that point. It must have been sheer reflex, because her brain was definitely not functioning.

He slid out slowly one more time before hitching her leg higher in the air.

"I can't wait to hear you scream my name."

Suddenly, he became a beast. With every thrust, she was melting further into him. Her skin began to tingle, and that slow pulsing throb in her core turned almost violent. That emptiness was now gone, and in its place was a fullness she'd never known she needed. She arched her body into his with each movement, desperate for more.

She was so close. She was teetering on the edge with no idea how to fall.

Then he reached between them to rub her on that one spot where her entire world began and ended, and her vision splintered in two as she screamed out his name over and over again.

Her name was a breath on his lips as he fell apart directly after her.

****

They were a mess of sweat and heaving breaths.

At some point, he had pulled her on top of him, and she was lulled into a gentle calm by the sound of his beating heart. There was a sudden new ache within her that she had never known. The kind that she knew would only ever be satiated by him.

She played with the damp tendrils of his hair that were draped across his shoulder. And without notice, she burst out in the biggest grin against his chest.

"What?" Callum questioned, still trying to catch his breath.

"Is it normally that good?"

"No. It's not. At least it never has been for me." He pulled her up to him then and placed a gentle kiss on her temple and then her nose, each cheek and then finally her lips. Then he buried his hands in her hair. "Are you in pain?"

"Not really."

He pulled back then to look her more fully in the eye, silently pleading for her to tell the truth.

"I'm sore and kind of achy, but trust me when I tell you it is one hundred percent worth it, and I want to do it a million more times." Her face turned red with the admission.

He kissed the tip of her nose and shifted them slightly, cocooning his body around hers.

"Can we do that again?" She shuffled against him, feeling the definite soreness starting to set in and added, "Maybe a little later." She turned back to face him, an almost drunkenly giddy expression on her face.

Callum burst into a fit of laughter.

"Yeah, baby. We can do that again. But in the meantime, there are a lot of other things we can do that won't make you more sore."

"I think I would like that very much."

And then they did.

Chapter 46 - Sam

The sound of cars pulling away from the house was what finally dragged them back to reality. Callum reached over to check his phone and groaned when he noticed it was already past seven in the morning. They had spent more hours of the night wrapped up in each other than actually sleeping.

"Good morning," Sam whispered into his chest.

"Good morning." Callum's voice was deep, and groggy, and sexy as hell.

"Do you think they heard us?" Sam asked as she peeked open her eyes to note that the sun had now fully risen.

Callum laughed into her hair as he tightened his hold around her middle and pulled her to him.

"I think most of the eastern seaboard heard us last night."

Sam swatted his arm.

"I was not that loud."

Callum shook his head. "I didn't take you for a liar."

Sam narrowed her eyes at him. "You weren't very quiet, either," she countered.

"I never said I was."

Callum buried his face into her curls and took a deep breath. Then started to pull away.

"Don't go," Sam pleaded.

It may have been the fact that they were still in the dreamy morning state of a new day, not yet able to absorb the consequences of their actions, but Sam couldn't quite figure out why they ever fought so hard against this.

"I have to get to the festival."

"Don't go," Sam begged once more. This time, she slid her body more fully onto his and wrapped her legs around him.

Callum groaned into her neck then closed his eyes and peppered a thousand tender kisses to her face, barely touching his lips to her skin. His stubble was lightly tickling her cheeks and a sleepy smile spread across her face at the sensation. The feeling was maddening, and further deepened her need to feel him inside her again.

He quickly flipped them so he was now hovering above her.

"How are you feeling?" Callum asked as his hand snuck down between them to tease her bundle of nerves. She arched up into him.

"I'm just sore. But it's not bad." Her words were breathless.

They had taken a break after that first time last night. Half of Sam wanted to jump right back to doing it again. The other half, the half that was throbbing from what had just occurred, was begging her to wait. She let him lull her to sleep with the finger drawings he made on her back.

All in all, she was only able to hold out a short while after she woke up the second time to him stirring behind her before she convinced Callum to take her once more. After that round, he stepped out and grabbed a warm cloth that he then placed between her legs. It felt odd, and embarrassing, and magnificent all at the same time.

But now that ache was barely there and she wanted nothing more than for him to take her again.

"Please. I need you," she whined into his mouth.

"Do me a favor," he stated as he brought his lips back to hers.

"Anything." She could feel him hard and ready above her.

"If I ever turn you down, have me committed to the psych ward."

Sam laughed out loud.

And then her laughter was drowned out by the moans that

spilled from her lips.

****

Sam grabbed Callum's discarded shirt and threw it over her head. Callum had reluctantly left only minutes earlier, and Sam was teetering between the nervous energy that came following great sex and the nervousness of needing to talk with Kristin.

> **Sam**: Where are you?

> **Kristin**: In the kitchen.

> **Sam**: Has everyone else already gone?

> **Kristin**: Yeah, about an hour ago. Can you come out? Can I come in?

Sam had just made it through the door when she saw Kristin's excited face peer around the corner.

"So," Kristin stated.

"So," Sam repeated. She couldn't hide her smile.

Kristin's response was a bulging of her eyes as she silently pleaded for information.

"Come on, Sam. Talk to me."

"What do you want me to say?" Sam buried her face in her hands in embarrassment.

"I want you to tell me it was the best sex of your life."

"Kristin."

Kristin narrowed her eyes.

"Okay, yes. I have a feeling nothing could ever top how it feels with him."

Sam sighed, then burst out laughing at the deafening squeal that came from Kristin.

"Come on. Go get a bathing suit on and meet me outside by the pool. We have lots to discuss."

****

The morning went by in a blur. Kristin threw a myriad of questions at her as they lounged.

"How was it?"

"Was he rough or sweet?"

"Did he talk dirty?"

"How much did you actually sleep?"

"How big is he?"

"How many times did you come?"

On and on it went. But Sam didn't mind. It was the first time in which she'd ever felt that giddy excitement making her want to gush all about him. She felt ridiculous, and she felt amazing. They had officially crossed that line, and she knew she never wanted to go back.

It was noon by the time they were headed down King, and Kristin had them going in and out of almost every store they passed. This wasn't Sam's first shopping trip with Kristin, so she was well aware of the dent that girl could put on her parents' credit card. She sure did enjoy the fruits of the upbringing she seemed to loathe so much.

Sam also didn't hate the three outfits she had let Kristin talk her into buying, either.

"We need to have their lunch at the booth by one, which means we have just enough time to grab you something for tonight before we pick up the food."

"What's tonight?" Sam questioned.

"Tonight is when you pull out a ridiculously sexy outfit that brings that man to his knees."

"He was already on his knees last night," Sam said, blushing.

"Fair enough. That just means we need to find the most

perfect lingerie there is," Kristin said as she pulled Sam into a shop with barely clothed mannequins lining the windows.

Sam had never seen such naughty attire in real life. She had also never imagined a price could be so high for such little product.

Sam had no idea what to pick. All she knew was she wore a medium in underwear and a 32B in bras. The most luxurious one she owned was a simple pink set from Victoria's Secret that had just a hint of lace across the band. That set was nothing like what she was now looking through.

"Here, try this one on?" Kristin handed her a black lace set that left little to the imagination.

Sam groaned in embarrassment as she stalked off to the dressing room.

It had a tie over the breast cup that, when undone, caused it to pop open, revealing her nipple inside. The bottom piece wasn't a bottom at all. It looped around her ass on the sides, leaving her completely bare. She then realized the purpose of this particular piece was that it was left on during the main event.

"Can I see?" Kristin called out from the other side of the door.

"No you cannot see!" Sam immediately tried to cover herself, afraid Kristin would somehow burst the door open any minute. "It literally doesn't cover anything. Everything is on display."

"Does it fit?"

"Yeah?"

"That's perfect!" Kristin called out and then informed the sales lady she wanted one in each color and to go ahead and grab the other similar sets in Sam's size as well.

By the time Sam made it out of the dressing room, fully clothed, Kristin was paying the massive bill that was more than Sam's half of the monthly rent.

"Kristin!"

"Listen. I am not taking no for an answer, okay? And if you absolutely hate them, then just give them back to me. I'm sure

Micah won't mind." Kristin winked.

******

They had food in hand and were walking up to the booth when Sam stopped in her tracks. Callum was working on a woman's ankle and another, she assumed the woman's friend, was standing over them, inspecting the work.

It wasn't the fact that he was working on another woman, but the fact that the friend had her hand placed on Callum's shoulder and continued to lean down and whisper things in his ear. At one point, she even reached back to twist a tendril of his hair in her hands.

Sam had never been so mad.

"He keeps shrugging her off," Kristin said from beside Sam.

"What?"

"I see what made you stop, but look at Callum," Kristin urged.

She was right.

Every few seconds, Callum would adjust his position, thus causing the woman's hand to fall from him.

"Don't let your head go somewhere it doesn't need to go."

"I don't like this."

"Sam. He's brushing her off. He's just trying to be professional."

"No, not that," Sam quickly amended. "I don't like how pissed I just got. For a second there, I had an image in my head of walking right up to her and punching her in the face, all because she touched a guy I'm not even dating."

Kristin laughed then.

"Hormones are a funny thing."

Sam gave her the side eye.

"And I'm pretty sure y'all are dating, even if you haven't given it the label yet."

Ignoring that until she talked more about it with Callum, Sam asked, "What should I do?"

"Walk up to your man and give him a kiss."

"I'm not doing that. We're in public!"

"Sam. Just walk up to him. I'm sure it will work itself out."

Once again, Kristin was right.

Callum was standing, having finished his design, and was gathering some type of salve to cover it. As soon as his eyes found hers, he immediately froze. He discarded the container, nodded at Micah to take over with that and the bandage and met Sam halfway.

"Hey, baby."

It was loud enough that she knew everyone in the immediate area could hear. She blushed.

"You don't have to call me that."

"What if I want to call you that?"

She pretended to mull it over. "I'll accept it."

"Any names you picked out for me?" His eyes rose in excitement.

"Asshole," she deadpanned.

For just a second, his features went taut and then he saw the teasing in her eyes.

"But you're *my* asshole, and that's all that matters," she quickly added.

His grin covered his whole face, and he pulled her in for a kiss.

******

It only took an hour for Sam to figure out his routine. By the time he finished the third guy, Sam had the salve ready with the correct sized bandage to cover it with. She also became rather adept at taking people's payments.

It was their most lucrative day. Callum had done seven tattoos in all, and had scheduled half as many larger projects for later in the month. He may have also snuck in a kiss between each client, and Sam decided that was her most favorite part. By the time they had everything packed up in the trucks, she was no longer embarrassed that Drew or Micah, or everyone else for that matter, were witnesses.

Chapter 47 - Sam

Sam and Kristin had basically locked themselves in Sam's original room as they readied themselves for dinner. It took almost half an hour, but Kristin convinced Sam that, instead of wearing regular underwear, she most definitely had to wear the new lingerie set under the black dress Kristin had bought for her.

"This is ridiculous." Sam shifted the dress around her waist.

"No, it's not."

"We are all going to dinner. You want me to sit in this thing for the entire meal? He won't even know I have it on. I can just put it on when we get back home." For some reason, Sam was whisper-yelling which made no sense, because they were in a room by themselves.

"Sam. Go tease him with a peek of it, and I promise it will be enough to drive him nuts the entire night."

"You want me to go flash him?"

"Yes!"

Sam groaned more in embarrassment than frustration. Never in her life had she worn anything other than cheap cotton underwear. Tonight, what she had on wasn't cheap or cotton, nor did it, if she was being honest, even pass as real underwear. She should be in a panic. The only thing giving her an ounce of that needed confidence was that fact that she looked like a goddess in that dress.

She stared in the mirror for a moment. She was wearing a

fitted black cocktail dress that barely covered her ass, was sleeveless, and had cut outs around her waist. The gold strappy heels Kristin paired with it were massively high. So high, in fact, that she knew her hand would be glued to Callum's arm for assistance with balance alone.

She had worn dresses like this before. Her freshman year had seen its fill of scantily clad outfits, drunken parties, and cute boys. She wasn't an idiot. She knew how beautiful she was, and there had been a time, a few years ago, when she'd tried to use that to her advantage. That was, until she'd made it almost halfway through freshman year and decided to make a major mindset adjustment.

It was shortly before Thanksgiving break of freshman year. She'd known she would be sent with a random family she didn't know for the week while everyone else was spending time with those who truly mattered. She had just made a B on a stupid mathematical exam and she had seen Christian the previous night with his hand practically up another's girls skirt at a party.

She'd realized then what she had been doing. She had been spending her measly income on buying things to impress a boy who didn't want her.

For some reason it was that sight, that realization of what she had been doing, that had caused her to bag up every sexy dress or outfit she'd owned and take it to a local donation center. She'd decided that she wanted to impress him with who she was, not what she wore. She'd wanted him to love her for how she thought and what she said, not for how easily he could get to where he wanted. That was the night she'd decided to love Christian from afar; to stop focusing on what he wanted in a girl and start focusing on who she wanted to be as a person.

She stared down at the dress one more time. In a way, it reminded her of those nights two years ago, but, in a way, it didn't.

Tonight felt different. Tonight, she wasn't desperate to make someone want her, she was desperate to take control of her own sexuality for the first time in her life.

She blushed the entire way downstairs. Her new underwear was missing that very important strip of fabric down the middle, and she felt every burst of air as she moved.

She didn't know why, but she knocked on his bedroom door. She was being ridiculous. They'd had sex in the room less than twenty-four hours earlier and she was absolutely positive she would be staying in there that night as well. And it wasn't like she hadn't seen him completely naked.

When he opened the door, he gave her a quizzical look.

"You don't have to knock."

"I know. I don't know why I–"

"Is that new?" Callum quickly cut her off as he reached out to grab her waist exactly where the cut outs were. His fingers felt like fire against her skin.

"Yes."

"I like it."

"Thank you."

It was then that she noticed his outfit. Black dress pants and black shoes, a black dress shirt with the top two buttons left open and the sleeves rolled up his forearms, leaving a perfect view of his tattoos. His long hair was pulled back into a perfectly effortless messy bun.

"I like your outfit as well." Her voice was an octave higher than usual and she watched as Callum's smile spread across his face at her reaction.

"I'm glad you like it. I hope you plan on taking it off of me later."

Sam blushed and then leaned up against the wall as she tried to steady her breathing. She couldn't hold in the giggle that started to erupt. That she always felt the urge to laugh at the most inopportune times was something she absolutely loathed about herself.

He was doing exactly what she was supposed to be doing.

She had come down here to tease him with her new, barely there strips of lace, not to be the one who was basically drooling at the mouth.

Sam groaned. "I'm not very good at this."

"Good at what?" Callum furrowed his brow and crossed his arms over his chest, causing the muscles of his biceps to bulge out. She had to shake her head to refocus on the task at hand. She would *not* get lost in staring at his arms.

"This whole thing where I..." Sam paused and started to nervously laugh once again. "You know, where the girl teases the boy."

"What does that mean?" Callum tilted his head to the side.

"I bought new underwear," the words came out in a rush.

That piqued his interest.

"But I was supposed to come down here and be sexy or something and tease you with them, but I'm not good at that. I can't even tell you the last time I wore a dress this tight or heels this high." Now she was rambling. "I'm going to have to hold onto you just so I don't fall flat on my face." She turned then, ready to bolt from the room. She froze when Callum reached out to grab her arm.

"Sam?"

She turned back to face him. Her cheeks now felt almost as red as her hair.

"You look beautiful in that dress."

"Thank you."

"But you want to know what my absolute favorite outfit you have is?"

"I'm scared to ask." She crossed her arms over her chest and nervously sifted from one foot to the other.

"That first night you showed up at my house."

"I don't even know what I was wearing." She tried to quickly run through her memory of that night, but could only recall how frustrated he made her.

"Jeans and a t-shirt."

"That's not sexy at all."

"You had on this green shirt that said *better luck next time*; it looked like it was left over from St. Patrick's day or something. But it matched your eyes. And it made your freckles stand out. You didn't have on a lick of make-up and your hair was pulled into a bun. I decided right then that you were the most beautiful woman I had ever seen."

"Callum." She wasn't sure why, but she felt the urge to blink away the wetness that gathered in her eyes.

"I don't care what you wear. I care about you." He reached out and grabbed her hand, turned it upward and kissed her palm. "But..." He gave her a devilish little grin and chuckled against her hand before slowly dropping it to her side. "I'm also very attracted to women, and the woman I like has informed me that she purchased some new sexy underwear that's intended purpose is to drive me wild."

"This is true."

"Are you wearing them right now?"

"Yes." For some reason, she was already breathless.

Callum let go of her arm, slowly stalked backward and away from her, and then sat on the edge of the bed. She wasn't sure what he was waiting for.

He pointed to the bottom of her dress and flicked his finger upward, indicating for her to shimmy the hem high enough for him to see.

It took her a moment to build up the courage to show him.

It was not the middle of the night.

They were completely and totally sober.

This was not a dimly lit room.

Everything would be on display.

"Sam. I'm waiting." Callum raised his eyebrows.

She couldn't look him in the eye. Instead, she focused on the swirling design of the rug as she moved. Her fingers shook slightly as she grabbed the hem and slowly pulled the fitted dress upward.

She heard his very audible gasp just as she felt that familiar burst of air. The noise caused her gaze to flit to him.

Callum licked his lips and then began exhibiting an odd breathing pattern.

"You're wearing that? Tonight?"

"That's the plan." She smiled at her sudden burst of bravery.

He looked down at his watch. "We are supposed to be leaving in five minutes."

Sam nodded.

"We are going to miss our reservation."

Sam laughed.

"No." Sam dropped the hem, letting it fall back down to her thighs. "We are not missing it."

"Sam," Callum growled as he stood and walked the few steps toward her.

"Callum." Sam pushed her finger into his chest, keeping them separated by only a foot.

"Don't make me wait. Please let me touch you." He was begging.

She was surprised at the amount of bravery that flooded her system. "I'm glad you like them. I hope you plan on taking them off of me later."

He growled in frustration as she turned to walk out the room.

****

The car ride into town was torturous. They had rented an Uber, knowing they would all be far too wasted to safely drive back by the end of the night. Callum was quieter than normal. He kept his hand on Sam's leg and each time she looked over at him, she found his gaze firmly planted on the apex of her thighs.

Maybe she did enjoy this teasing thing after all.

"Where are we eating?" Sam asked anyone in the van.

"S.N.O.B." Drew quickly replied.

"We're eating somewhere named snob?" She scrunched up

her nose.

"It's short for Slightly North of Broad," Callum amended.

"What kind of food does it have?" Sam was surprised the question came out as smoothly as it did. With Drew in the front, and Micah and Kristin in the row behind them, it meant Callum was not so sneakily running his hand up her thigh and getting that much closer to where there was nothing but *her* on display.

"It's fine dining. Takes weeks to get a reservation. I set this up the same night I booked our spot for the festival. I had a feeling we would need somewhere to celebrate." Drew added with a smile.

That caused Sam to snap to attention. She tilted her head backward just enough to catch Kristin's gaze.

Fine. Dining.

That was just another way to say expensive. That meant there were probably various utensils and glasses, and she was going to look like an idiot.

It was one thing to work at Topline where all she had to do was keep quiet, take orders and refill drinks. It was an entirely different thing to be on the opposite end of that scenario.

She felt her phone buzz just before the panic set in.

> **Kristin**: Calm down.
> The boys are paying.
> It's not like a five
> course meal kind of fine
> dining. Sit next to me.
> You will be fine.

Sam quickly hid the phone before Callum could read the message. In all honesty, he probably hadn't even paid it any attention. He was too busy staring at the one place she desperately wanted him to be.

It was only a few short moments before they were getting out of the car and walking into the restaurant. It was definitely fine dining and it was beautiful.

"What kind of stuff do they have on the menu?" Sam questioned Callum, but he just shrugged.

"They use fresh ingredients, so the menu frequently changes. Just depends on what they have that day." He added without removing his gaze.

Sam nodded then took a breath. It was one of *those* kinds of restaurants.

It wasn't a long wait, and by the time they were seated at a table, Sam was practically hyperventilating.

"Are you okay?" Callum questioned, whispering so only Sam could hear.

"Callum. I don't think I can afford this," Sam whispered back.

"In case you forget, the guy you're dating just made an astronomical amount of money over the last few days, so you don't need to worry about it. Let me spoil you a little bit."

"The guy I'm dating?" Her eyebrows rose in surprise and the butterflies in her stomach were doing barrel rolls.

"Yes. The guy you're dating." All of a sudden, his rather cocky demeanor turned nervous, and she could tell he was worried he had crossed a line.

She leaned in then, a devilish smile playing on her lips and brushed her nose against his ear. "I wasn't aware Drew and I were dating."

"Samantha Williams." Callum squeezed her thigh in mock frustration. It was the first time he had ever said her full name, and she was surprised by how much she liked it when he did.

She shrugged her shoulders with a smirk. "*He* never asked me out."

"Does *he* need to?"

"Yes. *He* does."

Callum quirked a brow at her. "I thought you didn't need labels?"

Sam paused. She had definitely said that exact phrase the night before. "I don't *need* them. But I *want* this one."

"Can you two lay off each other for just a few hours?" Drew asked.

"You're just jealous Melanie is stuck on weekend rotations and couldn't make it." Micah stated with a laugh.

"Yeah yeah yeah." Drew rolled his eyes.

"Who's Melanie?" Sam asked as they were handed the menus. It took considerable effort to pull her gaze from Callum.

"Drew's girlfriend. She's a nurse at the children's hospital down here. Got stuck on a full weekend rotation, so we won't be seeing her this trip," Micah answered.

"I was wondering if we were going to meet up with Mel," Kristin said as she and Micah decided on which appetizer they wanted.

Sam sucked in a breath when she saw the prices listed next to the items. Most entrees were around fifty dollars a piece, if not more, and that didn't even count the sides. Once you added in drinks and dessert, each person would most likely be spending well over a hundred.

She looked around to find a plethora of people she didn't fit in with. These were the exact people she'd always wanted to impress. She didn't know what half the items on the menu were. She didn't know how to properly pronounce her order. She didn't know what wine paired with what. She didn't want to have a water glass, a wine glass, and a sweet tea glass. She didn't belong here.

"Callum?"

He looked at her then. His excited and somewhat devilish smile from staring at the spot between her legs quickly turned down.

"Are you uncomfortable?" he whispered into her ear.

"It's just—" She once again looked around, trying to find the words to explain it. She didn't want to admit it out loud. She was a fucking foster kid. She could usually adapt to any situation thrown her way. But for some reason this beautiful room with the chandeliers and the beautifully dressed people and the thousand dollar bottles of wine was too much.

Callum squeezed her hand then and reached into his back pocket to pull out a card. He tossed it between Micah and Drew.

"Get whatever you want. Doesn't matter the cost. Put it on my business card."

"Where are you two going?" Micah asked in confusion. Kristin just had a devious smirk on her face.

"Text me when you all are done and we'll meet you at the bar."

He grabbed Sam's hand and pulled her toward the front of the restaurant before anyone else could utter another word.

Chapter 48- Sam

"What are we doing?" Sam asked while being gently pulled past the numerous people still waiting outside for a table.

"You weren't comfortable there," Callum stated as if the answer was obvious.

"Drew said that place was hard to get into."

"It is." Callum nodded.

She stopped then.

"Callum. Why did we leave?"

"I refuse to be in any situation in which you are not one hundred percent at ease. I know another place you might like better, and I thought we could go there instead. We can meet up with them for a drink after we eat."

"You know..." She leaned up then, grabbed his cheeks, and placed a very deep kiss on his lips. "You are damn near perfect."

He pulled her back in and let his kiss linger on her lips.

She could get drunk on him.

That realization brought with it a slight epiphany. Maybe she had always been able to adapt to any situation because she didn't have the option *not* to. Now, with Callum, she felt safe enough to allow herself not to adapt. She didn't *have* to put up with situations she didn't want to be in. The thought sent warmth through her body and she suddenly longed for more.

"I'm not very hungry. Not for food, at least," she whispered against his lips. His eyes darkened. "We could probably make it all the way back to the house, have a little fun, and then make it back here all before drinks."

"Sam, if I undress you right now, there won't be drinks. There won't be anything for at least another twelve to twenty-four hours. It may even take me weeks to do everything I want to you."

"I can't wait," she muttered against his chest.

And then her stomach growled.

"Not hungry, huh?" He lifted a brow at her.

"I lied." She crossed her arms in frustration and wanted to yell at her stupid stomach for ruining the moment.

"How are you with walking in those heels?"

"It doesn't hurt. Yet," she replied.

"If they start to hurt, let me know."

"Okay."

And then they started walking. It was only five minutes before they ended up at a pizzeria.

"Dianne's may be your favorite, but I prefer Pizzeria Di Giovanni."

"That sounds fancy." Sam smiled.

"It's not. But it's absolutely delicious."

They walked inside and Sam laughed. "We're far too dressed up for this place."

Callum raised an eyebrow. "Actually, if I remember correctly, you are not dressed up at all. You are missing a very vital part of your outfit."

"Don't act like you don't love it."

"I definitely love it." He gave her a devilish grin. "I'll love it even more once you let me play with you in them."

Sam shook her head in embarrassment as they made their way up to the counter.

"What do you want?" Callum asked.

"Two slices of pepperoni and a coke."

"So boring." Callum rolled his eyes. "Two slices of chicken

and pineapple and a beer."

"I remember the pineapple. But chicken? On a pizza?"

"Don't hate on the most delicious pizza known to man."

Sam scrunched up her nose and then grabbed his arm when he pulled out his wallet.

"Callum?"

"Yeah."

"Let me pay this time. Please?"

He waited for just a moment before he slid his wallet back into his pocket. "Just this once. Okay."

"Yes, sir." She over emphasized the words and swore she saw Callum's eyes darken a shade.

****

"You are going to ruin your clothes!" Sam laughed out loud as Callum tilted his head back in order to catch all the falling cheese and sauce from the slice he had positioned in the air.

He shrugged his shoulders just as a splatter of red sauce hit his collar. "It's a black shirt."

Sam laughed again.

She was happy.

Despite all that had happened over the last week. Despite losing a portion of her funding, and going through all the emotions that came along with that. Despite how Christian basically left her to fend for herself after the meeting. Despite her self-thrown pity party that had occurred the following days.

Sam was happy.

"Just try it." Callum pinched off a portion of his slice with both pineapple and chicken on top.

"I don't know. It just feels wrong." Sam scrunched up her nose.

He lowered his voice. "If you try this, I promise to spend an hour with my face between your legs tonight."

Sam cut her eyes upward then smirked. "Callum. Let's be honest. You are going to spend *at least* an hour with your face between my legs no matter what I do."

He narrowed his eyes. "This is true."

"But I guess I'll try it anyway." She reached out to snag the piece from his grasp and popped it into her mouth.

She moaned in delight. Callum's eyes darkened.

"You're right. This is good." She moaned once more. "But it still doesn't beat pepperoni." She slowly licked each one of her fingers.

"Sam." Her name was a blatant warning on his lips.

He wiped his fingers with a napkin and suddenly got up and came to her side of the booth.

"Pepperoni is still better," she repeated with a smile. "Do you want a piece of mine?" Sam questioned as he slid in beside her,

"I want a piece of you," he murmured into her hair and ran his fingertips across the skin of her thigh.

"Callum." Her eyes went wide when his hand slipped under the hem to skirt the side of the barely there fabric.

"I can't stop thinking about you in this." He teased the side of the fabric.

"It's supposed to be a treat for later. You are being bad." She was breathless.

"I was never very good with patience. And besides, I'm always bad."

Sam swallowed and stifled a moan when his fingers reached the area of missing material. He nuzzled into her neck.

"Are you always this wet for me, baby?"

She couldn't answer. She was far too focused on not making any inappropriate noises that might gain the attention of those nearby.

He quickly removed his hand, licked his fingers, and went back to eating his pizza as if nothing had happened.

Kristin was right. And wrong. This underwear definitely did it's intended job on Callum, but his reaction was also now making *her* needy and breathless. By the time they finished the pizza, she could barely think straight. She was going to kill Kristin.

******

The walk from the pizzeria to the bar was even more torturous.

Callum never once let go of her. Either his hand was holding hers or his fingers were trailing up and down her arm. If he didn't stop, she was going to make him take her up against the wall of a side street, onlookers be damned.

By the time they made it to the bar, Kristin, Micah, and Drew were waiting outside.

"Where did you two run off to?" Drew questioned.

"Pizza," Callum answered matter-of-factly as they walked inside.

The bar was darker than she'd been expecting, with neon strobe lights shining through the air. The DJ was on a stage, and there were girls dancing in cages hanging from the ceiling above them. It was loud, and exciting, and somewhere she would normally never go.

"This place is insane!" Sam exclaimed in excitement as she looked up to Callum.

He brought his arm around her shoulders and pulled her in close as they made their way through the chaotic mess of half-drunken dancers.

It was so loud, there was no way Sam would be able to hear Kristin, who was currently yelling something to her from the other side of Micah.

Sam threw her hands up in the air with a wide-eyed laugh and Kristin rolled her eyes before turning back to Micah.

Callum waved the bartender over. "Sazerac and Negroni," he requested, and Sam burst out laughing.

"Are you serious?" she asked incredulously, still basically yelling in order to make sure he could hear her.

He leaned down to her ear. "What? Those are the two drinks

that kind of brought us together, you know."

Sam shook her head in disbelief. She truly couldn't believe he actually remembered what they were called.

"I was sure we would never speak again after that night," Sam admitted to him as the bartender handed over their drinks. She took a tentative sip. "Ew. This is disgusting," she said as she pushed hers back toward Callum.

He laughed. "I figured you wouldn't like them. What drink do you want?" Callum asked.

"I'll take a beer. Michelob Ultra."

Callum quickly ordered one for her. She swirled her stool toward the dance floor to take in the mayhem occurring before her.

"Full disclosure," Callum said as he leaned in toward Sam. "I was pretty much sucked in by the end of that night."

"What?" She had no idea what he was referring to.

He downed one of the cocktails in just a few sips. "I saw you earlier in the night waiting tables. I decided well before you asked me for those drinks that I wanted you. Well, I didn't know you yet, but I at least knew I wanted to grab your ass." He wiggled his eyebrows as Sam burst out laughing.

"Oh my God, are you already buzzed?"

"Maybe." His smile was so infectious she couldn't help but reciprocate it. She knew he'd had two beers at the pizza shop, and he and Drew had also busted open some ridiculously fancy bottle of scotch at the house before they'd left. She kind of liked the tipsy smile he now had on display.

"Did it live up to your expectations?" She thought she might as well continue this line of questioning, knowing he was getting drunk and thus probably more willing to talk.

"Your ass?" he questioned and Sam nodded. "Far exceeded anything I had imagined."

Sam laughed so hard she choked a little on her beer.

"Jeez. How have I been able to resist you when you talk like that? True Casanova right here."

She didn't expect him to continue talking, so she was surprised when he divulged further, "When you walked into our apartment that next week, I almost shat myself. I was literally contemplating how to talk to you during our next shift together just minutes before and then you just walk in my house."

She laughed and then that smile turned down as she recalled exactly how he had treated her that first night. "Why were you so mean to me that night then?"

He shrugged. That beautiful smile turned into an apologetic smirk. "I don't know. I didn't mean to be. It's kind of my default." He reached out and interlocked their fingers. "I'm sorry. I'm truly sorry for the things I said and how I acted. I hope you know now that that is not me. That's not the real me. That was just this persona I put on because I'm a dick and don't know how to deal with emotions."

"I know that's not you."

"Good." He squeezed her hand. "I promise to never, ever, ever act like that again."

She wanted his smile to return.

"Did you plan the whole going to Social thing with me?"

He shook his head with a laugh. "Nope. That, my dear"—he tilted his head down and his glassy eyes became even clearer in the light—"was fate."

Sam laughed again. "You want some water next?" she asked as he waved the bartender over.

"Why ruin the fun?"

"You are much more talkative when you've had a few drinks. I should have been plying you with them for the last few weeks."

"But not as forthcoming as you are when you talk in your sleep." He wiggled his eyebrows again, making her cheeks turn red.

Chapter 49 - Sam

The night was a blur of flirting, laughing, shots, and a now drunk Kristin pulling her out onto the dance floor just as Callum walked off to the bathroom.

Sam laughed as she and Kristin danced. Well, Sam danced, Kristin just kind of did her best not to fall. Sam made sure to have a steadying hand around her best friend's waist.

"Oh my God! Sam!" Kristin yelled far too loudly into Sam's ear as they moved to the music.

"What?"

"It's so perfect! You and Callum. Me and Micah. Our kids will get married and we can officially be related!"

Sam burst into a fit of laughter at her friend's level of drunken ridiculousness. "Kristin! Calm down."

Kristin grabbed Sam's face and placed a kiss on her cheek. "You are my bestest-estest-estest friend in the whole wide world!" Kristin's words were more than slurred.

Sam laughed and pulled her into a hug. "You are my bestest-estest-estest friend, too."

And then she slowly guided a very drunk Kristin off the dance floor and back to waiting Callum and Micah.

"I think it's time for this one to head home," Sam said as Kristin basically fell into Micah's arms.

"I can't take you anywhere, woman," Micah called out and

then kissed Kristin on the cheek. "I'll call an Uber. Do we need a van for all five of us, or are y'all staying out?"

"We haven't even danced yet," Callum said into Sam's ear.

"Just for y'all," Sam replied as she hugged Kristin and helped Micah get her to the front entrance. Drew would have to help him get her inside the house. They were lucky there was an elevator.

By the time she made it back to Callum, he was standing on the edge of the dance floor. She stood in front of him and he wrapped his arms around her from behind.

"I'm not a good dancer." She leaned back to see his face.

"I don't believe you. Anyone with hips and an ass like this"—he grabbed her for extra emphasis—"has got to have good moves."

She twisted around to face him, still encircled within his arms. When the next song started playing, he pulled her as close as possible, further moving them into the middle of the crowd. The beat of the music was fast and frantic and if they had been going along with the rest of the people around them, they would have been drenched with sweat by now. Instead, Callum had them locked together, slowly shifting from side to side. No words were needed between them as they soaked in the feeling of their bodies moving as one.

She leaned against his chest and listened to the beat of his heart. It seemed to match hers perfectly, and she wondered why she'd ever questioned this thing between them. When she looked back up to him, she found his eyes planted directly down at her.

She realized then that it didn't matter what her plans were. It didn't matter because she had no plans if they didn't involve him. In a matter of two months, she had gone from built up walls and unyielding resolve to happiness and peace.

Sam wasn't sure how many songs they went through, swaying in their own little world. It was only when she felt the subtle buzz of her phone and checked it to see that Micah had texted to let her know they had made it back to the house safely and Kristin was fast asleep that she looked up to Callum.

"Callum?"

"Yeah?" He was looking at her with the most beautiful smile she had ever seen. He had drunk a little water and slightly sobered up while she and Kristin had been busy dancing.

"I'm sorry." Her voice broke and Callum jerked back, obviously unsure as to where this was going.

He cupped her face then. "Sorry about what?"

"The other day at Topline when—"

"Wait. I can't hear you. Follow me." He grabbed her hand and had them outside in a matter of seconds. "What are you saying?" His lingering buzz seemed to melt away the moment he saw how distraught she was.

"The other night when I ran out of Topline. I told you that you fucked up my life, but you didn't. I'm so sorry. I'm so so sorry."

"Sam. It's okay. You were dealing with something and were upset."

"That's not an excuse. I've been meaning to apologize, but I just didn't know what to say and"—she started to laugh then—"and then you started distracting me with...other things and, well...I forgot."

"I like distracting you."

She tentatively smiled then. "You promise you're not mad?"

"I'm not mad. Can I ask you something, though?"

"You just did."

He rolled his eyes. Apparently this whole asking a question to ask a question was their new thing.

"I didn't want to ask, but since you brought it up."

Sam took a deep breath. She knew where this was going. "I lost part of it."

He pulled them over to a bench a few feet away. "Your scholarship? You lost it?"

"I lost it for the fall semester. I'll have to take out a loan to cover my expenses, but they told me that if I do well, then I can possibly have it reinstated for the spring semester."

"This is all my fault." He buried his head in his hands.

"No, it's really not."

"I told you I would mess things up. I literally fuck everything up for everyone." He stood then and started to pace.

"Callum, no!"

"I'm so sorry."

"It's not your fault. It was because of something I did back in January, weeks before I even met you."

He stopped then and turned her way. "What did you do?"

"I messed up my class schedule. I thought I was taking enough classes to hold the scholarship and, technically, I am. I just didn't realize it, and so I haven't been going to one of my classes all semester."

He looked utterly confused. "What?"

Sam smiled, pulled him back down to the bench, and explained about her scheduling mistake and the decision of the board. She was surprised she didn't end up in a puddle of tears. She had spent more time secretly crying over that mess the past week than she cared to admit. It was only then that she realized she had barely even thought about it over the last two days. Somehow, being with Callum had caused every worry to slip away.

"I wish you would let me help you." Callum brushed her hair back and cupped her cheek.

"Callum, I can't take your money. You worked hard for that and you shouldn't have to give it to some random girl just because you feel sad for her."

He looked at her sternly. "You're not a random girl."

"What am I then?"

"You're *my* girl." She couldn't stop the smile that encompassed her entire face. It spread like wildfire, and before she knew it, her entire body was alive with want.

"You know. You still haven't asked me out."

"I might be bad at it," Callum admitted with a shy smirk.

"How can you be bad at asking someone out? It's four, no,

five words." Sam started laughing nervously, hoping this wasn't a sign that he did not, in fact, want to ask her out.

"No. I mean, I might be bad at being a boyfriend."

"Why do you think that?"

"Because, outside of work, and Drew and Micah, I have pretty much fucked up every other relationship I have ever had."

"I have the utmost faith in you." Sam gave him a tentative kiss.

"What do I say? 'Let's make this official?'" Callum scrunched up his nose in embarrassment.

Sam sat up straighter. "Repeat after me." She cleared her throat. "Sam, you are the most amazing person I have ever met."

Callum rolled his eyes.

"Sam, you are the most amazing person I have ever met."

"And you have superb taste in pizza toppings." She started to laugh.

He furrowed his brow in mock disgust. "I'm not sure you are worth giving up chicken and pineapple."

She swatted his arm.

"Ugh, fine. And you have superb taste in pizza toppings," Callum stated as he glared at her.

"Will you be my girlfriend?"

"Will you be my girlfriend?"

"No," Sam deadpanned.

Callum looked at her in startled confusion.

"I'm just kidding," she quickly added with a laugh. "I just wanted to see your reaction."

He took a steadying breath and leaned down to rest his head on her shoulder. "I hate you so so so much right now." He then buried his face in the crook of her neck and started peppering kisses everywhere he could touch.

"You don't hate me at all," she said, laughing.

"You're right, I don't hate you at all." He gave her lips a quick kiss and then looked into her eyes. "Promise me something."

"Anything."

"One day, in the future, when I ask you a similar, but much more important question, don't joke with a no, okay? Just say yes." He barely breathed out the words.

Sam was frozen. He couldn't have meant what she thought he did. That would be absolutely and totally insane. She blinked her eyes a few times, trying to figure out how to respond as he stood and pulled her along with him.

"Come on. I need to get you home so I can spend the next hour between your legs as promised."

Chapter 50 - Sam

The ride back to Callum's place wasn't quite as frantic as it had been the previous night. This time, he slowly tortured her as he lightly ran his fingers across every portion of skin he could reach.

She wanted to enjoy every second of it, but her mind was slightly distracted by what he'd said before.

"What's wrong?" he murmured against her neck.

"Nothing."

"Samantha Williams..."

At this point, she knew she couldn't hide a thing from him. Why even try? She turned to face him then.

"I don't think you're real."

His lips pulled upward in an amused smirk. "I'm not real?"

"Sometimes you say things and it just doesn't feel real. It's like you're a fictional boy in one of my books."

"I'm not sure how to take that." He laughed nervously.

"You're perfect, Callum. You are absolutely and totally perfect."

She kissed him then.

****

When they entered the house, it was quiet and dark.

"I guess we're all alone," Sam observed as they made their way to Callum's room.

"Try not to wake everyone up tonight, okay?" He looked down at her with a smirk.

"No promises."

She turned to face him just as they entered his room. She wanted to kiss him then, but his finger came up to rest against her lips.

He walked backward and sat back on the bed just as he had done earlier in the evening.

"Take it off." His voice was a devilish command as he pointed to her dress.

She stood there in contemplation.

Her skin immediately felt as if it were on fire. She wasn't sure how he was able to do this to her. How he was able to turn her into this person who wore crotchless panties and stripped for him. She hadn't even opened a book all weekend and she couldn't remember the last time that had occurred.

"I don't know why I'm nervous. It's not like you haven't seen me before."

He stood then and walked back to her. "You don't have to take them off."

"I want to."

"But don't do it just for me. I want you to be comfortable around me."

"You make me more comfortable than anyone else ever has."

He ran his fingers through her hair.

"Can I kiss you?" he whispered against her temple.

"You don't have to ask that. The answer will always be yes."

He smirked at her response and brushed his lips against hers.

It was much slower than the previous night. He took his time teasing her, then commented that she deserved it due to the fact that he had barely been able to focus most of the night knowing exactly what she was hiding underneath her skin-tight black dress.

When said dress was finally pulled over her head and he found the small little ties covering her nipples, he let out a slew of curses in a few different languages, then added with a wide eyed grin, "This feels like the best treasure hunt of my life."

Sam laughed.

He slowly pulled one of the ribbons, letting the fabric fall away from her breast, then he tugged free the bow on the other cup as well. He leaned back to admire the view.

"I like this."

"I have three of them. Black, red, and white," Sam said with a smile.

"Where are the red and white ones?"

"In Kristin's bag. I'm saving them for another day."

He licked his lips and growled, "Woman, you are going to be the death of me."

Sam burst out in a fit of laughter. "Maybe I should wear them under my work uniform."

Callum groaned out loud and buried his face between her breasts.

But then he tilted his head and bit her nipple. She sucked in a deep breath, which quickly turned into a moan as she felt his fingers slip down to where that missing strip of fabric should have been.

******

He only took her once that night, but it didn't matter. Sam had no sense of time or space, or truthfully anything other than what it felt like when he filled her; when he stretched her; when he made her whimper, and cry, and scream out his name.

When it was over, Callum spent a few minutes kissing the skin of her back and watching as the sheen-covered canvas filled with goosebumps.

She had no idea what time it was—that small alarm clock that had been sitting on the bedside table had been knocked to the ground at some point—but she was surprised how wide awake she felt.

"Can I ask you a question?" Callum whispered as he pulled her body close to his.

Sam's response was a nod and a giggle.

"How have you been able to avoid sex for so long?"

She turned back to face him.

"I don't know. There were a lot of factors that probably played into that."

"Okay."

She was glad he didn't feel the need to pry any further.

"Can I ask you another question?"

Or, maybe he *was* about to pry. She narrowed her eyes at him, not sure where this would lead.

"You promised before, when we were at the beach, to tell me about your past. Do you feel like you can talk about it now, or do you need more time?"

She rolled over to lay on her back and stared up at the ceiling. She didn't want this bubble of perfection to burst. She didn't want this to end, or for anything to change between them. She was about to open her mouth when he spoke.

"When I was a kid, I thought my father walked on water. He was everything I wanted to be when I grew up."

She turned back to face him.

"My mom always said I was a carbon copy of him. I wanted to be an architect just like him, too. They spent so much money on drawing lessons and art classes for me. I loved it."

"What happened?" Sam asked as she began to draw small circles on the palm of his hand.

He smiled at the gesture.

And then his smile fell.

"When I was a freshman in college, I spent a lot of time at my father's firm, learning from his team. Connor was always going to be a doctor, and we knew Millie would be in some form of healthcare from the time she was a toddler, so my father had planned to hand his firm down to me one day. I had a 4.0 GPA and a ridiculously bright future ahead of me. At least, that's probably what everyone would have said if you asked them."

He took a deep breath and then his sad smile faded as he continued.

"I walked in on my father fucking his secretary. It was obviously *not* their first time and, once I knew, I guess he didn't feel the need to hide it anymore. He tried to win my silence with gifts and money, and, for a while, I kept my mouth shut. But by junior year, I couldn't even keep count of the number of women he'd snuck into his office at all hours of the day. Literally, my mom would stop by for lunch and then as she was hopping on the elevator to head home, Julie from marketing, or Janet from billing, or Heather from HR was hopping off the elevator and heading into his office. I think I finally cracked when I caught him fucking one of the interns I went to class with. I was twenty-one at the time, the intern was eighteen. I told my mom and ruined my perfect family."

Her heart broke. He had blamed himself this whole time for what his father was actually at fault for.

"Callum. That's not your fault."

"They're still in the process of the divorce. Apparently, it takes longer when you have a shit ton of money and assets to divide. I became the black sheep when that happened."

"You aren't a black sheep to me. You're just Callum." She quickly added, "*My* Callum."

He turned to fully face her and smiled.

"I have my degree."

Sam furrowed her brow in confusion. "What?"

"Everyone thinks I dropped out. But, in reality, I just changed my major from architectural engineering to business. It took a little over a year to finally graduate since I had to backtrack some classes, but I'm not the college dropout everyone thinks I am."

"I wouldn't have cared either way." She gave him a quick kiss to comfort him.

"I know. But I wanted to tell you in case someone said that about me." He ran his fingers through his hair. "I didn't tell anyone. No one even came to my graduation, but I can't blame them for that since they didn't even know it was happening in the first place."

"I would have come."

He smiled at her words and then he continued.

"Connor hated me for what I did. I had told him about what was going on and he'd told me to keep my mouth shut. That it would hurt our mom and ruin their marriage. But I couldn't keep watching it happen every day and not say a word." Callum shook his head as he gathered his words. "My dad had never really accepted Connor for who he was, but they had somehow found some kind of peace between them once he had gotten into medical school. We haven't really discussed it, but I think, even though he hated our dad, he still needed his approval for something. Our dad wouldn't accept who he was, but maybe he would accept his job. And then he could be proud of Connor. I think that's all Connor really wanted. He wanted our dad to be proud of him. But then I fucked up and broke our family apart, and it gave more fuel to the *my sons are massive fuck-ups* fire and my dad stopped coming around. There was a fight, and it was like Connor and I no longer existed. He still sees Millie from time to time, but we are dead to him. It won't matter if Connor becomes the head of the largest hospital in the world, just as it wouldn't matter if I became an amazing architect or not. We will never measure up."

She hated the look of pain that covered his features. She was desperate to take it away. Her mind raced with what to say or do. Then her lips rose in a slight smirk and he cut his eyes over in confusion.

"You know, if your sandcastle building skills are anything like your architectural skills, then it's probably a good thing you changed majors." She covered her mouth to try and conceal the giggle that was about to burst free.

"You dork," he stated with a laugh and pulled her closer. "I'll have you know I have excellent sandcastle building skills. I just had faulty equipment. Next time I take you to the beach, we are stopping by Costco and I'm buying the biggest damn sandcastle building kit they have."

She wasn't sure if that was really a thing, but she liked the sound of it.

"Next time, huh?" She pushed a strand of his hair behind his ear.

He gave her a quick and sweet kiss on her lips. "Yep. Next time."

He turned to play with a tendril of her hair as he spoke. "That's what my tattoo is." She furrowed her brow in confusion and he clarified, "The one you asked about that night we went to Social. It's an architectural compass that is broken and a navigational compass that isn't pointing north. It represents how I fucked up the path my parents laid out for me, and how I probably will never go in the right direction. I'll never be on a path that points north."

She waited for a moment to make sure he was finished speaking.

"Thank you for telling me. It's truly beautiful." She smiled. "And it makes so much more sense now."

He laughed. "Thank you."

"I think I'm starting to realize something, though."

"And what is that?" he said as he pulled her closer to him.

"Maybe it doesn't matter what path someone is *supposed* to take. Maybe, instead of a path, it should be called a series of turns. Some turns are good and some are bad. But sometimes taking that wrong turn may be exactly what you need to lead you in the right direction."

He kissed her brow.

"You wouldn't be where you are today without all those turns. Good and bad. And I guess, good or bad, I wouldn't be where I am either."

Callum smiled. "I have to say, I very much like where our paths are leading us now." He pulled her in for a deep kiss.

"Me too. And I think maybe I'll love where this path ends up," she whispered against his lips when they finally separated. "But, I'm sorry about your brother."

Callum flopped back to stare at the ceiling once more. "Me, too. He used to be my best friend."

"Maybe you can get back to that one day?"

He looked back at her then. "I would like that, but I don't know if he would. I don't even think he would answer if I called. He may have even blocked my number by this point."

He ran his hands over his face and she watched as his shoulders sagged into the bed.

"I also lied to you."

Concern coated her features. "About what?"

"When I told you I don't date. I did date. Once. And then I messed it up."

She wasn't sure whether to let him work out what else to say or to start asking questions. Thankfully, he started talking before she had to decide.

"Her name was Rebecca. It was the end of my sophomore year of college. She and I had been friends in highschool, but nothing more. She had a full ride to Georgia for nursing. We happened to meet up on spring break and then just hit it off. We dated for the entirety of our junior year. She ended up leaving Georgia and her friends and her scholarship to move to Columbia so we could be closer. So we could be together." A sad smile played on his lips. "But then everything happened with Millie, and then my dad, and then Connor decided I was worthless, and...I don't know. I kind of broke down. I broke up with her three weeks after she moved here. She moved here for me, and then I ended it, and she had nothing. I think she even had to delay graduation by a year because some of the courses didn't switch over."

Her fingers traced the line of his jaw. "Callum." She wanted to tell him it was okay. That he wasn't a bad person just because he did an inconsiderate thing when his life was falling apart.

"I just wanted you to know. I'm sorry I lied, but I just didn't want to screw you up, too. I didn't want to fuck up your plans like I fucked up hers."

"You won't. You haven't. And you can't really blame yourself for what happened. Sometimes good people make bad decisions. They make a wrong turn, or they do the wrong thing. But that doesn't mean they are bad people, it just means they are human. You were going through something, and you did what you had to do at the time. I'm sure she forgives you."

He nodded, but she could tell he didn't really believe it.

"Have you kept up with her?"

"I snoop through her social media every now and then. She's engaged. His name is Chad." Callum made a gag noise and Sam laughed.

Then he turned over to face her and kissed her cheek.

"But in a way, I'm glad it happened the way it did."

"And why is that?"

He lifted her chin to make sure they were staring directly at each other. "Because, if we hadn't broken up then I would have never met you." He gave her another kiss, then turned back to face the ceiling.

When she realized he had said his piece, she knew it was time to say hers. She could have kept her mouth shut. She knew that if she changed the subject and never said a word, he would be okay with it. He would never truly push her. But she needed to get it out. He had trusted her with a very important part of him, and it was now time for her to do the same.

It was now or never.

She took a deep breath and then placed her hand on his chin, pulling his gaze back to hers.

"I'm an orphan."

She wasn't sure why she started to cry. She hadn't cried over it in years. It just was what it was.

He reached up to wipe away the tears from her eyes.

"I grew up in foster care, and I lived in so many different places. My life was this chaotic shit hole that I was desperate to get out of. The scholarship was like my ticket to freedom."

He looked at her for a moment and then shook his head with a smile. A sudden burst of relief seemed to fill his features.

"I don't care. I don't care who you were, or where you lived, or how much money you did or didn't have. I don't care about your past. I just want to be a part of your future."

She really started crying then. Why did he have to say the most perfect things? Why did his every word cause her stomach to tighten and her heart to skip? He thought she was too good for him, but he had it all backward. He was *far* too good for her.

He tried to pull her in tighter, but she pulled back.

"You might think differently once you know everything about my past." Her lips were trembling.

Callum took her face in his hands and said, "I won't. But you can tell me if you're ready."

She took a deep breath and squared her shoulders. Her face turned back to the ceiling.

She couldn't look at him while saying this.

"Not everywhere was bad. There were a few homes that I wish I could have stayed in permanently, but things don't always work out the way you hope. There are two families I still keep in sporadic contact with even now, so please know that it wasn't all bad."

He nodded.

She wanted to say something else. Something to prolong the truth from being let free, but she knew there was nothing else. With a final breath, she let it all out. This truth that she had never told anyone but Kristin.

"When you asked me earlier if I was a virgin...the answer I gave you *is* how I feel. The concept of virginity is bullshit. But what I wasn't saying was that the answer to your question would have been...complicated."

Callum tensed then; she felt every muscle in his body go rigid.

"The first time it happened, I was eleven, and it was another boy in the house. He was sixteen. He convinced me that in order to be a *good sister*"— she swallowed at the words—"I had to do certain *things* to him. I didn't even know *that* was a thing you could do. But I was so scared and alone, and I just wanted to be perfect so they would love me. That lasted for a little over six months. Christian finally found out and beat the absolute shit out of him."

She steadied her breathing before she went on.

"Then, when I was thirteen, my foster father would sneak into our room at night. It was only Sara and me in the bedroom at that time; Christian was down the hall. She was older and took the brunt of it, and whenever he tried to come to my side of the room, she would entice him back to her bed." Her voice shook with the words. "Most of the time, that worked. But some nights, he sent her to sleep on the couch so she couldn't intervene. I think I blacked out most of it. To be honest, I'm not one hundred percent sure what exactly happened. Sometimes, it feels like I've just made it up in my head." She ran her hand over her face. "That lasted for over a year."

Callum grabbed her hand and squeezed, letting her know he was there.

"I would hear her crying sometimes"—her voice started to break and her lips began to quiver—"but I just turned over, covered my ears, and pretended it wasn't happening. That's why I thought something was wrong with me. I only cried when it happened to her. I never cried when it happened to me. I think he took that as me being okay with it. It took me a long time to realize I wasn't crying because I was just shutting it all out."

She paused for a moment and closed her eyes, willing the memories she did have to go away.

"Sara aged out while I was still at that house. I was transferred to one other house when I was fifteen, but then I was sent back to that house when I was sixteen. I joined every club and team I could find that didn't cost any money, and I only entered the house when it was absolutely necessary. He barely touched me then. I think I was too old." She heard Callum swallow, and she knew he was most likely holding down the rising vomit she had also experienced each time she thought about it. "I spent as many nights as possible in Sara's dorm, and later her apartment. She breezed through college, graduated early, and started med school before I got out of high school. She wanted to be a cardiologist, but she ended up in pediatrics. I spent every waking moment with her that I could. She even snuck me into some of her med classes. I technically aged out of the system at the beginning of March my senior year, but I stayed to finish school, and planned to stay on Sara's sofa over the summer."

Sam felt the edges of her lips lift up as she recalled their times together. Then she felt the smile slowly shift with the weight of what she was about to say.

"The week after I graduated from high school and finally moved out of that house, Sara killed herself. After that, I had to move into that little motel room with Christian. He worked a construction job and I worked at a pizza place so we could make ends meet until the fall when we both moved into our dorms."

Chapter 51 - Sam

Callum was frozen against her. He barely breathed. If she hadn't known with absolute certainty that he was still there, based on the hand wrapped around her middle, she would have assumed she was all alone.

Then he buried his face in her hair and kissed her temple.

She stilled when she felt a drop of wetness running down her cheek. She was no longer crying. Now he was the one with tears spilling forth.

His voice broke when he said, "I want to tell you I'm sorry. But I also know that nothing I say will ever take away the pain."

"You don't have to say anything. I just didn't want it hovering between us anymore. I wanted you to know everything before we took this any further."

He twisted their bodies so they were now directly looking at each other. His eyes were red.

"You do know nothing that happened to you was your fault, right?"

She nodded in agreement.

She had spent far too many hours consumed by her own self-hatred, but she had finally accepted the fact that nothing that had happened to her had been her fault.

She stilled her features and spoke as clearly as she could. "I know it wasn't my fault, and that you're going to say you still want to be with me, but I also know this has changed the way you look at me. How could it not? So, seriously, if you walk away right now, it would be completely understandable. It's a lot of emotional baggage to take on."

"It doesn't change the way I feel about you in the slightest." He tilted his head in thought. "Well, actually, it does."

For just a moment, she was paralyzed with fear.

"I knew you were amazing and strong, but I had no idea just how amazing and strong you were until this very moment. Samantha Williams, I have underestimated you."

She sighed with relief. "I don't feel very strong," she admitted.

He brought her hand up to his face then and kissed the center of her palm. "Have you been to therapy?"

"No." She quickly shook her head. She knew that was probably what she needed, but the idea of rehashing it all out felt almost as dreadful as the memories of what had happened.

"I think you should maybe do that. I can go with you, or just sit outside, or maybe–"

"Callum," she quickly cut him off. "No. I can't. At least, not right now."

Though she could tell he didn't fully agree with her decision, he nodded his head in acceptance. "Do you want to talk with me about it more?"

Sam shook her head. "It's in the past, and that's where I want it to stay. Honestly, I would be perfectly fine if we never spoke of it again."

He took a deep breath. "Millie said the same thing."

She furrowed her brows in confusion. Before she could ask what he meant, he stood up and lifted her from the bed, cradling her in his arms.

"I know it's well after midnight, but I'm not tired."

"Me neither," Sam quickly agreed as she wrapped her arms around his neck.

Callum's eyes narrowed in concentration. "Do you like ice

cream?"

Sam mirrored his expression. "Normally, I take the stance that there is no such thing as a dumb question. However, I am going to redact that sentiment for this one instance."

Callum laughed. "Come with me." He quickly set her down and tossed some clothes her way while he threw on a pair of shorts. Then he grabbed her hand and walked to the kitchen.

"We have vanilla, chocolate, strawberry, and rocky road. Although you can't have rocky road. So you have to choose between the others."

Sam furrowed her brow. "Why can't I have rocky road?"

"Because, I am allergic to nuts, and if you eat nuts I can't kiss you."

She looked at him with a wide-eyed expression as realization set in. "I guess I'm never eating nuts again."
Callum smirked in triumph. "Good call."

"I'll take the chocolate," she said with a definite nod.

He lifted a finger into the air. "Also a good call."

He lifted her up on the counter as he fixed their bowls. She had expected him to bring her hers when he was finished, but instead he walked toward the back door, slipped on some flip flops, and winked as he walked outside. She followed him.

It should have been pitch black at this time of night, but with the illumination in the sky from Charleston off in the distance and the lights that followed the path before them, she could see exactly where they were headed.

"The dock?" Sam questioned as they slowly inched further and further away from the pristine white house and manicured lawn behind them.

"It's my favorite spot. I tend to balk about coming here, but to be completely honest, it's my most favorite place. Well, it *was* my most favorite place."

She scooped up another bite. "Where's your favorite place now?"

He looked down at her then. "Wherever you are."

She stopped and pulled him down into another kiss, but he quickly pulled away.

"If you don't stop, I'm going to end up taking you on the dock."

"I wouldn't mind it." She shrugged her shoulders as she continued on ahead of him.

****

They sat outside, eating ice cream and talking for the better part of five hours. It wasn't until the sun started to rise on the horizon that he picked up their bowls to head back to the house.

"Aren't we supposed to be waking up in an hour?" Sam questioned as she leaned against the railing.

"Supposed to? Yes. But is that really going to happen? Probably not." He laughed a little. "I'll set an alarm for noon in case we aren't up by then. My guess is Kristin's still going to be out for a while as well."

"Probably," she agreed with a laugh and a yawn and then she felt him wrap his arm around her waist and lift her over his shoulder. She screamed in delight. "What are you doing?"

"I'm taking you back to bed."

"I can walk." She laughed with the words as she watched the dock slip further away.

"You can. But this gives me a perfect view of your ass." She guessed he was going to slap her butt then so she tensed, but with the bowls in his other hand, he couldn't. Instead, she felt him tilt his head and place a kiss directly under where the hem of the shirt fell.

She burst out laughing. "Did you just kiss my ass?"

"Yep." He slowly placed her on the ground as they reached the back door. "And I have a feeling I'm going to be doing a lot of ass-kissing in the future. Both metaphorically and physically." He wiggled his eyebrows as he ushered them inside.

Chapter 52 - Callum

He had never been so happy. He had also never hated the sunrise so much. Because once that light started to rise above the horizon, he knew the weekend was over. He said a silent prayer that this didn't mean their little bubble they had cocooned themselves within would pop.

When they crawled back into bed, he contemplated how he would get through the next days and weeks without being constantly by her side. He wasn't sure if that was love or infatuation; maybe a little of both.

He had never been in love. Not really. He'd thought he'd been in love with Rebecca, but he was beginning to realize he'd never before understood what true love was. He knew he loved his mom and Millie, and probably Connor, too. But he somehow equated that love with sacrifice; it was the only word he had ever thought of that compared. He would hands-down sacrifice his life for his mom, Millie, and Connor. He knew that. And he now knew he would do that for Sam as well.

But with her it was so much more.

His mind didn't immediately go to sacrifice or death as it did with anyone else when he tried to reason what it was between them.

It wasn't only that he would willingly die for her, when it came to Sam, he had decided he would gladly live for her.

And that was the difference.

She made him want to live.

He wanted to wake up every day and live for *her*.

Chapter 53 - Sam

The ride home was probably Sam's most favorite drive of her life. She spent the entire two hours running through every one of her most favorite Taylor Swift songs. Most Callum liked, a few he loved, and a few more he scrunched up his nose at. He quickly changed his expression to a wide-eyed smile when Sam informed him that if he didn't absolutely love every song then he could no longer kiss her.

When they pulled up in front of her house shortly after five, she paused, not wanting the weekend to finally come to an end. There was this irrational fear lingering over her that if he drove off, then their perfect little weekend would end and everything would go back to the way it was.

"I don't want you to leave." Her face was red with the admission.

"You could invite me inside?" Callum turned off the truck.

She raised her brow. "Last time I invited you inside, you—"

He quickly cut her off, "I promise not to turn that down this time."

She kissed his lips then and jumped out of the truck to head inside. When she made it to the front door and noticed he was still sitting exactly where she left him, she quirked an eyebrow.

"Are you coming or not?"

He jumped out then and made it to the door before it shut behind her.

****

The next few days were a wonderful, chaotic blur. The only times she wasn't with Callum were when she was in class or studying for final exams the following week. She also hadn't taken a single bus ride that week. Before they went to sleep that first night, Callum asked her to send him her class schedule, and then proceeded to spend the following hour alternating his schedule at Topline and the tattoo parlor in order to be at every single class the second it was over to shuttle her to the next.

She finally understood Kristin's constant need to be around Micah. At some point in the middle of the night, she'd decided she would be perfectly fine if Callum never left her side.

The four of them were alternating houses. Sometimes, if they stayed up late watching a movie or drinking, all four slept at the same house. Sometimes, Kristin and Micah would stay at her place while Sam and Callum stayed at his. At one point, Micah made a joke about the four of them finding two townhomes next to each other for the following year, if only to save money on gas. They soon all realized it wasn't really a joke when each had started nodding their heads in agreement.

Her life was perfect.

Absolutely perfect.

She had no idea how she'd made it here, but she was glad she had.

******

Sam had one more hour left in her shift, but there was barely a soul in sight. Her last table had left thirty minutes before, and Jess had spent the time since telling Sam all the ways in which Gwen had stolen her heart.

When another twenty minutes went by and not a single person walked in, she packed up her stuff and headed to the back. Not everyone knew about her relationship with Callum, so when she made it to the office, she still politely knocked.

"Come in," Callum called out from inside.

She slowly opened the door, walked in, and then quickly closed it behind her.

"Can I help you?" Callum asked, his back to her and without

even looking up from the computer.

"I'm wearing those red panties with the missing fabric."

Callum froze. Whatever he was working on was surely long forgotten.

"You are?" He still hadn't turned around.

She walked right up behind him and leaned down over his shoulder.

"I told you I would save them for a special occasion. I feel like being officially done with junior year is occasion enough to seduce you on your office desk for the first time."

He turned then and looked her up and down. She was still wearing the black dress pants, white button up and black tie. He reached forward, grasped the tie and pulled her down to him.

"I don't see any red, Sam."

"You need to undress me first."

He shook his head and licked his lips.

"Go lock the door."

"Yes, sir."

He growled in response.

She slowly made her way back to him as she undid the tie and began unbuttoning her top.

"Give me that." He reached out just before she dropped the tie, indicating for her to place it in his hands.

"Is this in one of your fantasies?"

"I think it's about to be," he replied with a smirk.

She wanted to tease him further, but he was having none of it. In a matter of seconds, he had her up against the far wall with every button of her shirt undone. He smiled when he noticed that her bra clasped in the front.

"Well, this is convenient," he said with a smile as he popped it open to let her breasts free.

Then he devoured her.

His hands were everywhere, and his mouth quickly followed suit.

Sam bit the inside of her cheek, desperate to keep from screaming out as he slid a hand into her pants to find the exact treasure she had teased him with, then she whined at the loss of contact when he pulled back after only spending a few moments touching her.

"I want to try something," he stated and then looked up toward the ceiling.

The exposed pipes and rails which had been left visible as part of the rustic aesthetic would now be used for something far more exciting. The lowest hung just inches from her head.

"I want to tie you up."

"Callum." His name was a desperate plea on her lips.

"Are you okay with that?"

She quickly nodded and brought her wrists up between them.

"Do I need a safe word?"

"Not unless you want one. All you need to do is tell me to stop or take it off, and I will."

He wrapped the tie around her wrists. She tugged once and realized there was no way she would easily break free from its hold.

"I told you. I was an eagle scout. I'm good at knots." He smirked then, and the sight of it made her lean forward and kiss him deeply.

When she pulled back, he looked at her once more, as if making sure this was okay. She quickly nodded. Then he was bringing her hands up and securing the tie to the bar above her head.

"Is this okay?" he asked once everything was in place.

"Yes," she whispered.

Her heart was frantic and her breaths were ragged. She was so worked up, she thought she would combust the moment he touched her.

He stepped back then and studied her.

"You are so goddamn beautiful," he said as if it was a prayer. "Tell me to stop at any moment and I'll stop, okay?"

She nodded. There was absolutely no way she could bring herself to speak.

He stalked back to her with a devilish grin plastered across his face.

His hand slipped between the skin on her stomach and the band of her pants. She clamped her mouth shut. She was in the office at Topline. There were people outside. There was literally a table of people eating on the other side of this wall. She could not make a sound.

His exploration halted just before he touched where she desired it the most.

"I have a challenge for you."

Her eyes shot to his in question. She could tell he was trying not to laugh.

"If you can keep quiet, I'll get you Dianne's pepperoni pizza anytime you want it for the next month." Her brows lifted in excitement. "If you make a noise, then you can only eat the chicken and pineapple."

She shook her head as she tried to stifle the laugh. She'd never known anyone else who could make her so breathless yet so invigorated at the same time. The thought that he could make her immensely happy.

"Challenge accepted," she managed to whisper against his lips.

He stepped back and quirked a brow. "You should know, I very rarely ever lose. And I sure as hell don't plan to tonight."

He looked down at her then and slipped his hand back inside her pants. She arched upward as he found her.

"You're so fucking wet, Sam." He smirked against her ear.

Then he took his time torturing her with pleasure. She wanted to beg for more, but she couldn't. Sam didn't actually care about the pizza. She just wanted to win.

He admired his hand as he pulled it from between her legs and took his time sucking each finger clean.

"You're perfect."

And then her pants were yanked to the ground. He stepped back to fully take her in.

She wanted to keep eye contact.

She wanted to watch him drink her in.

But it was too much.

Between her body fully on display and her hands being tied up, every single one of her senses was on fire. She closed her eyes as she tried to calm herself down.

She heard rather than saw him move. When she opened up her eyes once more, he was kneeling before her.

"Not a sound," he whispered. "By the way, I like the red." And then his mouth was on her.

By this point, she was very well acquainted with what his mouth and tongue could do, but that knowledge still did nothing to stifle the moan that threatened to erupt from her lips as the tension coiled in her core and that icy sensation swept through her curling toes. When he hitched her right leg over his shoulder, she knew she wouldn't last. Not like this. Then he added his finger and she all but lost control. She turned her head sideways as she bit into the fabric of her shirt and shattered against him.

"I'm impressed," he cooed into her ear as he slowly undid the tie and she all but collapsed into his arms. "But I don't think you will be able to hold out." He carried her over to the desk and faced her away from him.

Sam was still panting. She hadn't yet caught her breath, but he was pushing her forward and then she was laying face down on top of the weekend schedules. He grabbed her wrists and pulled them behind her back as he tied them together once more.

"Just tell me to stop and I will."

She nodded.

There was no warning. In one swift move, he separated her legs and slammed directly into her.

She lost the bet.

Her scream of pleasure was so loud there was no way it wasn't heard by at least a few patrons and staff. But he didn't stop. He wrapped his hand around to cover her mouth and stifle what noise he could as he pounded into her again and again. She knew they should probably slow down or hold off until they were home, but they were both too far gone to end this without definite release.

She collapsed into his lap when it was over.

She had no idea how she was ever going to show her face out there again. If their relationship was a secret before tonight, it definitely wasn't anymore.

"You might need to fire me." Her words came in pants.

He laughed into her hair. "And why would I do that?"

"I don't think I can work here anymore. Each time I come into this building I'll remember what you just did to me, and then I won't be able to focus."

"Maybe we should just make this a nightly, after-work ritual."

Chapter 54 - Sam

"Callum?" Kristin called out from across the boy's kitchen table as Sam nudged him in the shoulder. He had been so focused on his phone he hadn't even heard her.

He jerked his head up from his phone. "What?"

"I asked when our next Charleston trip was going to happen. I didn't get to take Sam shopping everywhere I wanted to, and now that it's officially summer..." Kristin gave him a pleading smile.

They hadn't again broached the subject of his family, and she wasn't quite sure what his relationship was like with his mother. He periodically mentioned her in passing, and she figured they must speak being as the beach house was technically his parents' and not his, but she was filled with curiosity on how exactly that relationship worked.

He shook his head and looked between the two girls. "Just name the date and I'll make it happen."

Kristin looked back at Sam. "I'm definitely going to enjoy the perks of you dating a guy who has a beach house."

Sam burst out laughing.

Kristin continued, "By the way, shouldn't you be thanking me?"

Callum quirked a brow in confusion.

"Thanking you for what?"

Kristin shoved a piece of the garlic bread into her mouth. It didn't stop her from talking.

"I'm the one who bought Sam those unmentionables."

Sam's face went bright red.

"I heard you thoroughly enjoyed them." Kristin winked.

"What are you talking about?" Micah chimed in, half oblivious to anything other than the delicious pasta sitting on his plate.

"Nothing," Sam quickly interjected. "She is talking about nothing," she said through gritted teeth and a pleading smile, begging her friend not to continue.

Unfortunately, it was Callum who then carried on.

"Kristin, I sincerely thank you for that. Best night of my life." He winked at Sam, who in turn let out a groan.

This was not happening.

Kristin couldn't hold in the laugh that bellowed from her as Micah sat there utterly confused.

A buzz from his phone caused Callum's mood to suddenly change.

"Give me a second." He kissed Sam on the forehead as he walked toward the front door.

"What's going on?" she called out, confused at his sudden shift in demeanor.

"My mom just got here. I need to sign some papers. I'll be right back." And then the front door shut behind him.

"His mom," Sam whispered to Micah and Kristin. "I haven't met his mom."

"She's so sweet," Kristin chimed in as she took another bite. "She used to come over to my parents' place all the time, but my guess is since she and Mr. Barker are no longer a thing, she doesn't feel the need to come play nice with my mom."

Sam frantically looked between her friends and the window that faced the front yard. "Would it be weird if I snuck a peek through the blinds?"

Micah eyed Kristin with an amused smile. "I mean, yeah, maybe a little weird, but who cares? Go snoop on your future mother-in-law," Micah said with a laugh.

"Oh, shut up!" Sam whispered as she stood and crept over to the window.

Kristin started laughing. "Why are you whispering and walking like that? They are in the parking lot. They can't see or hear you."

"Shhh!" Sam said as she peered out from behind the blinds. She was desperate to sneak a peek at the woman who raised Callum. She wondered if they would look similar. Sam had met his father and siblings, and they all had the same dark hair and bone structure. But Callum had the brightest blue eyes which none of the others possessed. They had to have come from his mom.

She slowly slid open the blinds. Then immediately snapped them shut.

Sam couldn't breathe.

It wasn't possible.

She peeked out again, hoping her eyes were just playing tricks on her. When the second look confirmed what she knew in the first, she abruptly stood and jumped back.

"What's wrong?" Kristin questioned from the dining room table.

Sam couldn't speak. There was absolutely no way this was truly happening. She pinched her arm. It had to be a dream. But no, that pinch hurt. This was not a dream.

"Sam? What's wrong?" She felt Kristin's hand on the back of her shoulder.

"What's her name?" Sam asked, tears filling her eyes. Kristin furrowed her brow. "Who? Callum's mom?"

"What's her name?" Sam asked more urgently.

Kristin gave her a confused look. "Mrs. Ashlyn. Ashlyn Barker."

"No," Micah quickly amended. "She took her maiden name back in the divorce. It's Ms. Ashlyn Clemmings now."

Sam's heart stopped.

Ashlyn Clemmings.

The head of the Giving Hearts board. The woman who controlled her future and had taken away a portion of her funds.

She made it downstairs and into Callum's bathroom before she heard the front door shut. She was pacing when he tentatively opened the door.

"You okay?" He slowly walked over, placing his hands on either side of her face. She leaned into him.

"That was your mom?"

"Yeah."

"That was your mom," she said once more. This time it wasn't a question.

Callum swallowed then took a breath. "Listen. I've never really done this before. This is new, and I'm not sure I want my family meddling in our relationship yet. I didn't realize you would want to meet her."

She wanted to laugh through the tears that had now sprung forth. He thought she was upset because he didn't introduce her to his mom. The irony of this situation was astounding.

"If it means that much to you, I promise that—"

Sam abruptly cut in, "I've already met her."

"What?" Now he looked even more confused.

"Your mom is Ashlyn Clemmings."

"Yes." Callum stared at her, mouth slightly agape.

"You said she works for the university?"

He nodded in response.

"Do you know what she does?"

"She is over a couple committees."

"She's over the Giving Hearts Foundation."

He shrugged his shoulders in response. That phrase meant nothing to him.

"Okay?"

Then it all came out in a rush.

"That's the foundation that pays for my schooling. They

support foster children. The email that I got that night at Toplie when you found me crying outside on my break…that email was from her. The next week, I had to sit before her and plead my case. It was absolute hell. She knows everything about me. Literally, she has my entire file and my history at her disposal and I have meetings with her scheduled all throughout the next semester. She is the one who will decide if I get my money back for the spring semester."

He stared at her in disbelief. "Are you sure?"

"Absolutely. She was a foster kid, right?"

He nodded. "My grandparents adopted her when she was twelve."

"It's her."

He stepped back then. She could tell he was unsure what to do with that news. "I had no idea. Sam, if I had known I would have told her, I would have–"

"No. I'm glad you didn't know. What happened happened because of my own mistake, and I'm not taking that out on her or anyone else. I just…" She tried to wipe the stress off her face. "Just imagine how hard it is knowing that the woman who has the power to decide your future is the mom of the man you are fucking."

He eyed her then. "We aren't *just* fucking."

She shook her head and amended, "You know what I mean. She's the mom of the guy I'm dating. What if she hates me before she even really knows me? She could find out *anything* about me by just opening a folder."

Callum laughed and kissed her brow. "No way she could hate you. No one could ever hate you, Sam."

She wanted so badly to believe him.

Chapter 55 - Sam

The buzz of her phone was what finally pulled Sam from sleep. Callum groaned when she pulled away to see who was texting.

In reality, it was already midday. After driving back to her townhouse, they had spent half the night wrapped up in each other's arms.

Sam had begrudgingly pulled herself out of bed for her eight o'clock lab. When she and Kristin had returned home around ten, Sam had had to stifle the laugh at Callum still snoozing away and wrapped up in her pink sheets. She desperately needed to study for final exams in the upcoming weeks, but this sight was too tempting. She crawled in beside him, promising herself that she wouldn't fall back asleep.

She didn't keep the promise.

The second buzz had her reaching forward and reading the message.

Christian: Can't get together today. Can we switch it to lunch tomorrow? Dianne's? 11:30?

Sam: See you then.

She and Christian still hadn't spoken since he'd stood her up after her meeting and he'd sent her that text that she promptly deleted. But it had been over three weeks now, and she knew she could only put off their usual lunch dates for so long. She decided to hear him out. They had been best friends for the better part of fifteen years. The least she could do was let him explain why he'd left, and then she could make him grovel by buying her dessert.

"Who in their right mind messages people this early?" Callum groaned out as he pulled Sam in closer.

"Callum, it's almost one in the afternoon." She kissed his nose.

His eyes shot open. "What?" He quickly let go of her and rolled over to check his phone. "My alarm didn't go off. It was on silent." He rubbed the sleep from his eyes as he sat up to give her another kiss.

"Where do you need to be?" she asked as she threw him the pants he was now looking for.

"Topline. I ordered some new barstools and chairs. I probably spent way too much money on them, but I'm trying to update the place." She gave him a nod. The place definitely needed some updating, especially if he was going to pull in a younger crowd as was the plan. "I want to make sure they look as good in person as they did online."

He nodded his head toward her phone as he threw his shorts on. "Was that Kristin?"

She gave him a timid glance. "No. It was he-who-shall-not-be-named."

Callum initially laughed at the reference, but then went stone-faced when he realized who exactly she meant.

"Why is he texting you?"

She could tell it was difficult for him to keep the edge out of his voice.

"We were supposed to get lunch today, but he's busy, so just rescheduling it for tomorrow."

Callum sat back on the bed and ran his hands through his hair. The topic of Christian hadn't come up once in the two weeks they'd been back from Charleston. In all honesty, they had been far too busy with more enjoyable things to really worry about anyone else. But she'd known this conversation was coming.

"I don't want you to see him." Callum stared at the ground as he spoke.

"Callum–"

"Please. I will literally do anything. Just tell me what to do so you don't see him anymore."

She wanted to scream.

"Give me a valid reason."

Callum paused.

She watched as he weighed the options in his head. She was desperate for him to come clean about Christian and Millie's relationship. That's what Christian had said was the reason. Christian and Millie had dated, and Callum had gone all crazy protective older brother on him.

A part of her knew that wasn't the entire story.

She knew Callum now. If she were a betting person, she would bet that she knew him better than any other person in his life, and she just didn't see him as the type to try to beat up another person just for dating his sister. But, then again, she'd never truly had an older brother, so she wasn't really sure what that dynamic was like.

"Callum, just tell me. At this point, based on the amount of hatred between you two, I know it's not just about me. There is something else there that you aren't saying."

"I promised her I would never speak of it again. Truthfully, the records are sealed, and I planned to never see him ever again. I thought that chapter was over."

Sam rolled her eyes. "You're speaking in code. Please just say it."

He looked up at her then. "I need to be honest with you

about something first."

She nodded her head, unsure of where he was taking this. "Okay."

"I knew about your past before you told me."

Her body physically recoiled.

"What?"

He quickly shook his head when the words had officially hit her. "Wait. I said that wrong. Not the whole thing. I didn't know about what happened to you, I just knew you grew up in the foster care system." He rushed the confession.

She took a step back and cocked her head to the side in confusion. She wasn't sure whether she was more angry, confused, or impressed. She'd kept that lifelong secret guarded better than most could.

"How?"

"I know Christian. I know he was a foster kid, and since you mentioned that you two were lifelong best friends, I just put two and two together. It wasn't confirmed until you told me, but I had a suspicion that was at least in part what you were hiding. I just didn't want to force it out of you or embarrass you and tell you I already knew. I wanted you to tell me when you were ready."

She was definitely impressed with the deduction he had made.

She took a deep breath. "That doesn't explain why you hate him?"

"No. I guess it doesn't." His hand made another path through his hair, which Sam now recognized as a nervous habit of his. "He met my younger sister Amelia, Millie, while they were in highschool. He was seventeen, she had just turned fifteen. They were friends, if you could call it that. I think they just kind of knew each other and hung out periodically when they happened to run into each other at school events. Anyway, there was a basketball game between his school and hers. They saw each other, and he made a move. She let him know she didn't see him in that light. He initially was okay with it, but then they saw each other that night at a party. All I know is that the mom whose kid hosted the party found Millie lying in the bushes when she walked out the next morning to get the paper. Millie was completely incoherent and there was blood. She was covered in bruises and vomit. But the thing is, Millie doesn't drink. Ever. I'm not just saying that or being naive or anything. Millie is the *definition* of a rule follower. So anyway, they immediately took her to the hospital, and after, she woke up and pieced it all together—well, what she could remember—and then, with the lab results and footage from the security cameras at that house, we figured out that Christian had drugged and raped her."

Sam was absolutely frozen. She saw Callum look up at her, but she wasn't sure she could form words.

There were very few times in Sam's life in which she'd felt utter shock. Now was one of them. Her heartbeat picked up and then it slowed. Her hands became clammy and then her throat felt too tight.

"They had it all on video. And the idiot still had the fucking pills in his pocket when they picked him up later that day. He was arrested, and then, because he had no family to bond him out, he stayed in juvie for the better part of six months while we waited for the trial. His defense played the card of a tough life and blah blah blah. Anyway, because it was his first offense and he had good grades and was a supposed good guy, he got off with time served. I think he had his eighteenth birthday in the middle of the trial. All I knew is they released him and he moved into a shitty motel for a few months with some girl until he started college. I now know you were that girl."

Sam stood then, if only by pure will alone, and promptly walked straight to the bathroom where she proceeded to vomit up everything in her stomach for the next five minutes. She was vaguely aware of Callum coming in and pulling her hair out of the way.

When she finally stopped, he lifted her up from the floor and carried her back to bed. Then he brought her a glass of water and rubbed her back in soothing circles.

"That's why he lost his scholarship." She wasn't sure why that was the first thing to come out of her mouth, but how could anything have made sense in the moments after her entire view of life had been shattered into a million tiny pieces.

"What?"

"He won the same funding as I did, but he lost it right before college started. He said it was due to poor grades his senior year." She closed her eyes and tried to steady her breathing.

Callum reached out to hold her hand and began drawing little circles there. "Honestly, I didn't think you would believe me. I had this whole speech planned out in case you didn't."

"There is a small part of me that doesn't, but then again I know you wouldn't lie to me."

"I would *never* lie to you."

His mouth kept moving. He kept talking, but she didn't hear the words. There was a deafening silence that consumed her. In that silence, she found the truth. She ran through every memory of his time away, every memory of the days, weeks, months after he had returned. She thought about how she'd suddenly not been allowed to watch the news, or how when he came back, her foster father wouldn't allow him in the house to visit. It was why she had lied and snuck away to the dilapidated playground two neighborhoods over to meet him. It all made sense.

"We had never been separated. Not once. And then I came home one day during senior year and he wasn't there. They told me he was transferred to another house out in the country. We didn't see each other until the week after he aged out."

"I'm so sorry, Sam."

She looked at him then and intertwined her fingers in his. "You're sorry? No, I'm sorry." There were tears in her eyes.

"You don't have to apologize. Millie is okay. She still goes to therapy and deals with it in her own way, but–"

"No, I wasn't apologizing for that." She couldn't get the right words out. Everything was jumbled together and nothing made sense. "I mean, yes, of course, I'm sorry that happened to her. I'm so, so, so sorry that happened to her." The tears stung as they fell down her cheeks. "And I'm sorry that happened to your family. But I'm also sorry about him showing up at your house because of me, and then when you saw us playing disc golf, and—"

"You can't take the blame for something you had no knowledge of," he stated as his fingers brushed away the fallen tears.

He then reached across the bed to grab his phone.

Whoever he called must have picked up on the first ring.

"Hey. Do me a favor and send a few pictures of the chairs, okay? I can't come in right now." He waited for a moment and then spoke. "Thanks. I'll try to come in later." And then he hung up the phone.

"Who was that?"

"Chase is on shift at the moment. I'm not leaving you. Not after telling you that." He curled up behind her and kissed the back of her neck.

****

She didn't speak for the next two hours. She knew he didn't care. Callum just held her tightly and rubbed her arm, her back, her neck. He drew his little circles on her hand, and kissed her temple whenever the tears started to come.

It was midafternoon by the time she finally got out of bed and shuffled downstairs to the kitchen to eat. She was thankful Callum didn't hover when she walked out. She needed a few moments alone to think. She was standing at the counter, attempting to eat a slice of toast when she heard his conversation.

"I can't come. Just have them take back the broken ones and I'll get in touch with the company." There was a brief silence. "What do you mean we ran out? There were three boxes in the storage room when I checked yesterday." Another pause. "Jesus Christ, Chase. Just find a way to—"

"Callum!" she called from downstairs.

She heard his rushed steps pounding down the steps before

she turned around to find him staring at her, worry etched across his features.

"You okay?"

"Go to Topline," she urged.

"What?"

"I'm okay. Honestly, I could use a few moments alone. I'll meet you for dinner at y'all's house tonight."

He shook his head. "I don't want to leave you."

"Callum." She placed her hands on his cheeks. "Let me have some time alone, okay? I'll be okay."

He stared at her for far too long before placing his forehead against hers.

"Call me the second you need me. I don't care if it's two minutes after I walk out that door. Call me." He kissed her, grabbed his keys out of the bowl, and walked toward the front door. He stopped right before he crossed the threshold. "Are you sure?"

"Go. I'll call if I need you."

And then he was gone.

Chapter 56 - Sam

She had lain there in bed for far too long after Callum left, every scenario playing over in her head a thousand times. There was the thought of what Christian had done and how he had hurt Millie. There was the thought of what would've happened if Callum actually tried to hurt Christian over their last few encounters. And then there were the memories that she and Christian shared. In that one moment, she realized she'd never really known him.

How can you think you know someone so completely and then realize they are everything you despise?

When she was six and had fallen off her bike (the one that had been far too big for her, but was the only functioning one left in the house, and damn if she was going to be the last kid left who didn't know how to ride a bike) he'd helped her hobble home and then rubbed her cuts down with water when they couldn't find any antiseptic. When she was eight, he'd saved up enough money to buy her a new backpack so the other girls would stop making fun of her on the bus. When she was eleven, he'd punched Aaron Hedges in the face for calling her a fugly freckle face.

He was supposed to have been her person. He had helped her. He had fought off that boy when she was a kid, and he'd done everything he could to protect her from her foster father a few years later. He'd seen what those actions did to someone. He'd known Sara. He'd seen her pain and watched her cry. He knew she had died due to the fact that she couldn't live with herself anymore after what she'd endured. Sara couldn't take the blame nor the guilt she'd placed on herself, and she'd done the only thing she could think to do to stop it.

He had seen it all. He had known it all.

And yet he'd gone off and done the same exact thing to someone else. He'd shattered someone's world.

Sam didn't really think through what she did next. She just knew she needed answers.

> **Sam**: Where are you?
>
> **Christian**: My house.
>
> **Sam**: We need to talk.
>
> **Christian**: Can we talk tomorrow? I'm working on a project
>
> **Sam**: Callum told me the truth about Millie.
>
> **Christian**: My front door is unlocked. I promise he didn't tell you the entire truth. At least hear my part before you decide to hate me.

She quickly threw on some clothes and grabbed her purse and her water bottle. It was then that she realized she would have to take the bus. She hadn't taken it in almost two weeks now, and hell if she had time to wait through four stops before it arrived at his house.

> **Sam**: Can I borrow your car? I have an errand to run before dinner tonight at the guys' place.
>
> **Kristin**: Sure! Keys are in the bowl. See you at dinner!

She didn't even remember driving over. Her mind was racing with what to say. Or really, was there anything to say at all? Maybe she should just walk right in and punch him in his stupid fucking face.

She had thought about cutting him out of her life right then and there after Callum told her everything. She could delete and block him from her phone and never think about him again. But they had a history. A fifteen year long history. And he had never once laid a hand on her. And as much as she hated to admit it, she needed closure.

When she looked up from her death grip on the steering wheel, she found him leaning against his porch railing.

She saw him walking up the stairs to his room just as she made it into the house.

He pointed to a chair at his desk.

"Sit," he said as she walked into his room. A room she had been in countless times over the last two years.

"I'm not here to sit," she looked at him with utter disdain. "I just have one question. And I need to see your face when I ask you. Did you do it?"

He turned back to face her then and sat onto the edge of his bed.

"You aren't going to believe me no matter what I say. Your mind is already made up."

"I need to hear it from you."

He stared at her for a long moment then, leaned his head back to look at the ceiling. "Yes. I did it."

She physically recoiled. That was not what she'd expected. She'd expected him to come up with an elaborate lie. She had an entire speech planned out to prove him wrong. A surge of hot anger rushed across her skin. She turned and walked straight into his bathroom. She slammed the door shut and leaned over the sink to splash water onto her face, trying to ignore the sound of his pleading from the other side of the door.

The water did nothing to cool her down. She stared at her reflection in the mirror and knew there was no going back to what they had been before. He was now dead to her.

When she stormed back into his room, she grabbed her bag and water bottle, then turned to walk away and out of his life forever.

"It's not exactly in the way you're thinking." He rushed after her. His eyes were red with unshed tears. "Jesus, Sam. You look like you're about to have a stroke." He reached out to touch her arm, and she physically recoiled.

"That's a pretty good representation of how I feel at the current moment." She was practically spitting the venom-laced words at him.

He reached out and grabbed a glass from the table, poured himself a drink and threw it back in one swift motion, then cleared his throat.

"Just do me a favor. Let me get this entire story out before you take your side." He pointed at the chair beside her. "You might want to take a seat."

Sam didn't want to sit.

She didn't want to do anything but punch him and kick him

and hate him for all eternity.

She wanted to leave.

"Please, Sam. We have been best friends for the better part of fifteen years. You know me better than anyone else."

She scoffed at that. Her feet begged to move forward and away from him.

"At least hear me out."

She didn't move.

Christian pushed the chair out next to him. "Just sit and talk with me. Do I not at least get that after fifteen years?"

She felt her heart break for what she was about to lose. What she had already lost. That anger was still there, growing in intensity with each passing second. She was sure the beads of sweat that fell off the sides of her water bottle matched the ones now rolling down the back of her neck.

She popped open her water bottle and downed half its contents, begging for relief from the heat, and hoping she would have the courage to let him know that their fifteen-year friendship was now coming to an end.

"I'm giving you five minutes, and that is only because of our past. After that, I plan on never seeing you ever again." Her lips trembled with the words. She was losing a part of herself with him.

He buried his face in his hands. He lifted up more than once, mouth agape as if the words were about to spew forth, and then his face would fall back into his palms.

She waited.

And waited.

And waited.

The five minutes he'd requested were long gone, and she had just about decided to stand and walk out when he finally looked at her.

With a final deep breath, he spoke, "Are you and Callum officially a thing?"

She rolled her eyes. "That's not why I'm here."

He cracked a knuckle. "Just answer the question."

She was gripping the arm of the chair so tight her fingers were practically white. "What does it matter who I'm with?"

His too-quiet words dripped with barely restrained rage. *"Because you are supposed to be with ME."*

He ran his hands through his hair.

She flinched when he slammed his fist down on the top of the table.

"What?" Her eyes went wide at his abrupt change in demeanor. He didn't get to be angry. Not now. Not after she'd found out this horrible truth.

"You and me." He pointed a finger between them. "You. And. Me. That's how this is supposed to end. Not you and Callum fucking Barker."

She wanted to laugh at the absurdity of this conversation.

"There is *no such thing* as you and me! You are..." She shook her head. "You *were* my best friend. I thought I knew you! I *trusted* you! At one point, I would have said I loved you. What about everything from before? Did you just forget all the shit that happened to me in those damn houses? *What about Sara?"*

Her breaths were coming in pants.

"I wanted you for so long. I bared my heart to you three years ago on that fucking swingset, and you acted as if it was a joke. Why would I sit by and wait for you?"

"Sam," he shook his head in frustration. "It was never that I didn't want you. You were always going to end up with me, anyone with eyes or half a brain could see that."

"I'm not ending up with you." Her grip tightened on the arm of the chair.

"Yes, you are." He leaned back as he spoke the words with sheer confidence.

"No. I'm. Not."

He shook his head with a little laugh. "Listen. I had my fun. I did the whole college experience, but I'm done with that now."

"Are you serious?" Her words were barely a whisper.

"Of course. I'm ready for you and I to get together."

He was absolutely delusional. She wanted to burst out laughing in hysterics.

"You can't honestly think I would just wait around for you while you fucked everyone you laid your eyes on. I'm not just your doormat to walk all over," she stated through gritted teeth.

Those unshed tears were long gone. Now she was filled with seething anger, and she knew without a doubt she would be perfectly fine never seeing him ever again.

It didn't matter what story he had to tell her.

It didn't matter if some of the details were twisted.

It didn't matter.

He had hurt someone in a way that was absolutely unthinkable, and she would never be able to forgive him for it. He had thought he basically owned claim to her all these years. She was nothing but a possession to him.

Closure be damned.

She knew then that she didn't need an answer.

She already had one.

"Goodbye, Christian." She stood and walked to the door. It took all of her restraint to walk away instead of toward him. It took every fiber of her being to hold back the punch she wanted to land on his stupid face. She grabbed hold of the doorknob just as her vision started to blur.

Sam wiped her eyes.

She would *not* cry for him. She would *not* cry for the years and memories she was walking away from. But when her hand pulled away from her face, it was dry, and she realized there were no tears being shed. She turned to face him and the room tilted. He caught her right before her knees hit the ground.

"What is..." Her voice was too soft, and it felt as if it was moving a million miles faster than her lips. "What are you..." She looked up then to find the face she'd thought she knew better than any other now contorted into someone she didn't even recognize.

"I saw her at your meeting. That's why I wasn't there when you left."

He wasn't making any sense. "What?" She blinked her eyes, willing her vision to clear.

"Millie's mom. Mrs. Barker," he let the name slip from his lips with about as much disdain as one could muster. "After you walked into the room, she walked into a side door. Her car was parked on the street. They have a restraining order against me. So, I had to leave. I guess it's lucky I wasn't able to go to the luncheons with you this year." He shrugged.

He led her to the bed where she practically fell onto her side. She was so damn tired all of a sudden, and her arms were so heavy.

It didn't make sense.

She and Callum had spent most of the day in and out of sleep.

She should be wide awake right now.

"Why him?"

Sam tried to focus, but his voice was so far away. "What?"

"It was so easy with the other guys. You know, I think Jared was actually head over heels in love with you, even though you only went on four dates."

Her brain was so foggy.

It took far too much effort to comprehend what he was saying.

"I thought he was going to be the hardest to convince to back off. But no, you had to go and find Callum fucking Barker."

Jared?

Jared?

Who is Jared?

Then it clicked.

Jared and Sam had gone on four dates the previous summer. It may have been short lived, but they'd seemed a perfect match, and she'd been more than shocked when he'd stopped returning her calls and texts. They'd gone from spending almost every day either studying together, or getting dinner or coffee together, or going to the movies together, to complete and absolute silence. Three weeks later, when she'd seen him in passing between classes, he had all but run in the other direction.

"I didn't even have to work at breaking up you and Jackson. By the time I realized you two were getting serious, you went ahead and caused that blunder by telling him everything about you."

She was so tired.

She could barely hold her head up.

Maybe she should call someone to drive her home.

"You don't get it. Never have. But I think you will understand more after today."

"Christian. I need my phone." It took more effort than she expected to get that sentence out completely clearly.

He snickered. "So you can call your boyfriend?"

"Christian, please. Hand it to me."

She tried to reach out her hand, but it didn't move. It was so heavy.

And her brain felt as if it was rushing through a thousand clouds, each neuron firing off into oblivion with no final destination in sight.

"Please." Her whimper was so low. He probably didn't even hear it.

She breathed a sigh of relief when he walked over to her purse and dug out the phone. He walked right up to her and reached out as if to hand it over. She felt her fingers move, and her hand inched up just slightly in reach. Right before she grabbed it, he held down the button and turned it off.

"Uh, uh, uh." He pulled it back out of her reach. "I'm assuming you and your new little group all follow each other in some way. Best not to let them know where you are." Then he threw her phone on the ground.

"Why would you do that?" She tried to lunge forward to grab

it and promptly fell off the bed. There was a realization that the fall should have hurt more than it did. The floor was hard. But she barely registered the pain of the impact over the nauseating weightlessness as she'd tumbled down.

He left her laying there as he kicked the phone further away and under the desk chair.

"You know what is probably the worst part about all of this? It's that you became the exact thing we hate."

"What?" Her brain was so foggy, and he wasn't making sense now.

He bent down so he was now hovering over her. "We are different from them, Sam. They are soft, and weak, and grew up without knowing what a tough life really was. They grew up with a fucking silver spoon in their mouths while we dumpster dived after class. Remember that?" He jerked her chin around, forcing her to meet his gaze. "Remember jumping the school fences every week to see what supplies the rich kids threw out that we could use? It was their trash we were living off of. You and I are just trash to them. Callum doesn't really love you. Hell, I doubt he even likes you. This is probably some little experiment he will get a good laugh from down the road."

"Christian, you have no idea what you are talking about." She barely recognized her own voice now. Her mouth didn't feel like her own, and half the words came out completely slurred.

"It was the same with Millie. I knew she wanted me, but she wouldn't admit it. I was not the cookie cutter picture of perfection. I didn't fit into her world. I didn't fit the mold. That night she turned me down was only because she was around her snooty group of friends. But she got what she wanted in the end."

"Call Callum."

Christian started to laugh. "You're not his. You never were, and you never will be." He bent down to face her more fully. "You are mine. You always have been."

Christian reached out to pick her up. She was practically

dead weight at this point. She tried to grasp onto him, but her fingers felt so weak. She knew then that something was very wrong.

"I need help."

"That's the most honest statement I've heard you say as of late."

"Please." It was then that she realized she was scared. Christian was scaring her, and that was an emotion she wasn't sure how to handle.

"I didn't want to do this." Christian stood over her as he spoke.

"Call an ambulance." She was frantically trying to dislodge her mind from whatever had taken hold.

"Have you already fucked him?"

"Please call someone."

Her vision was going in and out of focus, but this time she felt the wetness running down her face and she knew she was crying.

The hardwood floor underneath her suddenly became soft.

And then it was dark.

And then she was cold.

Christian always kept his room so cold. She'd never understood why. A few minutes ago, she'd been so filled with burning rage that she hadn't even noticed.

But she no longer had the energy for such rage, and the light had gone away.

Now, she was so damn cold.

She rolled over and tried to grab the covers at her side. Maybe if she pulled them over her naked body, she would warm up. But her fingers wouldn't grasp the sheets, and her eyelids felt so heavy.

A hand ran down her back and then a kiss was placed on her shoulder. She wasn't sure when Callum had arrived, but the thought somehow calmed her.

"Callum?" She turned her face to kiss him. A lazy, drunken smile covered her face.

"*Not* Callum," came Christian's voice from behind her. Her heart rate picked up and she blinked her eyes open.

"Christian?"

She tried to scoot away. Her eyes, still barely able to focus on what was in front of them, shot from one end of the room to the other.

She wasn't in her room.

She was in Christian's room.

Why was she here in Christian's room?

Why was she naked in Christian's room?

"Christian, stop." The words, barely loud enough to be considered a whisper, sounded so far away. Like she was in a tunnel and yet she was calling out from the other side.

"Stop what, baby? I can tell you like it. I've been waiting so long to give this to you."

He dug his fingers into her thighs to keep her legs apart, and that action brought back far too many memories.

Memories of that boy and that man.

Memories of being held down.

Memories of Sara screaming.

Memories of rough, unwanted hands and lips and...

Memories of her tear-filled nightmares that had followed.

She felt the too-familiar urge to slip away into oblivion, and thought perhaps it would be easier in her current state.

"Christian. Stop!" Her voice was louder this time.

She couldn't move to stop him; her arms still wouldn't obey her. They might as well have belonged to someone else.

"Shh. It's okay. You're mine," he cooed into her ear. That voice that had once calmed her, that had once brought her so much happiness and joy, was now a vile melody she longed to never hear again.

She felt her chest tighten and bile rise as his hands roamed her body, holding her steady against him.

She hated him.

She hated him more than she had ever hated anyone.

"No! Christian. Stop! Stop!" She screamed this time. She screamed it over and over and over again. She wasn't sure if she was saying it out loud or just in her head. But after a moment, she heard his bedroom door burst open. And then he was no longer there.

"Sam?"

She knew that voice.

It was quiet and calm and familiar.

The light turned on and she had to squint her eyes. It was so bright and loud and it was too much all at once. She curled into herself as she felt the sobs race through her.

"Sam?" the voice called out once more. This time it was closer. This time it was louder. This time it was sad.

Then there was fighting and yelling, and things were breaking in the background.

"Sam!" Her face was being held. Someone was shaking her. She was going to vomit. "Sam, look at me! Open your eyes!" They sounded upset. So upset.

But she couldn't open her eyes.

She was too tired. And too sore. And too cold. Then that cold disappeared as she felt a heavy softness cover her skin.

And then she accepted oblivion at last, and it all went quiet.

Chapter 57 - Callum

"Where is Sam?" Callum asked as Kristin and Micah walked into their living room.

"She isn't here already? I thought she was for sure going to beat us?" Kristin said as she hung up her raincoat on the half-broken stand.

"What?" Callum questioned.

"She took my car. Said she had to run an errand and then would be headed here for dinner. But that was, like, two hours ago?"

Callum had only ever had that sick-to-your-stomach feeling two times in his life. Once was the night he'd found out about Millie. The other was during the twenty-seven foot walk it had taken to go from his car to his parents' front door the day he'd told his mom about his dad. Tonight was now the third time that feeling made itself known.

He reached for his phone and let out a curse when he saw it was dead.

"Call her," he all but demanded of Kristin. His voice was frantic and foreign.

Kristin furrowed her brow at his tone. "You okay?"

"I'm going to grab my charger. Just call her, okay?"

He didn't even wait for her to respond before he was downstairs and yanking the cord from the wall. By the time he made it back to the living room, she was setting her phone down on the table while Micah was fixing them a drink.

"It went straight to voicemail, but I left her a message. I'm sure she'll be here soon."

Callum opened his mouth to tell her to try her again when Kristin's phone lit up with Sam's name and photo on the screen.

A sigh of relief slipped past his lips.

Kristin answered with a laugh as she said, "Listen. Callum must be super horny because he is over here—" She abruptly clamped her mouth shut and a confused look covered her face. "I'm sorry, what?"

That feeling in Callum's stomach came back, and this time it was ten times worse than it had ever been before.

"Who are you?" Kristin questioned an unknown person on the phone.

"What's going on?" Callum was across the living room before he had finished the question.

Kristin sucked in a shaky breath and then reached to grab ahold of Micah. "Oh my god." The words were barely a whisper.

"What is going on?" It took every ounce of restraint Callum possessed not to yank the phone from Kristin's ear.

This time it was Kristin's voice that became shaky and foreign. "What hospital is she going to?"

He couldn't breathe.

His chest caved in on itself and his stomach flipped upside down.

He couldn't think or focus or breathe.

He wasn't sure how, but in a matter of seconds he had on a pair of shoes, had found his wallet, and was reaching for his keys. Micah jumped in front of him to swipe them away.

"You aren't driving." Micah ran to the banister that led upstairs. "Drew! I need Mel's car keys! Now!"

"Just let me drive my goddamn truck," Callum yelled out.

In reality, he didn't even know where he was headed. He was waiting for Kristin to give away some more information, but she stood still and stone-faced as she listened to whoever was on the

---

other line.

"No, you'll get in a wreck trying to get there. We're taking Mel's car. It's the only one that will fit all of us if she ends up being able to leave the hospital tonight."

Callums' mind went in a thousand different directions.

If she ends up being able to leave the hospital...

If...

If...

If...

"Why wouldn't she be able to leave?" The myriad of possible answers to that question raced through him along with a crumpling weight that settled in the pit of his stomach.

"What the fuck is going on?" Drew came bursting down the stairs at the commotion. Melanie was right behind him.

"Sam's in the hospital. I'm not letting Callum drive. I need Mel's car so the four of us will fit." That seemed to be all the explanation they needed, and without a word, Melanie was digging in her purse and tossing Micah her keys.

"What happened?" Drew asked as they all headed for the door.

Micah looked to Kristin who was still listening too intently to the person on the other line. "I don't know. I'll call you as soon as I find out."

****

Callum was shaking.

It took three tries and they were already on the main road before he was finally able to click in his seat belt.

"Go to Baptist." It was the first utterance Kristin had made, and Callum could tell her voice was breaking.

His mind raced through a thousand questions at once. "Is she okay? Did she have a wreck? What happened?"

"No" was Kristin's only reply.

"No, she isn't okay, or no, she didn't have a wreck?" Callum raised his voice, earning a sideways glare from Micah.

"She didn't have a wreck. She is at Baptist. Go there."

"Damnit, Kristin. Tell me what happened!" He reached out and grabbed the headrest as the broken words left his mouth.

"Calm down, Callum," Micah all but yelled back at him. "Or I'm dropping you off on the sidewalk."

"Stop. Everyone. Just stop," Kristin was crying now which wasn't good. "It's not fair. She is too good for this shit. She doesn't deserve this. Not again."

Callum opened his mouth. He wanted to yell at her to stop speaking in codes and tell him what the hell was going on, but he caught Micah's warning glance in the rear view mirror.

It took significant restraint to lower his voice. "Kristin, hey. Turn around and look at me." He almost wished he hadn't asked. The look on her face caused every possible horrible scenario to race to the forefront of his mind. "Is she okay?"

Kristin nodded. Tears still streaming down her face. "Yeah. I think so. She is now."

"Thank God," he whispered into his hands as he tried to calm every bubbling emotion that threatened to burst free.

They were halfway there, but it was taking too long. If Micah hadn't taken his keys, Callum knew he would already be with her.

"What happened?" Micah asked Kristin, much kinder than Callum would have.

Kristin turned to look back at Callum and then to Micah. He wasn't sure why she hesitated, but he knew it couldn't have been good. She couldn't quite seem to formulate what she wanted to say. She then took a deep breath as if mustering up all her courage to get it out.

"Sam went to Christian's house." She looked back to Callum just as his jaw tensed. "I don't know everything. The girl, Amanda, I think was her name, didn't know all the details either. But, they think Christian drugged her."

Callum punched the seat.

"I'm going to kill him."

His mind began to race. This wasn't happening.

Not again.

Not again.

Please, not again.

If he had just kept his mouth shut and not told her, then she wouldn't have gone. She would be back at his house sitting beside him instead of inside of a goddamn hospital.

"Why couldn't you talk to her?" Micah chimed in as they pulled into the parking lot.

Kristin was still a mess of tears and frantic movements as if she still didn't believe what she had been told. "I don't know. Amanda said she was still really out of it from whatever drug she had in her system and didn't know what was going on when they left her in the ambulance. They are meeting us at the hospital with her purse and stuff."

"What about him?" Micah questioned.

"He was arrested."

Callum sighed in relief.

His only regret in hearing that was that he would have to wait till Christian was bonded out before he could kill him.

"Callum." His name was a warning on Micah's lips. "Don't go there." He snapped his head up to find Micah in the rearview mirror staring him down.

Callum furrowed his brow. "What?"

"I know what you are thinking. You aren't going to kill him. It sounds like he got caught and he will have to pay for it, okay? Don't do something stupid and get yourself locked up as well."

When they pulled up to the hospital, they parked and made it inside in record time.

"Sam. Samantha Williams. Where is she?" Callum all but yelled at the receptionist behind the desk.

He needed to get back there. He needed to be with her.

The woman didn't even blink at his outburst. Apparently, this kind of frantic behavior was fairly normal in the emergency room.

"Give me one moment," she said as she walked to the back. That moment felt like a lifetime.

He paced the floor and then counted the thirty-seven black tiles that lined the checkered design of the walls. When the woman still wasn't back at that point, he counted the lights in the ceiling; twenty-one. He had to keep his mind busy or else he would punch something.

"She is here, but I'll need to see your ID's."

They all frantically began yanking out their licenses and handing them over.

"I'm sorry. None of you are listed on the emergency contact form from the university."

"What?" Callum wanted to scream. "I'm her boyfriend! I need to be in there," he stated at the same time Kristin yelled something about being her best friend. He was going to tear this whole hospital down if he couldn't see Sam soon. He had to make sure she was okay.

"I'm sorry, sir. Hospital policy is to only allow emergency contacts until the patient is able to state otherwise."

Callum furrowed his brow and his heart just about stopped as it hit him.

"She can't talk?"

"I can't release any information, I'm sorry."

It was then that Micah finally chimed in. "Who is the contact?"

"Someone by the name of Christian Phillips."

Callum's eyes went wide and he punched the counter top.

He was pretty sure that punch caused a sprain, if not a mild break. The pain lanced upward, but he didn't even flinch.

"Well, sorry, but that asshole is currently in jail for assaulting her, so he isn't coming!" Callum screamed out. The woman flinched and then waved over a security guard as Callum started pacing the floor, his hands fisted into his hair.

Micah threw up his hands as he turned to the guard. "I'm taking him outside. I'm going to get him to calm down." It was a plea, and thankfully the guard stopped his forward movements. The last thing they needed was Callum placed in a cell beside Christian. "Kristin. Do whatever–"

"I'm going to get us into that room. Just calm him down."

Micah nodded as he dragged a practically hyperventilating Callum from the waiting room. He managed to get Callum outside to a bench before he took a breath.

"Fuck," Callum dragged out the word. "FUCK!" he screamed to the parking lot full of cars. Never had he felt so helpless and angry and sad all at the same time.

"She's going to be okay." Micah placed his hand on Callum's shoulder to comfort him, yet all Callum felt was a mixture of physical pain and unending anger.

"I did this," Callum's voice broke.
Micah wasn't sure what he could mean.

"I did this. I told her about Millie."

"What about Millie?"
Callum took a steadying breath. He hadn't spoken of this in years, and now he was mentioning it twice in less than a day. He hoped Millie could forgive him.

"Millie was raped a few years back. The guy who did it was underage, so he only served a few months in juvie. It's a sealed case, so I'm not supposed to talk about it. More so, I promised Millie I would never speak of it again. She wanted it to disappear and be as if it never happened. I kept my promise and I haven't said a word. Not until this morning. I told Sam."
Micah sat there for a moment in utter shock. He opened his mouth more than once, willing the words to come forth.

"I never knew. I'm so sorry." Micah squeezed his shoulder, clearly unsure of how he was supposed to react.

Callum shook his head. "It is what it is."

He buried his face in his hands and replayed their entire

conversation in his head. Then he replayed the sounds of her barely audible whimpers as the tears fell. He wondered if she was crying right now.

Was she alone and scared?

Were the doctors and nurses being kind to her?

Was she still stuck inside the haze of whatever drug had been used on her?

He was rocking back and forth, begging the multitude of what-ifs to end, when he heard his name being called and felt his shoulders rattle.

"Hey," Micah timidly caught his attention. "I'm sorry. I'm so sorry that happened to Millie, but what does that have to do with what happened tonight with Sam?"

Callum looked back at the ground between his legs.

"Christian was the guy that raped Millie."

Micah's eyes went wide in shock. "Holy shit, dude."

"I know." He covered his face with the collar of his shirt as he wiped away the tears and snot that had started to form. "I shouldn't have told her. But she wanted to go have lunch with him and I was so mad and I didn't want her to ever see him again. I told her this morning. She was so upset."

Micah pulled his face upward then. From the look reflecting in Micah's eyes, Callum was damn sure he had never once looked this pained before.

"Dude, this isn't your fault."

Callum pushed away.

"Yes, it is. If I hadn't..." Callum stopped.

He couldn't breathe.

He tried desperately to suck in air as he felt his chest compressing with the weight of all that was happening, but the air wouldn't come. And then his palms were sweaty and his head felt heavy and his view was spinning.

He had to get to her.

He would break down the damn door if that's what it took.

They would probably take him to jail for it, but that was what he wanted. He felt his fist clench and expand as the vision of what he would do once in that cell became clearer.

"Callum. Man." Micah reached down to grasp his hands and then pulled him in. "Calm down. You're going to hyperventilate."

Callum felt the tears hit his cheeks before he even knew he was crying.

"Shit man. Okay. Okay. It's okay. Let me check, and I'll try to get us back there."

The second Micah stood up, Kristin walked through the sliding doors.

"It's useless. She is still somewhat out of it and can't really talk, and they won't let us back there until she gives the okay."

"This is fucking insane!" Callum screamed through the tears.

"What about Connor?" Kristin asked.

That got Callum's attention. "What?"

"What about Connor? When I saw him at my parents house, he mentioned he was on a rotation this semester at Baptist ER. He could be in there right now. See if he can get us in there." Kristin was pleading now.

Callum hadn't spoken to Connor in months. Theirs wasn't necessarily the worst relationship, but since everything had gone down with their parents, they had barely spoken. None of that mattered. He hit the button before he even thought twice.

Connor answered on the second ring.

"What's wrong?" For some reason, his older brother's voice was exactly what he needed to hear.

"Are you at Baptist?"

"Yes." Connor's reply was quick.

"I can't get in. My girlfriend is inside, and they won't let me in." He wasn't even sure if the words were clear. He just needed to get it out as quickly as possible.

"Where are you?"

"Outside the ER on a bench by the parking lot."

"Give me five minutes and I'll be there."

The line went dead.

True to his word, Connor came directly outside. Callum had been able to hold in most of his emotions until that point, but for some reason seeing his older brother—the brother he hadn't spoken with for months, the brother he was sure still hated him for breaking up their perfect little family bubble, the brother who used to be his best friend—it broke him.

He crashed into Connor, wrapping his arms around his neck.

"What happened?" Connor questioned anyone who would listen as Callum let the dam break.

Micah gaped, clearly unable to voice anything. Kristin was sobbing along with Callum. When it was clear that no one else was able to answer, Callum pulled back and looked Connor in the eye.

"It's my girlfriend, Sam. Samantha Williams..." And then Callum explained what had happened and the connection with Christian.

"Oh my god," Kristin stated in utter shock, slapping a hand over her mouth as the reality of how they were all intertwined came to light. "Oh my god!" She kept repeating it over and over, as if saying it out loud would somehow make the situation more real.

"Okay." Connor took a deep breath and looked between them. "Let me go in and find out what's going on. I'm still technically a resident, so I don't have that much sway, but I can maybe get one of you in or find out more about her condition." He started to walk off, but then turned back to grab Callum by the face. "She isn't currently my patient, but even if I can't get you in there, I promise to try and have her switched to my care. Okay? I'll make sure she is taken care of. I'll park my ass in her room for the remainder of the night if needed, okay?"

"Thank you." There were still tears running down Callum's face when Connor ran off. "Connor!" Callum yelled. "Tell her I...tell her I'm here, okay? Make sure she knows I'm here."

Chapter 58 - Sam

The light was bright, and there was so much beeping. She tried to turn her head, but her disorientation brought on a wave of nausea that sent her vomiting into a blue bag.

She reached out to grab the arm of the person holding that bag, but she was too unsteady.

"It's okay." The man held her hair back and rubbed her shoulders as she emptied what was left in her stomach.

His voice was so familiar, and yet it wasn't. When the heaving ceased, she looked up to find Callum. Except, this Callum had somehow covered up all his tattoos and now had a full head of short, gelled down hair.

"Am I drunk?" Sam's voice was so dry and raspy.

"No. You're not drunk."

"You're not Callum," she stated and blinked a few times, making sure what she was seeing wasn't a hallucination.

"No. I'm Connor, Callum's older brother. We met at the Hadley's a few weeks back."

She nodded her head in understanding.

"What's going on?" Her voice was raspy and quiet.

"What do you remember?"

She blinked again and tried to recall anything. Her mind was blank. "I don't know." She looked around then as she finally realized where she was. Her eyes went wide. "I'm at the hospital?"

"Yes."

"Is Callum okay?"

Of course her first thought was about someone else.

Connor frantically nodded his head. "He's fine. He's here, outside in the waiting room."

It was then that a nurse walked into the room.

"She's awake?"

"Yeah," Connor answered for her.

"What happened?" Sam questioned.

The nurse motioned for someone else to enter the room. In a matter of seconds, another nurse, a doctor, and a police officer walked in.

"I'm your nurse. My name is Bella. This is Dr. Guine and Officer Palotte. I think you already know Dr. Barker. Is it okay if we ask you a few questions?"

"What happened?" She felt like she was on repeat.

"That's what we are trying to figure out," Dr. Guine stated. "What is the last thing you remember about tonight?"

She sat up more fully then, and Connor passed over a cup of water which she graciously accepted.

"I was at my house, and then I left to go talk to..." Her eyes shot up then as the fuzzy memories started to flash through her mind.

"Who did you go see?"

"I went to see Christian. I was going to confront him about Millie." Connor audibly swallowed. "We were in his room. We started fighting. I tried to leave." She took another sip of her water. "I don't know. I just remember being so mad and trying to leave, but..." Sam paused for a moment as she tried to recall what exactly had occurred. "I think I was walking to the stairs and then I was back in his room. It was so cold."

Her voice broke as her eyes shot forward.

She knew then.

She knew where this was leading, and why there was an officer in the room.

"Do you remember anything else?" Officer Palotte questioned.

"I remember he kept saying 'mine' over and over again. And then I didn't have on my clothes, and I tried to pull the blanket over me, and..." she paused, taking a steadying breath, "I think there was a fight. I remember yelling and something shattered in the background." Her voice was trembling as she whispered the truth to what had happened to her. She couldn't say it any louder. If she did, it would make it more real.

She frantically looked between the group.

"What happened?" her voice broke as she repeated the question.

It was Officer Palotte that filled in the rest of the story.

"A woman named Amanda went upstairs to find you. She said Christian's door was locked, but she heard you screaming from inside. Her boyfriend and another guy busted down the door. They called 911 and held Christian down until we could get there. She said there was no way you were drunk, because she had seen you walking in the house twenty minutes prior and you were completely sober then."

Sam was shaking.

And then she was vomiting once more.

Connor held onto her as the bouts of dry heaving took over. Then he wiped off her tear-stained eyes when she finished.

For a split second, when she first awoke, she'd been confused as to how she had gotten so drunk that she was sent to the hospital. She would never have let that happen. Now she realized she didn't feel drunk at all. She didn't even feel like she had a hangover. She just felt confused and as if she was missing an entire portion of her life. She felt dirty, and angry, and she wanted nothing more than for Callum to be in that room.

"Where's Callum?" She looked at Connor for the answer.

"Is it okay if I bring him in? It's him, Micah, and Kristin."

Sam frantically nodded her head as the sobs took over.

She looked around to find the room had all but emptied except for the nurse while she'd heaved over the side of the bed.

At Sam's request, Bella had brought over a mirror when Connor left the room.

The sight looking back at her was nothing like she had ever seen.

It was only then that she realized she wasn't wearing her clothes from earlier, but was sitting in a hospital gown. Her hair was a mess. There was a bruise forming on her left cheek and her upper lip was split open with one suture keeping it closed. There was what she believed to be a handprint on the bottom of her neck and a bite mark on her shoulder.

"There are some other bruises on your hips, and then on the insides of your thighs," Bella said gently as she reached out to take the mirror back.

Sam just nodded. She didn't want to see those bruises yet. She hoped she never would.

She steeled her face, not sure whether grief or anger or hate was about to take over. The silent tears continued down her face as if a river had burst through a previously unmovable dam.

It was only seconds after the nurse walked out before she heard running and the curtain being yanked back. She had turned over and was facing the wall, but she knew it was him. She didn't hear him move, but she was sure he was looking at the apparent bruises on the back of her arms. She knew she looked like a mess, but she couldn't bring herself to care at the moment.

She heard his footsteps inch closer. She thought for a moment that she may have still been experiencing the effects of the drugs because, when he finally came into view, she swore it looked as if he'd been crying. His eyes were bloodshot. His face was tear-stained.

He really did need a haircut. This was the longest she'd ever seen it, and he had to push it back away from his face. That's when she could really focus on his features.

He reached out to touch her arm, and she involuntarily jerked away. She didn't mean to, it just happened.

"It's just me. I'm not going to hurt you." His voice was so low it came as barely more than a whisper. He bent down so they were eye level. He slowly placed his hand on her cheek, and she reached up to grab it. He must have thought she was flinching again, because he quickly started to pull back.

"No, come back." Sam still didn't recognize her voice. She was barely audible.

As he replaced his hand, he leaned over so their foreheads touched.

"I'm sorry. I shouldn't have–"

"Sam, stop. Please. I'm so sorry. Don't blame yourself for this, okay? Don't do that."

She heard more footsteps and Kristin's audible gasp as she and Micah made their way into her room.

This didn't feel real.

It was as if she was watching everything happening from the outside. Like she was floating outside her own reality and Callum was the only thing anchoring her to the world. She would wake up in a few minutes and all of this would be a bad dream. She closed her eyes and tightened her hold around her middle, willing herself to wake.

"Sam?" Callum furrowed his brow as he tentatively sat on the bed next to her. "Sam, give me your hands."

He reached out to slowly pry her fingers from the grip they had on her arms. He sucked in a shaky breath.

"Hey! Connor!" Callum urgently stated as he began to rub his hand across her arm.

She heard Connor's quick footsteps and in moments he was standing beside Callum. It was odd to see them side by side. So alike and yet so different.

"Get something to wipe this off and maybe a bandage. She dug her fingernails into her arm."

Connor ran his hand through his hair just like Callum did. Apparently, that habit was genetic in nature. She almost wanted to laugh at the movement. But then she thought she might not know how to laugh anymore, and that bubble of humor that had started to seep upward was halted by a new invisible brick wall within her mind.

The nurse came in before Connor had a chance to respond, stating they still needed to collect evidence for the rape kit. That phrase caused another wave of nausea to race through Sam. She closed her eyes and tried to shut out the world as the nurse explained the process. She vaguely remembered nodding in agreement, asking Kristin to stay, and then Kristin ushering Micah and a very unwilling Callum out of the room.

It was amazing how well someone could disassociate from what was occurring around them—to them. Sam focused on Kristin's arms that encompassed her and listened as she hummed along to a broken tune as the nurse did what needed to be done.

They both cried when it was over.

She had no idea how long they stayed in that room. At some point, Kristin had found a comb and managed to somehow tame the mess on her head. She had also spent a considerable amount of time wiping off the mascara stains that her tears had spread across Sam's cheeks.

When she was being discharged, the nurse rolled in a wheelchair for her to use. Callum quickly shook his head and then proceeded to pick her up and carry her all the way to the car.

She wanted to tell him she could walk or that she was fine, but in all honesty, she was too tired to even force the words out.

The ride home was silent and all she could focus on were the circles Callum traced on her hands.

Callum all but carried her into the house while Kristin ran upstairs to start a bath. Sam had no idea what time it was, but as Kristin was washing the soap out of her hair, she saw the light from the sunrise flow in from the bathroom window.

By the time she got into bed next to Callum, the sun was completely up and she was barely able to keep her eyes open.

"I'm here, okay?" Callum said as he ran his fingers through her damp hair.

"I'm scared to go to sleep," she admitted as tears filled her eyes. It was the first time she'd spoken since leaving the hospital.

At some point over the last two weeks since they'd returned home from Charleston, she had told him about all the nightmares that had plagued her after enduring life in that foster home all those years ago. She knew even worse nightmares were about to come.

"I know. But I'm here, and I'm staying up. I'll wake you the second they start."

She rolled into him then and buried her face in the crook of his neck. She breathed him in. That smell—*his* smell—was somehow the one thing she needed to help calm her.

Chapter 59 - Sam

Five Weeks Later - June

"Hi," Sam timidly stated as she walked down the steps.

"Hey," Callum replied as he slowly lifted his hand to reach out and touch her.

Five weeks of therapy later, and she still sometimes flinched when someone touched her. Even him. She knew it broke him every time, but she couldn't make it stop.

But today was a good day.

She melted into his arms and said, "You didn't have to stay. Kristin said she could pick me up."

"I know. I still wanted to be here." Callum kissed her cheek.

He never missed a session. He was always there. She'd come out to find him sitting in the lobby, or the car, or on the front porch steps after every single session.

She had initially balked at the idea of weekly therapy sessions at the trauma counseling center. She was supposed to be able to adapt to anything that was thrown in her face. She was supposed to be resilient. She'd quickly learned it didn't matter how strong you were, there were just some things you shouldn't have to go through alone.

It also helped that it happened to be only a mile or so away from Topline. And if she was being completely honest, the therapy wasn't horrible.

Her therapist, Irene, didn't push her at all. She let her talk when she was ready. That may have meant spending the first forty minutes of that first hour in almost complete silence, but now talking to her felt like talking to an old friend. Their sessions mostly covered things that had happened to her in her childhood through teenage years. Those experiences were so far in the past and somehow felt like safer topics. It was like peeling back an onion. Each session she offered up a little more information, and each session she left feeling a tad bit lighter.

She hadn't yet broached the subject of Christian. That pain was still too fresh. There were a few rare moments in which she opened up to Callum. She could tell he wanted her to talk about it more but, just like Irene, Callum never pushed her. And at night, when the nightmares became too much to bear, he held her close.

They hadn't spent a single night apart since she'd left the hospital. That was probably the reason he had pretty much moved into her room. Paint supplies and all. They were actively discussing the possibility of moving into a place together for her senior year, but that was an entirely separate process she just didn't have the mental capacity for at the moment.

"What's for dinner?" Sam asked as she hopped up into his truck.

"I need to grab some paperwork from Topline, so I was thinking we could swing by and get something off the menu, that way we don't have to cook."

Sam gave him a large smile in place of a yes. She had always loved the food at Topline, and dating the owner meant she no longer had to pay a thing for meals. She didn't hate that at all.

By the time she crawled into bed that night, Callum was right behind her. He was mentally exhausted from spending any free moment with his head bent over a canvas.

It was his therapy.

She still held onto the hope that he would agree to go to the center and find someone to work through his own trauma with but, just as he didn't push her, she didn't push him.

There were days when she hated walking into that room and sitting on that couch, and then there were days when she practically ran inside.

Grief was a funny thing. It made itself known in the most random of places. It would hide away for a few minutes, or hours, or even days, and then just when she thought she was getting better, just when she forgot exactly why she needed to remember it in the first place, it would insert itself exactly where she didn't want it to be.

"Even the most perfectly paved roads have bumps." That's what Irene had said that one day when Sam was bursting with anger.

"What?" Sam had questioned through the tears.

"They can level the dirt and smooth out the clay. They can level the gravel and put the lines in exactly the right place, and a tree limb, or hurricane, or hot day will cause the road to split, or bend, or break."

Sam had just stared at her then, her lips slightly trembling.

"Your road started off with a few bumps. Hell, your road started off missing entire pieces. But you worked hard, and you smoothed that road out. You filled in all the little cracks and potholes, and you painted the lines exactly as they should be. You paved an immaculate road. One that most anyone would love to travel. And then a wayward root that you never planned for sprung up from the depths of the earth and tore a seam directly down the middle."

Sam had found herself nodding.

"You can plan and organize and detail out every single scenario you can think of, but there will always be things outside of your control."

"I just want to go back to before." Sam's voice had come out as a whisper.

"You can't. You can find what you need, and you can patch the hole. You can fill it, and smooth it out, and make it look perfect on the outside. But deep down under the surface, there will always be a small crack. You may even patch it up so well that no one may ever even know it's there. But it won't just go away. You can't go back to before the crack formed. But, you can stop it from spreading."

You can stop it from spreading.

That was the phrase that kept spinning through her mind as she lay in bed, snuggled up to Callum.

"I want to volunteer at one of the group homes," Sam blurted out as Callum drew lazy circles along her back.

His hand paused. "Where did that come from?"

Sam shrugged. In reality, the thought had popped into her mind a few times over the last few weeks.

"I don't know."

"Okay. I'll go with you if you need me."

She looked up at him. His face was barely visible in the darkened room, but his blue eyes still seemed to glisten.

"Have I ever told you how much I love your eyes?"

He batted them for dramatic effect and she laughed into his chest.

"Quite a few times, I believe." He kissed the top of her head.

It was true. She had recently started telling him everything she loved about him. Sometimes it was his eyes, sometimes his hair or tattoos. Sometimes it was the way he folded the bath towel or loaded the dishwasher. Sometimes it was just how he let her be. It was her way of telling him she loved him without saying the actual words. That was still too frightening of a concept.

But she did love him, and that scared her more than she wanted to admit.

August

She had been rushing around all day, trying to make everything look perfect. She had swept three times and vacuumed twice. The counters had been wiped down, and she had fluffed the pillows each time she walked by them.

Fall semester of her senior year was less than a month away, and they were still in the process of looking for a place to rent for that year. There were only two more weeks left on her and Kristin's lease, so they needed to hurry. But tonight Sam wasn't worried about moving, or rentals, or credit checks.

Tonight, she was having Ashlyn Clemmings over for dinner.

"Can you calm down?" Callum laughed from his spot on the couch.

Kristin had left about an hour ago, shortly after helping Sam get ready, and was at Micah's for the weekend. Tonight it was just her and Callum...and his mom.

She was hosting her boyfriend's mom for dinner for the first time. Sam felt like that was a completely normal reason to be nervous. The twelve panic attacks she'd had over the past three days were more because this would be the first time she and Ms. Clemmings had sat down together since that disciplinary meeting back in the spring.

"What if the chicken tastes horrible?"

"We both already taste tested it. It's amazing, as always," he tried to calm her.

"What if she thinks the house is a mess and thinks I'm a pig and doesn't want us together?"

Callum shook his head.

"Have you forgotten what my room looked like before?" Then he gestured to the room around them. "This place could be on the cover of a magazine."

Sam assessed the space. She and Kristin had spent the better part of the last week cleaning, and organizing, and buying decor to make it look absolutely perfect. Which was silly, really, since they were only going to be here a few more days. She was thinking through all the extra stuff they needed to pack when a rapid knock on the door brought her back to the present.

Callum stood and opened it. Sam stood a few feet behind him.

"Hi, sweetheart. I brought some wine. I wasn't sure what Sam preferred, but this is a favorite of mine. I hope she likes it."

Sam couldn't see Ms. Clemmings, but she could tell from her voice that the woman was all smiles.

When she tilted her head around Callum to find Sam, that inkling was confirmed.

"Samantha!" Ms. Clemmings left Callum standing at the door with the bottle of wine in his hands as she rushed inside and wrapped Sam up tightly in her arms.

Sam gave Callum a wide-eyed stare.

Ms. Clemmings lingered for just a moment and then pulled back.

"You know. I knew there was something special about you. I just wish I had known how important you were that day. I would have kicked all those other fussies out before it even started."

"Hi," Sam awkwardly stated and then started to laugh.

Ms. Clemmings hugged her once more, and this time when she pulled back she surveyed the room.

"Oh, this place is so lovely!" She squeezed Sam's hands as she spoke. She was really glad her brain allowed her to enjoy all this physical touch from Ms. Clemmings. The therapy was really helping.

Callum promptly poured them each a glass of the wine his mom had brought. Sam was beyond thankful. It was only then that she realized she should have probably taken a shot—or two or three—before Ms. Clemmings arrived.

As Callum plated dinner, the two ladies sat on the couch. Sam was so very nervous that Ms. Clemmings would bring up her classes, or future plans, or Christian, or really anything else that might have been in that folder that held the secrets to Sam's life. She had hoped tonight would be free from the constraints of her past and, true to Ms. Clemmings's character, she didn't bring up a word.

They instead spent the better part of the evening discussing Callum's newfound success at running a restaurant and how well the tattoo shops were doing. Ms. Clemmings beamed with pride with every word that came from Callum's lips. She also gushed over how well Sam was doing in classes, but didn't stray too far away from safe topics.

By the time the evening was over, Sam and Ms. Clemmings had made plans for the following week to go shopping with Millie as she prepared for her sophomore year. Millie was moving out of the dorms and into her own place, and needed an abundance of things to fill the space. Sam gleefully agreed.

"She loves you," Callum told her as they watched his mom drive off.

"She loves *you*," Sam amended and then added, "And she is so proud of you, Callum. Did you see the way she was looking at you as you spoke? I bet she can barely get through an hour of her day without beaming about all of your accomplishments."

He kissed her cheek, then they headed back inside to clean up from dinner.

September

"You know, you don't have to do this," Callum stated as he buttoned up the black dress shirt.

"I know."

Sam was standing in their bedroom, staring into the mirror.

The bruises had all faded, and most of the scars were disappearing as well. There was still a miniscule line that hovered over her top lip from where Christian had apparently hit her when she'd tried to fight back. Callum kissed the spot daily. But more than anything, the nightmares were still there. She knew in some small part that they always would be. They weren't as all-consuming as they had been those first few weeks after it happened, but they still lingered.

"Kristin and Micah just pulled up," Callum said as he poked his head back into their room.

In truth, she hadn't even heard him walk out. When she looked down at her watch, she realized she had been standing there, staring at herself for the better part of twenty minutes.

"You don't have to do this," Callum said again more forcefully.

"Yes, I do. I have to do it for me, and for Millie, and all the other victims."

"He's getting put away for a long time whether or not any of the victims speak before the judge. But I understand, and I will be there." Callum wrapped his arms around her middle and she leaned back into him.

Four more girls had come forward over the course of the investigation into her assault. Four more girls he'd drugged and raped. Four girls whose lives he had ultimately shattered. Three of them, including Sam, had agreed to stand up and speak about the marks he'd left behind, in hopes he would receive an even longer sentence.

He had officially been convicted the previous month. Thankfully, it had been a short trial, and none of the victims had been required to take the stand. There were enough eye witnesses and blatant evidence to convict even without their testimonies. Now, it was time for sentencing.

Sam and Irene had spent the better part of each recent session going through what to say. Irene had reassured her that she could stop in the middle and walk out if needed, that she didn't need to say anything at all, that she didn't have to look at him, that she didn't even have to go. But in the end, she'd decided to stand up and speak. She wanted him to see her face one last time before they locked him up for however many years. She wanted him to know that, after that day, she would never think of him again. He would be but a tiny crack in her past and nothing in her future.

When they walked out of the courtroom after it was all over, Sam and the two other girls who'd come to speak walked off to the side. They sat on a bench and laughed at a dog chasing his tail across the street. They spoke about the outcome of the football game the previous week and made bets on the possibility of their team going to a bowl game. They traded numbers and made plans for dinner a few weeks later. Then they sat without speaking for a long time, knowing they now had an unshakable bond that would last forever.

The ping of her phone made her stop just before she reached Callum.

Cass: Is it over?

Sam: Yeah

Cass: How long did he get?

Sam: Not long enough.

Cass: I'm sorry I couldn't be there with you today. I just am not ready for that yet.

Sam: Don't ever apologize. What about dinner this week? My place?

Cass: Definitely!

October

"Which one should I get?" Millie asked as she held up both options. Her eyes were beaming in excitement.

"I can't decide. My vote is both." Sam smiled as she assessed the two dresses in her hands.

"I agree!" Millie exclaimed with a firm head nod and swung them over her shoulder to head to the register.

Millie had her fall sorority formal coming up, and Sam and Callum had offered to take her shopping for the perfect dress. Sam could tell by the look Callum was giving her that he'd completely underestimated the amount of damage the two girls could do in one shopping trip. He may have also underestimated the cost of formal dresses.

"Why does she need both?" Callum looked at them with wide-eyed shock.

"Because she does," Sam answered. And that was that.

Millie continued, "Next is shoes, and I need some new make-up, and–"

"Why do you need new..." Callum questioned with a furrowed brow and then abruptly stopped when Sam cut her eyes over at him. "You know what"—he reached into his wallet and passed over his card—"get whatever you want. I'm headed next door to look at art supplies." He kissed Millie on the cheek and Sam on the lips before he walked away.

"I've literally never seen him smile this much," Millie said as they walked through the shoe department.

"He's so happy that he's getting to spend some time with you. I think he's been kind of jealous of our lunch dates. I'm debating whether to ask him to join us on the next one." Sam was smiling as she spoke.

Millie laughed. "I think he is just happy in general. And I think you have a lot to do with that." Millie nudged her in the side. "You know, he told us about his degree."

Sam abruptly stopped walking. "He did?"

"Yeah. Last week when you and Kristin were outside with Micah checking on the burgers, he told me, Mom, and Connor that he graduated. That's why mom was crying when y'all walked back in."

Sam almost wanted to cry then, too.

"Mom is so proud of him. We all are. But he is so hard on himself and always thinks the worst. Even as he was saying it, you could tell he was so nervous. It was like he was scared we would laugh at him or something."

"He started therapy last week," Sam added as she sat down on one of the benches meant for trying on shoes.

"Yeah. He mentioned something to Connor." Millie scooted in beside her. "It's about damn time. None of us blame him for what happened between Mom and Dad. We never have. It was just...well...I think we all processed it a little differently, and it took a while to all come together. Mom goes to therapy. I go. Callum goes. Now, if we can just get Connor in there, we will be all set," Millie said with sad eyes.

"Connor is going to need to choose that on his own," Sam added.

"Doesn't mean I still can't be the annoying little sister and badger him about it." Millie smiled.

"No, I guess it doesn't." Sam stood then, nodded her head for Millie to join, and picked up a pair of ridiculously shiny heels she thought Millie might like. "Do you think you'll see your father again?"

"Ha." Millie started to laugh as she slipped the shoes on and then stopped to look at Sam. "I don't know. I still kind of hate him. I know I shouldn't because he is my dad, and I should–"

Sam quickly cut her off, "There is no should or shouldn't. Just because you are related by blood doesn't mean you owe him anything. He messed up, and it's on him to fix it. I'm not talking about with your mom, I know that's over, but with you three. He broke that trust and then basically walked out when everything went to shit. You don't owe him a thing. And, if we're being completely honest, your dad is an absolute asshole. You all are better off without him," Sam stated.

She recalled the night Callum had further explained what all had happened with his dad. How Mr. Barker had never truly accepted either of his sons. Connor was too gay, and Callum was too rebelious. Neither were the picture perfect creations he had planned. Neither would ever achieve or *be* enough to stand on that pedestal Mr. Barker had built so high up in the sky.

Callum had explained how, when the affairs came to light and he had told his mom what had been going on right under her nose, his dad had beat the absolute crap out of him in the living room. Connor had tried to intervene and ended up with a busted lip and a black eye. Apparently, and even though Callum wasn't aware of it until years later, Mr. Barker had done the same thing to Connor the night he came out and introduced his dad to the guy he'd been dating.

Mr. Barker had never apologized for any of it. Not to their mom for the affairs, not to Callum for the fight, and not to Connor for never letting him know he was enough just the way he was.

Mr. Barker had promptly walked away after that last blow, gotten into his fancy sports car, and driven off. He'd periodically come back to shower Millie with gifts to try and win her affection, hence the awkward dinner party at the Hadley house all those months ago. Sam had found out later that the only reason Connor had even gone to dinner that night was to keep an eye on Millie; to make sure the abuse that had been experienced by both brothers didn't reach their sister. In reality, Mr. Barker was now just a name attached to a person they didn't really even know.

"I guess you're right." Millie carried the new shiny shoes and the other three pairs she decided to buy (with her brother's card and would thank him later) to the counter. "Can I ask you something?"

Sam wanted to laugh. Millie and Callum were so alike, they even spoke in the same way.

"Of course."

Millie caught her eye and then clarified, "It's about Christian."

Sam nodded.

They had spoken a few times about their shared history with that horrid excuse for a human being, but had usually ended up being cut short by someone else walking into the room.

"I didn't really know him when he hurt me. But it was different for you. He was your only family for so long. I just can't wrap my head around that. I know it's not the same as what happened with my dad, but I think a part of me will always feel this need to try to fix the relationship or forgive my dad because he is my dad and he is my family. But Christian..." She paused and took a deep breath. "I just can't imagine having that relationship and then..." Millie paused again, then awkwardly laughed. "I don't know what I'm trying to say."

Sam wrapped her arm around Millie and thought for a minute, trying to find the words.

"I think I've realized that you don't have to forgive someone to move on. If it's toxic, and has really only ever been toxic, then what are you going to do? I couldn't control his actions any more than I can control the sunrise. What I *can* control is how I react to what happened. A few weeks ago, I made the decision that I wasn't going to let him control any other aspect of my life. I won't forgive him, but I *am* forgetting him. And that's all I can do. With your dad, all I can say is you didn't do a damn thing wrong. If he wants to repair the relationship, then he needs to put in the effort. Don't let anyone guilt you into thinking you need to be the one to reach out. That's on him. And if he doesn't, then just know he's the one missing out."

Millie nodded just as Callum walked up with bags of new paint and brushes thrown over his shoulder.

"What's the damage?" Callum tentatively asked as he surveyed the two women with forlorn looks on their faces.

Millie perked up then. She yanked Callum's card out of her back pocket and teased him as if she was going to hand it back, but then quickly shoved it in her purse.

"Only three, no, four pairs of shoes. Make-up is next!" she exclaimed as she shoved the two dresses and the bags filled with shoe boxes into his hands and walked ahead.

"I'm going to go into debt with her, aren't I?" Callum asked as he looked back at Sam.

"I think that's a pretty fair assumption," Sam agreed as she gave him a quick kiss. "Good thing you're such a successful business owner so you can afford to spoil us." She gave him a wink and then ran ahead to catch up with Millie.

November

Sam was trying to decide how exactly she was going to get through this meeting. Not due to nerves, but due to the fact that anytime she caught Ms. Ashlyn's eyes, she knew she would break out in the biggest smile.

She knew this meeting was a serious matter, but she also knew Ms. Ashlyn was presiding over it and, even though it was a topic they had yet to speak about due to a possible conflict of interest, she had no doubts that her funding would be reinstated. She was almost through with Bio 428 and hadn't received anything below an A on every single assignment. She would have to completely fail the final just to end up with a B. She had also overheard Callum telling his mom one night at dinner about Sam's 4.0 GPA, and about how she would likely get into any med school of her choice.

Ms. Ashlyn pretty much frequented their apartment on a weekly basis by that point. They had dinner together almost every Tuesday night. And then there were the random girls days Ms. Ashlyn would come up with out of nowhere. She, Millie, and Sam would tell Callum they were going to the mall and somehow wind up in Charleston, or Charlotte, and one time even Atlanta. By all accounts, Sam was just family at this point.

When she came walking into the house with bags of new things, Callum would just shake his head. But deep down, she knew he loved it.

Sam would always have Kristin. They were like sisters. But there was something different about the relationship she'd formed with Millie and Ms. Ashlyn. Something more.

"Miss Williams?" that same short man from before called out, indicating they were ready to begin.

Sam walked into the bright room with a wide eyed smile. She just wanted to get this over with so they could head to lunch before her afternoon lab.

That smile quickly faded when Ms. Ashlyn was nowhere in sight.

"Where's Ms. Clemmings?" Sam questioned as she looked between the six member panel before her. The same fussy man from the previous session now sat in what should have been Ms. Ashlyn's seat.

"She will not be attending this meeting. It has come to light that you and Ms. Clemmings have a closer relationship than she has with the other recipients and, due to that, it was decided that she would not be a part of this meeting."

Sam swallowed. Her nervousness had somehow come careening back and slammed directly into her chest.

She slowly sat down in the seat and waited for the panel before her to speak. Thankfully, she didn't have to wait long.

"We have reviewed your transcript and your current standing in Biological Sciences 428 and find that you have adequately met the requirements for reinstatement of your funding." She almost couldn't breathe. Less than a minute ago, she'd been more than sure they were about to strip it all away. "However, if any more errors come to light over the next few weeks, then we will be forced to rescind that."

The man stated each word with utter disdain, as if it pained him to give her back the money that she had rightfully earned.

The next few minutes were a blur. A wonderful, relief-filled blur.

When she finally made it outside, she ran up to Ms. Ashlyn and wrapped her arms around her neck.

"I'm so sorry I couldn't be in there. They told me right before the meeting started so I couldn't even text you to give you a heads up," Ms. Ashlyn stated as Sam held her tight. "But at least now you know you rightfully earned it yourself. No one can say you were given any edge over the other recipients."

"Thank you." Sam was all but crying into Ms. Ashlyn's hair.

"Shh. It's over. You have your funding, and I am starving." Ms. Ashlyn pulled back and brushed the curls off Sam's shoulder.

"Thank you."

"Sam, don't thank me. You did that. You worked your butt off."

Sam nodded as she wiped away the tears, then asked, "Mexican or Italian?"

"I will never be a woman who turns down queso," Ms. Ashlyn replied with a wink as she ushered Sam into her car.

December

"Absolutely not," Callum and Connor stated their refusal at the exact same time.

"Come on." Sam threw her hands up in the air as both men adamantly shook their heads. Even Justin, Connor's boyfriend, gave them a pleading smile. Nothing worked. Not until Millie walked over to her two big brothers with that bottom lip pushed out just about as far as it could go.

"Please!" Millie clasped her hands in a pleading gesture. "For me?"

Sam wanted to laugh. Millie sounded so meek and sad, which was definitely not her normal. But it seemed Millie knew exactly how to get her brothers to cave to any request.

The two brothers looked at each other and then back at their baby sister.

Callum then shot a glance at Sam.

"I better get laid tonight," Callum grumbled with a smile as he yanked one of the adult-sized Christmas onesies out of Sam's grasp.

"Ditto," Connor stated as he looked at Justin.

"Ew!" Millie called out to her brothers with a scrunched up nose. "I want to know nothing about either of your escapades."

Sam laughed even harder then.

It reminded her of a few weeks back when she and Kristin had snuck Millie into a bar and had all gotten rip roaring drunk. On the ride home, Sam and Kristin had practically peed themselves from laughing so hard. Sam had started detailing out exactly what Callum could do with that tongue of his while Millie covered her ears and began intermittently humming a melody to drown out the words and screaming at them that she was going to truly vomit if they didn't stop talking about Callum.

"Go put them on so we can take pictures before the sun goes down!" Millie ordered as she pushed the two guys into a bedroom to change.

Sam, Millie, Justin, and Ms. Ashlyn had already put on their sets earlier while the two guys made a quick run to the store up the street.

Sam burst out laughing as the two brothers walked back into the living room, a beautifully begrudging look plastered on each of their faces.

It was Christmas Eve. And it was Sam's first Christmas Eve where she was actually excited about the holiday festivities. Everyone had congregated at the Barker's home, the one that was currently on the market, for one last family get together before Ms. Ashlyn moved into a ridiculously fancy, but much smaller, high rise apartment in the city.

It was also the first holiday she could recall ever not spending with Christian. But that was okay. She hadn't even thought about him once in the last few weeks. Not intentionally, at least.

The month prior, she and Irene had finally broached the subject of her assault which had resulted in Sam practically using an entire box of tissues during each of their next four sessions. Every time she'd walked out of that building and into Callum's arms, she had all but collapsed in relief that she had him to lean on in those moments.

It was a process. A process that was going to take years to get through. But she was making progress every day.

There were setbacks, as was to be expected. But with the support of Irene and her new family, she was able to break out of most any funk her mind would throw her into.

So this Christmas, instead of buying the customary cookie plate she had given to each of the families that had taken her and Christian in during their school breaks the last three years, she had bought personalized gifts for each person around her. Sam had never much liked spending money. That thought had changed, however, when the people she was buying gifts for mattered more to her than anyone else on the planet.

She could barely contain her excitement when she, Millie, and Justin were going through the photos they had taken on the dock later that night. There was one of her and Callum that she kept going back to. He'd had a grumpy expression plastered on his face, but Sam had reached behind them and pinched his butt just before Connor snapped the photo, resulting in his wide-eyed grin and a laughing Sam. It was her favorite photo to date.

She promptly added it to her Instagram account. The same one Christian had made for her all those months ago.

She had thrown the phone on the floor the day she went to upload her first post, a photo of Callum hunched over a canvas, only to find that she'd never deleted the one Christian had taken of them at Dianne's. She'd buried her face in the pillow, refusing to look at the screen until Callum had deleted the photo and put theirs in its place. Now her feed was full of photos of her and Callum, Kristin and Micah, Connor and Justin, and Millie and Ms. Ashlyn.

Looking at it now, there was no trace of how her page had first come to be.

"How long do we have to wear these?" Connor asked as they sat down, matching PJ's and all, for dinner.

"We are sleeping in them, and then opening presents in them in the morning," Millie proudly exclaimed.

Both brothers groaned.

February

"Well, hello," Callum stated with wide-eyed excitement as he walked into their bedroom.

"Hello to you, as well," Sam replied.

Callum stood there, slowly unbuttoning his shirt as Sam stalked toward him.

"What's the occasion?" Callum asked as his smile grew.

Sam shrugged her shoulders. "Nothing crazy, I just love you, and missed you, and to be honest, I'm just really horny."

Callum practically howled with laughter.

"I can work with that." He eyed her from head to toe.

She and Kristin had just come back from a shopping trip in Charlotte and Sam had bought another barely there black lace set for Callum to enjoy.

This time, the set came with a little more fabric, but it didn't really matter as the entire thing was constructed from sheer material. It may have also come with thigh-high stockings and a black silk robe. Sam was currently using every piece of the ensemble to her advantage.

It had taken them a while to get back to this place. After what had happened with Christian, they'd gone from practically consuming each other on every surface they could find to barely more than the occasional comforting touch. Callum hadn't seemed to mind, and he had never once pressured her. The night she'd made the decision that she was ready, he had been slow and gentle, and had worshiped her as if it was their first time all over again.

She'd cried after.

But now, they were back to what Sam would say was their normal, what she hoped would always be their normal, and she couldn't get enough of him.

The days when he was away from sunup to sundown checking in at the various tattoo shops and Topline and then scoping out new locations for other ventures were the worst. Both mentally and physically. Some days, when Sam had nothing left on her checklist to complete, she would tag along with him. She loved those days. It's how she became very well versed in the nuances of life as a business owner, she was particularly interested in exactly how many flat surfaces there were in each building that he could lay her out on.

But the days in which she didn't—or couldn't—go were hard. No matter what they entailed, Sam would spend the majority of her time missing Callum. She was still learning how to be alone, how to not jump at any odd sound, how to muster up enough courage to try new things by herself, how to cope with the emptiness that crawled its way back in when the house was quiet. What Christian had done had changed Sam in more ways than one. It had shattered that invisible stronghold she had placed around herself from all those years where it had just been the two of them fighting against the world, and it was going to take years to get back to where she wanted to be.

But tonight something was different. Tonight, she was finally taking back all of herself and giving it back to Callum.

He sat back on the bed as he assessed what stood before him. Sam let him look. She no longer felt shy under his gaze. If anything, the way he looked at her made her feel empowered.

"You are a fucking treasure. You know that, right?"

"Maybe you should unwrap your treasure and find out what's underneath?"

Callum reached out then to pull her on top of him, and she let her legs fall on either side of his body.

"What's on the menu for tonight?"

"Whatever you want," Sam whispered against his lips.

"I want it all," he answered as he let his hands run up and down her thighs.

"Take it."

He did just that.

Callum flipped them over as he laid her out on the bed. Then he let his eyes linger on the expanse of her legs.

"I was about to take these off." He brushed his fingers over her stocking-clad legs. "But I think I want them to stay on."

"Whatever you say, sir."

He gave her a knowing look.

Then he slowly undressed her. Each time a piece of fabric fell to the side and exposed more of her skin, he used his lips, and tongue, and teeth to devour her.

When she was finally bare, except for those damn stockings, he stood up and slipped off his shirt and pants. He was reaching for the condom when she stopped him.

"Wait," Sam quickly blurted out. She had a plan, and dammit, she wasn't going to let him completely derail her.

He quickly looked her up and down. "What's wrong?"

"Nothing." She smiled to let him know she was okay. Then she stood and pushed him backward on the bed. She slowly slipped his boxers down his legs and kneeled before him.

"Sam. No. You don't need to do—"

"I want to."

It was the one line they hadn't yet crossed. It was the act she'd been made to do by that boy so many times all those years ago. She knew he wanted her lips around him, but he had never once brought it up or even hinted at the notion. But tonight, she was in control.

He let out a stream of curses as she gripped him in her hand and then he damn near spasmed in relief when that hand was quickly replaced with her lips.

It wasn't long before he jerked her upward and away, stopping her just before he came.

"I need to be inside you." It was a plea.

"I think I would like that very much." She stood then with him and froze as he swiped his thumb across her swollen lips.

"So beautiful," he whispered just before laying her back down and taking his time worshiping each and every inch of her body.

Epilogue - 3 Years Later

CALLUM & SAM

Sam had barely slept and, unfortunately, it had nothing to do with Callum keeping her busy with his fingers and tongue and cock till the early hours of the morning. She finally got out of bed when she noticed it was now only one hour until her alarm clock was supposed to go off.

She showered, scrubbed, and shaved, making sure everything was exactly as it should be. When she stepped out of the bathroom, she smelled bacon and eggs, and sighed in relief, knowing Callum had probably gotten up directly after her to start on breakfast.

She was dressed and in the kitchen in under fifteen minutes.

He looked her up and down. They had been together for over three years now, and he still damn near lost his breath every time she walked into the room.

"You ready?" Callum asked as he passed over a plate and kissed her brow.

"No." She shook her head as she started shoveling eggs into her mouth.

He quickly yanked the plate back before she could stab the next bite, which resulted in her stabbing the pretty blue nautical themed placemat she had purchased at a home goods store the previous week.

She gave him a death glare.

Callum laughed at her attempt to appear stern. Even her death glares were stunningly beautiful.

He was lucky it was only a placemat and not one of the sweetgrass baskets he had filled their home with.

Then he sat himself in the chair beside her, the plate still pushed to the side. "It's 5:45 in the morning. You are already dressed and you don't have to leave for another hour and a half. Slow down or you are going to choke." He slowly slid the plate back to her.

She swallowed the massive amount she had already stuffed into her mouth.

"It's just so delicious."

He eyed her knowingly.

"I'm nervous."

He started to laugh. "I can tell."

"What if I mess up?"

"Sam, you're just observing right?"

"Right. But this is the exact place I want to work once I get my degree. These kids, they literally have nothing, and...Callum, I just want to help them. I just want to make a difference. I want them to know they are safe with me. I want–"

"Take a breath." Callum cupped the side of her face in his hand. "You are going to be the best damn therapist in the world. You are going to change lives. But you can't do that if you die the morning of your final practicum from choking on your eggs."

Sam groaned.

Callum was completely correct. It didn't lessen the fact that she was still the most nervous she had probably ever been.
If things had gone the way she'd originally planned, she figured she would be finishing her second year of med school now. At least, that's what Kristin was doing. But people change, and with those changes, so do their plans.

She had spent far too many hours, days, and weeks contemplating it. Becoming a doctor was supposed to have been her dream. A dream that would get her out of that cycle, and would give her a way to prove everyone wrong. Her freshman year at South Carolina all those years ago had been filled with visions of her showing all those fussy people at Giving Hearts up when she emailed them a copy of her medical degree.

It had taken Callum and then a good many hours sitting on Irene's couch before she'd figured out she didn't need to prove them wrong. She didn't need to prove anything to anyone.

She was herself, and she was enough.

She had promptly walked into their apartment after her last class of her senior year, thrown her bag on the ground and stated, "I'm not going to be a doctor."

Callum had timidly looked up from his computer. "Okay?"

"I'm going to be a therapist or counselor. I need to figure out the difference. I'm going to get my master's in counseling or psychology, or something of the like, I still need to look that up as well," she'd quickly added with a tilt of her head. "But I am going to help foster kids, and victims of sexual assault, and anyone else who needs it. I don't have to cut open a body to make it mean something."

"No. You don't," he had confirmed while shutting his computer. And then he'd stood up, walked over to her, and kissed her till she was breathless.

Callum had known this was the route she was going to take for a few months. He'd just been waiting for her to come to the realization herself.

Halfway through her senior year, she had stopped talking about medical jargon, and instead had started spending her days visiting the local homes of foster kids, doing artwork with them, painting their nails, helping with homework, and at times just being present. It was supposed to be a part of her own therapy. At the end of those days, she'd walked back into their place with the biggest smile on her face.

It made her happy.

And he just wanted her to be happy.

"Are we still going for ice cream tonight when I get back?" Sam questioned once she started eating again, this time at a much less alarming speed. The question roused Callum from his thoughts. "As long as you're not too tired by then, yeah, I'd love to." He kissed her cheek. "I'm going to jump in the shower. Don't leave before I'm out."

She nodded as he walked off into their room.

****

They were now living in Charleston. It had been two years since Sam had realized med school wasn't what she really wanted, it was what Sara had wanted. It was the safe place she had found in Sara, and she'd gravitated to it because, at that time, it had been her only safe space.

But now she had Callum.

Upon this realization, she'd then immediately applied to every graduate counseling program in the southeast with a focus on trauma and adoption counseling. She had gotten into seven. Due to her late applications, most of the acceptances were for the following spring semester and not the fall, but that just meant she had a full six months to prepare for classes and help Callum finish opening a second Topline location down in Charleston.

They had shared a small one bedroom apartment in Columbia for her senior year. Then one day, shortly after Sam had proclaimed her new path, Callum's mom had shown up at their door. She had been by countless times over the last few months, so it wasn't completely out of the blue.
Callum walked her in with a smile as they found Sam sitting at the table.

"Ms. Ashlyn!" she said, beaming as she reached up to give her a hug.

"I told you, it's just Ashlyn," she stated and Sam's smile grew. "Or, Mom from here on out."

She had made that remark a few times, but Sam was still too nervous to actually call her that.

Callum, thank goodness, decided not to comment on it this time. "I didn't know you were stopping by. Want to eat with us?"

Callum started plating their dinner as Ashlyn shook her head.

"No. No. I have a million things to do tonight. But I wanted to stop by and give you this." She reached out and placed a manila folder in Callum's hand.

"What is it?" he tentatively pulled back the seal.

"It was one of the stipulations I put in the divorce. You'd be surprised how much I got out of that wretched man. He had so many accounts filled to the brim that I'd had no idea about. Anyway, I thought about selling this, but honestly, it's always been yours. It's where you are the happiest, and I wanted you to have it."

Callum's head jerked forward as he started rapidly breathing. "Mom? You know I can't accept this."

She shook her head. "Nonsense. Think of it as a congratulations present for opening up the new restaurant and shops. I am so proud of you!" She quickly looked between both Sam and Callum. "I'm so proud of both of you."

It wasn't until Ashlyn had already walked out the door that Sam got Callum's attention.

"What is it?"

"She paid off the beach house and put it in my name." He flipped the folder upside down and caught the keys that slipped out.

"Oh my God!" Sam stared at him wide-eyed.

"You got into that online grad program, right?"

"Yeah?" It was her first choice, as Charleston was where Callum would have most likely ended up, but they were still trying to figure out the living situation and student loans aspect.

"I think we just figured out where we're going to live."

She crashed into him then, wrapped her legs around his waist, and kissed him until she had to come up for air.

They didn't eat dinner that night.

Instead, they spent the better part of the next three hours making each other scream the other's name across every surface of that small apartment.

By the next week, they were boxing everything up and loading the moving van.

****

Sam was fidgeting by the elevator door when Callum finally walked back into the living room.

"What's wrong?"

"I know I still have another thirty minutes, but I think I'm going to go ahead and head out. I'm worried about parking and what if there is a wreck or maybe road work, or what if–"

"Sam. It's okay. Go be an amazing therapist." He cupped her face and kissed her. "Let me know you got there safely."

"I will." She squeezed him one last time and then stepped onto the elevator.

He laughed as he heard her nervous squeal of excitement as the elevator lowered her to the garage.

The phone rang just as he fidgeted with the box sitting in his closet.

"You ready?" Micah asked when Callum answered.

"I'm nervous." He opened the box once more and then promptly closed it once he realized its contents were safe. This had become his hourly ritual over the last few days.

"Why?" Micah questioned, and from his tone, Callum could tell he had an incredulous look on his face.

"What if she says no?"

Micah burst into laughter.

"Stop being ridiculous. Also, our flight should be a little early. I'll let Drew know so he can get there earlier and then we will all be at the pier so we can grab a drink while we wait for the big moment."

"Have one waiting for me." Callum ran a hand over his face.

"Stop worrying. Sam will say yes. She and Kristin have damn near already planned out both our weddings and she and I still have two more years before we walk down the aisle."

Callum laughed.

Micah had planned to wait to propose till match day when Kristin found out what her med school specialty would be. But he had never been one for patience. He'd popped the question three weeks into Kristin's first year at Duke. Kristin was still going to make him wait till she finished school before she walked down the aisle, though. Something about getting her own last name on that degree.

"For some reason, I don't think Sam is going to want a long engagement."

"God, I hope not," Callum agreed.

****

This had become somewhat of their thing. Ice cream and walks on the beach. It was rather cliche, and Callum gave the customary groans whenever Sam brought it up but, on the inside, he absolutely loved spending this time with her. He had just discarded their empty paper bowls in a trash can when the sun started to set.

Sam had spent the last hour gushing over her day, but he'd barely heard a word. She was so wrapped up in how much she loved her new placement that she couldn't tell his mind was on something else, or that his fingers kept reaching into his left pocket, or that his eyes kept darting up to the pier, making sure their best friends were ready.

She had just started to explain the discharge process for the older kids when he cut her off.

"Sam?"

Her eyes quickly cut to his. "Yeah?"

"I want to hear all about that. I do. But if I don't get this out, I might just have a heart attack right here and now."

She froze. "What's wrong?"

"I love you." It wasn't the first time he'd said it. That had been after a practical marathon night where they had made love until the sun came up. Now, he said it almost every chance he got. "I've loved you since the moment you walked into work and spilled those drinks on me. I want you to know that no one ever truly saw me until you walked into my life, and I can't thank you enough for what you have given me."

She took a step back. In some way, she knew what was happening, but in another, she felt unimaginable shock. "Callum?"

"I know your life hasn't been what you would have hoped for, but I plan to change that. I know that all you have ever wanted is somewhere to call home. I want to be that somewhere. I want to be your home. I want you to know you belong with me, and that nothing will ever change that."

He pulled out the ring then and promptly began to kneel.

"Yes!" she blurted out before his knee hit the ground.

Callum laughed.

"I haven't even asked yet."

She buried her tear-soaked face in her hands as she laughed with him.

"Samantha Williams. Will you marry me?"

"Yes. A million times yes!"

She heard the screams of excitement from on top of the pier before the ring was slipped on her finger, and through tear filled eyes she could just make out the rest of her family. Kristin, Micah, Drew, Melanie, Connor, Justin, Ashlyn, and Millie were all sharing in their own excitement at what they'd just witnessed.

It was Kristin who made it down to the beach first. She crashed into Sam so hard they both fell to the sand.

"You're getting married!" Kristin yelled out.

"I'm getting married." Sam laughed through the tears as the boys helped them back on their feet.

It was a moment filled with wonderful chaos and hugs and laughter and, thanks to Millie, a thousand pictures.

"Where should we go to celebrate?" Ashlyn questioned as they all started walking back to the car.

Callum kissed Sam on the cheek and then said. "I know just the place." He gave her a wink and directed the group to their favorite spot for pizza.

The End.

Acknowledgements

Okay guys...this book came out of left field. I'm not even sure how this happened. I remember chatting with my team, fussing about fantasy worlds and how I was in a bit of a writing rut and somehow stepping away to do something else was recommended. That recommendation then turned into a book.

And that book was somehow completed in less than a month (don't expect this level of productiveness to happen on the regular lol).

But here we are with a new book (in a completely different genre) and I can't tell you how absolutely ecstatic I am about it.

First and foremost I want to thank my amazing husband, Martin, who didn't fuss when we had constant left overs or the laundry wasn't done or if I stayed up into the wee hours of the morning writing. He has been my constant support on this new journey and I know I wouldn't be able to do this without him by my side.

To my family. Again, thank you for watching the boys, helping me with any and everything I needed so I had a few moments to steal away and write.

To my Illustrator, Editor and one of my best friends, Marcia. Girl....How have you not been there my entire life. I don't know what I will do if we ever stop constantly texting about books and babies. You have literally been there from step one and I am so excited and lucky to have you on my team!

Rachel, my amazing Developmental Editor and Alpha Reader. I have gained some amazing friends along the way. I am so happy that I now can say you are a "real-life" friend and not just some random girl I met on the internet. Your insight and suggestions literally MADE this book! Thank you for all that you have done.

Liz, Taylor, Jessey, Ally, Ashley, Tamara, Kelly and Krystal. I have the best Betas in the world. No one is ever allowed to steal you away. You provide so much support, insight and advice and I know I wouldn't be able to do this without you. I love how most of our conversations end with side talks that have nothing to do with books haha

Made in United States
Troutdale, OR
08/26/2024

22323415R00268